QUEEN'S REVENGE

6-20-13

*To Connie
May God Bless You
So Nice to Meet You and
Neil.*

QUEEN'S REVENGE

A NOVEL

Ray Lett

RAYMOND LETT

© 2012 by Raymond Lett. All rights reserved.

WinePress Publishing (PO Box 428, Enumclaw, WA 98022) functions only as book publisher. As such, the ultimate design, content, editorial accuracy, and views expressed or implied in this work are those of the author.

No part of this publication may be reproduced, stored in a retrieval system, or transmitted in any way by any means—electronic, mechanical, photocopy, recording, or otherwise—without the prior permission of the copyright holder, except as provided by USA copyright law.

Scripture references are taken from the *King James Version* of the Bible.

ISBN 13: 978-1-4141-2102-4
ISBN 10: 1-4141-2102-4
Library of Congress Catalog Card Number: 2011931812

Thank you, Sharon, for making this second book about my great-great uncle, Ben Lett, possible with your constant love and prayers.

I dedicate this book to you, my love, for your tireless efforts and encouragement.

May our family, friends, and historians enjoy this history of the Lett family and its early days in northern Illinois.

ACKNOWLEDGMENTS

MY THANKS TO Loretta Stenger, who gave so much to this book. Her professional abilities in editing the book helped me make this another great book.
Thanks, Loretta.

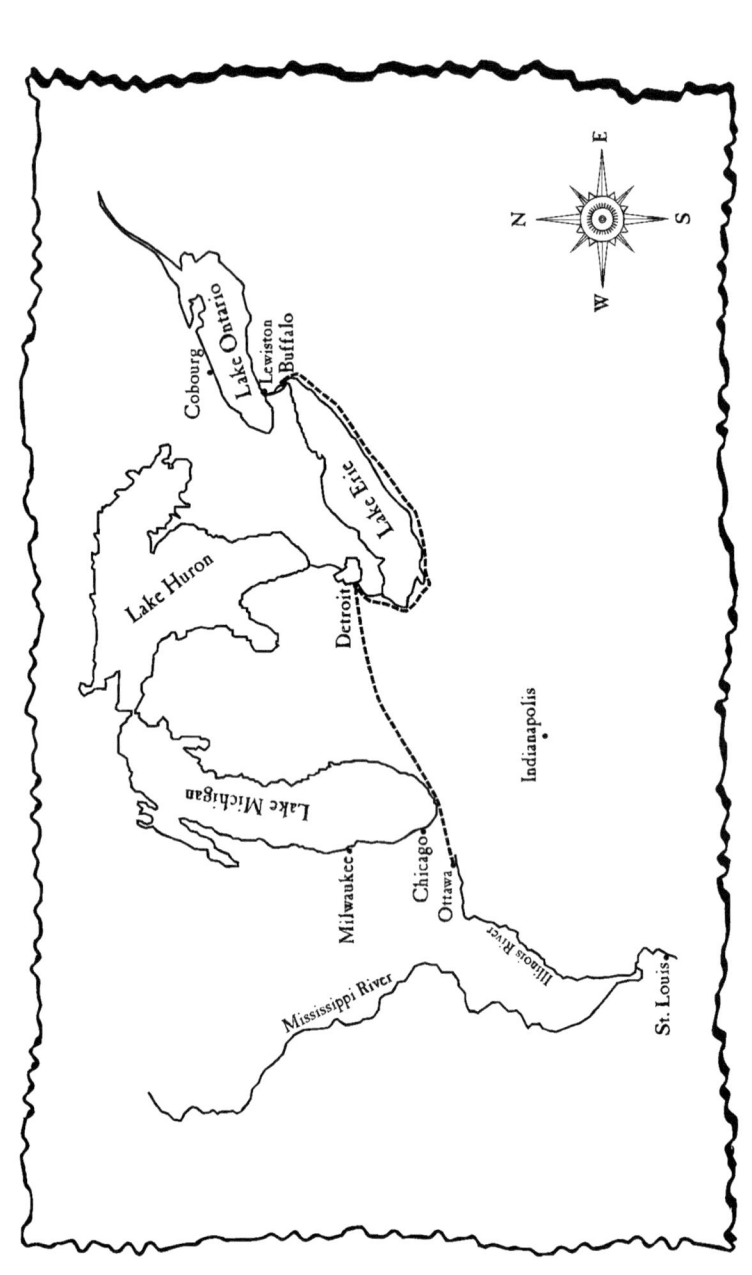

CHAPTER ONE

BEN'S SHIRT WAS soaked with sweat born of anger and tension as he hunkered down with Ed in the dense thicket looking for three Indians spotted earlier in the area. He strained his ears.

With a venomous whistle, an arrow sliced through the branches, just missing Ben. He turned right, took careful aim with his rifle, and shot. The scream confirmed that Ben had hit his target.

One down; two to go, he thought. *Might they have fled?*

Ed started to rise, but Ben's hand on his arm pulled him back down. Just then two more exploratory arrows skimmed through the bushes at different angles.

Ed whispered, "Thank you."

Soon Ben heard movement in the bushes straight ahead and behind them. He saw a feathered headband on an Indian crouched beside a small tree. Ben took his Bowie knife from his hip.

"Take the one behind us, Ed; I'll take the one straight ahead," he said.

QUEEN'S REVENGE

He crawled toward the brave ever so quietly. The brave became edgy and stood up. Ben threw his knife straight for the man's back, but the brave turned just as the knife lodged in his shoulder. He fell to the ground.

In the meantime, Ed found the other brave. They met each other with knives poised high above their heads.

Ben approached from behind, holding a thick branch. He brought it down hard on the brave's knife arm, breaking it just above the wrist. The brave yelled in pain. When he tried to run, Ben tripped him from behind.

Falling on his broken wrist, he yelled out again. Ben struck him again, knocking him out.

"What shall we do with them?" Ed asked.

"Let's find their ponies," Ben said. "We'll tie them atop the ponies and send them home. They won't bother us again."

The men dressed their wounds, tied the braves to their ponies, and whistled for their horses.

"Take us to the wagons, boys," Ben said.

Some distance east, Ben's wife, Debra, stirred a large kettle of stew not far from two covered wagons. Her family, the Letts, and their good friends the Doyles, were traveling to Illinois from Lewiston, New York.

The aroma was wonderful. Debra and Janice Doyle began to fret about what might have happened to their husbands because they usually returned from their scouting trips by dark. Their children—seven-year-old Jackson Lett, five-year-old Sam Doyle, and almost-four-year-old Sophie Doyle—were playing at the nearby stream, skipping stones.

The campfire flames cast dark shadows through the nearby trees. An owl screeched deep in the woods, sending chills up Debra's spine. The women knew of recent renegade Indian sightings. Might Ben and Ed have met them and been wounded or killed?

CHAPTER ONE

Just then a bright smile came over Debra's face as she heard hoofbeats approaching.

"Children, I think your fathers are coming," she called. "Jackson, you help Sophie and Sam wash up for supper."

Debra wiped her hands on her apron and smoothed her hair. She caught a glimpse of Ben's broad-brimmed black hat. Her heart leapt for joy as she ran toward the approaching horses.

Ben pulled on the reins, swung from his horse, and gathered Debra in his arms. Ed put his arms around Janice, then Sophie, and tousled Sam's curly blond hair. Ben grabbed Jackson by the seat of his pants and lifted him in the air. Jackson tried to break loose, but Ben held him tight.

"What happened to you, Ben?" Debra asked when she saw his torn shirt and bleeding arm.

"I was crawling through the thick underbrush," he lied.

"Let me help you," she said.

Debra carefully moved Ben's arm and used a knife to cut away the crimson sleeve. She studied the deep slash on his upper arm.

"Janice, would you please collect some water from the stream and boil it?" she asked. "It looks like I'll need to prepare a poultice for this wound."

"If you ask me, Ben Lett, I'd say you have been hit by an arrow," she said evenly as Ben avoided her eyes.

Debra washed the wound and dabbed it with alcohol before applying the herb leaves. Then she took needle and thread and sewed shut the gash. When the sting and pain caused Ben to jerk, Debra said, "You big baby."

"I'll make some willow bark tea," Janice offered. "That poultice should help draw out the infection. My tea should help keep down a fever and restore his strength."

As Ben lay resting in the wagon that night, he thought of Gad Nichols and the nice party the Nichols family had given just a few weeks ago upon their departure from Lewiston, New York. The Nicholses had offered prayers for their safety, and he appreciated them now more than ever.

Ben believed God had his angels watching over them. He was glad God was keeping his family and friends safe for the moment on this journey. And he allowed himself to dream of freedom from old threats that had dogged him since his involvement with those who fought in the 1830s for Canada's independence from Great Britain.

In the morning, Ben and Ed were up before dawn, preparing for that day's journey. Ben's arm still gave him pain, but he couldn't wait for it to completely heal.

Debra awoke and began making breakfast while Ben and Ed hitched the teams of horses to the wagons and tied the cows behind. They enjoyed sourdough biscuits, gravy, bacon, and strong coffee before the men gave orders to climb aboard.

"It's time to move out and explore more territory," Ed called.

"Westward we go!" Ben said. He focused his eyes on the horizon.

"I dreamed last night about the prairie grasses, the small wooded areas, and the beautiful streams passing through our new homeland in Illinois," Ben said. "I expect it will take another month before we arrive, but we'll stop in Detroit first. Ed and I will need a few days to set up our trading business there."

The days became as rhythmic as the swaying of the wagon, and a familiar pattern developed. Breakfast around a campfire preceded lunch on the trail along a brook or stream

CHAPTER ONE

with a good stretch or rest for the animals and travelers. A campfire dinner finished the day.

The only time Debra and Janice felt uneasy was when Ben and Ed rode off to scout the trail ahead. The women stayed alert, acutely aware of their responsibility for the children. They had two cap and ball rifles, and they knew how to use them. Debra also kept a pistol near her bed in the wagon.

Already it was mid-October, so dawn's early light made long shadows on the trail ahead as the wagons moved along through the trees. The men and children walked, and the women drove the horses pulling the wagons. The next several days passed without any signs of trouble. The air was cool and crisp, and ducks flew overhead. Leaves on the trees were changing colors and had started to fall to the ground.

Each evening Ben played his guitar, Ed played the harmonica, and Debra and Janice led songs and hymns. Ben danced with Debra and Janice while Ed played, then they switched. Jackson and Sam played games in the wagon with Sophie.

In the fourth week of the journey, the expedition entered a deep green valley skirting the southern edge of Lake Erie. In the bright, still morning air, the lake's expansive waters looked bluish green.

Ben was talking to Ed about the sighting of Indians the previous day. He suddenly stopped; his eyes were wide open.

Ed twisted around to see what had caught Ben's attention, and at the same time the women said, "Well, look at that, will you?"

An enormous black mother bear had emerged on all fours from the shadowed timber. She began to growl and rise up on her back legs. A pair of hawks screeched and flew from a nearby tree.

5

QUEEN'S REVENGE

Ben said to Ed, "I've got to bag me that bear."

He moved the wagons along with the wave of his hat while he prepared to return to the bear.

"Are you sure you want to do this?" Ed asked.

"Sure do," Ben said, yanking his rifle from its place in his wagon. At the same time, Ed slid from his wagon and followed on Ben's heels. The women drove the wagons on with the children inside.

"I'll fire if necessary, Ben," Ed said.

"I'd appreciate that," Ben responded, still moving toward the bear, his rifle cocked as he gripped it tightly in his right hand.

The bear's mouth was open wide, and Ben's muscles tightened as he moved forward to face the bear ready to protect her territory. The bear began to charge Ben and Ed, so from fifty feet, Ben shouldered his rifle, drew a bead, and fired. The bullet hit square between the eyes. The bear stopped and roared, shook her great head, took one more step toward Ben, and slumped to the ground.

Ben cocked his rifle again and cautiously moved up to the large black heap of fur. Ed stayed at his side.

Ben nudged the bear's head with the muzzle of his rifle; the eyes were closed, no movement.

Ed went to bring the women and children to see the fallen bear.

"Daddy, that is some bear," Sophie yelled. "Did you shoot her?"

"No! Uncle Ben shot her," Ed responded.

"What you gonna do with this animal?" Jackson asked.

"We don't have time to skin the animal, so we'll just leave it for the forest animals and birds to feast on for the next few weeks," Ben replied.

CHAPTER ONE

As the days passed, and they drew nearer to Detroit, Ben warned everyone to keep an extra sharp lookout for thieves and Indians.

On the morning of November 2, 1845, Ben's brother, Tom Lett, stepped from the two-story brick building used for the post office into the brilliant sunlight. Wagons and buggies passed on the wide, dusty street. People strolled along the boardwalks going into stores and shops, often stopping to talk with friends and acquaintances.

Tom pocketed a wad of cash he had just withdrawn from the Cattleman's Bank in Ottawa, Illinois. He ran his hand through his hair, twisted the ends of his curling mustache, and looked around on the sunlit Main Street. Holstered on his wide belt was one silver-plated Colt® .45 revolver.

Tom glanced left, and his eyes fell on his brother. He grinned and said, "Well, howdy, Robert!"

Robert smiled and said, "I expect you're about to buy that team of oxen to finish the harvest and use for next spring's work."

"You're right! Why don't you join me, and we'll go down to the livery stable together and look the teams over," Tom responded.

Tom and Robert had come to Illinois in the spring of 1840 and established themselves on separate farms some twenty miles north of Ottawa near the Fox River a half mile north of Sheridan.

The Lett brothers found the owner of the livery stable to discuss their interest in obtaining a team of oxen. They inspected the five teams on hand. Robert, a better judge of horses than oxen, yielded the selection to Tom, who was an old hand at farming with oxen.

Tom chose a fine well-muscled, three-year-old roan team. Tom also bought a grain wagon that day. With the team hitched to the wagon, he drove to the elevator and filled it with wheat for seed and grain. Then Robert and Tom headed for home.

Halfway there, the brothers noticed two farm wagons stopped on the side of the road, heading toward town. Tom recognized the two families as neighbors to the west of their farms. Charles Parker had his wife, teenage son, and a young daughter with him; Doug Brown was with his wife and two teenage sons. The farmers and their sons were examining a rear wagon wheel on the Brown wagon.

Suddenly, four Indians galloped up the hill, firing rifles as they rode hard toward the wagons. The women and children scrambled from the wagons to hide underneath.

Tom and Robert grabbed their rifles from under their seats and began firing at the Indians as they urged their teams along. They closed in rapidly on the scene. The teenage boys and their fathers joined the fight.

The shots echoed across the small ravine, and smoke filled the air. Tom pulled hard on his reins to halt his wagon near the others. Robert took cover with the neighbors. One Indian crawled toward his rifle with a slug in his leg. Another lay on the ground a few feet away, face down.

A third Indian rode Tom's way, whooping and hollering. Robert shouldered his rifle, took aim, and squeezed the trigger. The Indian dropped his lance as the slug hit him in the chest. The Indian on the ground fired at Tom but missed, the bullet whizzing past his head. With a cartridge already in the chamber, Tom fired back, delivering a fatal blow to the head.

Robert took aim and fired at the Indian on horseback who had just shot Doug Brown in the left arm. The Indian continued riding for a few minutes but eventually fell from his horse with a bullet in his groin. The one remaining Indian turned his horse for the woods and fled.

CHAPTER ONE

Tom stood up from crouching behind the Browns' wagon and went to Doug, propping him against the wagon wheel. Betty Brown wiped away dirt and blood with her scarf while Ann Parker kneeled and offered to get some water to wash the wound. Doug needed to get to a doctor as soon as possible.

Robert came to where Tom and the others were already gathered, compassion on his face. He lifted his broad-brimmed hat, ran his hand through his hair, and said, "Folks, my brother Tom and I were on our way home when we heard the shooting. I'm sorry we didn't get here sooner."

Betty rose to her feet, the strain deeply etched into her features. She put a hand on Robert's shoulder and said, "Robert, if you hadn't come along when you and Tom did, we might all have been killed.

"Now if you would be kind enough to take my youngest son home with you, my son Tim will help me get Doug to the doctor in Ottawa. We appreciate your kindness to our families."

Tom helped Betty onto the wagon seat, and Tim climbed up beside his mother. Tom and Robert laid Doug into the back of the wagon. Doug winced but tried to smile in appreciation. Tim snapped the reins over the backs of the horses and the wagon headed for Ottawa.

Moments later, Robert and Tom rode away, leading three ponies and carrying the three dead Indians in Robert's wagon. Charles and Ann Parker followed Tim and Betty into Ottawa.

Robert and Tom took the Indians' bodies to the sheriff's office in Sheridan. Sheriff Dan Hendricks and his assistant, the deputy sheriff, had heard what had taken place earlier that day. The deputy took the bodies from the Lett brothers and placed them behind the jail for the undertaker.

The doctor dressed Doug's wounds and said, "It's a good thing you got him here fast. He might have died from bleeding or blood poisoning. I'm hopeful he will be all right. He must rest for at least a month. I'll check on him a week from tomorrow."

Once home, Robert and Tom related the story of the incident. All gave thanks to the Lord that all members of the families had survived the attack. Tom led a special prayer for Doug Brown's rapid and safe recovery.

Later in the month, Tom made a special trip to Doug's farm to check on him and found him up and in good spirits. Doug commented that he and his family and friends owed their lives to Tom and Robert.

"You should praise God for your delivery and your rapid recovery," Tom said. "Robert and I are glad he used us to help. I see you're able to get around some now."

"Yes, I'm able to do light chores. Come on in, Tom, for a cup of coffee and some sweet rolls. Let's visit about the price of corn. It really is low."

The next day, November 3, Ed and Ben drove their wagons into downtown Detroit to lay the groundwork for opening a new branch of their trading business.

In late 1836, Ed had purchased a warehouse in Cobourg, Canada, and started a fur trading business. He had asked Ben, his friend since he was eleven years old, to be a partner. Now that they were moving west to Illinois, Ed had decided to expand the business. Many fur-bearing animals lived in the area forests, and demand for furs was high.

Their first objective was to find the office of Dr. Duncombe and renew their acquaintance. Dr. Duncombe had worked on the American side of the Canadian border to assist William Mackenzie when he organized skirmishes and rebellion against British rule in Canada in the late 1830s. Ben

CHAPTER ONE

had worked with Mackenzie for this cause; Ed had helped fund these efforts and transport messages through Ben.

It didn't take long to find the good doctor's office, and what a reunion they all had. Debra and Janice took the children shopping with Mrs. Duncombe leading the way. The children delighted in exploring the sights and sounds of the big city.

"Take your time shopping," Ben shouted to them as they left. "Ed and I have a lot of catching up to do with the doctor."

"We'll take your advice, Ben, and return about dinner time," Debra responded. Debra and Janice had their own money pouches but were inclined to be very frugal. Today they knew they were free to buy whatever the family needed.

After spending most of the afternoon reminiscing, the men got down to the business at hand. Ed and Ben needed Dr. Duncombe's help finding the right warehouse for a trading business.

"I suggest you visit the mayor's office and ask for his help," Dr. Duncombe said. "He owns a large hotel in the center of the city and would benefit from your trading business. Mayor Brannon is a tough old warrior, but he knows everything about business in this city. He fought in the War of 1812 against the British and lost part of his right hand. He loves anyone who fought the British and will be delighted to hear your story, Ben. I wouldn't be surprised if he knows just the building for you and Ed to rent."

When the women returned from shopping, all agreed to dine at the mayor's hotel restaurant that evening.

"Maybe the mayor and his wife would join us for dinner tonight," Debra suggested.

"Sounds like a great idea," Ben responded. "Dr. Duncombe, could you invite the mayor and his wife to join us?"

"Let's make this a social evening," Janice suggested. "Perhaps you men can wait until tomorrow to talk business with the mayor."

"We agree!" Ben responded.

They met for dinner at The Hotel Detroit, a beautiful old four-story colonial building with ornate trimmings and plentiful lattice work. The entry door was cut glass, and the magnificent glass crystal chandelier in the hall entrance sparkled. For a moment, Debra thought she was back in her childhood home in Old England enjoying a night in Her Majesty's court.

What a grand evening after more than a month on the dusty, dirty trail! She and Janice were as excited as two debutantes. They couldn't stop staring at the ceiling and wall decorations.

Lillian Brannon, the mayor's wife, approached them accompanied by Gloria Duncombe. Both smiled, extending their hands in friendship. Soon Lillian pulled Janice and Debra aside into a parlor to share the history of this landmark hotel.

The Hotel Detroit had belonged to Lillian's father's family since the 1700s. Her father and mother had lived in the hotel. Her father's name was John Daukins, and he fought the British in the War of 1812.

The hotel became the social center of Detroit because of the many important matters of business and government discussed and settled there.

"Our husbands will be tempted, but they promised us no business will be discussed at dinner," Janice said.

"We'll make sure of that!" Lillian said, laughing.

The head butler spoke privately to Lillian a few minutes later before escorting the ladies into a private dining room

CHAPTER ONE

off the main hall. Debra was seated to the right of the mayor, who delighted in having such a lovely, intelligent dinner partner.

What a gracious evening was had by everyone. Two lovely young ladies sang opera for the group, and Lillian was fascinated by Ben and his tales of hunting, fighting, and escaping from many battles. She especially enjoyed tales of how he used disguises to fool his enemies and avoid arrest when he traveled back to Canada.

Ed and Ben spent the entire next day selecting a building to rent and hiring a young man to run their business.

David Bristol, a tall man with a light complexion in his early thirties, filled every requirement. David's temperament emitted confidence, self-assurance, and honesty to all he met, and the mayor could vouch for his honesty. David was a leader in his church and strong in defending America. The partners sought a man like this, and they were convinced God was answering their prayers.

In the next days, Ed and Ben worked with David to set up the office and warehouse for the trading business. So many trappers and hunters wanted to sell their wares in the Detroit area that David had a backlog from the first day in business.

Ed told David he had permission to seek the mayor's advice when the business grew enough to add a second man.

"I'm flattered you have that much confidence in my judgment, and I'll not let you down," the mayor said.

CHAPTER TWO

THE BITTER COLD wind blew from the west, and the breath of animals and humans plumed in the air as the Letts and the Doyles bid their good-byes to the Brannons and Duncombes.

Ed and Ben would return in years to come to check on David Bristol and their trading company. Years from now, Ed and Janice would stop on a trip to visit family in Cobourg, Canada. And Ben and Debra would return as well.

They began their journey with Ben and Ed astride their favorite horses. Debra and Janice drove the wagons with Jackson, Sam, and Sophie inside. Debra's heart soared.

Now, today, she thought. *The beginning of our dream starts now! Ben and I and Jackson are going to live in freedom from terror and have our own farm and business. Our children will grow up educated and prosperous. I really believe the Lord will reign in our hearts forever and ever.*

After the noon stop, Ben and Ed tied their horses behind the wagons and climbed up beside their wives.

"Westward we go," Debra said excitedly.

CHAPTER TWO

Ben and Ed had been leading their families farther into the wilderness for weeks, and still they had encountered neither friend nor foe.

"I thought we'd have seen someone by now," Debra said to Ben.

"Worried?" he asked.

"No."

"Scared?" he added.

"A little," she admitted.

She lifted her eyes toward the sky and looked at Ben from the corner of her eyes.

"Ben, I believe this is what the Lord wants us to do, and he's led us this far safely. I know we have strong, smart men taking care of us, but it's OK for us women to be a little scared, isn't it?"

She laughed and looked at him carefully.

"Aren't you just a little scared?"

"Not yet," Ben responded. "Life in Illinois won't be easy. I know scary times will come. Let's don't borrow from tomorrow."

They forded the Portage River in Michigan with only a little difficulty.

"The Lord is surely taking care of us, Ben," Debra said as the back wheels of their wagon hit solid ground. Ed and Janice had no trouble following them across the river.

Debra's eye swept the vast countryside.

"When we decided to come out here, I was certain. But at times I have wondered if we'd done the right thing," she chuckled. "If we keep our eyes on the Lord, we will have victory like David the shepherd."

Ben nodded his head in admiration of her faith.

Debra climbed from her seat beside Ben and lifted a blanket at the back of the wagon. She tested the cottage cheese ripening there. It crumbed nicely. With her fingers, she compressed the curds and put them in flour. She was getting ready to make bread.

These ingredients would go in the Dutch oven in the coals when they stopped tonight. The smell of fresh bread drove Ben crazy. She wanted this evening to be special for both of them.

When evening came, they stopped by a stream. Debra and Jackson built a fire so she could begin baking the bread. When it was time to eat, she cut pieces of warm bread for the entire group. She watched carefully while Ben took a slice of bread and put it into his mouth.

"What did you do to the bread? This is the best bread I've ever eaten," Ben shouted.

With great pride she told him of her idea to put some cinnamon in the dough.

"I may need to buy you some more cinnamon," he joked.

"By the way," Debra said, "our flour and coffee are getting a little low. I hate to think what you might do, Ben Lett, if we run out of coffee!"

She and Janice put up a brave front at the mention of a needed supply trip. Indians could be near, so they dared not leave their wagons unprotected. The women and children would stay alone while Ben and Ed went for supplies.

That night before bed, Ben comforted her.

"Will you be all right?" he asked.

"Of course," she said.

He pulled her into his arms.

"I'll do everything I can to make it easier for you and keep you and the others safe. Maybe Ed should stay with the wagons this time."

"No," she said, looking at him in the dark, barely able to discern his features. "We'll trust the Lord to take care of us, too."

CHAPTER TWO

Ben took Debra by the hand and suggested they go for a walk to the opening by the stream.

"Just look at those stars. It appears we could almost reach up and pick one out of the sky," he said.

"What would you do with a handful of stars?" she teased.

"Why, I'd give one to my best girl and keep the others for another night," he grinned.

The moonlight revealed the smile on his face, and his blue eyes shone as he spoke of his great love for her. Ben guided her to a log at the edge of the clearing. There was no need for words as they sat on the log in the clear moonlight with the cool breeze blowing.

The couples had been on the trail for six weeks, and it was mid-November. They had left Michigan several days earlier and were almost across Indiana. The next day they would arrive in Illinois.

Ben and Ed scouted the next morning. Debra and Janice scanned the horizon where the dried grass stood tall from summer. They topped a small rise to find a large stand of timber as thick and dark as velvet drapery. The wind rubbed the blades of grass together, creating a symphony that welcomed them to the land of their dreams.

Debra and Janice reined in the horses and stopped the wagons atop the rise. Ben and Ed rode up, waving their hats and shouting.

The men helped the women and children from the wagons and gave them all big hugs. They stood, arms around one other, looking into the beautiful sunset. The sun and clouds and glorious array of colors formed a tapestry only God could create.

Debra gasped and raised her arms in tribute to the God of heaven for such a beautiful sight. She began to cry.

"It's been a long time since I have seen you cry, Debra," Ben said.

"Some people cry when they're sad. I cry mostly when I'm happy," she replied.

That night, Debra carefully noted the date—November 16, 1845—in her Bible. She wrote about how thrilled she was to be settling in such a beautiful part of God's creation.

"We should be at the home of my brothers in the Sheridan area in three days," Ben said.

"I can't wait until we reach our new home and you carry me across the threshold," Debra added.

Ben and Ed left the women and went to the nearby town for supplies the next morning. Debra and Janice played with the children while they washed some clothes in the nearby stream.

"Let's take this opportunity to spend this day getting ourselves and our children ready to visit the Lett relatives," Debra said to Janice.

"The more we spend time getting ready for our visit, the more organized we'll be to move into your new home," she replied.

Before the men left to get supplies, Ben came to Jackson. "Watch over Sam and Sophie, Jackson. Their father and I must go to town on business. Your mother is resting, and Mrs. Doyle will be bathing in her wagon. We shall be back soon."

"But, Dad!" Jackson protested.

"Do as you are told," Ben said firmly. "Each must do his bit, and this is your part. Be kind, now."

To keep them entertained, Jackson decided to tell Sam and Sophie some scary stories.

Sam was a very thin boy with large eyes that seemed even darker in the darkness. He listened intently as Jackson told him and his sister tales of the Tommy-knockers who

CHAPTER TWO

haunted the mines underground. Then Jackson told of shipwrecks and storms along the rocky coast of Lake Erie. Little Sophie just hid her eyes behind her hands.

The two wagons stood together, but another wagon stood at a campsite at least two hundred yards away beyond a roll of the hill and some trees.

The campfire had burned low, and Jackson could hear the water splashing in the tin tub where Janice was bathing.

The children sat at the edge of the brush. Jackson kept his voice low so as not to disturb his mother, who rested in their wagon. Suddenly he became aware of a mutter of voices—drunken voices.

"We've got to move fast," somebody said in a voice not at all drunken. "The wagons will be empty, and their money is hidden," the voice said.

The sound trailed away, and several men came into the circle of light. Instinctively, Jackson put a hand over Sophie's mouth and pulled her back under the brush. One of the men took a pull at a bottle, and another grabbed it from him.

"Hey! That's mine!" he protested.

"Ed?" It was Sophie and Sam's mother.

"Is that you, Ed?" she called.

One of the drunken men lurched toward the rear opening of the wagon and jerked back the canvas.

"No, this here is George, this here's . . ."

His voice broke off sharply and then . . . a scream. A shot followed. George flew back out of the wagon.

Holding Sophie and Sam tightly, keeping their faces against his chest, young Jackson watched in horror. He heard a stifled scream and the sounds of men brawling.

Another shot rang out, and a man yelled, "I'm hit."

At least four men were at the wagons. Another shot sounded, and one of the four fell to the ground wounded.

Several men rushed from the wagons, almost falling over one another. The men outside the wagons turned and rushed to their horses. Jackson picked up his rifle and aimed it at one of the fleeing would-be thieves. He pulled the trigger and down went one of the men.

Suddenly someone shouted, "Look out! Run! Here they come!"

As the robbers scattered, Jackson saw Ben and Ed riding as fast as they could toward the wagons. Ed flew off his horse while Ben pursued. Ben caught and shot two of the three men trying to escape. The remaining man turned his horse into the shallow stream. Ben let him go and rode back to the wagons.

Jackson had taken the children by the hand and returned to the wagons where Ed and Janice hugged. Jackson waited while Ben and Debra embraced. He then clung to his father's hand; his other hand was around Sophie. He stared at the dead men lying on the ground.

Ben and Ed buried the bodies of the six men side by side on a little hill not far from the nearby Kankakee River.

When it was over, Jackson asked, "What will we do now?"

"We'll notify the authorities and continue our journey to Sheridan, Illinois," Ben said.

The next morning, Debra and Janice served cottage cheese flour bread along with a hearty helping of fried meat.

"Nothing like the smell of fresh ground coffee cooking in the morning," Ben said happily.

Debra stood by the makeshift table as she finished meal preparations.

"Ben, why don't you pray for our journey? Today might be our last day on the road."

Ben bowed his head and said, "Dear Lord, we humbly bow before you, thanking you for watching over us during

CHAPTER TWO

this trip. We ask for your continued care on what we hope will be our last day on the trail."

Ed took a big bite of his food, chewed thoughtfully, wiped his mouth with a piece of cloth, and said, "I've heard this part of Illinois is a good place to farm now that the Injuns are pretty well taken care of, but we still need to be careful. We have to be here a while to know the good Injuns from the bad."

He talked to them all about his idea to trade with the Injuns if they wanted food.

"You might call it a peace policy," Ed said. "If we trade, maybe that will prevent them from attacking us or stealing from us. I say we should try and get along with 'em as best we can. As always, though, we have to be ready to defend ourselves."

The sun was setting over the Fox River Valley as the wagons reached the crest of the hill. Ben got off his horse and bid everyone gather around. Looking in a northwesterly direction, he pointed to the smoke coming from the chimneys of several houses north of the river.

"Those are the Lett family homes just north of the little town of Sheridan," he said with pride. "We could reach them tonight, but it would be dark. Let's make camp here, and we'll reach them before noon tomorrow."

Debra grabbed Ben around the neck and almost squeezed his breath away.

"Hurray!" Debra said. "Janice and I have already planned what we and the children will wear. We'll wear the dresses we wore in Detroit. Mine has that pretty lace around the collar," she added. "We will dress in the morning and be ready to meet them at their homes."

Early the next morning, Debra and Janice moved in a blur. They insisted Ben and Ed draw pails of water from the nearby stream for bathing. The entire family was ordered to scrub despite the chilly temperatures. A mile away you could hear the families scrubbing and laughing and playing. It was a good sound.

When Ben got up out of the water, he reached for his clothes.

"Oh, no! Don't put on those dirty things!" Debra scolded. "I have clean ones laid out for you in the wagon."

So it was that the scrubbed and happy families went calling. Debra and Janice had baked pies that night and had them in baskets ready for the family reunion.

They approached the Tom Lett farm home the morning of November 19, 1845. Tom rode out to the farms of his other siblings and asked them to come greet the travelers. His siblings then took turns greeting them all.

Tom introduced his wife, Merrilla. Robert, at that time, was a bachelor farmer. All of Ben's sisters had married Springstead brothers who had settled in the area. In 1841, Maria had married Hiram, and Betsy had married David. And in 1843, Sara had married Harvey.

The men sat at a table in the living room while the women pulled chairs up to the kitchen table. The children all ran outside to chase the chickens and dog.

Merrilla was an able hostess, and Tom and Robert were as warm and inviting as anyone could imagine. The men drifted outside to look over the property.

The women talked of babies and cooking and recipes, and eventually Debra told Merrilla of the people they had met in Detroit and how much fun they had with Mrs. Duncombe and the mayor's wife. To Merrilla and the Lett sisters, it sounded wonderful. They asked a lot of questions and began dreaming of the time when they might make a trip to Detroit.

CHAPTER TWO

By mid-afternoon the travelers were eager to be on their way to Leland. Debra and Janice hugged the entire group and thanked Merrilla for the wonderful lunch. Tom and Robert shook hands with Ben and Ed before the men helped their wives and children into the wagons and climbed up themselves.

It took about two hours to reach their new Illinois home. Otto Gilbert, the caretaker, came from the barn to greet them. Otto was one of the men who had helped Ben build a strong barn to hold the grain, hay, and animals during the cold winter days. It had been an enormous undertaking.

When he first saw the barn, Ben recalled the celebration he had held when the barn was completed. He had invited Tom and Robert to join him and the neighbors for one big feast with lots of dancing. Otto had asked a young woman he was courting in Leland to be his date that evening back in late spring 1841.

Ben remembered that Otto had brought his friend to the party in a borrowed buggy and introduced the young lady to the Lett family.

"This here is Miss Ginny Burns," he said proudly. "Ginny, this is Miz Merrilla Lett, Mr. Tom Lett, Mr. Robert Lett, Miz Betsy Springstead and her husband Mr. David Springstead, Miz Maria Springstead and her husband Mr. Hiram Springstead, and Miss Sara Lett."

"I'm pleased to meet you," Ginny said. She was medium height and slender with long, straight, blond hair. Some of her hair fluffed over her slender face in a very attractive way.

Otto planned to take care of the farm while Ben was in New York the following year. However, Ben was gone for five years instead of one, so Otto stayed on and kept the farm in first-rate shape. He married his sweetheart, Ginny, and they built a cabin and settled down on the farm. The

Gilbert family awaited the day Ben and Debra would return to claim the house and farm for their own home.

Ben had rented the farm to Otto on a fifty-fifty basis. He raised corn, wheat, barley, oats, hay, and meadow. Otto hired extra help during the planting and harvesting season, and Ginny fed the crews and raised a very large garden. They had forty hens, one sow and her litter of pigs, three milk cows, and two calves being fattened as beef. They also cared for four oxen, six work horses, a driving team, a Shetland pony, a dog, and five cats.

Otto and Ginny now had two children—Robert, a stocky boy of three who followed his father helping with any job his dad would permit, and Susan, two, who loved to be out of doors playing with Shep, the farm dog.

When the Letts and Doyles arrived, Otto quickly helped the children from the wagons and welcomed Debra and Janice.

"Come on, Ben, I can't wait to see our new home," Debra said.

They acted like newlyweds, holding hands as they ran toward the house. It looked very similar to the one Ben had built for them on the Nichols land in Lewiston, New York. The site of this beautiful new house made Debra feel right at home.

When they reached the porch, Ben scooped Debra up in his arms and gave her a squeeze before carrying her across the threshold.

"Here we are, Mrs. Lett. What do you think of our new home?" he asked with a laugh.

"It's magnificent and so similar to the home I loved in New York. Hallelujah!" Debra cried. "It's so familiar that it helps make me feel like I'm home."

Light was fading fast, so Otto unhitched the team of horses and turned them out to pasture while the men

CHAPTER TWO

unloaded the wagons. Soon everyone gathered around the dining room table for the first dinner in their new home.

Ben asked everyone to stand and hold hands. Ed offered thanks for their safe trip and wonderful welcome by Otto and Ginny.

"Tonight after our meal, we will retire to the living room around the great fireplace and read from the Bible," he said. "I'd like to read about the children of Israel arriving in the Promised Land. We need to dedicate our lives to the Lord for safekeeping and service to his holy name."

When they had gathered, Ben picked up the family Bible and began reading from the book of Joshua. This book shows so clearly how well the children of Israel were blessed because of love of God and obedience to his will.

Ben read, "After the death of Moses, the servant of the Lord, it came to pass that the Lord spoke to Joshua, the son of Nun, Moses' assistant, saying, 'Moses, My servant is dead; now therefore, arise, go over this Jordan, thou, and all this people, unto the land which I do give to them, even to the children of Israel' (Joshua 1:1-2).

"The Lord gave us this land, and we should be ready to work, struggle, and sacrifice for our home and family," Ben said. "I've given each one of you a candle tonight to light. I will light the first candle from the fireplace, and then I'll light Debra's candle from mine. She will light Jackson's from hers and so on around the circle.

"Think of how the Holy Spirit might be speaking to your heart," Ben said. "Think about putting the Lord's power to work in your life for people in this area or for this place. When everyone's candle is lit, I will pronounce a blessing on each of you in the name and power of our Lord Jesus Christ."

Ben started. "I'll give supplies for winter to widows and poor families."

Debra thought for a minute. "I'll open our home to teach children reading and music."

Jackson said, "I will teach children how to ride ponies and how to rope calves."

"I can help build things for the neighbors," Ed offered.

Janice smiled and said, "I want to help teach the Bible to children."

"Sophie and I will play with the children," Samuel said.

"Our family will continue to farm the land, raise horses, cook, clean, and sing," Otto said.

"I'll have prayer meetings every day in the Lett kitchen before the day starts," Ginny said.

"Now why don't we sing some hymns and songs?" Ed asked. "Janice, why don't you lead our first song?"

When they had finished, Ben called everyone to sing "Blest Be the Tie That Binds our Hearts in Christian Love."

"It's time to get ready for bed, but before we do, let me pray a blessing on each of you," Ben said.

As Ben prayed for each person, they felt God's power flow through them. Each recognized how ready he or she now was for a new mission.

Ben and Debra gave each of the Gilbert family members a big hug. Otto thanked Ben for the wonderful evening and said how thrilled he was to be a small part of such a wonderful family.

Ben said, "You have such a wonderful family, Otto. We are so happy to partner with you on this farm."

Ed and Janice and their children headed upstairs while the Letts retired to their rooms on the first floor. These would be their arrangements for the time being.

CHAPTER TWO

"Ben, what a beautiful evening," Debra said with a sigh. "You couldn't have found nicer people to help with the farm work. Ginny and I will become good friends in no time at all. I'm glad you suggested they eat most of their meals with us. It will make our living here so much more pleasant."

"I'm glad you like Ginny and Otto," Ben answered. "I hoped they would be special company for you."

Then he added, "Well, Mrs. Lett, it's time for you and me to have a special time tonight in our new home."

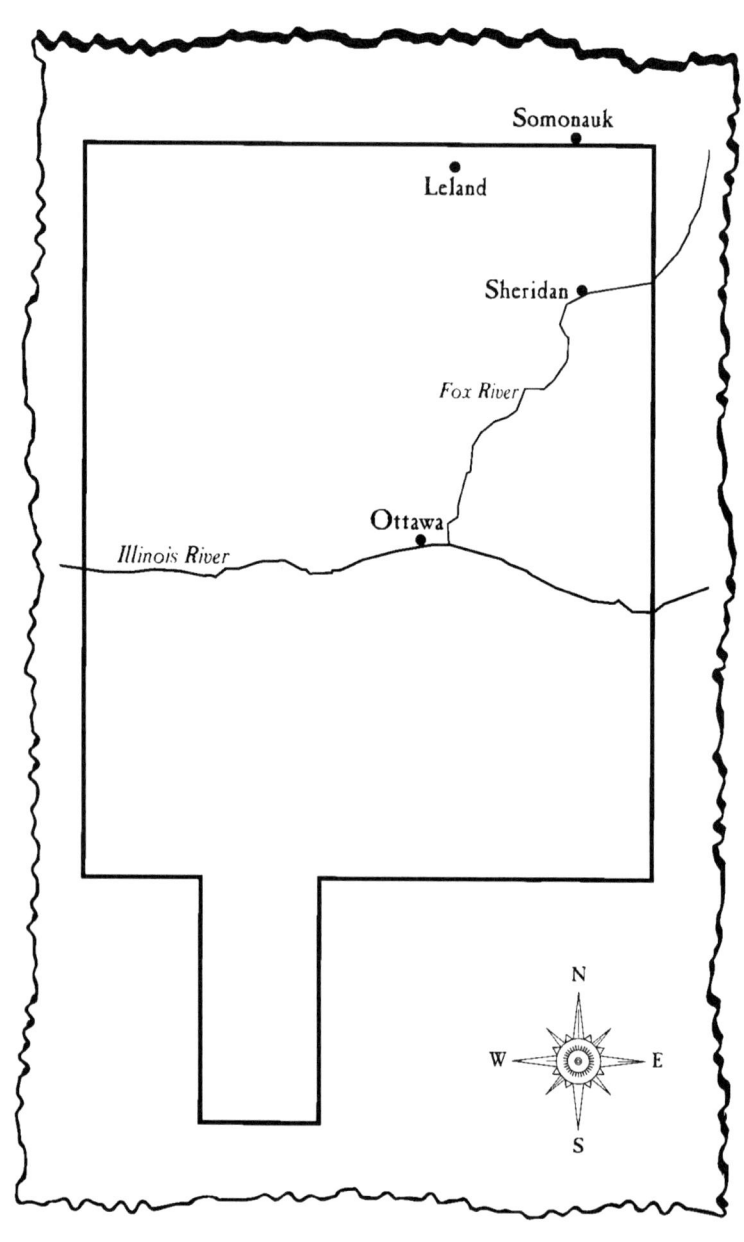

CHAPTER THREE

BEN AND ED worked inside the barn the next afternoon, spreading new straw on the floor with pitchforks. Ed began recalling how God had spared Ben's life in prison.

"You were hated for trouble you were accused of causing along the border in Canada," Ed said. "I'm surprised they caught you. It took a traitor turning you in for the reward money for them to catch you. We had better always be on the alert for trouble. After all, the queen would like nothing better than to get revenge for you being free today."

As he looked out through the open double doors, a rider came into the yard.

"Looks like we've got company, Ben," Ed squinted. "Oh, it's Tom!"

Janice was on the back porch of the house, shaking dust from a small rug. Ben and Ed saw Tom draw rein at the porch, tip his hat to Janice, and speak to her. Janice smiled and pointed toward the barn.

Tom smiled in return and guided his horse in that direction. Pitchforks in their hands, Ben and Ed stepped out into the sunshine, and as Tom approached, they saw a folded newspaper in his hand.

Ben said, "Morning, Tom. "What brings you out here? Did you want to pitch some hay?"

Tom laughed as he dismounted. "Ah . . . no. I'm here for a different reason. Hello, Ed."

"Greetings to you, Tom," Ed nodded.

Tom stepped close and waved the folded newspaper.

"I have a copy of yesterday's Ottawa newspaper. Have you men seen it? An article in here says the army is interested in buying horses for their cavalry."

"I'm way ahead of you, Tom," Ben said. "I already have a contract with the U.S. Army to supply horses in any number I choose.

"Otto has been expanding the herd for the last five years. We have more than a hundred horses now ready for sale," Ben continued. "This news will give Ed and me something to do next week. We will round up twenty of these horses and drive them to Chicago. I plan to start the drive Monday, the twenty-fifth of November. Will you join us on the drive?"

"I sure will, and I'll check with Robert. Maybe he'll come along as well. As you no doubt remember, he's a good horseman," Tom said.

"I would really appreciate having you and Robert with us on the trip. With you along we could take more horses. You men also would give us more fire power in case we have trouble from thieves," Ben added.

"I'll ride over to Robert's on my way home and check with him," Tom said. "We'll look forward to seeing you early Monday morning."

CHAPTER THREE

On Friday, Ben, Ed, and Otto began to round up the herd of horses. They planned to bring at least half the herd to the corral next to the barn to sort the best for sale. These would be the first horses he would sell to the army, and Ben wanted to make sure these were some of his best.

The profit from the sale of these horses would allow Ben to buy more breeding stock from local horse breeders and more land for pasture. Ben had a good eye for the best horse flesh and a knack for arriving at a fair price for buyer and seller.

The morning they left, cold air hugged low to the ground and filled it with frost. The full moon dropped in the western sky, lighting the smoke plumes coming from the houses in town. The plumes coalesced into broad bands in the north central Illinois sky. Clouds hung heavy in the west. The temperature hovered around thirty degrees Fahrenheit.

An army lieutenant rode into the farmstead just before Ben began preparing the horses for the drive.

"I'm Lieutenant Moorman," barked the cocky young man who sat on a prancing red roan. "I'm here to buy horses."

His arrogance irritated Ben, but the possibility of getting cash from the government right there at the farm kept Ben from the hard reply perched on the tip of his tongue.

"I'm about to sell to the army in Chicago," Ben replied. "How many horses did you have in mind?"

Ignoring Ben's perceived rudeness, the lieutenant got off his horse and dusted his clothes.

"That depends entirely on the quality of the animals," the lieutenant responded.

"Been here long, Lieutenant Moorman?" Ben asked casually.

The man blushed slightly. "A month," he replied.

"Then you should know that horses sell well. Especially when they are high-quality horses like mine. Quality is a point of honor with me," Ben said.

Silently he led the lieutenant to the corral where Ed and Otto were already working with the horses. The lieutenant was clearly pleased with what he saw.

"I can use twenty horses like these," he said. "I'll give you ten dollars apiece."

Ben decided to speak up for more money. He asked for fifteen dollars.

"We'll split the difference," Lieutenant Moorman offered.

"I'll take fourteen dollars," Ben responded.

"It's a deal. We'll be back in a week. I'll bring you the money at that time," Lieutenant Moorman promised.

"You just bought yourself some horses, Lieutenant," Ben said.

"That's what I wanted," he answered.

He mounted his horse and rode down the lane and across the bridge over the creek.

"Well, men, we're richer now, if we get paid," Ben said.

"Of course the downside is that we need to break more horses." He threw a wave to Otto. "Go to it, man, and be sure and take some men with you."

Ben, Ed, and Otto came to supper that night exhausted. After washing up, Ben sat down and bowed his head to pray.

"For what we are about to receive, O Lord, and the surprising sale of the horses, we give you thanks."

The three men sat by the fireplace that evening to finalize their plans for their horse drive to Chicago. Ben used a piece of brown wrapping paper to draw a rough map, indicating the trails known to him.

CHAPTER THREE

After the children were in bed, Debra and Ben sat at the kitchen table discussing the day.

She said, "Ben, I sense you're uneasy about something."

Ben stared into his coffee cup, watching the lantern light reflect in the black liquid. After a pause, he admitted, "You're right. No matter what I do, I have the feeling our herd of horses is vulnerable to attack, and there's nothing much more I can do to protect it."

Quietly she said, "I think you need to spend a lot more time in prayer. No one on earth can keep your herd together all the way to Chicago. Give your worries to the Lord and let him take care of things."

Ben looked down. Finally, he set his cup on the table and stood up.

"Debra, love, I need to go out and do some talking with the Lord. Why don't you get some sleep? I'll be joining you later," he said.

As he headed for the door, Debra reached out to grab him by the arm and give him a kiss on the cheek. Her gentle smile was the last thing he saw as he closed the door behind him.

Ben walked out past the barn and leaned on the corral fence. He looked at the horses and up into the sky full of stars. Looking at the black heavens filled with tiny pieces of mirror put his life in perspective.

"Lord, it's time you and I shared our hearts. You know I have trouble relying on anyone other than myself," he prayed. "I've depended upon my wits and human strength to get me out of trouble most of my life. But I'm facing a situation that I can't handle myself.

"Would you transform my mind and give me your mind on the matter of driving these horses to market? I need your protecting hand over our herd and our journey. I need your watchful care over Debra, Janice, and the children while we're gone."

Ben awoke refreshed and eager for the new day. Otto and Ed were out early getting the horses ready for travel. Ben separated the horses sold to the young lieutenant and then chose forty horses for the drive. He was certain Ed and Otto, along with Tom and Robert, could handle the herd. He trusted that they wouldn't have any trouble along the way.

Trouble could come in the form of storms, thieves, rivers to cross, wolves to encounter, and possible stampede. This trip would not be easy.

He wanted to build a solid reputation as an honest man who only dealt in quality stock. He recalled Debra's advice and prayed, "Lord, be my peace of mind during the days and weeks ahead."

Ben decided to lash eight horses in a group to trail behind each man. Ben would lead the group because he knew the trail better than anyone. He planned to make the trip in three days given good weather. If it snowed, they could still arrive in four.

Debra took one look at Ben's face and said, "I can see in your eyes you are about to leave."

"We'll leave in two hours if Tom and Robert have arrived," he confirmed.

He pulled her away from her work and put his arms around her. Pain clouded his loving blue eyes.

"Try not to be mad at me for leaving," he asked.

"I know you have to go. I just can't stand to think of something happening to you," she whispered.

"I made it through the war." He grinned wickedly. "Didn't we agree that the Lord was in charge?"

"I miss you already," she said and then kissed his mouth carefully.

"I love you."

CHAPTER THREE

"I'll bring you some peppermint," he said and smiled, hoping to coax a smile.

"That'll be wonderful, but don't forget the money, too," she teased back.

Ready to move out, Ben saw Tom and Robert coming across the bridge, heading for the corral. He waved at them, turned away from the family, and mounted his horse. His black mare was a beauty and full of energy. She responded to Ben's knee movements.

Ben greeted his brothers and gave the order for each man to grab the lead rope for his group of eight horses. Ben was on the point. He pulled his broad-brimmed black hat down a little tighter over his forehead as he led the procession down the lane, across the bridge, and onto the open trail at a fast gallop.

The first day tired them to the bone. They hoped to make it to Geneva on the Fox River by night. Tom and Robert weren't thrilled at riding drag, but everyone had to take his turn at the back of the group. The dust of the herd and the constant smell of warm droppings were tough on the men. The next day, Tom and Robert would rotate to another spot. They planned to stay west and north of the Fox River and approach the river toward evening.

A sudden rifle report threw the horses into wild contortions. Ben pulled hard on his lead rope, trying to keep control of his group. Each of the men did the same. Looking over his shoulder, he could see a group of riders bearing down on them. His men began firing into the approaching raiders.

Ben tried to see the attackers and hold his horses at the same time. The screams and gunshots reminded him for one awful moment of his days back in the Canadian War. The fear in the pit of his stomach knotted his muscles, and he fired at any target that presented itself.

Ben's crew got off better shots than their attackers, so they staved off the determined efforts of the bandits. A few at a time, the attackers dropped away. Ben and his men pulled their horses into a circle and checked for any injury to the horses. They found none. Ben breathed a prayer of thanksgiving.

"We are only five miles from Geneva, so let's move it out. I would like to be settled for the night somewhere along the Fox River," Ben remarked.

"Find us a place to bed down. We can shackle the horses for the night along the river. We've come far enough for the first day," Robert said.

Ben expected the men would all want to talk about the encounter with the bandits, but most were too tired to do much more than eat and roll up in their blankets. Otto took first guard duty until midnight. Even Tom was asleep before Ben laid out his bedroll close to the banked fire.

It had been a rough beginning, and the men had fought the bandits and controlled the horses even better than Ben had hoped. Now they were veterans. Surely they could handle anything.

CHAPTER FOUR

ON TUESDAY, OTTO moved the herd away from the Fox River and headed east toward the Des Plaines River. No more attempts to steal the horses had occurred, but Ben knew too many miles lay ahead.

At the noon break, Ben and Ed leaned against a tree. It was cold, and the wind was blowing hard from the northwest.

"Only one attempt at stealing our horses," Ed said, grinning. His voice sobered.

"You know we'll get hit at least once more before this trip is over."

"I can understand why the outlaws would try again to steal my horses," Ben remarked with a smile on his face. "These horses are worth a lot of money. With more and more immigrants coming to this country from out east, it is getting harder for thieves to make a living. These pioneers are brave men and prepared to fight for their family and property.

"I came out here to make a living for me and my family, too," he added. "I have no intention of letting some thief rob me of my possessions."

He focused his thoughts on Debra waiting for him at home. Her absence was like a living thing within him. Half of him was at the farm, and half of him was there. It still amazed him that his love for one woman could have remained so strong through all those years. It had grown from the first desires of young love to a deep need of being together.

He loved Jackson, the extension of their love for each other.

The cold, hard winds and low-hanging clouds meant an early snowstorm loomed. Ben shivered. He scanned the horizon but saw clouds floating like fully spread blankets. They bedded the horses that night beside a large spring that fed Lake Michigan.

"Men, build a large fire tonight so Otto can cook us his famous rabbit stew," he said. "Tomorrow about noon we should make it to our destination."

The clouds began moving away, and the sky cleared. Never had the moon been brighter.

In a strong voice, Ben said, "I'm planning on wearing my hat to bed and keeping my gun in it. If robbers try again to hit us, I'll be ready."

"Did you notice that Robert puts his rope in a circle around his bed at night?" Tom said. "Our father told him that a snake won't cross over a rope, but who expects snakes in this kind of weather?"

"He hasn't been bitten yet," Ben said with a poker face.

The north wind and the songs sung by the men before turning in helped soothe Ben's nerves. He slept soundly despite the cold and woke about three o'clock in the morning

CHAPTER FOUR

to snow on his face. He woke the men to begin the last phase of the trip.

The men roused themselves with the aroma of strong coffee and the sweet smell of bacon crisping in the frying pan. Otto also had bread warming in a towel by the fire. The wind had changed direction, now blowing from the east off the lake. That could mean trouble.

Ben encouraged the men to hurry and move out. As they mounted, the snowfall began accumulating in drifts along the trail. The wind off the lake was moist and bitter cold. The men pulled up the collars of their coats around their necks and pushed their broad-brimmed hats down over their eyes.

"We've got about a four-hour ride ahead of us. Let's move along as fast as we can," Ben yelled over the wind.

The snow soon blinded them and covered the trail. They moved along using the lake shore to guide them. A sudden first-rate blizzard made the going really slow. A four-hour trip became an all-day ordeal. Ben began to wonder if they would ever make it, but he also knew his men were tough and would not quit on him.

At noon, they found a grove of trees and some slight shelter. The horses shivered and the men's faces froze over from the steam of their breathing. They chewed some beef jerky, drank cool water from their canteens, and refreshed themselves enough to continue. The horses resisted moving from shelter, but whips and the firing of their guns got the herd moving.

Some four hours later, Ben thought he heard a dog bark. He listened for a moment but heard only the howling wind and blowing snow. He halted the group and listened. There it was again! Truly, this time he was sure he heard a dog.

Ben shouted at the men, "We're here!"

He began pulling harder on his team of horses and moved in the direction of the barking. Soon he saw the massive gates of the army's fort and shouted at the watchman with no response. He took out his revolver and fired it into the air. After what seemed like an eternity, the gates began to open. The frozen men and horses were led to a barn to warm up and get some food.

Ben went to the commander's office to settle up for the horses. Captain Riley welcomed Ben and offered him a cup of coffee.

"Thanks for the coffee, and thanks for inviting my men to a meal," Ben said.

"We are very happy you made it here in the storm. We desperately need the horses you brought us. I'm prepared to pay you a premium," Captain Riley remarked.

"My brothers, my best friend, and my partner are some of the best men you will ever encounter for operating under such harsh conditions. They know how to find their way in a storm," Ben said. "Captain, what do you intend to offer for my horses?"

"You know how to get right to the point, Ben Lett," the captain said, smiling.

"I believe in talking straight, Captain, and I don't talk around the bush," Ben answered.

"Normally I might offer sixteen dollars per horse, but because yours are such fine horses and because we are in desperate need, I'm willing to pay you eighteen dollars."

"Captain, you are indeed a generous man," Ben responded. "I'll take your offer, providing you promise to come to my home someday soon and look at our entire herd."

"I'll agree to visit early next April and look over your horses. I may buy the entire herd. What do you think of that, Ben?" he added.

CHAPTER FOUR

"I'll be looking forward to your visit," Ben said as he shook his hand.

"Let's have some food and drink together then," the captain said.

The men chatted about Ben's experiences in the war, and Ben told the captain how glad he was to be free and farming in Illinois. He also told him that he really looked forward to selling horses to the army.

"I promise you, Ben," the captain said, "for the foreseeable future, the army will buy all the horses you can raise or purchase."

"I'm pleased to hear of your interest," Ben answered. "Come see us in the spring like you said, and I'll have a couple hundred horses for you."

The storm had subsided by morning, and Ben was anxious to hit the trail for home. With saddlebags loaded with pouches of gold coins and supplies for the families, they began their trip home.

"We should be able to get home in two days if we ride hard," Ed remarked.

Ben, Ed, and Otto arrived home and spent an evening handing out gifts purchased in Chicago. With the three couples together, everything seemed funnier and even the food tasted better. They were good friends gathering together to celebrate the successful sale of many fine horses.

Ben had paid the men well for their work. He also had shared rewards with Tom and Robert before they left for home. Ben was a generous man, and people appreciated his kindness to them.

"Ben, get out that fiddle of yours. I'm pining to be dancing with my wife," Otto called.

On the hardwood floors of the dining room, they spun and wheeled to Ben's fiddle, and the gingham skirts whirled. The music slowed, and for a while each couple seemed wrapped in their world of memories.

Otto spelled Ben with his harmonica, and Debra found herself in Ben's arms, waltzing to the sweet strains of "Sweet Amy Lee."

She thought, *How strong and handsome my Ben is. I think he's probably the best-looking man here.*

She felt so secure in his arms, gliding across the floor to the music. As they danced, she reminded herself to concentrate on what she had today, to forget about yesterday, and to keep her eyes on Jesus. She laid her head down on Ben's chest and gave herself up to the rhythm of the music.

The December wind had an ugly bite to it a few days later as Debra and Janice worked to carry the frozen clothes into the house from the clothesline. While Ben, Ed, and Otto were doing chores that day, a visitor arrived from Leland to talk to Ben.

Ben introduced himself to the visitor, who seemed quite reserved about introducing himself. He also introduced the visitor to Ed and Otto. The men talked about the harsh winter weather, the price of grain, and the possibility of war between the northern and southern states. In time, the visitor said his name was Tom Bracken.

"I didn't come here to waste your time. I came to try and interest you in my horses," Bracken remarked. "Would you be interested in buying ten well-bred geldings for riding horses? I'll let you have them for eleven dollars apiece."

"All I can say today," Ben said, "is let's set a time to look them over. Then I'll let you know if I'm interested."

The men agreed to meet the next Tuesday morning at the Bracken farm. Ben warned him that they were good judges

CHAPTER FOUR

of horses. If any of the horses were lame or defective, there would be no deal.

Shep monitored Bracken's arrival and his departure down the lane and over the bridge. Debra brought some scraps from the kitchen and tossed them to him. As he gulped down the food, she stroked his black and white coat. His long tail beat the air in pleasure.

Debra left the dog and went back into the house. It was bread day, and she looked forward to getting her hands into the fragrant dough. She had just put the first batch into the fire to bake when she heard the dog's low warning growl. She looked out her kitchen window and saw a buck deer crossing the frozen creek near the house. She shaded her eyes, looked a second time, and observed seven does following the buck.

My, they look beautiful, she thought.

Debra's pounding heart settled a bit. She loved to see these beautiful animals, especially in the winter.

At noon Ben and Ed came in from the barn hot and dirty.

"Got the barn cleaned and the manure hauled away into the corn field," said Ben. "We certainly have some beautiful colts. Maybe we'll expand the barn to make room for more colts."

Debra and Janice put the hot stew and fresh bread in front of the men and children. The children had been in classes with Janice all morning and were looking forward to going for a sleigh ride after lunch. Jackson was old enough to drive the sleigh himself and take the other children.

"Ed and I are going to take some horses to Aurora tomorrow," Ben announced.

Debra wanted to argue with him—to ask him to wait a day or two as though that would make some difference—but she knew it would be useless. Selling horses was their primary source of income, and Ben needed to be about that business.

"We have an opportunity to sell ten horses to the livery stable there," he continued. "You'll have Otto and Shep to protect you."

Ben and Debra exchanged glances.

"We'll be fine," Debra said.

"We should only be gone two days. We don't have a big herd to move, but we need to do it before the next storm sets in," Ben said as he took a drink from his cup. "Make me a list of things you ladies need from town."

When the men left the following day, Debra hugged Ben tightly.

"God, watch over our husbands," Janice and Debra prayed throughout the day. "Please take care of Ben and Ed."

Being in the saddle again feels good, Ben thought as he began the drive.

It was a welcome break from his steady chores at home. Rocking in the saddle of a good horse, new sights, and a feeling of adventure made him feel alive.

He and Ed pushed their horses hard and fast, getting them away from the horses back home.

"Don't give them time to think," Ben remarked to Ed.

They finally reached the livery stable in Aurora, quickly concluded their business, and turned their horses back the way they had come. The skies rumbled over them and darkened. They turned up the collars on their overcoats and pulled their hats down lower. The day's ride was long and cold.

That night they made a crude shelter from the wind and snow. They expected to be home the next day.

CHAPTER FIVE

AS WINTER CLOSED in on them, Debra and Janice filled their days with ease. They schooled their own children and twice a week held classes for the neighbor children. Debra taught piano, singing, and sewing. Janice taught reading, writing, and spelling.

Once a week, Ben and Ed taught classes in math, science, and carpentry. The children delighted in learning all they could. The textbooks came from Janice and Ed's personal library carried all the way from Cobourg, Ontario.

Cooking, cleaning, and laundry never seemed to end. Otto's wife, Ginny, did most of the cooking and some laundry for the two families living in the farmhouse. Ginny did her own cleaning and laundry on Mondays and spent every morning helping at the Lett house.

Dr. Paul Hudson, a dear family friend of the Letts from Canada, had followed them and became the physician in Sheridan. He came calling every two weeks to make sure they were in good health. He usually renewed their supplies of cough medicine and castor oil.

He made sure the children gargled with salt water and brushed their teeth with a salt solution. His idea was to make sure the family stayed free of upper respiratory infections and diarrhea.

The family loved his visits because he always told stories of his life in Canada. Some were true, and some he made up. It didn't matter to the children.

When the weather was too severe in the winter, his visits were less frequent. For the sake of the families, however, he remained their most confident friend and health advisor until he retired some years later.

Ben, Ed, and Otto wrapped in many layers of clothing to tend the animals. Even so, their faces were red with the cold as they came stomping into the house.

"I don't like this weather, Otto," Ben said. "It feels like the temperature will drop tonight way below zero."

The men took off their work gloves and hats, shucked their heavy coats, and hung them in the closet by the back door.

"We have some bone-warming supper for you men," Debra said as she rose from her chair by the fire.

The men dug into the thick meat pies.

"This is really good," Ed raved. "How about some more?"

"Ed, I've been thinking if we get a good January thaw, we should take some time and go up into Wisconsin. We need to do some hunting and trapping," Ben said.

"Maybe we could line up some fur suppliers for our business in Detroit. Wisconsin is full of fur-bearing animals just waiting to be harvested," Ben continued. "I think we could be gone about three weeks, and I know Otto will take good care of the farm and our families."

CHAPTER FIVE

"That sounds like a great idea to me," Ed answered between bites of the meat pie. "I can be ready to travel almost any time. We might even bring home enough furs to warrant a trip to Detroit. We need to touch base with David and check on our business there."

"I'll talk to Otto this afternoon. What do you ladies think of us going off on a hunting trip for three weeks?" Ben asked.

Debra got up from the table silently and called the children to the living room for their studies. Without a word, Janice pushed her chair back and began clearing the table.

"Wow! I think we have our answer," Ben remarked. "Ed, you'll have to talk privately with Janice, and I'll do the same with Debra tonight."

Pushing away from the table, Ben turned to Ed and said, "Let's finish our work in the barn before I talk with Otto."

Looking out the kitchen window, Ben noticed that a sleigh drawn by two stunning black horses had pulled up in front of the barn. One of the two men in the sleigh got out, went to the barn door, and walked in. He soon reappeared with Otto following him and pointing toward the house.

Ben began putting on his boots, overcoat, and gloves. "I'll see what these two fellows want," Ben said.

Greeting the stranger on the back porch, he said, "Hello there. What can I do for you?"

"Hello, are you Ben Lett? My friend and I would like a word with you," the tall stranger remarked. "My name is Barnes. Manly Barnes. My friend here is Steven Bradshaw."

"Yes, I'm Ben Lett. Let's go into the barn where we can get out of this wind," he said.

The three of them walked to the barn, where Ben introduced the visitors to Otto and shook hands. Then Otto returned to his work cleaning stalls.

"Well, what brings you to my place on such a cold, miserable day?" Ben asked.

"We've traveled from Detroit the past week, and we came to talk trading with you. We represent a large fur-buying company in Montreal and would like to buy furs from your business in Detroit," Barnes remarked.

"May I call you by your first names?" Ben asked.

"You may," Manly responded.

Manly was a tall, broad-shouldered man with piercing dark eyes, black eyebrows, and a gun stuck in his belt. His partner, Steven, had a scar on his right cheek. He was very lean, but muscular, and had a mean-looking grin.

To Ben, they looked like outlaws. He wondered about their real mission and wondered why they had come so far. Could their company be a front for The Family Compact in Canada or the Queen of England? Could these men have been sent to hunt Ben down? The people in Canada loyal to the Queen wanted Ben hunted down and killed for the damage he did to their country. They thought of him as the "Rob Roy" of Canada.

"Why didn't you just deal with our man David in Detroit?" Ben asked. "David has the authority to check out your company and sell you the furs."

"We like to deal direct with the owner," Manly responded.

"I don't believe you. And furthermore, you look like hired guns to me," Ben said.

"You certainly are touchy, Mr. Lett," Manly sneered.

"I am aware that the queen isn't going to stop trying to hunt me down," Ben said.

"Why don't you get off your high horse, Lett, and do business with us? Or will we have to deal with your partner Ed?" Steven responded.

"I think you men better leave now before you make me mad," Ben demanded.

CHAPTER FIVE

"OK, just settle down," Manly replied. "We'll be on our way, but you can expect to hear from us again."
The men headed for the barn door. Steven turned and gave a hateful look at Otto as they left the barn.
"Hey, boss, those guys looked like trouble to me," Otto remarked.
"Don't say anything to our women," Ben said. "We'll simply tell them they were fur buyers and that I didn't want to do business with them, which is true. I'm headed for the house now to tell Ed and our wives what I just told you."

As February locked her wintry arms around the earth, Debra and Janice began dreaming of a warm spring. They both hated the long winters and suffered in the frigid temperatures when they had to be out of doors hanging clothes to dry.
March followed its normal course and came in with angry growls. The women decided to host a party for Jackson's birthday, and Debra made honey cakes with the precious little sugar they had left. Provisions were growing slim in spite of careful stockpiling. Debra knew it wouldn't be long before Ben and Ed would leave on one more hunting trip.
Debra could feel spring coming. She imagined she could smell roses from the garden back home. Little by little, winter began to lose ground to the insistent sun, and the days began to hold the promise of warmth.
The women's spirits rose with the temperature. They both yearned to feel the rich soil of the new garden. They took more trips to Leland and to Ottawa to revel in the sweetness of the still-cool air.
Ben and Ed made their hunting trip to Wisconsin in the late days of winter looking for furs, so Otto and Shep took

care of the wives and children. Debra and Janice asked the Lord for his guardianship for all of them.

Late March rains washed away the last of winter, and the whole earth seemed to open its eyes at once. Debra felt excited and thrilled with the fullness of spring.

"We made it through our first winter," she remarked.

Debra worked in her herb garden every day except Sunday. She knew she would need an extensive one to supply enough herbs for food and medicine. Back in Cobourg, Canada, a good friend who ran a boarding house and kept a garden had taught her a lot about herbs for cooking. Doc Hudson also had spent time with her during his visits, instructing her on medicinal herbs.

One of the books she had brought with her at her cousin's insistence was a book on herbal healing. The frontier needed people who could help treat illness. Debra soon became the area's best herbalist.

As she worked in the garden, she also looked forward to a new baby. She suspected she was pregnant because of her morning sickness, and Doc Hudson told her the baby should come in October. She was in excellent health, and he said Debra should expect a good pregnancy. She looked forward to a baby girl for whom she could sew pretty dresses.

Debra loved being out in the garden and working in the soil. Jackson helped her build raised beds for the vegetables and flowers. Then Ben created an English garden with beds of flowers and evergreen bushes. These raised beds helped keep the rabbits away, and the fence Ben and Jackson constructed around the garden kept out the deer.

One pretty day, Sophie threw a stick for Shep to retrieve while Debra gardened. Her long-sleeved dress and poke bonnet warmed in the sun, and the cotton gloves on her hands were damp with perspiration where she held her

CHAPTER FIVE

hoe. Carefully, she worked the rich soil around the tender plants. She looked up at the steady pound of horse hooves coming up the lane and across the bridge.

Shading her eyes, she recognized Otto. He was riding hard, a sure sign of trouble. He headed straight for the corral where Ed and Ben were breaking horses.

"We got trouble," he shouted. "Someone has broken down a fence on the west side of the farm, and some brood mares are missing."

Ben came to Debra with the news about the horses. His face was set hard as stone.

"Oh, no!" she gasped.

"We're going to try and get them back," he promised.

Debra watched the men ride away while Janice took Debra's hand and sent up a prayer.

"Lord, why can't someone sit down to work out the problems between thieves and the farmers so everyone is happy?" she said. "Lord, please keep our men and horses safe."

Tears filled Debra's eyes. Her heart was nearly broken over the stealing that went on out there on the prairie.

Ben and Ed didn't come home for dinner, but the women didn't expect them. Debra and Janice fed the children and prepared them for bed. There would be no singing that night, only sincere prayers. The women could not sleep until Ben and Ed returned.

It was close to dawn when the men arrived, dragging ten mares behind them. Debra and Janice peered from the kitchen window cautiously before they opened the door. Ben's grin was tired but victorious.

"You got them! Are they all right? Were any of them hurt? Poor horses, they must have been scared to death. Oh, Ben, tell us what happened!" Debra cried.

"I'm just waiting until you catch your breath," Ben said, giving Debra a hug. "We followed the thieves to their camp and waited until they bedded down. We cut our horses loose and shot two of the thieves. The others surrendered, and we took them to the sheriff in DeKalb. We killed one and wounded one. It couldn't be helped."

Ben was tired and wanted to rest. Ed did not want to talk about the ordeal.

Debra said, "Come, and we'll feed you."

"We're too tired to eat right now," Ben replied. "I just want to go to bed."

He knew nothing would stay in his stomach if he ate. It had been an ugly scene, and Ben wanted to try and forget about it.

Janice noted a similar look on Ed's face as he headed into their bedroom. She lay next to the man she loved most in the world, wondering if she could ever really know everything about him. Had God changed Ed's heart through this incident?

It seemed to her that Ed would like to be free from this kind of frontier life. His life as a businessman suited him better than chasing thieves and possibly killing them.

Janice had read Ed's face correctly. The sights and sounds of the firefight had sickened him. Thieves or not, the death of that one man was more than Ed could stand. He tried to tell himself it was like killing a mad animal to put it out of its misery.

Janice had noticed that Ben had a similar look of regret or worry on his face. Ben knew full well what these thieves might do in retaliation. Otto, Ed, and Ben would have to stay alert until this matter was well behind them.

Time would tell whether these thieves might try again to steal from them or if the county court would order them

CHAPTER FIVE

hanged. Horse thieves often hung for even trying to steal horses.

When Debra and Ben were in bed, she sighed deeply as she turned toward him.

"It's beginning to feel like our dreams for our home in Illinois are really taking shape," she said. "We have our horses, barn, corrals, a garden, buggies, and our own little school here at home." She smiled.

Ben was lying on his back beside her and added his deep sigh.

"Yes, I guess we do. Once I dreamed of helping to save Canada. Those dreams of glory faded real fast in the face of the awful battles."

His face was sad, then hopeful. "Now I have new dreams of glory. The Bible says our dreams should be about Him and His kingdom, not about our life here on earth and building kingdoms for ourselves.

"I do want to build our farm and horse ranch for God's kingdom so our children can learn and grow up to love Jesus Christ," he said. "If we could also help build a school for our community, that would be the most important part of our lives. I'm looking forward to the day when we can build a school and hire a full-time teacher."

"How long do you think it will take?" Debra asked.

"With the help of our friends and neighbors, we could have a building up and finished by this fall if everyone pitches in and works long hours," he guessed.

Ben turned toward Debra.

"Illinois is the one place God is allowing our dreams to come true. He gave you to me so we could work as partners for this dream, and for that I am eternally grateful.

"I think we can make the finest farm and ranch in this part of northern Illinois. People will come for miles to sit at our table and listen to our children sing and recite stories of the frontier," he said.

"We'll build on to this house and entertain everyone from the poor to business tycoons. And we'll educate our sons and daughters and help them take over for us when we're resting from our labors."

Debra felt the power of Ben's thoughts, and goose bumps rose on her arms.

"When you speak of our dream like that, I just want to get out of bed and fall on my knees and praise God," she whispered. "The Lord lives within us and watches everything we do. He reminds us to ask constantly for his help."

"He has blessed us so far, and I'm confident he will continue," Ben said.

CHAPTER SIX

BEN AND ED came in to supper that night exhausted. Ben's greeting wasn't as warm as usual.

When he sat down at the table, out of habit he simply prayed, "For what we are about to receive, O Lord, make us truly grateful for your bounty."

When the men had eaten enough to ease their hunger, they turned toward their wives. Both Ed and Ben had remained quiet during the meal. Debra burst into tears and sat down at the table next to Ben. Her crying made Ben put his arm around her and hold her close to his chest.

"Why are you feeling so bad?" Ben asked.

"You said it would take until fall before we could have our new school building finished. I wish it wouldn't take that long," Debra said through her tears.

"We'll get the Lett brothers and some of the neighbors together as soon as the crops are planted. Maybe together we can begin building that school in June," Ben offered. "I love you, Debra Lett. You are more beautiful to me every day. Is there anything else on your mind?"

"We'll need some work done on the guest bedroom . . . for the baby," she said.

"Oh, Debra, I'm thrilled!" Ben smiled, holding her close. "When will it come?"

"Doc Hudson says early in October," she said, looking into his blue eyes.

"I'll make sure we finish the school and fix up that room by the end of August. Anything for you, my love," Ben promised.

Ben, Ed, Otto, and Ben's brothers took a herd of horses to the army in Indianapolis, Indiana, in early April. The drive took all week, and each man was ready for a few days of rest and some good food when they arrived home. The army had agreed to buy the same number of horses at the same time the next year.

As the men rode into the yard after the trip, Ben sprang from his horse to fold Debra in his arms. Ed rode up to the porch and jumped from his horse to hug Janice. Otto rode to the barn to put up his horse before he went to his cabin to find Ginny.

Debra's heart swelled with joy as Ben swung her around and around. She felt his strong arms hugging her tightly around her waist. Tears of happiness slid down her face, but she made no attempt to wipe them away.

Ben tipped her head back to look at the beautiful face he had conjured in his dreams so many times during the trip. He kissed the warm mouth for which he had hungered.

"You're even more beautiful than ever," he whispered.

The warmth of the house and the greeting Ben received made him feel great. He presented gifts to Jackson and saved a special one for Debra. The sapphire and diamond bracelet looked gorgeous on her wrist.

CHAPTER SIX

"Oh, it's lovely," she breathed. "I'll wear it to our next community dance and keep it always as a reminder of this day."

"Praise the Lord for delivering us to this wonderful land of peace and freedom," Ben added.

Debra's countenance glowed.

"Oh, Ben," she said, "the Lord has been so good to us. I know all of it could be gone in a minute, but I'm just beside myself with joy for what God has provided. I never thought our lives could be like this!"

"You're right about how fast it could all be gone," Ben agreed, "but I want to bask in the blessings he's given us."

His eyes were full of love for her, and he handed her the deed for new farmland he had just purchased north of Leland. He was so happy, and he wanted his entire family and his friends to rejoice with him.

"We really do have this dream in our hands," she said softly. "What will we do with it?"

"We must use it for the Lord and our children and anyone else we might choose," he answered without hesitation.

He came to her and put his arms around her while she rested her head on his arm.

"Do you want to keep expanding our land holdings and become one of the dominant farmers in this area?" she asked.

Ben was quiet for a long while.

"Yes and no," he said. "I don't want to do anything to change the love between us, nor the love of God in our hearts. I want us all to stay as happy as we are now. I don't want wealth or land to control our lives.

"I believe," he continued, "that the Lord has blessed us so we can be a blessing to others. I want to use this blessing to build a home where our children can grow up and marry and bring their children back to visit."

QUEEN'S REVENGE

He held her closer.

"Debra, if I had to choose between our love and the money, I'd give the money away in a second," he said, gently taking her face in his hands and kissing her mouth as he had when they were first married.

"I never dreamed our lives could be so happy," Debra said, sighing. "I didn't think a love like this could exist."

Debra knew there would be pain and heartache in their lives. There had to be, for that was life. She only hoped she would be strong enough to meet the tests ahead.

When she went to bed that night, she spent extra time praying. She wanted to hear what God was saying to her concerning their future. Her heart was warmed by just knowing he was listening to her prayers. She stopped every few minutes and listened to what God was saying to her.

Ben kept his word and saw to it that the school was built and the guest room was made ready for a baby by the first of August that year. To celebrate, Ben and Debra planned a party on Saturday evening, August 20.

Debra, Janice, and Ben's sisters handled the details for the neighborhood event to celebrate the new schoolhouse. Days ahead of the event, Betsy and Sara did their part, shopping for decorations with their sister-in-law, Merrilla.

As Betsy moved down the boardwalk in Ottawa on that August day, threading between people in her path, she noticed two unkempt young men coming out of a saloon just ahead of her. They spotted her immediately.

The taller one said to his friend, "Hey, Tommy, watch me charm that pretty lass."

He grinned and stepped in front of Betsy, blocking her path. Betsy came to a stop, gripping her umbrella firmly in her right hand.

CHAPTER SIX

"You're in my way," she said coldly.
He grinned down at her with his broken teeth, scarred face, and foul breath. He reached for her hand and said, "My name is Harry Tomas, young lady. What's yours?"
Betsy didn't reply. Instead she stared right back at him. He moved to block her way. She jabbed him in the stomach with the umbrella, causing him to bend over. Pulling it back, she struck him over the head, knocking him to the ground.
Tommy couldn't believe his eyes. He fled for the nearby alley. People began to gather to stare at Betsy and her fallen victim. She stepped over him and continued down the street to the meat merchant's shop.
As Betsy finished purchasing some special cuts of beef, Sara and Merrilla walked into the shop.
"We found some beautiful decorations," Sara said.
"I suggest we go for tea and scones at Peterson's cafe to celebrate our successful shopping," Merrilla said.
The women walked two blocks, turned right on Center Street, and headed to Peterson's café. Mr. Peterson greeted them himself.
"Afternoon, ladies. It is so nice to welcome you distinguished ladies in my humble café."
"You sure know how to lay it on thick, Pete," Betsy said with a smile.
"I hear you know how to handle the rough guys in town, Miss Betsy." Peterson winked.
"The city should keep its dogs locked up," Betsy responded.
"I hear you hit old Harry hard enough to knock him out of commission for a while," Peterson continued.
"Is that true, Betsy?" Sara asked.

QUEEN'S REVENGE

"I cannot tell a lie," she responded. "Two bums tried to stop me on my way to the butcher. One isn't feeling so well now. I hit him with my umbrella." Betsy laughed.

"Let's order and find out more about Betsy's adventures," Sara suggested.

The afternoon passed quietly without any more drama. The three enjoyed their lunch and began the long trip home. They wanted to reach home before dark. Merrilla suggested Sara and Betsy spend the night, but they insisted on heading home to their own families.

"Let's get together again next Tuesday and work on the decorations," Sara suggested.

"That's a great idea. Can we meet at your house, Merrilla?" Betsy asked.

"I'd love that," Merrilla answered.

Debra, Janice, Betsy, and Sara did gather at Merrilla's home to prepare decorations for the big party.

"We will decorate the school building and our new room at the house for a party," Debra said. "I want the games and food to last all day and into the evening."

"We'll get those wonderful musicians, Barney and the Boys, to play for the dance. They could play square dances and mix in some waltzes. We can award prizes for the best dancers. Ben and I could even judge. Even the children could win prizes," she said.

"Let's have some of Debra's piano students play solos. Janice's students could recite and maybe even prepare a play," Sara suggested.

"Sara, would you consider preparing several poems for the occasion?" Betsy asked.

"Ben and Ed can sing and play their guitars. Oh, and we need someone to give a dedication speech," Janice said.

CHAPTER SIX

"Tom would do us proud," Debra said. "He has read more books than any person in our family. I'll ask Ben to approach him."

With just days to go until the dedication of what would become the local school, church, and community center, the women decided on the guest list.

Invitations would go to guests from as far away as Ottawa. Neighbors and friends would be asked to open their homes so the visitors could stay overnight.

As they agreed on the last details, Debra asked Janice to lead them in prayer, asking for God's help. When they had finished, Janice led them in a song of praise and thanksgiving.

CHAPTER SEVEN

DEBRA SIGHED DEEPLY as the baby began its usual night kicking.

"It's beginning to feel real. The dream, I mean," she said. She grinned largely in the dark. "We now own our own farm near a school and a town."

Ben was lying on his back beside her and added his deep sigh to hers.

"Yes, we do," he said in a soft voice. "After the war, I always dreamed of moving away from danger and having our own farm. Now I have a new dream.

"I know the Bible says the kingdom of God is within us. But I also wish God would put our farm and home inside his kingdom's protection. With his help we can do so much for this part of Illinois."

Ben turned to face Debra and said, "This is the place where all our dreams can come true. God gave us each other to work out these dreams. We can make a go of it together."

He talked on about how he wanted to make their farms the finest in their part of the state and how he hoped people

CHAPTER SEVEN

would come from miles around to join them for a meal or to spend the night.

As the baby she was carrying kicked, they talked about how they wanted to educate their children to be leaders in their growing country.

"I hope they will take over the farms when we go to be with Jesus," Ben said in a voice like the sound of a stallion leading a band of horses across the plains.

Debra felt his strength, and chills rose up her spine. Hope flashed through her mind. She had great confidence that Ben would succeed in his dream of growing the farm and raising horses.

"The Lord promises to watch over us. We need to ask, and it will be given," Ben said.

Debra took Ben by the hand and said, "Let's go outside and look at this land by the light of the moon."

Ben helped her sit up and said, "Come on, little mother. Get your robe. It's cool out there this time of night."

He guided her quietly from the house into the light of the full moon. The wind played the leaves like wind chimes, calming and soothing the hearts and minds of the young couple.

Ben stood behind her, holding her tight and keeping her warm. He kissed the back of her neck. She shuddered with the heat of his kiss.

"Lord, thank you for the blessings you've heaped upon us," Debra said, her heart filled with joy. "Keep us safe from Satan's claws and lead us into your ways."

She felt tears of happiness slide down her cheeks as Ben held on to her tightly. Both were filled with power and hope. With God's help, nothing would stop them.

Oranges, blues, greens, and reds patterned the prairie sky. Wisps of white cirrus clouds curled around the deep purples of the sunset. Raucous mockingbirds strove to outdo one another in announcing a sunset.

Ben could hear the soft sounds of the small stream behind the house, and the smell of Debra's and Janice's supper teased his and Ed's taste buds. The babble of their three children blended with the firm commands of their wives.

Ed and Ben sat reading the latest news from the *Chicago Weekly Democrat*. Ben leaned back in his favorite rocking chair.

"Ed, it says here that the government needs more horses. Maybe it's time to contact Captain Riley in Chicago," Ben commented.

The sudden nickering of horses in the corral made Ben sit up, alerting all his senses. Any sound of disruption with the horses concerned him because of the threat from wild beasts and the occasional horse thief.

The horses quieted, but Ben listened a minute more. Ed continued to read the paper. Ben stayed focused on the horses, for they were his prime source of income.

The noise and confusion of the Letts and the Doyles finding their places around the supper table quieted when Ben paused to say grace. As the baked beans, roast, biscuits, gravy, and corn from the garden circled the table, all conversation focused upon the possibility of selling more horses to the government.

During a break in the conversation, Jackson cleared his throat and hesitantly said, "Papa, I work with the horses every day. When can I go with you and Uncle Ed on a roundup and horse drive? I know I could help. Please?"

Ben looked at Jackson in surprise and glanced across the table at Debra.

CHAPTER SEVEN

"Son," he said gently, "I do appreciate how you've taken hold of the work around here and helped me and your mama. That's why I have to say no.

"While we're gone, your mama's going to rely on you to take care of the animals and help with the chores around the house. I'm depending upon you to be the man of the family while we're gone. Do you understand?"

Jackson's countenance fell. He quickly looked down at his plate and whispered, "Yes, sir."

"Jackson," Debra added, "I know this is a big disappointment for you. Waiting to take part in a big adventure isn't easy. But I can't tell you how comforted I am to know you will be here all those days your papa is gone."

Jackson gave her a big smile, but Debra knew how disappointed he was in his heart.

With supper over, the men went outdoors to continue talking horses. Janice and Debra took a few minutes to talk about the schoolhouse event.

"The children are tucked in, and the men are outside, so this is our chance," Janice said. She helped herself to a cup of coffee from the pot on the back of the stove and settled herself in a chair by the kitchen table.

Debra's eyes gleamed with mischief. "Wouldn't it be fun to go with them on the horse drive?" she said.

Janice was visibly shocked and said, "No! No! I would never even think of such a thing."

"But think of what we could do when we arrived in Chicago," Debra sighed.

"Some of the women in that town are the kind we don't talk about," Janice replied, looking suspiciously at Debra. "You've been reading those romantic stories again, haven't you?"

Debra blushed slightly and said, "Ben found a magazine for me in town last week."

QUEEN'S REVENGE

"And you didn't tell me?" Janice said, jumping up from the table. "Where is it? I want to see the latest fashions."

She tried to look stern as she said, "And there was a romance story in it, too, wasn't there?"

Debra clasped her hands. "Oh, it is so sad. I cried and cried after I finished it. I planned to give it to you as soon as I was done with it."

"You cried?" Janice said flatly. "You never cry."

"The ending of the story was so beautiful!" she gushed as she opened her brass-bound trunk, took out the magazine, and handed it to Janice.

Janice smiled, promising to return the magazine when she had finished it. Debra joined her at the table with her own cup of coffee. She sighed as she lifted it to her lips.

"I was thinking, Janice, of all the work you and I will have to do on our own in the next few days to get ready for the school celebration. The men will be gone, and we won't have their great help."

"No one realizes how much work this celebration will take. If we're real lucky, the neighbors—both husbands and wives—will be ready to help us," Janice said.

"It won't be luck, Janice. It will be God's love and mercy," Debra declared. "I don't believe in luck. God has plans for each of us. We may not understand and comprehend these plans or even like them, but what happens isn't luck. And nothing is written down.

"Different people make all kinds of decisions that somehow affect us," she went on. "Then the Lord makes good out of it to accomplish his ultimate goal for us. God's love and strength have brought us through all our trials to make us what we are today. Think of all the women who have suffered with their men.

"I'm glad I know the things I know. It doesn't mean I want to go through them again, but I will if I have to," Debra said.

CHAPTER SEVEN

On August 19, Debra and Janice went to the new school building and began decorating for the party. Thaddeus Peterson and his wife, Ella, drove by in their wagon and stopped to visit. Thaddeus offered to return the next day with Ella and neighbors Tom and Martha Morgan to help. Debra said she was delighted and thanked them.

Pretty soon most of the residents in the Leland area were helping decorate the school inside and out. The stage in front looked like a model classroom. Miniature characters sat in the seats near a model teacher that resembled Miss Hanson, the new teacher. Barney and the Boys had agreed to furnish the music for the dance that would follow the evening meal.

The Lett relatives arrived early to help with last-minute decorations, food, drinks, and organizing the games. Merrilla and Tom came as well as Sara, Betsy, Maria, and their families.

The newness of the school and grounds impressed everyone. The grass had been cut low, and the new well pump handle sported a ribbon. The whitewashed outhouse had flowers planted all around it. A hitching rail stood ready for horses and buggies.

Neighbors helped build tables for the food. A small diamond for the new game of baseball had been built for the boys, horseshoe pits sat ready for the men, and a croquet set awaited the ladies.

The whole community turned out for this special occasion. Ben and Debra hosted what was the most exciting thing to happen in Leland up to this time. Games, contests of all kinds, singing, dancing, and, best of all, eating, filled the day.

Debra and Janice helped set up the contests for the children, including an egg toss, three-legged race, drop the handkerchief, dodge ball, and apple bobbing. The men split logs, had a turkey shoot, and held knife throwing, barrel racing, and horse racing competitions. Ed and Ben took charge of the men's contests. Merrilla and Sara conducted the croquet contest for the women.

Four neighbor men judged the pie-baking contest. The winner would earn a special trophy Ben had carved himself over the course of the summer.

The musicians played and fiddled all afternoon and into the evening for the dance.

Debra was heavy with child, so she limited her activity to conducting games and serving food. When the dance started, however, she and Ben couldn't resist taking a few steps before she had to rest.

Ed and Janice really took to the dancing. Ben danced with Janice and most of the other ladies at the party at least once. He saved the last two dances for the beautiful Debra.

The only shadow over the event was the presence of the two fur buyers who had been run off by Ben early in the year. Ed wanted to run them off again, but Ben refused. The party was going too well to be spoiled with trouble from these men.

Ben introduced Tom Lett as the master of ceremonies. The crowd loved hearing the Lett family history. Their ancestors had moved from Europe to England with William of Orange to drive William's father-in-law off the throne for his efforts to convert England to Catholicism.

Tom also congratulated Ben, Debra, Ed, and Janice for the hard work and vision they had shown to build the schoolhouse for the community.

Ben closed the day by thanking everyone who had helped in any way to build the school and make the day and evening a success. He and Tom also introduced Miss Hanson. She spoke of how she was looking forward to

CHAPTER SEVEN

school starting the next month. She had met the students and thought they were really wonderful children.

Ed closed the ceremony with a prayer, and Janice led the singing of "Blest Be the Tie that Binds."

Riding home, Debra asked Ben about the two strangers who had appeared at the event.

"I don't know them very well," Ben said. "They came by the farm, talking about our trading business in the winter, and I asked them to leave. They seem to be up to no good. Maybe I can find out about these men in Ottawa," he added. "Please don't worry."

He reminded Debra that it was a day to celebrate.

"Ours is one of the first schoolhouses in this part of the country. I'm proud of all you did to make it a reality," he said, smiling. "Our baby-to-be has quite a special mother. I love you."

CHAPTER EIGHT

FALL BEGAN TO sprinkle a few colors about the trees, changing greens into vivid reds, deep purples, and flaming oranges. The nights became cool again, and everyone slept better. The cool westerly breezes blew across Ben and Debra's room from the open window. Debra would deliver soon, and the cool weather made her feel better in her heavy pregnancy.

Ben and Ed did their best to learn more about the men who had come to the school opening uninvited. John Curran, the president of the Farmers Bank, told Ben he had seen the two strangers enter the meat merchant's establishment in Ottawa by the rear door on several occasions. They looked suspicious and dangerous to him. Each wore a dark broad-brimmed hat and carried two firearms.

Ben went into Ottawa for his monthly meeting of the Horse Owners Association. Ed and Janice went with him, and they dropped Janice off at the white-planked church for the weekly quilting. Ed made his way to the general store for supplies.

CHAPTER EIGHT

Janice brought Debra's apologies for missing the gathering this time and then sat down to enjoy the harmless gossip, recipes, and remedy exchanges the quilting meetings always provided.

That day the ladies were working on a quilt with a picture of Ottawa in the center and discussing the need for new hymnals at the church.

"We need some of the families to give more money to the church. Then we could just buy the hymnals," Jessie said.

"She's right," Amy said. "I have given my tithe and others have not. What we need is a good sermon on giving."

"What we need is for every family to give its fair share," Gertrude Barnes said sharply.

"That'll be the day," mocked a stout lady with a florid face. "If that ever happens, I'd think faith and love had finally come to our church."

"Then why don't we just talk to the pastor about the subject of giving?" Janice asked reasonably.

"Seems when it comes to giving, we don't have the right spirit," Gertrude said tartly, "or we would have purchased the hymnals before now."

Janice took no offense at the rebuke as Gertrude was known for her pessimistic view of life. Janice often wondered what had happened to give her such a sour disposition and the will to express it at every occasion.

"We could sell our quilts and make box meals to be auctioned off, I suppose," Amy said.

"We'd be the ones to make the quilts and cook the meals for the box lunches," Gertrude said. "Might as well dig up the money out of our own pockets!"

"Morning, ladies," a cheerful voice called out. It was Gertrude's husband come to get her.

Janice was glad to see him, for a small pinch of Gertrude's outlook on life went a long way.

"We were just talking about you men," his wife said in a complaining voice.

"I'll just bet you were, darling," he said amiably.

How has he lived with her all these years and stayed so kind? Janice wondered. Then she said, "We're discussing how to raise money to buy hymnals for the church."

The women all looked at Gertrude to see if she would allow Janice to overrule her assessment of how to get the money.

Gertrude's husband was a tall, skinny man. He stood there with his hat in his hand, stroking his beard. He dressed as a prosperous man would and always gave the appearance of good humor.

"I'll tell you what, ladies," he said with a smile. "I know all about what goes on at these quilting meetings. I'll give you a hundred dollars to buy those church hymnals."

"What!" they responded.

"If you ladies," he said, grinning from ear to ear confidently, "can sit here for the whole day and quilt without talking."

Looking at one another, their anger seemed to grow.

"Well, how rude," began one lady.

"Wait," said Donna, who had listened quietly until then. "I think that's a wonderful idea. We'll take you up on your most generous offer," she said graciously, inclining her head toward him.

"But . . ." began Amy.

"Thank you for getting us our hymnals," Donna said. She winked at the ladies around the quilting frame.

Mr. Barnes was a bit taken aback by her confidence, so he said, "I'll send our son to sit with you next week. We surely want to do this fairly."

Janice could tell by his attitude that he felt sure his offer was safe.

CHAPTER EIGHT

On the appointed day, Mr. Barnes came by the church with his son Daniel and entered the room where the women already were busily working. He burst into loud, raucous laughter. He laughed so hard, tears rolled down his cheeks.

The ladies were sitting around the frame quilting steadily. Each one had a gag tied firmly over her mouth.

The hymnals were promptly purchased and a proper acknowledgement posted at the church honoring Mr. Barnes. The entire congregation praised him and his wife.

When Ed and Ben picked her up after that day of quiet quilting, Janice couldn't wait to tell them how she and the ladies had outsmarted Mr. Barnes. The men thoroughly enjoyed the story, and it became a favorite tale told around town for years.

Ben and Debra had their coffee on the shady side of the big porch on a large oak table set there for breakfast. Debra marveled at the swift passing of time. The baby would arrive within a few days, and even Jackson was excited about the coming of his new brother or sister. Jackson was very much like his father, and Debra had a sense of déjà vu as she watched the two of them working and playing together.

Many times Jackson asked how much longer he had to wait. Everyone was on pins and needles. When Doc Hudson agreed to come and stay until the baby arrived, it gave Ben great confidence and thrilled Debra to no end.

Although he was the youngest brother, Ben felt every inch the patriarch of the Lett clan.

"The Lord is good," he said as he took a bit of honey biscuit dripping with blueberry jam. "Did you think our lives would turn out like this, Debra?"

She looked at her husband with his new goatee and mustache. He looked dignified, but his eyes were still a youthful blue. He was lean from his hard work on the farm, yet a small spread across his girth hinted at his wealth.

"No," she admitted. "I never thought this far ahead. I spent most of my time worrying about what was going on right then. In the time I've had for reflection now, I am surprised to find myself no longer young. It seems like only yesterday I was eighteen. When I look in the mirror, I still can't understand where the time has gone."

In those early days of October, Ben and Ed began discussing an opportunity to sell horses in St. Louis, Missouri. Ben tentatively agreed to consider the possibility if Tom and Robert would help with the drive. He would ask each man to bring his hired man with him so they would have plenty of help.

Ben also planned a trip for supplies just before Debra expected the baby.

"I'll keep watch at the farm while you're gone," Ed said.

The day Ben drove the wagon and horses to Ottawa, the weather was tranquil. Debra and Janice spent some time in the garden, and Debra could feel her baby moving. She felt confident the Lord would protect Ben as well as the rest of them left at home.

When Ben returned, he brought supplies and news.

"First things first," he said. "Candy for you, Debra."

She broke into a huge smile for him. It was now a joke between them. Peppermint candy had been his first gift to her and probably always would be when he returned from any trip.

"What about us, Papa?" Jackson asked with Sophie and Sam on either side.

CHAPTER EIGHT

"Candy sticks for everyone," he said, laughing.

Finally, after everything was unloaded and put away, he shared the news.

"Everyone was talking about the new sheriff," he said. "I'm not sure how well he is going to work out. If he can cut down on crime and round up the thieves, it will be a blessing. There's also a plan in the works to round up the remaining Indians. The peaceful ones are still staying in their camps; the others are guarded by the army on the lower Fox River."

"We're still our own best protection," Debra said.

"Us and the Lord," Janice reminded her.

"Of course," Ben said as he took a mouthful from his tin cup. He had been so busy talking he had not noticed that Debra had handed him buttermilk instead of his usual cup of coffee.

"Where in the world did you get this cold buttermilk?" he asked.

Ed smiled and looked a little sheepish.

"Oh, it was just a little project Janice has been trying to get me to do. I built a springhouse down by the stream. The water runs through it and cools the milk and butter," Ed said. "It's working pretty good right now."

"Ed, you're brilliant! I love cold buttermilk," Ben smiled and savored another cup.

"I also stopped by Tom's place on the way back," he continued. "Merrilla sent a cake for all of us."

"There's something else you haven't told us . . . something good. I can see it in your eyes," Debra said. "Come on, Ben, don't hold out on us."

"Well, I did hire two men to help us deliver our horses. They'll be here tomorrow," he confessed.

Debra said, "That means the drive is beginning soon, doesn't it?"

"We're on our way to becoming successful horse traders, just like we promised," Ed said.

"We'll begin soon," Ben said.

Ben was up before dawn in anticipation of the men coming. Debra heard his unsuccessful attempts to make coffee quietly and finally gave up her sleep to help him get his breakfast.

"I don't know why everything has to start so early," she remarked.

"It's the best time to talk to Jesus," Ben said as he poured a cup of coffee for Debra and himself.

"It is not," she said, yawning. "I like to talk to him when the children go down for a nap. Janice and I read and pray at that time. We both love to read and pray together. Lately, I wish I could take a nap with them. It seems like I'm tired all the time. It isn't easy being pregnant."

"I get bigger and bigger every day. I can't bend over and get things I need. And someone inside me is kicking every time I want to sleep. My hands and feet swell. Soon I won't be able to see my feet. And I know how much it's going to hurt when that lump in front finally does decide to come out. This baby keeps me up all night, and then there's Jackson to care for, and . . ."

She laid her head on his broad chest and began to cry.

"What this?" he soothed. This was not the Debra he knew and loved.

"I just feel like crying, all right?" she said.

He stood there holding her, wondering what to do or say next. He was afraid he'd make things worse if he said anything. He was honestly confused about her feelings.

Jackson woke up, rubbing his eyes, and hung his head over the staircase.

CHAPTER EIGHT

"Why is she crying, Papa?" he asked. "Why doesn't she go back to bed?"

Debra cried a little harder knowing Jackson was awake; now she didn't have a chance of sleeping. She pushed Ben away and sat down in her rocking chair, tears streaming down her face.

Ben went ahead with breakfast preparations, but then dropped the big iron skillet just short of the fireplace. Everyone jumped. Helplessly, Ben looked from Debra to Jackson.

"Just go away," Debra sobbed. "You've helped me enough for one day. Go away. And don't come back until dinner."

Her angry words stung Ben. He stomped from the house without his breakfast and fed the horses in a very angry mood.

"Women!" he told the horses in the corral. "If I live to be a hundred, I'll never understand them!"

CHAPTER NINE

SUNDAY MORNING WHEN the Lett family arrived at church, Ben drew his carriage to a halt, hopped down, and tied the horses to a hitching post while Jackson helped his mother down. He turned to Debra and said, "Let's go in. The Doyles will be along soon."

Pastor David Stahl and his wife, Tammy, greeted them on the porch and, when they stepped inside, Ben leaned close to Debra.

"May I take you out for dinner after church?" he asked.

"I would like that very much."

"Would you like to eat at Mona's Cottage?" he continued.

"You really like that place, don't you?" she asked.

"I think it's charming."

"OK. Mona's Cottage it is," she agreed.

As Ben and Debra walked toward their pew, she glanced at Jackson, who already was on his way to Sunday school class talking with some of his friends. Ed was the boys' Sunday school teacher.

CHAPTER NINE

Debra was so proud of Jackson and his interest in the Bible. Ed was the kind of teacher who kept the boys' interest by having them act out some of the stories in class. In her heart she said, "Lord, help Jackson to trust you more and more and dedicate his life to you."

Monday morning, Ben and Ed were on the barn roof in a flood of golden October sunshine nailing some new shingles on worn spots in preparation for the winter snows. With the last shingle in place, they both sat down on the slanted roof to rest.

Birds sang and performed in the nearby oak tree as Ed said, "Ben, I've noticed how anxious you are to move horses to market. I see you out by the corral looking at them by moonlight."

"I'm getting nervous about the baby and about moving the horses," Ben admitted.

"A horse drive is a lot like an army maneuver. Both take teamwork and good strong leadership," Ed reassured him.

That night when quiet descended on the Lett home, Ben wrapped his arms around Debra and kissed her softly.

"I know you're worried about the horse drive, but you won't mind my leaving so much when I buy you a new fur coat," he teased and helped himself to a kiss.

In spite of herself, she felt the familiar stirrings.

"You're terrible," she breathed even as she returned his kiss.

"I know. All horse barons are alike," he grinned.

Later that night, Debra thought about the baby and her secret hope for a girl. A girl would fill a special place in her heart, and a little sister for Jackson would be nice for all of them. She loved the name Betsy Ann. She even dreamed of grandchildren a daughter might have someday. She fell asleep with plans in her head.

Ben woke with a start as Debra screamed and hit him in the nose with her forearm.

"What's wrong?" he said.

"The baby is coming. Doc Hudson had to ride to Ottawa today. I don't know if he is back yet, so please get Janice right away. Try not to wake Jackson. Be quiet!" Debra said. "And hurry up!"

"Hold your horses. I'm moving as fast as I can," he whispered. "Will you be all right while I'm gone?"

"I'll be fine, just hurry," Debra whispered back between pains.

Ben fumbled with his trousers and shoes. He put the left shoe on the right foot and had to change it around before finishing dressing. The right shoelace was in a knot, and he had to untie it before finally putting on his shoes.

"Oh! What's taking you so long, Ben?" Debra gasped.

"I'm hurrying; just hold on. I'll have Janice here in a few minutes."

Ben stumbled into the straight-backed chair sitting by the door, knocking it into the wall.

"Who left the chair in the doorway?" Ben said in a low voice.

"Be quiet!" Debra whispered back.

Ben opened the door to the bedroom and proceeded down the hallway to the stairs. He looked into Jackson's room as he passed by and saw he was asleep. Tiptoeing down the stairs, he managed to get to the back door by way of the kitchen in a few long steps. He let in the cool night air as he opened the door and then ran across the broad yard, praying as he ran that Debra and the baby would be safe.

Knocking loudly on the door of the small house where Ed and Janice now lived on the farm, he managed to awaken Ed from his deep sleep. When Ed saw the panic

CHAPTER NINE

in Ben's eyes and on his face, he guessed without asking what was needed. Ed let Ben into the kitchen and offered him a seat.

"It's Debra. She's having labor pains. We need Janice quick," Ben said with a gasp. His hair looked scruffy. His eyes were bloodshot. His shirt was half tucked in his pants with one suspender holding them up.

"How's Debra?" Janice asked.

"She's asking for you," Ben mumbled.

"I have some things packed. I'll be dressed in a minute. You go on home and stay with Debra and hold her hand. I'll be there in a minute," Janice reassured him.

"Ed, could you see if Doc Hudson can come?" Janice said.

Ben rushed back to his house and quietly slipped up the stairs to the bedroom.

"Darling, how do you feel?" Ben asked.

"Like a cow bloated from eating too much poison weed," she said.

"Janice and Doc Hudson will be with us soon. Would you like some cold water for your head?"

"Just relax, Ben. I'll be just fine when they get here. They know what to do in these matters," she said. "A cold cloth would feel fine."

Ben could hear the kitchen door open and someone move about.

"I'd better go and start a fire to heat some water. Will it be all right if I leave?" he asked.

"Go and help," Debra said and she began to moan again as the pain came.

Working together, Janice and Doc Hudson brought a new baby girl into the Lett family, and both mother and baby were doing just fine.

Debra took one look at Ben's face a month later and said, "I know. I can see it in your eyes. When will you leave with the horses?"

"In two days," he said as he pulled her away from the window and put his arms around her. Pain clouded his loving blue eyes.

"Try not to be mad at me for leaving. Janice, Doc Hudson, and Jackson will be here."

"I know you have to go," she said. "I just can't stand to think of something happening to you."

"Wasn't it you who told me to pray about everything and that the Lord would be watching over me?" Ben asked.

She turned, hit him with her hand, and then ducked her head.

"I did. And I meant every word of it."

She put her head on his shoulder and said, "I miss you already."

She turned and kissed his mouth carefully, adding, "I love you with all my heart."

"I'll bring you and Jackson some gifts from St. Louis."

"That'll be wonderful. Just don't forget the money, too," she teased.

The next day Ben and Jackson rode into Leland. They did not plan to stay very long, but Ben sought some more good horses before leaving on the drive. He asked Johnny, the livery owner in Leland, if any horses were for sale.

"A fellow brought some new mares in yesterday that might interest you," Johnny said. "I put them out back in the corral. Take a look."

Ben thanked him and headed for the corral. The mares looked wild and full of spunk.

"What price are you asking?" Ben said.

CHAPTER NINE

"These are really good mares, brought from the Langley ranch near Rochelle," Johnny said. "I think a good price would be seventy-five dollars each."

"Johnny, you're too high. I'll give you fifty dollars per horse," Ben countered.

"Give me $60 a piece for the lot, and we'll call it a deal," Johnny shot back.

"I'll agree to $55 per horse and not a penny more," Ben replied.

"Ben Lett, you're a hard man. I'll take $57.50 and not a penny less."

"I'll give you $56."

"It's a deal," Johnny grumbled, but I won't be making any money on these mares."

"I feel sorry for you, Johnny," Ben replied. "I happen to know you bought these mares for $50 each, and six dollars for handling them is plenty of profit for you."

Johnny got red in the face and spit a chew of tobacco. "Ben, you're nuts," he answered.

"Ed and I will come by tomorrow and get the mares. Have them haltered and on a line and ready to go. Nice doing business with you, Johnny. See you tomorrow."

As Ben and Jackson rode toward home, Jackson asked, "How did you know what Johnny paid for those mares, Dad?"

"I didn't. I just guessed. But do you think I guessed right?" Ben smiled.

"I sure do, Dad," Jackson said, beaming.

The grueling work of collecting the herd of horses continued until the last minute before they left. Ben felt the excitement grow by the hour. He also felt an increasing obsession with finding out everything he could about what was ahead on the trail to St. Louis. His head swam with the possibilities of delivering this herd of horses for a great price.

"Thank you, Lord, for the possibilities ahead," he prayed.

That night Ben, Ed, and Otto sat around Ben's table, drinking coffee and eating cherry pie.

Otto pointed to the map he had brought with him.

"See this?" Otto said. "We can move the horses through Ottawa and follow the trail near the Illinois River southwest until we meet the fork of the Mississippi. That will take us straight into St. Louis.

"I've heard tell of robbers west of Peoria in the hill country around Beardstown," he added, "so we'll have to be on guard. There isn't any other way to get there. Will we be leaving soon, Ben?"

"Yes."

Like little boys, their excitement showed even though they knew the serious nature of this trip. Before mounting their horses to depart, they stood together as if posing for a portrait.

Ben prayed silently, "Lord, protect my family and us on this trip."

Janice, Sam, and Sophie stood off on the side, crying.

"Take good care of yourself, Ed," Janice said.

"I'll bring you and the kids some presents," Ed promised.

The first day out would be rough because the men were not used to riding all day at a fast clip. Ben's brothers and their hired men joined the drive west of Sheridan on the way to Ottawa. Robert took a rope, leading the ten mares Ben had just purchased. Tom led a group of young stallions that took a strong man to hold. The next day the brothers would rotate to another group.

Otto pointed to the bluffs along the Illinois River in the distance and said, "I'll scout us a campsite for the night."

CHAPTER NINE

After eating an inviting meal prepared by Ed, the men lay down for the night. They were too tired to do much more than eat and roll up in their blankets. Robert guarded the horses and camp for the midnight shift. Satisfied all was well, Ben lay down.

He estimated it would take about fifteen days to travel to St. Louis. He wanted to deliver his horses, get paid, have a good meal, sleep in a real bed, and then head home. He did not plan to spend any more time in St. Louis than necessary. Ed, Robert, and Tom felt the same way.

When they finally saw the buildings of St. Louis, Ben thought that he soon would have this task done. Leaving the others in charge of the horses a few miles outside town, Ben and Ed went to strike a bargain with the buyer. They hadn't ridden far when a man met them.

"Hello there and welcome to St. Louis, the gateway to the west," he said. The man was well dressed and rode a beautiful roan mare.

"I saw your herd of horses and thought I'd be the first to welcome you," he said. "My name's Arthur K. Hubbard. I'm a horse buyer. Looks like you have a sizeable herd up there on the bluff."

Ben offered his hand.

"I'm Ben Lett, and this is my friend Ed Doyle."

"I'm here to offer you ninety dollars a head," Hubbard replied. "You won't find a better deal anywhere. I have cash money in the bank in town. I'll be glad to show it to you."

The two men looked at each other. The price seemed even better than Ben had hoped. He had figured he would be happy with anything over sixty dollars a horse. Ed cleared his throat, motioned with his head, and rode off a little way with Ben following.

"He may be on the level, but he's the only man we've seen," Ed whispered. "Horses could be going for a hundred dollars a head. We don't know."

"Let's go," Ben said.

"You won't find a better deal, of that I'm sure," Hubbard said when they returned.

The three men headed for town as Hubbard offered, "Supper is on me."

The setting sun created a haze over the city that darkened the houses and businesses. A northwestern breeze blew over the Mississippi River and sent a chill up Ben's spine. A flock of geese moved over the river, looking for a field of grain on which to settle for dinner.

They chatted with Hubbard as they rode and then took a barge across the river. They ended at the Hotel Quincy, where they took Hubbard up on his offer of a meal.

Everything checked out as Hubbard had said it would. They agreed to the deal in principle, and Hubbard gave Ben a large advance, promising to see him after the horses were loaded the next day.

"You're a fortunate man, Mr. Lett," Hubbard said. "Only a few herds came in ahead of you. You're getting top dollar."

That pleased Ben. He politely thanked Hubbard for the advance and headed for the nearest hotel with Ed. They tried to keep the money out of sight as they walked along the muddy boardwalk. Every stranger looked like a robber to Ben.

They took a room, hurried upstairs, and locked the door. Ben spread the money on the bed, and he and Ed stood there staring at it.

"I've never seen that much money since we were in Canada," Ben breathed.

"Me either," said Ed.

CHAPTER NINE

"Are you staying in town tonight, Ed?" Ben asked.

"Janice would have my head if I spent more than an hour in this sinful place," he grinned. "I'll go back to the horses with you. Maybe tomorrow we can enjoy the bathtubs and barbers."

"What a pleasure that'll be," Ben said, grinning. "Let's get back to the boys and the herd and see how they are doing."

CHAPTER TEN

BEN AND ED returned to St. Louis with Robert, Tom, and Otto and their two other hired men. Each man led ten horses on a rope line. They delivered their seventy horses for ninety dollars apiece to Mr. Hubbard. Ed divided the gold between Ben and Ben's brothers and him for safety's sake. They each hid more than fifteen hundred dollars on their person.

In St. Louis, they saw a few rowdy cowboys making a racket in a saloon. Ben could hear someone beating a tinny piano to death.

"I call this town an egg waiting to hatch," Ben said.

He observed a woman making her way down the plank sidewalk, swerving as she walked. Her skirts were dragging in the dust and mud, and she carried a parasol to shield her eyes from the evening sun. She returned his smile. Ben tipped his hat.

"She acts like she would enjoy knowing you better," Ed said, smiling.

CHAPTER TEN

"I guess we look like prosperous cowboys," Ben responded.

They eased their horses down the street. Pulling up behind the Hotel St. Louis, they dismounted and turned their horses over to the stable boy. Ben went up the hotel steps and entered the hotel near the main desk. He saw their three hired men waiting in the hotel lobby.

Otto asked, "Are we free to do the town?"

"As soon as I pay you some of your wages," Ben responded.

Later he told Ed, "I plan to use part of this money to buy some land north of Leland near the Somonauk Creek. Debra and I want to expand our farming business."

"That sounds like a great idea," Ed said. "Maybe Janice and I can buy the land next to it."

"Do you and Janice want to settle down in Illinois?" Ben asked.

"We've come a long way to be near you and Debra, Ben. And besides, I do like Illinois," he added. "Janice and Debra are best of friends, our children play well together and, most important of all, the Lord is leading us to stay here. We like teaching the gospel in the local church and school."

"Right now nothing would please me more. I'm happy to know you will stay in Illinois," Ben said.

"We could search our entire lives and never find a better place to live and work," Ed repeated. "God led us to be business partners in Canada and Detroit and now farmers and ranchers in Illinois and teachers in Leland. What a wonderful life we can have if we work hard with God leading and guiding our every move."

"You have made me so happy today," Ben remarked. "Let's have a steak dinner and celebrate."

They summoned the head waiter in the hotel dining room and, the next thing they knew, all seven men were seated at a large, round mahogany table in the rear of the hotel dining area. The men could not help their loud talking and storytelling.

Ben told them about his recent trip to Wisconsin to hunt for furs. He and Ed had hunted and fished the Wisconsin River for about four weeks in March. The weather was rough and stormy. It snowed half the time, and several snow storms dropped more than two feet of snow. Some nights temperatures dropped to twenty degrees below zero. The wind blew thirty or thirty-five miles an hour most days, piling snow drifts six feet high.

Ben and Ed spent their time in a small cabin with plenty of firewood piled high outside the back door. They studied and memorized the eighth chapter of the book of Romans.

Ben believed it was the most important chapter in the entire Bible. He wanted to memorize the entire book of Romans and encourage his son Jackson to do the same.

"I look forward to preaching about the life of Christ and the work of the Holy Spirit in our church," Ben had told Ed on those frigid days.

He and Ed were often invited to preach at the Sunday morning service, especially when the pastor had to be away. Ben included true stories of interest to the entire congregation from his experiences in the Canadian War. God had given Ben his guidance in many ways, and it was exciting for others to hear how he had protected Ben in those days.

When the worst weather had passed, they got out of the cabin and made up for lost time. They found abundant deer, fox, black bear, rabbit, raccoon, opossum, turkey, grouse, and pheasant through the entire area.

For two weeks, both men hunted and trapped night and day. They slept on the ground and cooked over open fires.

CHAPTER TEN

"We had some real fun with the black bears," Ben told the men around the table at their special dinner. "The bears would try and sneak up on us at night.

"I woke one night with a bear sniffing at our fire. I put my knife into my right hand and prepared to drive it into the bear's heart. I knew I would have only one chance and couldn't miss," he said, enjoying their attention.

"The bear opened his left side to me, and I struck with a swift blow. That bear didn't know what hit him. He was dead instantly. About then Ed woke up, saw that bear, jumped three feet in the air, and started running," Ben said, laughing.

"That's not fair!" Ed protested. "I didn't jump three feet in the air. You're not telling it right. I jumped, yes, but not three feet."

The men all laughed their heads off and couldn't stop.

"It's time to go to bed before Ed beats me up," Ben said.

Ben did a little jumping of his own that night when something awoke him. He lay perfectly still, listening. His life had taught him to sleep with awareness. He was quick to rouse at any light, sound, or strange movement.

His door was barred from within. The window was large enough for entry, but it was closed but for a crack at the bottom.

He slid his hand to the chair where his holstered gun hung from the gun belt, and then slid the six-shooter into his hand. He waited a long moment but heard nothing. Had a sound awakened him?

Easing from under the covers, he put the gun down on the bed. He slipped into his trousers, slung on the gun belt, and returned the six-shooter to its holster.

All the time he was careful to keep himself in complete darkness and not to lift his head high enough to be seen through the window. Knowing the position of what little furniture he had, he avoided it and got back into a corner from which he could see out the window.

Nothing. Then a movement. Only a glimpse.

He waited and listened, poised and alert. A shadow moved. It could be a friend who didn't want to disturb him. Only a fool shot at what he could not identify.

Was it one man out there? Or were there more?

A slight pressure pushed on the door. The bar did not give, and the door stood firm. One attempt, then no more.

A friend or acquaintance would knock or call out.

A shadow moved outside the window. Ben's left hand dropped to the stove poker. Outside the window, he saw the faint shine of a gun barrel. A face pressed against the window, peering in. He swung the poker with his left hand.

Glass shattered, but the poker struck something hard beyond the glass. He heard a faint cry, a moan of pain, and then staggering footsteps.

Someone swore and swore bitterly. Muttered words. Ben waited and felt the cold draft from the broken window.

He heard boots on gravel, muttered protests, and more anguished moans.

Convinced he was alone once again, Ben hung his coat over the broken window, opened the stove door, and added a couple of sticks to the coals. The fire blazed as he got back into bed and listened to the pounding sounds of the wheat mills in the distance. His pistol lay beside the bed on a chair within easy grasp.

At dawn, Ben was outside, repairing his window. He found shattered glass and some large drops of blood near a six-shooter with polished bone grips on the butt. He picked up the gun, puzzled at six letters engraved upon it, and stuck it in his belt.

Ed came to Ben's room and knocked on the door.

"Come on in, the weather's fine," Ben called.

CHAPTER TEN

"You have trouble last night?" Ed asked.

"An attempt to enter my room is all," Ben responded.

"Did you see anyone?" Ed asked.

"He left some blood outside my window, but I didn't see him."

"You must have wounded him," Ed guessed.

"I hit him with the stove poker, and it hurt," Ben said. "The most important thing is that the money is safe. We will leave after breakfast."

At breakfast, Ben asked Ed for his thoughts about the attempted break-in.

"Do you think my intruder was just trying to get my money, or could there be another reason for trying to break into my room?" Ben asked. "Those two men at the schoolhouse opening are still on my mind."

"They might have followed us to this hotel," Ed said. "Perhaps they were sent to Illinois from Canada. They could be out to kill you, Ben."

"I'm not worried about two strangers from Canada or anyone else," Ben said, pushing back from the table. "They may try to kill me, but they will not succeed because God will watch over me.

"If they bother my friends or family, then I will drive them out of this country. I might have to capture them, carve them up, and leave them for the birds," he added. "You see, Ed, they are the ones who ought to be afraid."

"The time will come when you and Debra will be free of men who want to harm you," Ed reassured him. "But in the meantime, please be on guard and watch out."

Debra and Janice were feeding cornbread and cold buttermilk to their families for lunch when Jackson held his piece of cornbread in midair, his mouth open slightly, and stared through the open door.

"What's wrong, Jackson?" Debra asked in alarm.

He didn't answer. Instead, he knocked over his chair as he bolted from the house. When Debra stood in the doorway, she saw the reason for Jackson's strange behavior.

"Well, I'll be double dipped in molasses," she said.

Janice looked over her shoulder. Pandemonium ensued as they all tumbled out of the house for a look.

"Daisy! Thank you, Jesus," Debra breathed as she ran out to watch Jackson throw his arms around the horse's neck and run unbelieving hands across her back.

Daisy was Jackson's horse, and she had been missing for several days.

"Look at that. She broke her rope," Debra sighed. "Daisy, we are happy you found your way home. Well, quit petting her, Jackson, and take her to the barn and feed and water her. She looks all right to me."

Debra turned questioningly to Janice.

"Daisy looks good to me," Janice said. "She hasn't been mistreated, and she was smart enough to find her way home."

"Well, if someone took her, they won't get her again. I can promise you that," Jackson said flatly. "I'm going to sleep with her all the time now."

"No, you're not, young man, but we'll think of something," Debra answered.

While Jackson led the procession to the barn, Janice said, "We can tie her inside the shed at my house if you like."

"No, I would like you at our house with us until the men return." Debra smiled grimly. "If someone did take her, he may decide to come back for a horse who will escape. A robber could come for her just to make a point."

"She is a special horse," Janice agreed.

"We'll put Daisy in the shed by the house," Debra said.

CHAPTER TEN

Janice didn't see the shadow that blended into the trees at the edge of the woods. The shadow's eyes mocked the little family gathering. Taking the horse was child's play. Next he would drive Ben Lett from his land.

The dappled sunlight barely revealed the stern, coal-dark facial features and the long hair covered with grease. As he strode toward his horse, the face of Jerome Banister was grim. His heart was like a stone in his chest.

Ben Lett had taken his brothers from him, shooting them down after he caught them leading away some of his mares. Well, now Ben must pay for taking away his family and everything that was dear to him.

He mounted his horse and rode away, still a shadow on the hill.

With a bit of shuffling, everyone found a place in Debra's house that night. Both Debra and Janice knew it was prudent for them to be together.

Debra thought of Ben and Ed on the trail and wondered if they had reached St. Louis yet. She prayed for them and their men, and she prayed for her family and friends there in the house.

The next day Debra was startled to see two men in dark clothing riding calmly up the road toward the house. They carried no drawn weapons, and she stood at the front door with her hand on a rifle. Janice also had a rifle in her hands as she walked out to meet the men.

After a few minutes of conversation, Janice came back to Debra. The men sat impassively on their horses, watching her.

"They want to see Ben, but since he isn't here, they want something to eat. They said they know only two women guard the house."

"So we're being threatened again," Debra replied angrily.

"I told them just because we are women doesn't mean we don't have more courage than they do. I assured them our hearts are like those of a wolf and tiger. I told them we are prepared to defend our home and children.

"They said since we are so brave, they are sure we could spare some home-cooked meat. What shall we do?" Janice asked.

Debra honestly didn't know. The two men didn't look hungry or poorly dressed. One had his hair parted in three ridges. The other man wore a long black coat and broad-brimmed cowboy hat. It made her shudder to think of what these men might have in mind for her and Janice.

From the corner of her eye, Debra saw a movement out by the corral. One of the men pulled a gun. Janice shoved her roughly into the house, slamming the heavy door behind them. They heard a thud against the door.

"Close the shutters!" Debra yelled to Jackson.

He sprinted for them and got his rifle. They worked together. Janice lifted the hinged door on the cellar, and then she carried the baby and led the terrified youngest children to safety.

"Mama!" Jackson screamed. "They're trying to get Daisy out of the shed!"

The horse was trying to pull away from the man in the black coat. Through the window, Jackson shot at the man, who fell gracefully from his horse. Jackson uttered a moan of anguish as another of the men took deliberate aim and shot at Daisy's neck.

"No, no," Jackson kept saying as he shot at the men.

The men surrounded the house and pelted all four walls with continuous fire until they finally made a retreat, taking the wounded man with them.

Jackson sprinted for the door, straining as he lifted the heavy brace that barred it.

CHAPTER TEN

"No, Jackson!" Debra shouted. She pushed him away from the door.

"But Daisy may still be alive!" he cried.

"We can't go out there yet."

Her voice was firm. She went to all the windows, peeking through the wooden blinds. It looked safe enough, but they still needed to wait to be sure the men were gone.

After a time, Jackson and Janice walked slowly toward the fallen mare. Jackson flung himself down on Daisy. The horse whinnied pitifully. A bullet wound appeared on her lower right neck, and blood ran down her beautiful mane.

"Can't we take it out?" he cried. "Mama, Mama, please take the bullet out. You can save her."

"Oh, Jackson," was all Debra could say.

Debra and Janice exchanged glances.

"She's lost a lot of blood, son," Debra said, trying to console him. "See if you can get her on her feet. We need to get her to the shed before I try to take out the bullet."

Daisy struggled to her feet while Debra marveled at her strength. Gently, they walked her to the shed. She lay down on the straw with a deep sigh.

"Get me the bowie knife," Debra ordered.

She prepared as she had before to treat bullet wounds for Ben or other horses.

She cleaned the wound with witch hazel after she had removed the bullet, then made a poultice of healing herbs, holding it in place with lengths of torn cloth.

"That's all I can do. It's up to Daisy and the Lord now," she said at last.

The moon began to lose its battle with the sun. It moved toward the other horizon and shone more brightly than it had all night. The sun slowly erased the moon, and the coming of the morning mist gave hope to the thought that Ben, Ed, and Otto would be home very soon.

At about noon the next day, Jackson came running into the house, yelling, "Daddy's coming!"

Debra and Janice joined hands and gave thanks to God for saving their lives and for bringing their men home.

As they stood in the circle of prayer, Debra heard Jackson say confidently, "I heard you say this is a miracle. Where is the miracle, Mama?"

She put her arms around him and said, "Right here, my son. Right here is our miracle. Everyone got home safely."

Two days later Daisy was on her feet and seemed to be recovering. Jackson got down on his knees and thanked God for making her well.

Life was getting back to normal. The Doyles had stayed with the Letts in case the attackers decided to try again, but all seemed to be peaceful.

"We'll be goin' over to our own house," Ed announced at breakfast that morning. "I think everything is all right."

He chewed a big bite of Debra's soft biscuit and added, "I'm sure glad you were able to drive them off."

Everyone around the table nodded their heads in agreement.

"I'm sure we don't want to go through that again, especially alone," Janice said firmly. She raised a cup of coffee to her mouth.

"We need to report this to the sheriff in Ottawa so he can be on the lookout for these men," Ben said.

"We don't want to leave to go to town right now, Ben," Ed said. "We don't know for sure where those men might be."

Ben considered what Ed had said and accepted the advice.

CHAPTER TEN

"We need to round up our mares and colts now anyway," Ben said. "It's time to wean the colts and put them in the pasture near the corral so we can train them."

He looked at Debra. "Will you be all right if we leave you women here so we can round up these mares?"

A sharp flash of fear came over Debra. She pulled herself together and, with bright eyes, said, "Janice and I can take care of each other."

She put the hot blue-enameled coffeepot on the table carefully. "I know what to do if those men come back."

Ben cut a big bite of bacon. "If they do, shoot to kill. We'll only be gone two days."

Debra looked to see if he was joking. He wasn't.

"Ben," Debra said hesitantly, "I don't think it's a good idea to go out after the mares so soon. You don't know who those men are or even if they'll come back. Please don't go yet."

Ben was afraid they truly might return, but he couldn't spend the rest of his life guarding their home and family. He put his arms around her and said, "I won't leave right away."

His eyes went to Ed as he spoke to Debra.

"We'll wait a while, but then we'll have to wean those colts. Being away from home will always be part of our work. With any luck, the sheriff ought to have rounded up those men by the time we have to move out."

Debra was relieved that Ben and Ed wouldn't be leaving anytime soon. As she lay in bed that night with Ben, she said, "Thank you for staying. I'm not sure I could cope with another attack—and especially without you."

He held her closer, running his fingertips over her soft face. He ached with love for her. "I won't leave you alone. You were so brave, my frontier woman. You have been through so much, yet you've never left me or let me down."

Gently, he added, "You do know we have to go care for those horses, don't you?"

When he felt her nod her head against him, he said, "Believe me, those men who attacked our home won't be back around here anytime soon. But I believe others will pick on us if we act afraid."

"Our home was surrounded by angels," she added, smiling at him in the darkness. "That's how I want to remember it. We were surrounded by angels, and the attackers couldn't get through."

"If you had run out of ammunition that night, you would have thrown sticks at those attackers to defend our home. You know it's true," he said.

Debra nestled deeper in Ben's embrace. She could feel the slow beating of Ben's heart under her head.

"I'm glad we don't have to do this by ourselves. If God blesses our dream, it will come true—not without hardship, but not without the Lord," she said, leaning up to give him a soft kiss.

"I've talked to the Lord a lot about the dream we share." Ben smiled in the night. "He isn't going to make it easy for us, but I don't think he's said no to it. I still think he supports our dream."

Ben turned over a little so he could see her beautiful face in the firelight. "I'm not able to put our dream into words for you. When I try it seems like, well, like I'm full of myself. I never want to be a failure in your eyes."

"Ben, that will never happen."

She used his closeness to kiss his mouth again.

"You keep that up, and you won't get a chance to hear my ideas for protecting our home from the attackers," he said, smiling.

"Ooh, tell me more," she teased.

CHAPTER TEN

"I'm thinking about a plan to trap these guys if the sheriff cooperates," he said. "If we spread the word that I'm at home ill and that Ed has left to get a doctor from Ottawa because Otto is taking care of the horses in our north forty, these men might reappear," he explained.

"With all the men gone and me sick in bed, these guys will come back again to try to kill me. If we can catch them, I think we can see that they are sent off to prison. If we are free of this threat, we could plan some special fun."

"Hmm, let me hear more," Debra said.

"I'd like to travel to some of those countries I've only heard about. My family roots go back to Ireland and Scotland. Why, the Lett family members are just waiting for us to connect with them," he said with a smile.

"Pioneering in Ireland sounds like fun."

"Thank you, my love, for sharing this dream with me," he said. "You're the biggest part of my dream. I had to find you before I could even think of starting it. God gave you to me, Debra, just as surely as he gave me the dream. And he will urge us on when we get discouraged and save us when disaster is near. He made us one."

Ben's kisses became deeper and more possessive as he said, "He made us one flesh."

Debra gave herself up to Ben and the dream.

CHAPTER ELEVEN

THE NEXT MORNING, Ben heard the sound of an approaching horse on the lane. He immediately grabbed his rifle and headed for the door.

"Well, I'll be. Tom is coming up the lane," he called out.

"Hello, Tom. Come on in and join us for some coffee," Ben said. "We have lots to talk about."

"I heard that Debra had some unfriendly callers while we were on our trip to St. Louis," Tom said. "These men should be hung for trying to kill your wife and children. They are out to get you, Ben. Someone needs to talk to the sheriff."

"Thanks for your concern, Tom," Ben said. "I would appreciate your help to make sure these men get what they deserve. I have an idea how we might be able to draw them out and work with the sheriff to capture them."

"You know, my neighbors are talking about the new sheriff. I hear tell he is a fine young man and a real hero," Tom said. "He and some farmers caught and arrested fourteen robbers and killers who were threatening men and women on farms twenty miles south of Ottawa."

CHAPTER ELEVEN

Tom explained how the sheriff had set a trap for the robbers. Farmers in the Streator area were invited to an all-day meeting in Ottawa, leaving their wives and homes unprotected. A posse led by Sheriff Dan Miller waited in the woods north of Streator until the attackers raided the first farm home.

"Everyone is talking about what happened next. It didn't work out too well for the fourteen bandits," Tom said. "Three were killed and seven were wounded. The rest were rounded up and taken to Ottawa to jail. They are planning a trial for the living.

"I know those farmers don't trust the banks, but they really need to place their gold into the bank. They are holding too much money in their homes," Tom said. "The robbers can't resist the temptation of hitting when farmers aren't home."

"Well, I have an idea of my own to take care of the fellows who attacked us," Ben said as he poured a second cup of coffee. "I'm sure these are hired guns, and we need to find out who is really behind them. Can I ask you to share the idea with the sheriff?"

"Remember, we are still our best protection from any attackers," Debra said.

"Us and the Lord," Janice reminded her.

"Of course," Debra agreed.

"The plan I've been thinking about should be foolproof because it involves our wives and children," Ben said. "I just don't know if the sheriff and his men will hang these fellows if they are caught."

"The sheriff knows Robert and me," Tom said, "and I'm sure he can be trusted."

Then Ben detailed the plan he and Debra had agreed to just hours before.

"Ed, you will leave from home in your buggy with your mount tied behind and drive toward Ottawa to get a doctor for me," Ben said. "Otto will put out the word and say you'll be gone two days.

"When you reach Sheridan, you will join Tom and Robert and a posse of farmers from the Newark and Sheridan area. At about the same time, Sheriff Miller and some men from Somonauk will gather east of Leland along the Somonauk Creek. They will wait for a smoke signal telling them when to ride toward our farm.

"Otto will ride north as if he is heading for the O'Brian farm to buy some horses. He'll meet up with O'Brian and his farm hands and ride back to our farm."

If the plan worked, horsemen would be coming toward the Lett farm from three directions, and the constable and local businessmen from Leland would approach from the west.

"Debra and Janice will be with the children at school all this time," Ben said.

"Where will you be, Ben?" Tom asked.

"I will be at home waiting," he said. "I'll make sure my horse is tied in the barn so they can sneak up to the house without arousing the horse or dog. I expect they will come into the house, guns drawn, looking for me.

"They'll walk across the center of the living room, and one or more of them will step on the rug in the middle of the room. Surprise! Away they will go and fall into the basement. Shep will take care of one or two of them very quickly. Another will be greeted with a pan of oil that I'll release from the ceiling. If there are more, I'll take care of them. Jackson will light the brush near the school on fire to signal the posse to ride to our farm.

"If you have any suggestions for this plan, speak up now before we send it to the sheriff," Ben said.

CHAPTER ELEVEN

"Let's pray over this plan," Debra said. "Please put the plan as written on the table, and we'll all lay hands on the paper. Ed, you lead us in prayer."

"Lord, this seems like a good plan, but maybe there is something about it that you would change. Please let us know before Tom takes it to the sheriff," Ed prayed.

"Lord, please help us catch these men and put them away so we don't have to live in fear," Debra prayed.

"Thank you, Lord, for protecting us thus far and helping us survive these awful men," Janice prayed.

"Lord, help us, we pray," Otto said.

"Maybe we will be fortunate and these men won't come back," Janice added, voicing the hope of everyone in the room.

"That would be wonderful, but I think we'd better be ready for another attack," Ben said.

"Ben," Debra said hesitantly, "I think it would be a good idea to put your plan into action as soon as possible. We don't know where these men might be holing up or even if they'll come back."

He put his arms around her and said, "I believe you're right. Let's put the plan into effect on Monday." Ben's eyes met Ed's. "Is Monday all right with you, Ed?"

Ed nodded his consent.

The next day Tom took the plan to the sheriff, and the Doyles helped Ben and Debra prepare to put it into action.

Monday morning, Ed started for Ottawa in his buggy with his mount tied behind. Otto left for the O'Brian farm. The sheriff made camp on the Somonauk Creek. The businessmen in Leland gathered at the coffee shop, talking about the day's events.

Word was out that Ben was ill and that Ed had gone to Ottawa. Debra and Janice were at school with the children, and Jackson had built a fire in the potbelly stove.

The trap was set.

Ben was ready for action. Loaded Colt revolvers and a Bowie knife hung from his belt. The trap door in the center of the room was set to release. Shep lay quietly in the basement.

No one knew if the raiders would come.

The weather was cold, the air hazy with snow. A smoke signal would be almost worthless, but it was too late to change plans. Ben would be on his own.

"Lord, you and I are alone now. If the raiders come, you've got to help me," Ben prayed.

In a matter of two hours, four inches of snow had fallen, and the wind had picked up. Ben began to sweat from the heat of the fire and his own anxiety. The clock over the mantel struck noon. It looked like nothing much was going to happen.

Jackson was watching the house from his hiding place in the back of the school building. Suddenly, he saw four horsemen coming up the lane. One man was wearing a black broad-brimmed hat pulled down over his eyes to protect them from the blowing snow. His collar was pulled up as high as it would go, and he was riding a jet black stallion with a white mark on his forehead and three white stockings.

The other three men were dressed similarly, but didn't appear to be as large. None rode as magnificent a horse. The riders pulled up to the front of the house and dismounted, giving the reins of the horses to one of the riders.

Looking around, they seemed satisfied that no one appeared in the vicinity of the house. The man with the

CHAPTER ELEVEN

magnificent horse approached the house with two guns drawn. Two companions followed with theirs drawn as well.

Jackson's heart began to pound and his hands started to sweat. He was scared out of his wits. His dad would be facing three men by himself. His job was to set the brush on fire, but the snow was blowing so hard no one would be able to see anything.

Jackson didn't know what to do.

He thought for a moment. If he shot the man guarding the horses in the leg, maybe he would let go of the horses. Then they could run away. And then his dad could chase the men out of the house.

But what if he missed? The men might come to the school and kill his mother and baby sister and all the other students and adults inside. Suddenly, Jackson heard shots from the direction of the house. He decided something had to be done, so he took aim at the guard holding the horses. Bang! His rifle went off, and the guard fell to the ground in pain. The frightened horses pulled back on the reins, breaking loose from the guard. The guard lay on the ground, grasping his leg, yelling for his companions.

More shots rang out. The men inside the home had approached the stairs leading to Ben and Debra's bedroom. They had walked around the small rug in the middle of the living room and proceeded up the stairs, guns drawn and ready for action. Arriving at the top of the stairs, they approached the door of the master bedroom, kicked the door open, and fired into the bed at what they thought was a person.

Jerome Banister, the leader, pulled the blankets off the bed only to discover the bed stuffed with pillows instead of a man. He realized that they were in some kind of a trap. At that very moment, he heard his guard yell out in obvious pain.

QUEEN'S REVENGE

"Let's get out of here fast," Banister yelled at his men.

They turned and ran down the stairs. Banister pushed the man ahead of him, and he tumbled down the stairs and fell on the throw rug in the middle of the floor.

The rug and the man disappeared into the basement.

Shep attacked immediately, biting into the man's arm with a viciousness that made the man scream with pain. By this time, Banister was out the front door whistling for his horse, which came running. The other man, Will, tripped and fell head long out the front door.

Ben had jumped down into the basement and was tying up the man who had fallen through and been bitten by Shep.

The businessmen from Leland arrived just in time to cover Will and Fred, the man shot in the leg. Banister beat a fast retreat toward Somonauk along the creek and into the path of Sheriff Miller and his posse. In the blizzard, they couldn't see him coming until they were right on top of one another.

Banister rode hard past the sheriff and posse, heading toward Somonauk. They turned and followed, but before long they had to give up the chase in the blinding storm. Sheriff Miller told his men to reverse direction and head for Ben's house.

Ben took his time bringing the outlaw in the basement upstairs because Shep was doing a good job of teaching him a lesson.

"You look like you've had enough roughing up by Shep," Ben said to him at last.

"Get this dog off of me," he shouted at Ben.

"I'll call him off when I'm ready and not a minute sooner," Ben responded.

The posse from Leland had taken the wounded Will to the local infirmary and put Fred in the jail. Ben brought

CHAPTER ELEVEN

James up from the basement and gave him over to the sheriff and his men.

"I'm sorry we let one of your attackers get away in the storm," Sherriff Miller said. "My men will hunt him down as soon as the storm clears."

"It looks like we have most of the gang. As soon as we find the other one, we'll hold a hearing," he continued. "Judge Peterson will be arriving in Ottawa next Monday, so they will be bound over to the grand jury for a hearing. You've got plenty of witnesses, but they will have to come to Ottawa for the hearing."

"I'm so thankful someone shot the man holding the horses. If these men had all had their horses, you might not have caught any of them," Ben remarked. "By the way, who shot that guy?"

Out of the corner of his eye, Ben saw Jackson coming from the schoolhouse with his rifle in hand. "Where have you been, young man?" he asked.

"I've been watching from the woodshed behind the schoolhouse," Jackson said sheepishly.

"Well, what did you see?" Ben confronted him in a stern manner. "Who shot the guy holding the horses?"

"I did," Jackson said with his lower lip quivering.

"You shot the guy holding the horses? But why?" Ben asked.

"I thought you might be in trouble with those other three guys who went into the house, so I took aim and shot him in the leg. Are you mad at me?" Jackson asked.

Ben took the boy in his arms and gave him a big bear hug.

"How could I be mad at you? You helped us catch these outlaws. You are our hero."

109

"Dad, will these men go to jail for a long time?" Jackson asked. "I am afraid they might come back and hunt me down."

The children were just beginning to sleep through the night without bad dreams. Loud noises could still make them jump.

"I'm sure they will be in prison for a long time," Ben said, reassuring his son. "The man who got away will be caught very soon. Then we can relax."

CHAPTER TWELVE

SHERIFF MILLER APPEARED in the lane with two men.

"Can I run out to meet him, Dad?" Jackson asked. "They'll be here in just a few minutes. Please, Dad."

"Go ahead, son. I'll be right behind you," Ben answered.

Jackson ran out the door and then slowed to a walk so as not to scare the horses.

"Hi, Sheriff Miller," Jackson called out to him.

"Hello, Jackson, and hello to you, too, Ben," the sheriff responded. "I rode up here today to tell you some good news.

"We caught that fellow who got away the other day in the snowstorm. His name is Jerome Banister. We caught up with him in Ottawa, leaving the shop of Watson, the meat merchant."

The sheriff continued, telling Ben and Jackson that one of his deputies had happened to be buying meat when someone came in the back of the store and called for Watson.

"Watson jumped like he'd been shot and left Deputy Parker standing there waiting for his meat," the sheriff said. "When the door to the back room swung open, Parker saw Banister's reflection in the mirror that hangs on the wall opposite the door."

Parker had recognized Banister's black features and triple-parted hair, but Banister had not noticed Parker.

The sheriff said his deputy had left the store immediately and ran down the street to tell what he had seen.

"Parker was breathing hard and barely able to talk, but he spouted out that he had just seen Banister at Watson's. I asked him if he was sure and he said, 'Yes, I'm sure.'

"We both pulled on our gun belts, I grabbed my shotgun, and we headed out. We came up the alley and saw a black stallion tied to a post. That stallion had a white star on his forehead and three white stockings just like Banister's horse," Sheriff Miller said.

"I told Parker to get that horse and lead him down the street and I would cover the back door and arrest Banister when he came out.

"'Be careful, Sheriff, he's a killer and fast with his guns. Remember, he killed two fellows in a Somonauk bar,' Parker warned me.

"The stallion didn't like being led away and began to whinny and stomp the ground. Banister came out the side door and began yelling at Parker, who was trying to hold the stallion.

"'Stop in the name of the law, Banister, and get your hands up before I blast you with my shotgun,' I shouted. That man stopped and turned around in the middle of the alley and began shooting at me with his two six guns. I was behind the building wall across the street.

CHAPTER TWELVE

"'Drop your guns and put up your hands,' I said. He could see the barrel of the shotgun pointing right at his belly. I was protected by the wall.

"He had no chance of escaping because Deputy Parker had tied his stallion and was approaching, gun drawn, from the other end of the alley.

"'Drop your guns like the sheriff told you, or we'll both fill you full of lead,' Parker said."

The sheriff then told Ben and Jackson how Banister did not drop his gun, but instead ran for the back of the meat store. Parker shot him in the leg, but he still managed to drag himself into the store.

The sheriff had followed Banister while the deputy covered the front of the store. Banister crawled behind the meat counter to hide, but Miller could follow a trail of blood.

"'Watson, get out of the store now before you get shot,' I shouted.

"Banister, I know you're hiding behind the meat counter. Throw out your gun now, and we'll get you a doctor. If you don't, we'll come get you.

"'Come get me, if you are man enough,' Banister hollered.

"Parker had entered the front door and stepped behind the counter, guns blazing. Banister was hit in the head and died instantly.

"Ben, you can rest easy. There won't be anyone out to get you now," Miller said in conclusion.

"Thank you, sheriff," Ben said. "I appreciate all you've done, but I am well aware that someday this could happen again. Another hired killer may find me, but for now, I am very relieved."

Life on the Illinois prairie settled back into a rhythm with nature, and the Lett family continued to marvel at the surprises and blessings they encountered.

One morning the next summer, Debra heard women's voices approaching the house, heading east on the road from Somonauk. True to her resolve, she went outside to greet them. Three Indian women approached, talking rapidly as they came. Debra called out to Janice to come and see them.

They were dressed in a combination of Indian buckskin and calico most likely purchased at the trading post in Leland. Lovely colorful beadwork provided a splash of color against the natural tan of the soft deerskins.

When they saw the white women, the Indian ladies suddenly grew very quiet.

Janice and Debra knew no Indian words, but they took the chance these women might know a few English ones.

"Good morning," they both said, smiling.

No response.

They tried again. "Hello."

"Hello," they all responded in unison.

"I'm Debra, and this is Janice," Debra said, pointing a finger at herself and then at Janice. The youngest Indian woman smiled and nodded to the others.

"Debra and Janice," Debra repeated.

The young woman giggled, hiding her face behind her hand.

Debra wanted to invite them in but didn't know what words to use. She tried in simple English and said, "Would you like to come in?" waving her hand toward the house.

They looked puzzled.

"Come in?" she repeated.

The woman in the middle seemed to understand, held up a basket she was carrying, and distinctly said, "Berries."

CHAPTER TWELVE

Debra and Janice understood they were on their way to pick berries and didn't want to take the time to stop. They nodded to assure them that they understood. The other two women lifted their baskets to show that they, too, were berry pickers.

The ladies nodded again to them. If only they knew a way to wish them great success in their picking. The young woman then surprised them by pointing a finger at them, lifting her basket in the air, waving a hand at the trail ahead, and saying, "Come?"

It caught Debra and Janice off guard, but they responded quickly with a "yes" and a smile.

"We'd love to come," Janice said. "Please wait until we get our pails."

Debra ran into the house while Janice waited at the door. She asked Ginny to care for the baby and the older children and quickly scribbled a note to Ben and Ed, who had ridden off to town. She grabbed two pails and the floppy hats and scarves she and Janice wore to ward off the mosquitoes and dashed back out the door.

The Indian women took one look at their hats, pointed at them, and began to laugh loudly. Debra and Janice laughed with them, even making the hats bounce up and down more than was necessary to give them a good show, which made them laugh harder. Then the five of them moved down the path together to the berry patch.

Debra and Janice had no idea where they were going, so they watched closely for landmarks in case they had to find their own way home.

They followed the path to the stream closest to the farm and then followed the trail that paralleled the twists and turns of the stream.

About a mile from the Lett farmhouse, they came to the berry patch. The canes were thick with black raspberries, and they looked delicious. The women talked excitedly as they pointed here and there, then they all set to work.

Debra and Janice couldn't keep up with the Indian women. Their hands seemed to whip berries into their baskets. At about noon, the youngest woman came to look into their pails, and then she showed them her basket. She had picked twice as many as Debra and Janice combined.

The young woman then knelt, quickly picked up a few handfuls, and threw the berries into each of their pails. The others came with their full baskets to help. With five of them picking, Debra and Janice's pails were full in no time.

They thanked these generous souls with their best smiles.

As they walked home, Debra said, "I wonder where they live and if we will ever see them again."

When Janice presented pies after supper, Ben and Ed looked very pleased.

Ed asked, "Where did you get the berries for these beautiful pies?"

"You'll never believe this," they both tried to answer at once.

"Some Indian women came by today. When we greeted them, they said they were going berry picking and invited us to go along, so we did," Janice said.

"We didn't quite fill our pails on our own. They helped us," Debra continued.

"These women could speak English?" Ben said.

"No, not really."

"Then how?" Ed asked.

"Oh, they said 'hello' and 'berries' and 'come,'" Janice smiled. "We sort of filled in the rest with gestures."

CHAPTER TWELVE

"We might have found some friends—and lost them—in the very same day," Debra mourned.

As they worked in the kitchen the next morning, Janice and Debra wondered aloud if their newfound friends would return. Janice let out a surprised, "Oh!" when she turned around to see the youngest member of the trio from the day before inside the kitchen door.

Debra smiled and indicated a chair for her. The young woman shook her head and held up her basket. She was going to pick berries again.

Debra and Janice decided then and there to go for berries again. Two additional Indian women had come this day, so Janice and Debra smiled at them, pointed at themselves, and said their names.

Again they picked berries until noon and again the Indian ladies helped them fill their pails after they had filled their baskets.

The seven women walked home single file, laughing and talking as they went. When they got to the Lett house, Debra invited them in and they accepted. Janice made some tea and they all sat down in the living room.

Janice spoke to the youngest woman and asked her name. The Indian women looked at one another and smiled.

Determined to learn more, Debra and Janice repeated their names, pointing to themselves. Debra then pointed at the youngest woman who had been the one to walk right into the house that morning. The Indian women looked at one another and smiled.

"Star Bright," the young woman said carefully, and then she went around the circle pointing her finger at each of the ladies and saying their strange mixture of names.

The oldest woman was Kiyemki; the middle-aged woman was Pale Moon. Then they learned the names for Lily and Robin. Janice reviewed each of the names once more to make sure that she had heard them right. The women looked at one another and smiled.

"Where do you live?" Debra tried.

Star Bright shook her head, not understanding. Debra looked at the other women grouped around her. They looked blank.

"Your house? Where is your house?" Debra said, pointing at her house.

Star Bright's face lit up.

"McMasters," she said. Debra knew the name of the Somonauk trader. She sensed the women were anxious to leave, so she smiled and stepped back, nodding them a good day. They smiled in return and started, one by one, down the path.

Robin, a small, thin woman with dark eyes, was the last to go. Just as she passed Debra, she stopped and leaned forward ever so slightly.

"Star Bright doesn't understand English talk," she whispered and then followed the others down the path. Debra and Janice stared after her with their mouths open.

On another outing to pick berries, Janice asked Robin more questions. She learned that all five women lived in a settlement north of Somonauk. Robin spoke English well because she had attended a mission school. Her education was the equivalent of about grade four. She did the figuring when she and her husband went to the trading post in Leland.

Debra and Janice were learning how to fill their pails quickly.

CHAPTER TWELVE

Janice talked to Robin on the way home the last day they picked berries. She wanted to be sure the women knew they were welcome at the Lett home at any time in the future.

"Why would you want us come?" Robin asked forthrightly.

"Well, to get to know you better. To make friends. To have some tea," Janice explained.

"Tea," Robin said. "That is good."

Robin talked again to her companions. The word *tea* seemed to be a drawing card.

"We come—sometime," Robin said.

"Good!" Debra exclaimed. "Tomorrow?"

Robin looked puzzled. "Why?" she said. "Why tomorrow?"

"We would like you to come as soon as possible," Debra said, smiling.

"Come when ready," responded Robin, and Debra and Janice nodded their heads.

Sunday arrived again, though Debra had a hard time really convincing herself that another week had gone by so quickly. Both families rose early to eat breakfast and get ready for church. Ben and Ed arrived early to stoke the fires and arrange the chairs for the service. The women would teach classes for the children and lead their singing.

The church was growing rapidly and the congregation would soon fill the school building. Pastor Johnson, who also served as the school principal, conducted the main service and usually preached a one-hour sermon. He told stories and made the sermon interesting for even the youngest child.

Monday was wash day. Janice and Debra really enjoyed wash day because, as they worked together ironing and washing the clothes, they also sang and told each other stories from their pasts. Debra especially loved telling stories of Old England.

Sometimes Debra shared details from her mother's latest letter from England. Mother McGirr loved to tell all about the wonderful things Queen Victoria was doing for England. Debra became very angry at these letters because she knew the queen still had a price on Ben's head. Despite the reminders of the queen, though, she did thrill at hearing from her mother.

The afternoon sun was very bright one Monday in fall. Debra was busy ironing when a call came from the doorway. There stood Pale Moon, Lily, and Robin.

Debra put aside her ironing and fixed tea. Janice got out a plate of fresh bread and spread each piece with black raspberry jam.

The Indian women seemed to enjoy the treat, smacking their lips appreciatively as they drank and ate. They had just finished when Kiyemki and Star Bright appeared. Debra made another pot of tea, and they started all over again. Debra and Janice talked to Robin about sewing, and Debra went to the bedroom trunk and brought out fabric that she had purchased to make pillows.

She gave each of her guests a needle and thread and proceeded to demonstrate how to go about stitching up the pillows. When they had finished, each woman handed the pillow to Debra.

"Please, Robin, tell them they may keep the pillows," Debra said. "Take them home with you. You can use them in your own homes."

They nodded and took their pillows with them.

Another time, Lily and Robin came with another woman named Little Fawn. Debra and Janice had much fun meeting with these ladies for tea and sewing.

CHAPTER THIRTEEN

IN SPRING 1849, budding leaves on the trees and cool breezes brought pleasant memories to Ben of his childhood home near Ontario, Canada. Butterflies and birds moving through the woods caused an ache of happiness in his chest. Life was becoming very good for him and his family in the three and a half years since they had settled together in Illinois.

He was proud of his children. Jackson, now eleven years old, had grown so tall. He was smart and very thoughtful of his mother and father. Jackson could handle horses almost as well as a man. He broke horses and trained them to respond to his commands.

Betsy was his constant delight. Now two and a half, she was narrow-faced and had long, blond curls that Debra kept in ringlets by wrapping them in rags at night. Betsy would crawl into his lap and look up at him with her blue eyes and smile her sweet smile. Ben would melt like butter on a hot summer day. He wanted to pull her to him and squeeze her hard. Somehow he hoped this could keep her from any harm.

He looked at his wife and children through the eyes of a man who could never see enough of them if he lived forever. He had dodged many a bullet and Indian arrow. He'd almost died before being pardoned from prison in New York. Now, though, he could feel the new life of springtime in his bones.

His love for Debra became his passion and feverish desire. He could barely wait sometimes until the children were safely in bed so that he could kiss her and pull her against him. He liked feeling her soft skin against his. He wanted to blot out all the ugly memories of prison with the fire of his passion, and she responded with an openness and desire that shocked him. The heat of their passion seared and removed the wounds of prison. Now he found peace in his memories.

The future looked bright, and it wasn't long before it became clear that Debra would have another child.

"Ben," she whispered, "I believe I will have another son. He will be part of our future—part of us conceived in our love for each other."

"I don't think it will be a boy," he said.

"It doesn't matter." She returned his kiss. "But I still think it will be a boy."

Samuel Jonathon Lett was born October 5, 1850. It took Debra longer to recover from this birth than from the births of the other children, but Samuel was a good and healthy baby.

Ben was careful of Debra, remembering how he had nearly lost her to sickness one winter. He took care of the children while she regained her health.

In the spring of 1851, Debra sensed a restlessness beginning in Ben. It seemed that he needed a new challenge.

CHAPTER THIRTEEN

He had been reading and studying about the gold rush in California. Ed and Ben had been speculating as to how much gold they might be able to mine in a year's time. They had tried to figure out how they could travel with any gold they found and get home safely.

Debra and Janice made some sumac tea for the men and served them some sourdough buns. They got cups for themselves and joined the men in conversation.

"I'm beginning to feel hemmed in, and I believe it's time to explore for gold so we can buy more land for our horses," Ben said. "The United States Army is trying to buy more horses, and we can't supply them fast enough because we don't have enough land for expansion."

"We could buy more land if we went to California and got some gold," Ed said.

"It's time for you to try, Ben," Debra said.

Ben looked at Debra long and hard.

"You know what it means, don't you, if Ed and I go to California and mine gold?" Ben said. "We might be gone for more than a year."

"Well, you won't be leaving us here while you're out there exploring the west," Debra said. "Janice and I will be going along!"

"If we take you and Janice along, who is going to watch the children?" Ben asked.

"Otto and Ginny will watch over the four oldest children, and we'll take Samuel with us," Debra responded.

Ben shook his head and said, "Ed and I will have to make this trip alone because of the hardships we'll face."

"We're going if you go, Ben Lett. I'm not staying here alone without you. If we have to, we'll take all our children with us," Debra said defiantly.

Debra took Ben's hand. "If you stay here, maybe in a few years we'll be able to buy that land even without gold from California."

He kissed her hand and looked deeply into her eyes. "I won't lie to you," he said. "It will be hard. But we can get rich in a short time if we're willing to work hard and contend with the Indians and desert heat. It's really what I want to do."

Debra saw a youthful spark in the face of the man she had married as he dreamed a new chapter of his dream. The two of them were now world wise and knew what lay ahead of them.

"I want us to pray about this, Ben. The Lord will let us know if we're to go or stay here. He has always led us in the past," Debra said earnestly.

"Lord, we need to know what you want us to do. We'll start working hard toward our goal," Ben said. "If you approve, make the way smooth. If you don't approve and want us to stay here, make it very clear to us that we are to stay. Amen."

"That's plain enough," Debra said and sighed. "Now we'll start getting ready and see what happens."

She looked up into Ben's blue eyes. "I'm really glad, Ben, that you like asking God what to do before going ahead with your plans. I watched you change from a skeptic to a man of God. And I praise God for this change in you."

"I know you spend a lot of prayer time on me." He smiled. "I have learned to be a patient man and listen to what he's saying."

As both families got ready for supper, the children helped their mothers prepare the meal and set the table. Janice talked about what it might be like in California. She said she thought the children should stay in Illinois but said she and Ed would like to join Ben and Debra on the trip.

CHAPTER THIRTEEN

When they had finished supper that night, Debra said, "Do you think any of your brothers or sisters might like to go with us, Ben?"

Ben shook his head and took a deep drink of buttermilk. "I doubt it. My brothers are well fixed, and my sisters' husbands are pretty happy farming. They enjoy their towns and especially Ottawa because it is growing so rapidly."

He looked at Debra soberly and said, "Do you still want to go?"

"I'm going unless the Lord tells me differently," she said confidently.

"Tomorrow Ed and I will ride down to Tom and Robert's and discuss the trip with them. Thursday, we'll go see my sisters and their families," Ben said.

Each night Debra and Ben measured the day's activities for a sign.

After several days, then weeks, Ben said, "I do think he wants us to go, Debra."

"It looks that way to me, too," she said. "The trip is hard to imagine. I feel we're on a mission with God's blessing. At first I wanted to go along to California because I love you and your dream of pioneering. But now, I feel the Lord has something he wants us to do. I don't know what," she admitted, "but he hasn't told us not to go.

"We'll wait and see what happens. It's all I know to do, unless he sends an angel messenger with a letter," Debra said with a laugh. "We must live our life and pray for his guidance—we must pray every day."

Debra wrapped her arms around Ben's neck and whispered softly in his ear. "I love you, and I thank God for the day he gave us to each other. I've loved you from the first time I ever saw you. But I love you more now. All the things we've been through, all the time we've spent together have changed both of us—for the better, I believe."

Reluctantly she let go of him and turned to work on the packing.

"It won't take Janice and me too long to get things ready. I believe you'll be glad you let us go with you to California. We can help you protect the gold on the return home."

The next day, Ed came to breakfast with an announcement.

"Janice and I have decided that she should stay in Illinois and take care of all the children," he said. "It's far too dangerous for any of the children to travel to California in a covered wagon because there will be Indians to fight and desert to cross. The possibility of getting sick or killed by Indians is so great that it isn't worth the risk to any of the children. We love you and don't want to see any of you hurt."

They all knew the trail to California would cross Indian territory much of the way. Although the women had had recent friendly exchanges with neighboring Indians, they also remembered when others had attacked them on their trip from New York.

"Do you think we can get along with them?" Debra asked.

Ben hesitated and cleared his throat. "All I can tell you is that we'll try."

He looked steadily at her. "You know I'll have to defend us if we're attacked."

Debra looked surprised and perplexed at Ed's announcement. What could she say? Ben just looked at Ed and smiled.

"You're right, Ed, we don't want to risk the lives of any of our children. No gold is worth their lives," he said.

"Maybe I should reconsider the trip, too," Debra said. "I don't want to be away from you for a year, Ben, but it's

CHAPTER THIRTEEN

true the children need me, too. I've been praying about this trip, and God seems to be laying a burden on my heart to stay with the children."

She wondered to herself how life would be, running the farm alone without Ben. Her enthusiasm for Ben and the trip were still strong, and she knew in her head it was the right thing to do to stay behind. She also knew that her heart was not as excited about a new adventure as it had been when they were first married and had traveled to Illinois.

She didn't tell Ben about her doubts for fear of disappointing him. She knew he needed his dreams. And she needed him.

"The Lord must want him to go," she said to herself. "He hasn't done anything to keep Ben and Ed from this trip. Lord, be my strength to help Ben fulfill his dream."

Friends and Ben's sisters and brothers gave Ed and Ben many staples and other items for the journey. Supplies were packed so tightly into their wagon that they wondered if some items should be left behind. They knew they might have to unload some things to cross streams.

The children were excited about seeing their fathers off on a wonderful adventure to California and about their prospects of finding gold. As a going-away gift, Ben gave Jackson the one thing his heart desired above all things—his very own rifle. Ben worked with him, teaching him the fine points of how to shoot it and care for it.

"You're my right-hand man now," he told Jackson. Jackson straightened his shoulders and held his head a little higher.

The last Sunday before the men left, the pastor asked Ben to preach the sermon, and Debra agreed to read a poem. The pastor told the congregation that a short time of prayer and dedication for Ben and Ed would follow the service. He would anoint them with oil and pray for the families staying behind as well as for the travelers. Lunch would be served by the ladies of the church.

The congregation was so pleased with Debra's poem and Ben's sermon that they tacked copies to the church wall for all to see. Ben took copies with him to share with families along the road. The messages of both were to trust in God the Father, rest in Jesus Christ, and be guided by the Holy Spirit.

Many times they would share these messages on the trip. Ben folded a copy of Debra's poem and placed it in his shirt pocket until he returned.

Trust the Father

Do not be anxious, said our Lord,
have peace from day to day.
The lilies neither toil nor spin,
yet none is clothed as they.
The meadowlark with sweetest song
fears not for bread or nest
because he trusts our Father's love
and God knows what is best.

Ben's sermon included the story of an old dog who gave his life when attacked by a bear. It touched on how God's love delivers, how God's love protects, and how God's love provides. And it reminded everyone that Christ Jesus lives within us, delivering, protecting, and providing.

The prayer service led by the pastor followed. Ed and Ben knelt in prayer while the entire church body gathered around and laid their hands on them in worship and prayer.

"We pray that God will be your blessing and protection on this trip," the pastor said. "All these things we ask in Jesus' name."

CHAPTER THIRTEEN

Janice sang "The Lord's Prayer," then each member of the congregation shook hands with Ed and Ben.

The lunch following the service was a special occasion. Ben's family stayed for lunch, and friends from Somonauk, Sheridan, and Ottawa joined in and wished the men well. Some of the families brought gifts for the trip, such as guns, ammunition, clothes, bedding, food, dried beef, smoked pork, and lard for cooking.

The children went outside to play hide and seek while the adults gathered at tables in the basement. The children were having such a good time that they didn't want to stop playing to come in for lunch.

The meal consisted of fried chicken, roast beef, pork chops, and all kinds of vegetable dishes to pass. Then they started in on the pies and cookies. Ed led them in prayer as everyone gathered around and held hands while he asked the Lord's blessing for the food.

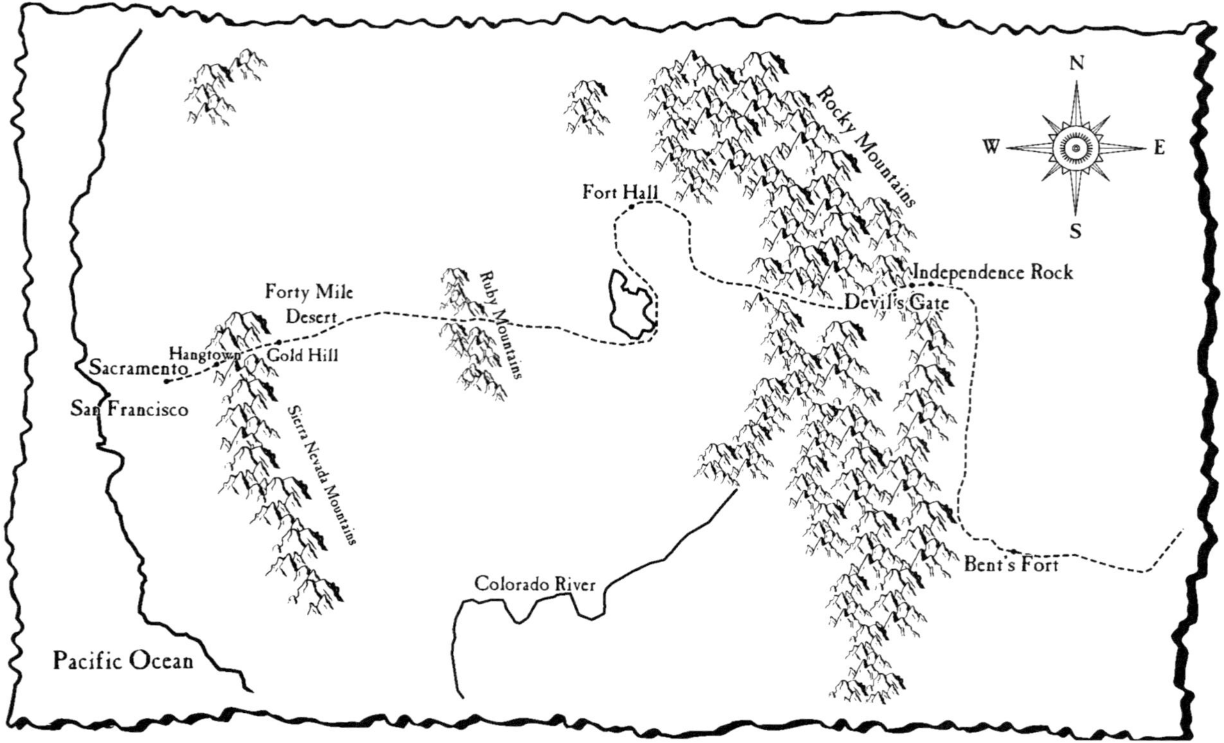
N
W
E
S
Rocky Mountains
Fort Hall
Independence Rock
Devil's Gate
Bent's Fort
Ruby Mountains
Forty Mile
Desert
Hangtown
Gold Hill
Sacramento
San Francisco
Sierra Nevada Mountains
Colorado River
Pacific Ocean

CHAPTER FOURTEEN

AFTER BREAKFAST ON the morning of April 7, 1851, Ben got up, put his hat on, and started for the barn to hitch the horses to the wagon. Ed saddled his horse and tied it to the back of the wagon. Ben would drive the wagon first while Ed rode next to him.

Ben saddled his beautiful black mare with the four white feet. He had trained this mare he called Lady to come whenever he whistled. She also would kneel and bow her head when asked. Lady was the envy of the community.

Their final good-byes said, they started. An overnight snow covered the ground, but the sun was coming up, and the snow would be gone within two hours. The wheel-o-meter, a crude mileage counter on one of the wagon wheels, tracked the very first of the hundreds of miles they would cover on this journey.

They stopped first in Melugins Grove where their friend John Hines and his family had a really good farm. The family looked fit, and John was getting equipment ready to till and

QUEEN'S REVENGE

plant the land. Ben and Ed camped the first night at Inlet Creek about fifteen miles from Dixon, Illinois.

Often Ben turned to prayer, especially after seeing something that made him think Indians might be ahead. He always took comfort in talking to the Lord. Vigilance kept him ready for any eventuality.

On April 19 they arrived in Fulton, Illinois, at about noon, then traveled another fifteen miles that afternoon. Fulton was a small, rather handsome place. The locals were at work on the Mississippi and on Rock River Road. The country around it was very poor indeed—the poorest they had seen yet.

They arrived at Fulton City on the Mississippi River the next day. The Mississippi was about as wide as the Hudson River at Stuyvesant Landing. Fulton City contained about five hundred inhabitants. For four dollars they hired a horse ferry there to take them across the river.

The mighty Mississippi lived up to its name. The horses were frightened of the large river, so Ben blindfolded them so they would not get too excited. So many families with their wagons and belongings waited for the ferry that it took a day for their turn to come. Two steamboats passed them while they waited to board.

On the other side of the river they entered Lyons, Iowa, a pretty town of about five hundred inhabitants. It was late when they got across the river, so they scouted for a place to camp. They found a cabin about two miles from the river.

A stiff-legged man came out the front door carrying a rifle loosely in the hand he wasn't using to support himself on his crutch. He waited until they got close enough to hear him and called out, "Howdy."

"Howdy, yourself," Ben said. He sat loosely in the saddle with his hand close to his pistol. "Mind if we spend the night here on your property?"

CHAPTER FOURTEEN

"Help yourself to the water in the well. You can sleep on the straw in the barn in back. Sorry, I ain't got no beds for you. Ain't been able to get around to making anything yet."

Ben nodded his understanding. "We thank you for your hospitality."

"Willard Bernanke is my name."

"I'm Ben Lett, and this is my partner, Ed Doyle," Ben said.

Ben tipped his hat, and Ed smiled at the ragged man. Ben unhitched the team and unsaddled the horses. Then Ben turned the horses out in the small pasture next to the cabin. Ed began cooking over the campfire behind the barn and was surprised to see Willard limp over to the fire.

"Them beans smell mighty good," Willard ventured.

Ed's heart went out to the starved-looking man.

"You're welcome to have some supper with us," Ed offered.

"You live out here by yourself, do you? Is that the way you want it?" Ben asked as he sat down across from the man.

"I do. At first it was right nice, but Injuns is running wild now. You got to be real careful out here. In some ways it's harder now than ever."

He accepted a plate of beans and campfire bread from Ed.

"Truth be told," he said, "I've been waiting for someone to come along so I could hook up with them."

The look in his eyes was shy as he asked softly, "Would you fellers mind me tagging along? I have what's left of a horse. I can help keep watch and do odd jobs to make the trip easier."

"It'd be good to have another man along," Ben said kindly.

That night as they slept in the barn, Ben said to Ed, "Things are really changing out here. Yes, things are always changing. We could get rich on this trip if we find gold. If not, though, we'll still have a great adventure."

"We are already rich," Ed responded.

"I knew you would say that," Ben answered.

Starting from camp at early morning, progress was hard. They traveled only about ten miles because of rain. They ran across another traveler with a team and wagon stuck in the mud. Another group of wagons came along and, together with six yoke of oxen, they pulled them free. They saw a great deal of good prairie but little timber.

They traveled next through DeWitt, Iowa, which was the county seat of Clinton County. It had about three hundred inhabitants at that time. They camped with two families and their drove of cattle. They placed two people on guard all night because of the danger of Indians or thieves.

At about ten o'clock the next morning Ed, Ben, and Willard stopped their horses well away from the fast-moving Cedar River.

"I was afraid of this," Ben said.

Ed squinted at the sky. "Don't think we better wait; it looks like a storm coming. We need to lighten the wagon so the horses won't founder in the water with the weight."

"Willard, you drive the wagon," Ben said. "Ed and I will secure the wagon with ropes on the other side and sort of ferry it across. Everyone pray hard. This is going to be a tough deal."

The men tied ropes to trees and the wagon to keep it from floating downstream. By the time they reached the other side, Willard's arms ached from the strain of urging the horses into the swift water. Ben helped Willard down from the wagon seat.

CHAPTER FOURTEEN

"I hope we don't have to do that again for a while," Willard remarked.

Ed was uneasy the next night when they camped. Something didn't feel friendly to him. He felt something or someone watching the camp with hateful eyes, and he was extra alert at every little sound and movement. Willard's dog prowled around, adding to his edginess.

Willard took the second watch. He also thought someone was watching them. Ben took the third watch.

In the morning when Ed and Ben were hitching up the horses, they found moccasin prints not far from where the team had been hobbled. They exchanged knowing looks.

"I'd say we're in for some excitement if we're not real careful today," Ben said. "I wonder why the dog didn't bark. It's a good thing he didn't, or they would have cut his throat."

They arrived at Iowa City in Johnson County at midday and camped until morning. Iowa City was on the east side of the Iowa River, a very handsome stream about as large as the Cedar River. It was navigable for steamboats in high water.

They crossed the Iowa River by horse ferry and moved west. Early spring was upon them, but the water in their pail froze a half-inch thick at night. They passed through better country that day, but water was scarce. They had to draw it nearly a mile away in the evening.

"I wouldn't live in this area if they gave me the best farm in the county," Ben remarked.

The next day was Sunday, and they camped near a little brook on a broad prairie. This was the largest prairie they had crossed since leaving home, and it stretched twenty miles across, timber to timber. California-bound travelers filled the road. Ed had the bowel complaint caused by being obliged to use so much poor water.

Out in the open air, the men had some time to talk.

"Willard, do you believe in God?" Ben asked. "Do you trust in him to keep you safe?"

Willard answered slowly, "I guess I do."

"You'd rest a lot better if you could put your faith in him. Our load of fear we're carrying now is too heavy for us. You won't be so scared and tied up in knots if you let the Lord do some of the watching with you when you stand watch at night."

Willard pulled his hat down harder on his head.

"I'll try to do it the way you said, but it ain't easy," he said. "Really doesn't sound like it would work."

"You saw the moccasin prints this morning, didn't you?"

"Well, yeah."

"And we are still just fine this morning, aren't we?"

"Maybe it was just dumb luck," Willard responded.

"Nope. We had the Lord keeping us safe last night. He'll do it all the way to California and back if we ask him," Ben assured him.

"I'm going to do a lot of asking, Ben. And I'll think on the things you've said," Willard promised.

That night, they put their backs against a low hill and camped in a piece of timber near a brook. Some dried cattails waved gently in the cool air. Ben walked along the brook very carefully. It was spring, and all manner of creatures were coming awake after the coldness of the winter.

He put his foot down and froze. A water moccasin sleepily moved away from the intrusion of his boot. Ben broke out into a sweat and stood perfectly still until he was sure the snake was out of striking range and that there were no more. He came back to the warm fire and sat down to eat supper.

"Stay out of the cattails," he warned Ed and Willard. "The moccasins are waking up."

CHAPTER FOURTEEN

Willard said, "Once I saw a whole passel of moccasins come together in a circle, and they raised up on their tails and swayed to the sound of the wind. Nearly scared me half to death."

Willard's eyes were wild and frightened.

Ben walked over to Willard's sentry post.

"Did you really see those snakes do that?" he asked casually.

Willard looked solemn as a preacher who finds a boy smoking behind the barn. "Yes, sir. But then, that was during my drinking days," he winked.

They crossed the Skunk River by ferry one afternoon not long after and then camped on the prairie beside a little brook. They made twenty miles the next day and crossed the Des Moines River by ferry late in the day, then camped one mile west of Fort Des Moines.

The next day, they came through a new town called Adel in Dallas County and crossed the Coon River, a beautiful stream and the first of its size they could ford.

As they crossed the plains, Willard often scouted for trouble by riding out ahead. From their seat on the wagon, Ben and Ed saw Willard in the distance coming at a gallop. Ben rode out to meet him.

"Trouble?"

"'Fraid so," Willard reported. "I saw a small band of warriors, or maybe a hunting party, out northwest of here about two hours ago."

"Could you tell which way they were riding?"

"If we keep going this way, we'll run into them. Let's turn more to the south. They weren't wearing paint or anything, but it won't take much to get them riled."

So far they had managed to avoid seeing any Indians, and that was the way they wanted it to stay. When they camped for evening, Ed made supper of hot coffee and rabbit stew.

"We'd better put two guards out tonight," Ed said.

"That's sure a good idea," Ben agreed.

Ben and Willard sat around the low fire and drank endless cups of coffee as the night deepened.

Stretched out in the wagon, Ed prayed, "Oh, Lord, we need help tonight. Send your angels to protect us and watch over us through this night. Help us, Lord. Help us."

He drifted in and out and was annoyed that the prayers he prayed did not ease his fears.

Ed awoke to the war-painted face of a Comanche warrior looking at him from the open end of the wagon. His knife was in a striking position over Ed's head. A single shot rang out, and the warrior's face lost expression. Shouting, screaming, and shooting echoed in the camp. Horses squealed in fright.

Ed grabbed his rifle as the cloth side of the wagon was ripped open. He turned and aimed at the dark hand holding the knife. Without hesitation, he fired and heard an awful scream that joined the sound of the rifle going off in the small space. Where were Ben and Willard? Were they still alive?

Ben came running from where the horses had been tied. He and Willard had killed two braves trying to steal the horses. The fight had ended with four dead braves.

They pushed hard the next day to reach Council Bluffs by dinnertime and camped on the Missouri River bottom three miles below the town. Wagons were parked everywhere, waiting for their turn to take the ferry across.

All night, heavy thundershowers kept them awake. A gale blew and made it impossible to keep dry.

CHAPTER FOURTEEN

Once they had crossed the river into the Nebraska Territory, they saw five graves the first day on the trail. Willard saw many Indians as he scouted ahead.

They washed up and baked bread before noon. The next day as rain fell, Ben washed two shirts for Ed and Willard and carried water. They had seen a black bear the day before while crossing the prairie creek. The prairie bottoms were beautiful along the Platte River. The only timber they saw included a few ash and elm and some cottonwood trees near the river.

"Ed, did you talk to any of the men in that last company that passed us?" Ben asked.

"Yes. Why?"

"One of the men told me they were robbed by Indians. They took all their clothing except what they had on their backs," Ben said. "One man was shot with an arrow in the chest near the armpit."

"Were any of the animals or women and children hurt?" Ed asked.

"Several of their horses were stolen, and two men were killed. The women and children survived, but they haven't a change of clothing left. Several arrows cut through the wagon covers," Ben said.

As the sun began to turn a bright shade of orange-copper and slide down out of sight, tension in the camp escalated. A full moon would rise that night. Pioneers called this a Comanche moon because this tribe conducted their cruelest raids under such moons.

"I've tried hard not to hate these people," Ben said. "It's hard for me to understand why they do the things they do."

"Do you think it's because they don't know our God?" Ed answered. "For them, life is different. They don't depend upon the heavenly Father the way we do. They have to do everything themselves."

"Why do they have to punish us?" Willard asked.

"I don't know the answer to that," Ben said, "but I do know that there's a chance we could get back some of the horses they have stolen. Ed, tomorrow you and I should go after some of the Indians and see how many horses we could get back from these raiders."

Ben's eyes detected a tiny movement in the trees along the river. His heart jumped sickeningly. The Comanches rode from their cover in the trees, painted with the glow of the moon. The horses' tails waved behind, plaited with ribbons so they looked like banners. Terrible screams flowed from the mouths of the Indians.

Ben and Ed started firing right away, for the painted men were close. Screams came from the men Ben hit, and the snorting of the horses seemed to go on forever. Their horsemanship was tremendous. Some clung to the sides of their horses and fired from beneath their necks. Ben started aiming not at where the rider was supposed to be but where he would probably show up at the neck of the horse. It was a very small target at which to shoot.

Bullets pinged and whined all around the wagon, and the dull thud of arrows and bullets buried themselves in the wheels of the wagon. As the battle unfolded, Willard found himself calmly following Ben's instructions. In his mind was a running prayer to the Lord for help. His body was busy fighting the Indians.

"Willard, watch out!"

Willard took careful aim and fired his rifle. The sound of a scream brought a brief smile to his face.

"You'll not get me," he promised beneath his breath.

Neither Ben nor Ed could estimate the casualties on the other side when the battle was done.

CHAPTER FOURTEEN

"I think I've shot at least fifty men," Ed exaggerated.

Ben and Willard laughed out loud. It felt good to laugh after the extreme tension. The men joined hands and gave thanks to God for saving their lives. Ben knew what a miracle it was that they all had survived.

A gentle wind stirred and blew through the nearby trees, pushing the smoke from the gunfire east and away from them. The battle seemed like it had gone on for hours, when in fact it was only about twenty minutes. The Indians retreated, and Ben slumped down next to the rear wagon wheel.

"We laid down a good barrage for them," he said, "but we could have used a cannon."

Ben looked back over the land. During the war in Canada, bodies lay everywhere after a battle—some dead and some screaming in pain and wanting help. Here, no sign of battle remained. The Indians worked in pairs and had swept up any fallen comrades. The quiet was unsettling.

"I think we'd better be ready for another assault," Ben said.

Everyone went on alert. The raiders were determined to get them and came straight at them this time. The men opened fire together, and several braves fell from their horses. The next thing Ben knew, the Indians had turned their horses and ridden out of sight.

CHAPTER FIFTEEN

THE MEN CROSSED the Arkansas River above Bent's Fort. From there, they traveled along the foothills of the Rocky Mountains, reaching the Platte River at the mouth of Cherry Creek to camp. They had passed three graves that day.

Next they passed over Diamond Creek where an Indian had killed a traveler a few days before. The grass grew tall and thick, and the horses ate it with great pleasure. The men shot an antelope and had steak for supper one night. They ate it with a full view of the snow-capped Rocky Mountains.

Ed woke everyone early, ate breakfast, packed up, and headed for Independence Rock. On the way they endured a severe sandstorm that lasted half an hour. Their faces and hands ached, and they rubbed mud on them to soothe them before they rested for the night.

They rolled out the next morning to a light snow, and Willard found bear tracks near the stream. They had situated their wagon near three small ridges and decided to get their rifles and head for the ridges to hunt the bear. Ed

CHAPTER FIFTEEN

took the right ridge, Willard the one on the left, and Ben the middle one. These open ridges were scattered with pine trees, but along the creek stood heavy timber and dense underbrush.

While walking along the ridge, keeping a sharp lookout for the bear, Ben saw Ed, who motioned him to cross over. Ed had found a small bear in the thicket. They both cocked their guns and started into the brush side by side. When they reached the center of the thicket, the bear reared on its haunches. The snow fell from the bushes so fast and thick that it was impossible to get a bead on him, but Ben fired anyway and hit too low, failing to bring him down.

The bear rushed for Ben, but Ed had saved a shot. The snow was falling from the thicket so heavily, though, that he could not get a shot at the bear. Ben and Ed both felt compelled to flee for their lives. Ed took to the hillside, and Ben made his way down the ridge, jumping small logs, falling over the large ones, and riding down the brush.

Just as Ben crossed a little opening, Ed fired, hitting the bear's jugular vein and his windpipe. With its windpipe severed, the bear made a louder noise than ever. Ben assumed the bear was nearer than ever and strained every nerve and fiber of his body to widen the distance between him and the bear.

Ed yelled, "Run, Ben. Run for your life!"

Ben came to a big log. He jumped, climbed, and fell over it. In fact, he never knew exactly how he did get over it. He ended up on one side of the log, utterly exhausted. The bear, unable to get over, fell on the other side and died.

Willard heard the two shots and Ed yelling. He had a little fun with Ben and teased him about running from so small a bear.

"If a little bear like that were to come at me, I would take it by the tail and beat its brains out against a tree," he said, laughing.

By the time Ed and Willard got the bear dressed, Ben had recovered sufficiently from his run and the excitement to help carry the meat to the wagon a few rods away. Ed and Willard had a great time making fun of Ben and often reminded him about the time that bear had hunted him.

They left camp early the next morning and passed Devil's Gate in what is now Wyoming. The Sweetwater River runs between two mountains four hundred feet high on the east side with a pine tree or shank growing from its crevices now and again. They came upon three trading posts within miles of one another. All sold dry goods, groceries, provisions, and ready-made clothing. The buildings were hewn of pine timber and quite large.

They camped for the night near one of the trading posts, and the next morning Ben took his gun to hunt mountain sheep. As he clambered up the mountain, he looked about one hundred yards or so ahead of him on a rock cliff and saw a panther. The panther appeared to be stalking some game.

Ben fired and killed her on the first shot. As he started to the cat, he heard her kittens crying up in the rocks. His first thought was what a nice pet he would have if he got hold of one of those young panthers. He was afraid to crawl into the cave for fear that the male panther might be around, so he decided to cut a forked stick. This he could twist into their fur and pull them out. He found two cubs and carried them back to the wagon.

In time, the female grew to be very tame and was an affectionate creature. The male, however, got very cross as he got older and he had to be tied. When Ben went to feed the male one day, the cat drew back and slapped at Ben. He shot him on the spot with his pistol.

CHAPTER FIFTEEN

The day after he had shot the panther, Ed and Ben spotted a large herd of horses driven by seven Ute Indians. Ben and Ed pushed the horses at the greatest possible speed in the direction of their wagon and called out to Willard. He grabbed his gun, mounted his horse, and hid with them, ready to receive the Indians.

The Indians did not see the wagon and the men until they had run the herd of horses almost into the camp. Ben, Ed, and Willard surprised them and succeeded in killing the seven Indians before they got far away. They captured the herd of horses, which proved to be a herd these Indians had stolen from an Arapahoe tribe the night before.

Ben later told the story of what happened next.

"We rounded up the herd and took the horses back to the Arapahoe village," he told the men at the general store. "Chief Gray Eagle thanked us and gave each of us a horse.

"Then we met an Englishman from London. He had come here from St. Louis in the company of two other men named Jim Lee and Oley Skinner," Ben told them. "This Englishman was named John Helder, and he dressed in fancy boots and a long black coat. He had a silver pistol in his waist belt.

"The Englishman took a fancy to my pet panther and asked the price for her. I told him that she was not for sale. Then he offered me a hundred dollars. I hated to part with her, but a hundred dollars would help us meet expenses for the rest of the trip, so I agreed," he concluded.

CHAPTER SIXTEEN

THE DAY BEFORE starting west, they had discussed their route and drawn a diagram of the country, showing the route by streams, mountains, and valleys and noting the tribes of Indians inhabiting each section of the country.

The Pimas were one of these tribes, and Willard said they were friendly toward the whites. He insisted that the three of them visit if they went that way. He had been at the Pima village in 1849, and at that time, they had told him he was the third white man they had ever seen.

To cross the Rocky Mountains, Ben, Ed, and Willard took the main trail west to the summit of these mountains. Then they crossed over to the headwaters of the Grand River and soon reached the village of the Goshoot Indians in what is now western Wyoming. They visited with them and bought some venison and beans.

Before long Ben and Ed would be in California, mining for gold. At night, lying alone, Ben thought of what some friends had said. They had encouraged him and Ed to

CHAPTER SIXTEEN

find gold and head for home. He considered his situation carefully and knew he needed to talk with Ed.

"Ed, we need to get going if we plan to make California a month from now," Ben said the next morning.

Ben and Ed both received letters from their wives when they arrived at Fort Hall in what today is southeastern Idaho. They spent the better part of the day reading their epistles.

The women and children reported they were in good health, and Jackson, with Otto's help, had the farm in good shape. Crops had been planted, and Otto was preparing to take horses to Chicago. Tom and Robert would go along on the drive. The sale of the horses would provide some income until the harvest.

Debra and Janice were busy caring for their children and the farm. Otto and Jackson did most of the work but sometimes hired help for plowing and planting. Debra wrote to Ben:

June 14, 1851
My Dear,

I want to tell you . . . about a letter that was written by a man, who had traveled, last season, all over California. The subject was the health of the miners.

He said improper food was the main cause of their sickness—that if they would use beef and fish instead of pork, use rice, bean, and wheat meal, instead of fine flour, use Indian meal and drink chocolate, boil their food instead of frying it, and work reasonably, resting in the heat of the day, they would enjoy as good health as at home. He thought the climate healthy.

I have many reasons for being anxious you should keep well, but the main one is that you may come home sooner.

I feel at times so lonely . . .

If it were not such a long, disagreeable journey, I would be in California before many months . . . I presume by the time you reach Sacramento, you will be so sick and tired . . . that you will almost shudder at the thought of anyone . . . attempting the journey . . .

A number of letters have come . . . since you left. Thomas Latham was in business in Sacramento and made $600 in a week . . .

I sold the wagon to Peter Dolben for $65. Everything in my care seems to be doing well. I have the calf pasture fenced and the calf in it. Mr. French has a Bible class at 10 a.m. the days he preaches, and there is a Sabbath school every Sabbath under the care of our people . . . .

Brother Moses wrote that he would have gone with you if he had known it in time. Oliver Pearson starts home October first. Perhaps you can send your journal by him. I hope you will do so well that you will be satisfied to come home a year from this month, for if you live through next fall, I do not want you to risk another there . . . .

The papers state more than forty thousand will cross the plains this summer.

For a recipe for fever. Put as much salt in any quantity of vinegar as it will dissolve. Take a tablespoon full at a time for an adult, as an emetic, at first, then continue it until there is profuse sweating.

CHAPTER SIXTEEN

When the fever is rising, take it as the stomach will bear, followed by copious draughts of warm herb tea—keep warm until better, be careful about diet and exercise for a few days.

It is recommended for all kinds of fever, pleurisy, sore throat, and dysentery.

I hope you will get some good dried herbs before you go to the mines.

Oh! I did not think I should feel as I do. Almost every hope of future earthly happiness is associated with your return, if disappointed, the future looks dark and unpromising to me.

I duly commend you to God, knowing he can preserve you from all evil, support you in every trial, and restore you to your family if it is his will. I rejoice that you have an arm on which to lean that can never fail you and that he has said, "My grace shall be sufficient for thee." Build on that foundation and it will never fail nor put to shame. I will kiss this spot and may your lips next rest on it.

Write as often as you can.

Your affectionate wife,*

Ben, Ed, and Willard later reached the Snake River and successfully got across without mishap. The spot where they forded is near where Pocatello, Idaho, now stands.

The first night after crossing the river they camped by a little stream that Ben named Rock Creek. That night the snow fell one foot deep.

Near Ogden, Utah, Ben's group fell in with an emigrant train of twenty-two wagons bound for California. The families insisted Ben, Ed, and Willard travel with them the rest of the

---

*see Author's Notes.

way to Sacramento. The company of these Illinois families suited Ben just fine, and he remarked to Ed that he had never traveled with or seen a finer crowd of people. They seemed more like brothers and sisters to Ed and him than strangers.

They resumed their journey toward Sacramento, heading west into the territory that one day would be Nevada, crossing the extreme northeast part of the Ruby Mountains.

Had it not been for the kindness of the Indians, they might have perished for want of water.

When they told a good Indian where they were going, he sat down and with his finger marked a diagram in the dust, showing the lay of the country over which they must pass. He marked every little blind spring near the trail and the mountains and valleys. He marked it so plainly that they could scarcely have made a mistake on the trip.

On their travels, only a few men spoke English. They traveled very slowly and cautiously, and at the foot of the mountains they met a party that had fought with the Indians in the mountains three days before. Several mules had been killed, and two teamsters were wounded.

The leader of that party told them the mountains were swarming with Indians, so Willard continued to drive the wagon while Ben and Ed rode ahead to scout for Indians.

On the third evening, just as the company set up camp, Ben and Ed surveyed the hill nearby and saw a band of Indians coming leisurely along, evidently bound for the same clearing.

Ben hurried down to inform Willard of the situation while Ed lingered to verify the Indians' position. What he saw made him put spurs to his horse and ride down as quickly as he could. Willard was flying around like a chicken with his head cut off to prepare the company to meet the

CHAPTER SIXTEEN

Indians. He barely had time to get the wagons in a circle and position the men to engage the Indians.

The Apaches they met stood their ground better than any Indians Ben had ever seen in battle. Beyond a doubt, this was the toughest little battle Ben and Ed had ever witnessed, but it did not last long.

The men remained in camp until they were sure the Indians were gone.

Four days later, they saw a band of Indians camped ten miles from the next fort in a valley nearly a mile wide. Ben knew this must be a new camp. Not a stick of timber stood on it except a few small willows that grew along the little rill that ran through the valley.

Ben and Ed could not get close enough to ascertain the number of Indians until after dark. They would have to count their fires to make an estimate.

As he watched, Ben sensed nervousness in these Indians. Little bands of them would walk from one fire to another. After about two hours of observation, he and Ed returned to camp and sat down with Willard to explain the lay of the land. Ben reported about twenty Indians in this camp.

"I think we should attack them at once," Willard said. He asked Ben if he had located the Indians' horses. Ben said he had. Ben gave the order for each man in the camp to mount up.

Ben and Ed were to take another man named John, make a dash for the horses, cut them loose, and stampede them. They had good starlight on their side that night. Willard and the other men rode within one hundred yards of the Indian camp before he gave the word to charge.

The Indians were immediately on their feet. Without their horses, which had been driven off, however, they had to try and run away on foot. The men led by Willard charged them on their horses, shooting the Indians as they ran away.

QUEEN'S REVENGE

The third day after the battle, Ben and some other men made a tour around the camp. Ed and two others went out hunting for fresh meat and killed four deer.

Ben started for Black Canyon to locate any small band of Apache that might be prowling around. He and the others traveled all day, saw no sign of Indians, and returned to camp.

A week later, Willard learned that Indians had attacked a train in Choke Cherry Canyon. They burned all the wagons, but no one knew how many persons had died or if some had escaped. Ben and Ed decided to check out the situation.

"Ed, you take the ridge, and I'll take the brush," Ben said. "If you see anything, whistle like a bird."

Soon Ben saw a small shoeprint, so he dismounted and tried to follow it. Soon the prints stopped. This confused him greatly. He said to himself, "This may be one of the victims. The prints are small. It could be a child or possibly a white woman."

He made his way to a patch of brush, drew a pistol in each hand, and peered in. Two Indians sprang upon him and grabbed his arms, which caused him to discharge both pistols in the air.

Ben quickly rolled on the ground with the two of them on top of him. They soon overcame him. They drove a stake into the ground, tied Ben to it, and gathered brush for a fire. This did not suit Ben a bit, but all he could do was struggle against the rope.

The Indians started a fire. Ben retained his nerve, struggling all he could.

Ed was moving as fast as he could in the direction of the gunshots he had heard up the canyon. He spotted smoke and dashed up to find Ben tied to a stake and two Apaches piling brush on the fire.

CHAPTER SIXTEEN

Ed fired at the Indians through the gathering darkness, killing one. The other ran off. Ed kicked the fire away from Ben and cut his bonds.

"How did just two Apaches take you prisoner?" he said.

Ben told him he believed a woman was alone somewhere in these hills. He suspected she had escaped from the Indians who burned the emigrant train. They agreed to search until morning.

They separated by a quarter mile and commenced circling a large hill, covered in some places by a dense growth of sagebrush as high as a man's head atop a horse. Ed and Ben agreed if either found something to fire two shots in quick succession.

They covered most of the hill, helloing every little while, until Ben finally thought he heard a faint answer. He called again and listened intently. He was sure he heard an answer. He mounted his horse, rode toward the answer, and called again. He heard a faint answer quite near and soon found a young girl of about eighteen. She was overjoyed to see him but too weak to rise.

Ben asked, "How did you come to be here?"

"The wagon train in which my family was traveling was attacked by the Indians," she said. "My family and the others were murdered and the wagons burned. My younger sister and I were taken prisoner. When night came, they tied us hand and foot and staked us to the ground, then lay down for the night.

"After we thought they were all asleep, I made a desperate effort and freed one of my hands, although it hurt terribly," she continued. "I soon released my sister, and we ran for our lives. We had gone but a short distance when the Indians discovered our absence. They raised a yell and started after us. My sister outran me. I hid in a little thicket, and they missed me. They may have overtaken her. I don't know."

Ben asked her, "What's your name, and where are you from?"

"My name is Mary Gordon, and my father's name was Henry Gordon. He was sheriff of our county in Illinois for two years before we started west."

Ben fired his gun to call Ed. It wasn't long before he rode up.

Miss Gordon said, "Oh! I don't know what I shall do in this desolate country without a relative or friend. Perhaps it would have been better if I had been killed with my father and mother. Sir, what will I do?"

Ben told her not to grieve.

"My friend and I will protect you and see that you get safely to civilization. We'll also see if we can find your sister," he said. "Are you hungry?"

"Yes, I've had nothing for three days."

Ben left Ed to care for Miss Gordon and swung into his saddle. Daylight dawned, and when he got to the top of the hill, he looked south and saw a fire. He went down the slope like the wind through the heavy sagebrush. As soon as he was near enough to distinguish objects, he saw a young girl near the fire.

He also saw two Indians. They had the girl tied to a stake and were preparing to burn her. He crept to within twenty yards of them and fired, killing one. As the other turned, he fired again and hit his target.

He approached the girl, cut her loose from the stake, and raised her into a sitting posture.

"I'm so tired and weak I can't stand," the girl said. "They have almost killed me dragging me over the cactus."

Ben asked the girl her name, and when she said her name was Maggie Gordon, he felt great joy. Ben put the girl on his

CHAPTER SIXTEEN

horse and asked her to hold on tight. Soon they reached Ed and her sister.

They shared a good cry in each other's arms. Ed and Ben saw to it that they ate something to build their strength. Four families besides the Gordon family had been murdered. These two young ladies were the only ones to escape.

CHAPTER SEVENTEEN

THEY CAMPED ONE night on a branch of Mary's River in what is now Nevada. Willard told the men they should fill the kegs and anything else that would carry water. He also told them to cut some grass for hay.

"We'll have no water or feed this side of the Carson River," Willard warned.

"What's the problem?" Ed asked.

"Desert . . . two days of it."

"We've seen a lot of desert, Willard," Ed responded.

"You ain't seen the Forty Mile. This is the worst of all, and none of the stock is in good shape. There'll be no water at all and no grass. There'll be dead animals every fifty yards. There is one spring of boiling hot water.

"It's about twenty-four hours of travel to get across. We'll not set out until afternoon; it's too hot. Every few hours we'll need to stop, feed a little hay, and give the horses water before we go on. Fill everything we've got with water . . . we'll need it all."

CHAPTER SEVENTEEN

With hand sickles they went to cut grass in a meadow close by. They carried it in their arms to the back of the wagon. Much of what they had started with was now gone. They had used their spare wagon tongue, and they had eaten most of the food.

The three men were still cutting grass when the sun went down. They slowly tied up their bundles and carried them to the wagon.

Ben slept part of that night. Ed seemed to be wide awake, staring up at the underside of the wagon whenever Ben opened his eyes.

The day dawned hot and still. Not a breath stirred. At noon, they led the draft horses to the wagon and hooked up. They tied the saddle horses behind the wagon.

Slowly, without confusion, the wagons moved out. Puffs of alkali dust arose from the rolling wheels and the hooves of the animals. Nobody talked. There was little yelling at the animals. As the day wore on, the sun grew hotter. Ben longed for a drink but dared not ask for one nor take one.

Ben caught a glimpse of the rib cage of a mule, half buried in sand. A little farther along, he saw the ruins of a broken wagon, gray and splintery from long exposure. He plodded on, walking beside the team. The wagon rumbled along, and they mounted a low rise to look over the land ahead. There—a miracle of miracles—a shimmering blue lake!

"Ed! Look!"

Other travelers had stopped as well, staring.

"Water! My God, it's water," Ben said. "But you told us . . ."

"Mirage," Willard said. "It just looks like water."

Ed turned hotly. "Are you trying to tell me that isn't a lake yonder?"

"You'll be seein' that every day. It's only a mirage. Caused by heat waves," Willard assured them. "Can't say I understand it myself, but it's a regular thing out here."

Slowly they moved on, the heavy wagons rocking and swaying over the desert. After sundown they stopped. They unhitched the horses from the wagons and carried a small bundle of grass to each. It was not enough by far, but it was something. When they had finished, each one was given a hatful of water to drink.

"We'll rest two hours," Willard told them. "Then we'll move on until midnight. We'll pull for a few hours after a rest and then take another rest just before daybreak or right after."

"And then?" Ben asked.

"The Carson River by noon, if we're lucky. Then we'll rest."

Ed lay down in the wagon, desperately weary. He heard Ben fumbling about and then it was quiet. The movement of the wagon startled him. He awakened and for a time lay still. Had Ben forgotten him? He crawled to the end of the wagon and got down over the tailgate.

Ben and Willard were plodding along near the horses, and as Ed spotted them, he saw Ben stagger. For a moment, he feared Ben would fall, but then he saw his good friend recover and plod on with Willard.

Catching up with them, Ed said, "Ben, why don't you get in the wagon? Why don't you rest?"

"Don't be a fool, Ed. They're doing all they can to pull the wagon now, let alone with me in it."

After midnight, they stopped again. In the clear night, the stars seemed close. The stench of dead animals and dust—ever and always the dust—surrounded them.

The three men sank and rested their heads on the ground. After resting for about an hour, Ed slowly took what

CHAPTER SEVENTEEN

remained of the grass to each of the animals and filled his hat with water for them.

They moved on for a time. The wind began to blow, irritating, fitful gusts that filled the eyes and ears with gray-white alkali dust that made the eyes smart and the lips crack. They stopped for a few minutes of rest, and started again. Only a few wisps of grass remained and almost no water. The water in the keg made a sloshing noise.

Ed walked, urging the horses when he could, his throat sore from dryness and dust. Walking ahead of him, Ben stumbled and fell. Slowly, heavily, he got to his feet.

Beside the trail some books lay in the sand, a six-volume set of *Rollin's Ancient History*. Just beyond sat a rocking chair and an old trunk. All had been left behind by overloaded wagons.

All night, they saw stark white bones of long-dead animals stripped by buzzard and coyote. They stopped again in the gray hours of morning to dip out enough water for coffee. They shared the rest—less than half a hatful each—with the horses.

"How far?"

Willard shrugged. "Ten mile, maybe more. The animals will smell water about midmorning, and you'll have to hold 'em, if you can. They'll stampede for it."

Ed shrugged. "They haven't strength enough, Willard. If they try to run, they'll fall."

"When they smell water, it gives them strength. You mark my words. If they start to run, just pile in the wagon and hang on!"

Red-eyed with weariness, their faces, hair, and clothing gray with dust, they started again. Each step was an ordeal; each step a victory. Twice Ed fell, and each time he crawled to his feet in time to avoid the horses.

Midmorning came and passed, and still the horses plodded steadily, hypnotically onward with heads low, leaning dumbly into their harnesses.

All about them was gray. Desolation littered with dead animals, parched and shriveled hides clinging to stark white bones, broken wagons, blankets, tools, odd bits of furniture, and the stuff of people's lives now abandoned.

Suddenly they felt a sharp gust of wind and a brief spatter of rain that vanished as soon as it came. And then the wind . . .

Ben saw a vast billowing cloud, black and ugly, rolling down upon them just before it hit. Sharp particles of sand stung his face. He saw Ed and Willard struggling to pull kerchiefs over their mouths and noses. In the midst of it, he heard a low moan from the nearest horse. The animals' pace quickened to a trot. Ben lunged for the tailgate of the wagon and pulled himself over it. They were running, rolling, rumbling, and bouncing off occasional rocks.

Ben clung to the wagon bow and prayed the wagon would hold together. Around him other wagons were rumbling and bouncing, banging into one another. Dust filled the wagon. The choking dust had him coughing and gagging. Everything inside the wagon was thrown together. The shotgun fell into the bedding, and the stove door slammed open. He closed it after cold ashes had spilled over everything.

From the right, Ben heard a splintering crash and a scream of pain. He caught one wild, fleeting glimpse of another wagon, turned on its side, wheels spinning, its horses gone.

They raced on, and he clung to the wagon in fear. Would it never stop? Would it never end? Where were Ed and Willard?

Suddenly, the horses stopped. Ben felt a delicious coolness coming into the wagon. Crawling to the back, he

CHAPTER SEVENTEEN

peered out. The horses were knee deep in water, their heads plunged into it. Slipping over the tailgate, he crouched down into the water himself and scooped great handfuls into his mouth. He threw it over him and dipped his head into it.

Willard and Ed soon joined Ben in the water. They had missed their wagon and jumped into one of the other wagons.

When they were all settled in for the evening meal, each told the story of how he had survived that run of the wagons.

They found Sacramento a lively place in this time of great California gold excitement. This was the first city of any size they had seen since leaving the Midwest. They observed gambling on a large scale. Games and all kinds of traps existed to catch the honest miner and rob him of money for which he had labored.

Ben, Ed, and Willard took in the sights of the city that first night. When passing one of the gambling dens, they saw two men leading another who was crying like a child, exclaiming, "I am ruined! I am ruined!"

They learned that this broken man had come to the city that day with eight hundred dollars in gold and bought a ticket for New York. He intended to sail the following morning, but had first gone out for a farewell spree with friends. He drank too much booze and started gambling, thinking he might double his money by morning. Like thousands of other miners in those days, though, he "played out of luck" as they termed it and lost every cent he had.

Ed, Ben, and Willard walked to their hotel. In a few minutes the broken man came in, still crying like a baby. The proprietor only laughed and said it was a common occurrence for men to come to the city with even twenty thousand dollars, gamble it off in less than a week, and then return to the mines to make another stake. He did say, however, that he had never seen a man before that took it so hard.

It was all new to them, and they agreed a little went a long way.

That night Ben told Ed, "I've seen all of Sacramento I care to; I'm ready to leave."

He and Ed and Willard camped on the edge of Sacramento the next night near their wagon. Ben was lonely and restless. He sensed that Ed felt much the same way. Now that they had traveled all the way to California, they wanted to get their gold and return to Illinois as soon as possible.

During the night, Ben sat up suddenly. He had acquired a plat of mines in the area that would come to be known as Gold Hill and Virginia City, Nevada. He pulled it out and studied the diagram. Some mines there had passed from the hands of discoverers into those of developers, and men were digging deeper and deeper to find gold.

If this plat were correct, and he was sure it was, no one had filed a claim on a corner of the Spanish mine called the Solomon. Surrounded by flourishing mines, it sat idle. Was he the only one who realized this? He decided then and there to file a claim on that corner.

The wind blew and stones rattled like hail against the walls of the wagon as they camped. Longtime residents of these Sun Mountains slept soundly, accustomed to the rattle of stones. Only the men in the mines were safe, and they had other worries.

Layers of clay kept pushing into the empty tunnels and filled any space left available. As veins of ore widened and grew richer, miners had to find ways to support walls and stopes. New methods were needed.

As he thought through his plans for the claim, Ben took a square of paper from his pocket. He knew he would

CHAPTER SEVENTEEN

face the same problem as other miners. How could anyone support the walls and roof in the mine as veins grew wider and wider?

Then it came to him—a honeycomb! If miners built supports with squares, one atop the other, these could be filled in with waste rock to add support. Surely it would work.

"I think I have some answer about what we do next," Ben told Ed when he woke up.

Together they walked outside the wagon, waited a moment, and studied the street. Nearby stood a bakery they had noticed the night before. They took a narrow foot path for an early morning cup of coffee and a roll. The path passed near some cabins, but all was dark and quiet. Lamplight filled the window of the bakery.

They waited, listening. They could hear someone humming softly inside and the heavy sound of boots walking back and forth. The baker came to the door and stood listening. After a bit, muttering, he turned and walked back inside.

Ben and Ed approached the open door of the bakery, but when they started to enter, the baker said "Hah! Got you!" and pointed a rifle at Ben.

Ben fell to the ground on his shoulder and spun around as a shot narrowly missed him. His instep caught the man behind the knee. The knee buckled, and Ben kicked him hard alongside the kneecap with his other heel.

The baker grunted with pain and fell. Like a cat, Ben was on his feet. He kicked the baker in the head as he fumbled to get the rifle in position. The kick knocked him sprawling, and Ben caught up the rifle.

"You're threatening customers," Ben said very softly. "Now crawl. You crawl back into the bakery and get some coffee ready for us. Next time I might hurt you."

"You've busted my knee!"

"Not yet. It will be sore for a while, that's all. Now get going with the coffee."

"I've got a job to do in the bakery! I can't just . . ."

"You had a job. You won't have it tomorrow if you don't move."

The baker tried to get up, cried out in pain, and fell.

"Just crawl," Ben said. "You'll feel better that way."

He and Ed watched the man get up and return to his baking and helped themselves to coffee. The room was warm with the smell of freshly made coffee and baking. Out the window, Ben could see half a dozen buildings going up, some stone, some frame.

"If the boom holds, ten thousand people will come here from the East by next year," Ben said.

"So many?" Ed asked.

"This community will grow and prosper. You can count on that as long as people find gold."

They stayed two more days near Sacramento to replenish supplies and file their claim. Then they pulled out for the Sierra Nevada Mountains by way of Hangtown, a little mining camp situated at the American Fork. They crossed over a pass that a friend had told them about earlier. It later became a splendid stagecoach road.

From Hangtown, they traveled down the Carson River some distance and met a party of miners. These miners said that a few days before, a band of Indians down on the Humboldt River had attacked an emigrant train. They cut off a portion of the train, stampeded the teams, killed all the people in that part of the train, and burned the wagons. Two weeks later, another train of emigrants crossed the Sierra Nevadas without a guide and paid with their lives.

CHAPTER SEVENTEEN

Ben, Ed, and Willard worked hard on their claim at the corner of the Solomon mine. They got out more ore, sorted out the best stuff, and had it milled at the local stamp mill. From time to time they thought of moving on or going to some other area, maybe to Austin on the Reese River. But Ben's good sense told him things would be no better there.

At night, he dreamed of Debra and the children. He considered quitting and returning to Illinois. But he considered their situation honestly and found it going pretty well. He had this as well as the adjoining claim on the east, and they were good claims. He believed they would take some very rich ore in the eastern claim.

His claims were surrounded by mines that were already producing well enough to keep going. Fortunately, nobody believed Ben and Ed had anything in their mine. The longer they believed that, the better off Ben, Ed, and Willard would be.

Ben decided to stroll down the slope that morning. He sat on a rock, looking up at the mountain. Of course, there was no telling which way that vein would go. He glanced at the claim adjoining his on the north. It belonged to a Dutchman, who kept a store and sometimes cut hair as a sideline.

Ben decided to pay the Dutchman a visit.

"How's for a haircut?" he asked.

"Sit over there—in the cane chair."

Ben dropped into the chair, studying himself in the mirror. It was time he had a haircut.

"If you find any dust in my hair," he commented, "don't bother to pan it out."

"What's the matter? Not paying off?" the Dutchman said, making conversation.

"I've got a claim up on Eight Mile. If I work, I can make a living," Ben commented.

"I own the one to the north."

"You do? Well, what do you know? If it was to the east, we could make a deal."

When the Dutchman had finished cutting his hair, he put his scissors down and said, "You'd not be interested in my place then?"

Ben picked up his coat, put it on, and headed for the door. The Dutchman spoke.

"Ben, if you want that claim of mine north of you, I'll let you have it for five hundred dollars. Take it or leave it."

"I'll take it," Ben said.

They shook hands.

"I appreciate doing business with you, although I should tell you you'd be wise to leave," the Dutchman said. "I hear things, and there's going to be trouble."

"Trouble?"

"Serious trouble. I'm going to pull out, now."

CHAPTER EIGHTEEN

BEN AND ED traveled to Sacramento to pick up mail and file more claims. Ben also wanted to learn what he could about the struggle between the Union and the Southern Confederacy. The struggle affected the mines. Each side wanted to control the mines for the riches they held. Ben had a letter from Debra.

September 15, 1851
My Dear Ben,

... In June I wrote you a full letter, but fearing something might prevent it reaching Sacramento, I decided to write again.... Last week's paper states that letters sent to California should be prepaid. I did not know it was necessary when I sent the last letter. I gave you all the news in the other and will only include a few bits in this. We are all well, and it is very healthy here.

Last week's paper states that grain and water are abundant on the plains, but that a number had died of cholera in some companies. The news came by emigrants, who, weary, had returned.

Letters have been received lately from California that came in six weeks. How glad I am they can come so soon. You do not know how pleased I was that I could hear from you so soon after you got there. Many rich mines have been lately discovered. Several from Somonauk have recently been heard from and all expect to do well this summer. If you have your health, I doubt not but you will, too. All write it is healthy there if they take care of themselves.

There were letters from Oregon in the last Repository that gave the country a great recommendation and I almost wish you were there instead of California. A man could make there all he would want in a few years and at the same time enjoy an excellent climate and health.

It will be . . . (many) weeks next Monday since you left and . . . months before we meet again.*

Jackson and Otto continue to buy more horses and prepare to sell to the army. Your brothers have been great help in locating horses to buy and delivering them to our farm. The oat crop was wonderful and so was the wheat. We have never had such a yield. You would be so proud of Jackson. Otto says that he is so strong and hardworking that he thinks of him as a man now.

Your lovely daughter is a great help in the kitchen and in the garden. She likes to ride the pony we gave her. She named it Buttercup. We never let her ride it

---

*see Author's Notes.

CHAPTER EIGHTEEN

with a saddle for fear she might fall off and catch her foot in the saddle. She loves to have me read Bible stories to her. Our baby boy is a joy to me each day.

    Janice and I have a women's Bible study in our home twice a week. The ladies bring their sewing and work on it after lunch. Otto and Jackson help them unhitch their horses and turn them in our pasture. When the ladies are ready to leave, Jackson catches the horses and hitches them to the buggies.

    . . . I fear this will try your patience, but there is so much I want to write. May God bless you and keep you from all evil. Receive this with much love from your affectionate wife.

Ben had prepared a letter to mail to Debra and dropped it at the post office that day. It read:

November 3, 1851
Darling Debra,

    I write a few lines with the wish that they may find you in the enjoyment of good health and all of the blessings that are promised those to whom God has chosen for His own . . . *

    The three of us are feeling well and are about to launch a new mine next to our present one. We believe the new vein will yield rich rewards. We will begin tomorrow working the mine. We are well equipped with blasting powder, picks, and shovels. Our mule is in good shape and ready to pull our cart filled with ore from the mine.

*see Author's Notes.

We want to take advantage of the good fall weather to get a lot of work done. My goal is to mine enough for each of us to have $3,000 worth of gold by spring. Then we can make plans to sail home by way of New York.

I am pleased to hear the children are doing so well in school and helping in the house and on the farm. There is no question in my mind that by the time we get home, Jackson will be man enough to take over for me.

We must think of him as a partner in the business if he is interested. He has the skills to make a great farmer. His love for the land and for horses is just wonderful to behold. You be thinking of how we should approach the subject with him.

Tell my lovely daughter and baby son to save up all their love and kisses for their daddy.

Debra, save all your love and affection for your one love.

Love, Ben

When they traveled on business to what would become the town of Gold Hill, the three friends stayed in a small cabin on the outskirts of town.

"Ben, what is one of your favorite verses in the Bible?" Ed asked as they rested by the fire that night.

"I believe it is Proverbs 3:5-6. 'Trust in the Lord with all thine heart; and lean not unto thine own understanding. In all thy ways acknowledge him, and he shall direct thy paths,'" Ben responded. "What is your favorite verse, Ed?"

"'They that wait upon the Lord shall renew their strength; they shall mount up with wings as eagles; they shall run and not be weary; they shall walk and not faint' (Isaiah 40:31)."

CHAPTER EIGHTEEN

"Willard, how about your verse?" Ben asked.

"'Whatsoever you do, do it heartily, as unto the Lord and not unto men' (Colossians 3:23)," Willard said.

"You men know I'm not much of a Bible scholar, but I do believe the Lord came into my heart when I asked him to when I was a seventeen-year-old boy. My father told me how Jesus died for me because he loved me and thought I was someone special.

"He also told me how God the father wanted me to join him in heaven someday. I liked the thought of being with him. Dad was a real man of God and wanted his children to be with him in heaven someday," Willard said.

Ben, Ed, and Willard decided to get some coffee in the local coffee shop the next morning. They accepted the coffee the cook poured for them, and Ben started telling them about a tall man he had met there the day before.

"He told me he owns a mine, a pretty good one, and he offered me a job," Ben said. "He told me if I wanted a partner, he had capital to invest, but I told him I already had a partner."

They finished their coffee and went back to the cabin. They decided to ride up the canyon to the site where they had first tried to pan for gold in a stream. They made camp near several gnarled, ancient cedars that offered shelter behind their trunks and twisted branches. The mountain rose steeply behind them, so they could not be taken from the rear.

They built their fire under the edge of the trees and set up a large, flat rock for a reflector. After Ed started their coffee, he got out the gold pans they had bought at the general store.

They heated the new pans over the fire until they took on a dull red glow to give them a proper burn. Then they dunked them into the stream to remove the oily film.

Burning also turned the pans a dark blue shade that better reflected gold particles.

When Ed's coffee was ready, they sat back under the trees, chewed some beef jerky, and listened to the sound of the creek and the stirring of wind in the cedars. When they had finished eating, they left the coffeepot on a rock amid the coals and went to the stream.

Filling their pans nearly full of gravel, they held them just beneath the surface of the water. With a pan in one hand, they broke up lumps of clay with the other hand and threw out the larger rocks. Then, holding the pans just beneath the surface, they proceeded to swirl the water about, first in one direction, then in the other, to settle the larger pieces.

Lifting them clear of the water, they tipped their pans slightly to allow the suspended sand and dirt to trickle over the edge of the pans. A few sharp blows on the edge of their pans helped to settle the gold particles.

By repeating the process, soon only the heavy sands and gold remained. With tweezers they picked out the more obvious fragments, put the material aside to dry, and started again.

They worked the afternoon through, and in four hours of hard work with each man handling six pans an hour, they netted approximately twelve dollars, which was good for the time and the place.

They had bought a half sack of barley, and they fed a little to their mule. They made some coffee and fried some bacon and sat down to rest and talk.

They sat talking about what they had heard at the coffee shop in town. Some men had been inquiring about Ben.

Ed wondered who would know about him out there.

CHAPTER EIGHTEEN

"Who could?" he asked. "Back in Illinois two of the men looking for you were caught. Who else would be looking for you?"

Darkness settled over the canyon, and Willard banked the fire. They spread their beds under the cedars. For a long time, they lay looking up at the few stars they could see through the branches.

Ed and Ben thought of their families back in Illinois. If they were careful and hid the gold they were panning and mining, they might each have three thousand dollars by spring.

Several times during the night, Ben awoke and listened. It was a habit he had begun to develop on the way west.

At daybreak in the canyon, the men were up and panning for gold. The water supply came mostly from melting snow, and that would end soon, so whatever they could find to supplement their stake would need to be found quickly.

The third week of panning they found a pocket under a boulder where the water spilled over to create a natural riffle. They netted six hundred dollars in two weeks. As their supplies ran low, they saddled their horses and, pulling the mule, they left most of their gear where it was. They rode down the canyon to its junction at Eight Mile and then down Silver Canyon, taking a roundabout route that brought them into town from the north. They did not want to advertise the location of their camp or direction of travel.

At least a dozen new buildings were going up, and perhaps three or four hundred men had moved into the area.

Melanie, the owner of the coffee shop, met them at the door. "I saw you fellers coming," she said. "My friend Jim's here. He has been waiting to see you."

Jim Ledder sat at the table with a cup of coffee and some doughnuts.

Ben, Ed, and Willard dropped into chairs and accepted cups of coffee and some hot doughnuts. Ben glanced up at Melanie.

"How are you doing?" he asked.

"You should do so well!" Jim said. "She can't make them fast enough! My guess is she's staked a better claim than anybody around here. How are you men faring?"

"We've been washing a little dust," Ben responded.

Ledder glanced at Ben thoughtfully but offered no comment. After a moment he said, "Before the year is over, there will be three or four thousand men here."

He sipped his coffee and then dunked a doughnut.

"Ben," he said, "you be careful."

Ben's expression did not change. Ledder was puzzled by him. When he smiled, which was rarely, Ben was a remarkably handsome man.

"Somebody's interested in you," he commented. "Asking around. Have you any enemies?"

"Who hasn't?"

"With your savvy, you could become a rich man," Ledder commented. "Albert Davis assayed some of the ore at Brown Valley, and I hear it runs four thousand dollars to the ton."

"Is this Davis the man who has been asking for me?" Ben asked.

"No, Davis is one of the richest men in these parts. It was a big, slow-moving man. Takes his time, I mean. Handlebar mustache and a bad scar over one eye. He's no miner, I'll bank on that. I never heard his name, but he seems to have money enough to live and get around."

Ledder finished his coffee and stood up. "Got to get back over to the livery stable. I'm meeting a man over there with some mules to sell."

"Business growing?" Ed asked.

CHAPTER EIGHTEEN

"Uh-huh. But one day I'm going to give it up and go back to southern Illinois. I'll buy a place there and settle down to raise horses."

Ben said, "See you on the road maybe."

"How about some more coffee and doughnuts, Melanie?" Willard asked.

Jim left and the men refilled their cups.

"He seems to have a plan," Ed commented. "He might never really do what he said, but at least he has it in mind. He has somewhere to go."

Ben gulped a mouthful of coffee, started to rise, and then sat down slowly.

A man riding by on a paint gelding—a big man with a handlebar mustache—had drawn abreast of the coffee shop. He squinted to stare within. Ben sat in a dark and shadowy place. Not a chance in a hundred could the rider make him out, but Ben noticed something. The rider had a deep scar over one eye.

Ben had no memory of the man. Watching from where he sat, he saw him dismount in front of Emery's and tie his horse there.

Ed spoke, "What are you staring at, Ben?"

His first impulse was to get up and go confront the man.

"The man Jim described has just ridden up in front of Emery's blacksmith shop. This man is looking for someone, and it may be me," Ben said. "Suppose he has been hired to look for me. Such men have a way of drifting, taking up with anyone to do whatever they have in mind."

Ben sensed something cold and calculating about the man with the scar.

Melanie returned to the table with a pot of coffee and refilled everyone's cups.

"Ben," she said, "there's a lot of talk going on about the Union versus the South. The men who come here for coffee

175

argue about it and sometimes they get very angry. I don't even know what they are talking about."

"It's a matter of state's rights," Ben said, "and the slavery question is involved. I believe the slavery question is secondary to the right of a state to do as it pleases for most men who come in here. Better than half the men in the mining camps are from the South."

"I wish they'd take their arguments somewhere else!" she said.

"Just listen," Ben advised, "and stay out of it. Keep your own counsel and let them debate the issues. Nobody is ever convinced by argument anyway. The thing for you to remember is that no matter what they believe, they all drink coffee and eat doughnuts and pies."

From where Ben sat, he could look out the door or the windows and see the paint horse still tied at Emery's.

Ed asked Ben, "What are your plans for the coming months?"

"If this place follows the pattern of other mining areas, the men mining here will sell out and move on, driven by the urge to discover rather than develop. In fact, few of them have the knowledge or the business skill needed to develop a mine," Ben said. "They are seekers and finders who only know placer mining and surface indications. They don't understand hard-rock mining or what it entails."

When Ben looked up again, the horse was gone. Irritated, Ben paid Melanie, and he and Ed and Willard moved on to the blacksmith shop. Emery's wife, Martha, had been washing clothes and cooking for miners for some time. She was a hearty, easygoing, friendly woman who stood for no foolishness and treated all the miners as so many unruly boys. They loved her for it.

CHAPTER EIGHTEEN

"Howdy," she said as she glanced at them sharply. "Haven't seen you boys for a while. Ben, you had a visitor just now—big man with a scar and mustache."

"I did? Do you know him?"

"He's a bad one. Leave him alone. I mean, even you. Leave him alone."

Ben and his men dropped on a bench. The place was empty, and Martha was cleaning up.

Ben got up. "What do you know about him?"

"He's always got money. Doesn't flash it around, but he doesn't count it either. And he's not prospectin', and he ain't lookin' for work. I'd say he's the kind to stay clear of."

"I'd like to know who his friends are, if he has any," Ben replied.

"What's between you?"

Ben stopped in the door as they were leaving.

"That's just it. I don't know, but he's been asking around about me," he replied.

CHAPTER NINETEEN

BEN STUDIED THE gold in his pan under a small glass. It was a very good grade of gold, and he had handled a lot of gold dust since arriving in California. So far, he and his friends had made a good haul panning gold in the streams, but he thought it was time they headed back to their mine.

The three friends had accumulated a lot of dust and a very good supply of nuggets of late, but the longing for a good cup of coffee and some decent food drew them down from the mountains. They took a roundabout route before they appeared at the coffee shop just as their friend Jim Ledder was arriving.

Jim wanted the three of them to join him handling mule trains over the mountains from San Francisco. Ben knew he would be fully exposed on the trail if he handled regularly scheduled mule caravans. He would be an easy target for anyone out there who wanted his scalp.

"We can't do it, Jim," he said.

Ben went to the door, glanced around, and went around the building to his mule. The three friends mounted their

CHAPTER NINETEEN

horses, leading the mule. Ben was concerned about getting back to their cache. They rode up the canyon where they had been panning for gold.

They took a trail east out of Gold Hill. They rode about a half mile, turned north, and then passed through the prospectors' holes and shacks into the rough country until they reached Eight-Mile Canyon. Several times they checked their back trail. No one had followed them.

At Eight Mile they turned east and rode up the canyon at a rapid trot. They did not slow their pace until they neared their claim.

The late afternoon sun was dipping down beyond the far mountains, casting shadows in the canyons, but no darkness fell as yet. They tied their mule with slipknots as usual and went to the cedars where they made camp.

The camp showed no sign that anyone had been there since they left, but Ben was jumpy and uneasy. Ed broke sticks for a fire and laid the sticks in order. Then he went to where Ben was checking their cache.

Ben squatted and saw the round white rock he had placed atop the rock near their cache. Right below it, barely visible in the low light, he saw a sharp white scar—a deep scratch made by a glancing bullet.

Ben let out a yell and threw himself to the right. He heard the vicious whip of the bullet and the snapping sound as it clicked off the rock, and then he was firing from his drawn Colt. Firing at the flash of a rifle, he and Ed ran. Another shot followed, a hasty shot fired by a man angry he had missed.

For a few minutes they waited but heard no sound at all. Ben expected none.

This gunman was a careful man, a most careful man. He had located their cache, had set the rock up as an easily seen target, and had checked the distance and range with at least one shot. And then he had waited.

For an hour the three men waited. By then it was totally dark. They went down to their cache and dug into the sand, into the hollow under the rock.

Their gold was safe.

"Ed, we had better make plans to move on. That bullet was for me. Someone wanted to kill me, but at least our gold is safe. When I squatted down to dig out our cache, I saw that small rock we place atop the one that marks the cache. That rock was no larger than my fist—nice and round and very white. I saw that scratch on the rock and instantly knew somebody had shot at it to test the range. So I yelled and hit the dirt, rolling just as he shot."

"That was very close," Ed said. "He'd been watching you then, saw you at the cache. Somebody's scared now that they missed you, Ben, and that's odd."

"Looks to me like somebody's out to get me," Ben said.

"Do you have any idea who it might be?" Ed asked.

"If I did, we might all saddle up and go after him."

Ben wanted no trouble. At the same time, he was perfectly aware that having missed once, the unknown marksman was unlikely to quit and go elsewhere. He had found their cache and had not taken it.

"A man was murdered on the trail only last week, struck over the head from behind and then robbed," Ben said, relating a story he had heard while they were in town. "The fellow who shot at me was no common thief."

"You've a reputation, Ben, whether you like it or not," Willard said. "I hear someone asked Miner Peel who was the most dangerous man around, and he did not hesitate. He named you."

"That's nonsense," Ben said. "I mind my own affairs, that's all. And I fight my own battles. Ed, you and Willard ride back into town and check out the latest rumors and see if you can learn anything. If you see any rough characters,

CHAPTER NINETEEN

keep an eye on them. Get all the information and gossip you can.

"See if there is anyone looking for me," he added. "Someone may come up to you and ask where I am. Just tell them you don't know. Tell them I left you on the trail."

The streets in Gold Hill were crowded, and a dozen new buildings were going up. The double row of structures that faced one another across the narrow street was now a quarter mile long and lengthening each day. The gambling houses were open all night. There was even talk of trouble with the Indians.

George Hearst came into town and made an offer for a one-sixth share of McLaughlin's mine, taking an option on it when McLaughlin agreed. He rode out of town for Orange City to borrow the money.

The coffee shop was becoming more and more a meeting place. Ed and Willard chose Melanie's table, but she was rarely there now. She had three bakers working shifts around the clock.

Ed and Willard began talking to her and asking about the business. They also asked her if she had seen the man with the handlebar moustache.

"I haven't seen or heard of him lately," she said.

"We think he shot at us yesterday near our campsite," Willard said.

Ed bought Willard another cup of coffee. They talked mines and mining.

"I heard tell about a vein at the Montgomery mine. The gold doesn't always lie where you figger. Sometimes you strike a rich pocket, and then she plays out," Willard said.

"Often as not there is more that lies beyond. Folks decide they were wasting money, and maybe they were. Anyway, they quit and take off on another tangent."

"What do you think?" Ed asked.

"I think the men at Montgomery should've kept on the way they were going, but who am I to say? They took plenty of samples. They knew what they wanted to do. You and me, Ed, we got to take a walk. Show you a thing or two about this here layout."

He gestured widely at the hillside.

"You mind what I say. Pretty soon the money boys from Frisco will be coming in, buying everything in sight."

When night came, Willard and Ed rode up the canyon as if returning to their original claim near the Sugarloaf. They circled back to reach their campsite near the Cameron River. They found Ben working the site.

"Ben, it's good to see you," Ed said. "We didn't learn much in town, but we know no one has been looking for you there lately."

"Men, the gold I'm finding here is the best by far," Ben said. "I have found several neat pockets of alluvial gold in natural riffles and a clean-up on the bedrock trench dug along an old streambed. The gold I found here is better quality than what we found in the other canyon and will run about sixteen dollars to the ounce."

They all got busy and worked there another two weeks. Working from daylight until night, sometimes they didn't even stop for lunch. By the end of the second week, the water had almost ceased to flow, so they could work no more. Most of the intermittent streams had long since dried up.

"Ben, it must be time to move on and work our mining claim near Clover Mountain," Ed said.

"You're right. Let's saddle up and move on," Ben replied.

About an hour after starting, they paused to water the animals at a spring beneath a steep bluff. After a brief rest, they started on down the canyon. They knew of a settlement of miners nearby, but they had never visited the place.

CHAPTER NINETEEN

In time, they found three shacks and a somewhat larger structure that doubled as a store and saloon.

Leaving the horses and mules at the hitching rail, they went into the saloon. A bald-headed man with a red fringe of hair glanced around at them.

"Howdy! We got whiskey, and we got some cold beer."

"No thanks," Ben said.

"Are you Ben Lett?"

Ben looked around at the speaker. He was a slim, handsome young man with a wave of red hair and a friendly smile.

"I'm Slim Broorman," the man said.

"Heard of you. I am Ben Lett."

"Hear you're mighty good with a gun."

Ben looked at him coolly and replied, "When I have to be."

Slim laughed. "So am I," he said.

Ben was irritated, yet Slim was warm and friendly, and something about him made Ben like him.

Ed and Willard walked up to Slim and suggested they needed to get going. Ben put down his cup of coffee and started for the door. They saddled up and looked back at Slim, who had walked to the edge of the porch. Ben lifted his hand and Slim waved, then walked back inside.

The three men rode west into the bitter wind off Clover Mountain. Ed, Willard, and Ben pulled for San Francisco by way of Los Angeles. They made the trip inside of a month.

As soon as they arrived in San Francisco, they put up at what was known as the Fashion Stable. It was run by a man named Kiefer. They found him to be a perfect gentleman. This was the first stable built on the city's Market Street.

They remained in the city three weeks, getting supplies for the next trip to the mines. During this time, Ben spent much time training his new horse, Black Bess.

"Ed, this is a very intelligent animal, and she follows me like a dog wherever I go," Ben bragged. "I am teaching her to perform many tricks, such as to lie down, kneel down, count to ten, and tell her age. I can throw my gloves or handkerchief down and leave her for hours without tying her, and she will be there when I return. What do you think of her?"

Ed said, "I wager you can't saddle Black Bess up and have her follow you to the Wells Fargo & Co.'s Express office and back to the stable again without touching her on the way."

"Ed, if it will be any accommodation to you, I will have her follow me there and back, and it will not cost you anything," Ben said with a smile in response.

"All right," Ed said. "About one o'clock, meet me at the stable, for I have made a bet of fifty dollars with a man from the country that she can do this."

The Wells Fargo & Co.'s Express office was eight blocks away from the stable, and on Ben's return he found quite a crowd waiting to see the performance.

Ben threw the saddle on the mare, put the bridle on her just as though he was going to ride, took his whip in his hand, and started down the sidewalk. The mare walked down the street. Montgomery Street was always full of teams at this time of the day, and the sidewalk was crowded with people. Bess picked her way along the street among the teams as though Ben was on her back, and kept her eyes on him all the time.

When Ben arrived at the Wells Fargo & Co.'s Express office, he picked a handkerchief from his pocket and threw it down at the edge of the sidewalk, walked into the office, and remained there for five minutes. When he came out,

CHAPTER NINETEEN

she was still standing with her head over the handkerchief as though she was tied. Ben picked up the handkerchief and started down the sidewalk. She took to following him down the street to the stable.

Ed walked over to the farmer with whom he had made the bet and put out his hand. The farmer started to argue with Ed until Ben walked up and asked, "Is anything wrong?"

The famer realized he was outnumbered and reached into his pocket for a fifty-dollar gold piece.

Before putting Black Bess back in the stable, Ben had her perform several tricks and then bow to the crowd, which by this time had grown to more than a hundred people. Several different men asked Ben what he would take for her, but he informed them money would not buy her.

This black mare proved to be the most intelligent animal Ben had ever owned. She disliked nothing more than the sight or even the scent of a wild animal such as a bear. The moment she saw or caught the scent of anything strange, she came to Ben and pawed until he looked in the direction of whatever object she had seen, heard, or smelled.

Ed, Willard, and Ben were drilling for gold in a mine owned by Ben. If one man held the drill while the other struck it with the eight-pound double jack, the drilling was easier. Then the third man could clean out the holes.

"Let's take a rest for five minutes," Ed said. "Ben, you're a good man with that sledge."

"Swinging the sledge is good for a man's muscle," Ben said. "But then, in my time I've done a lot of things that could be called muscle building. You men keep on drilling. I think I'll go to town and file a new claim."

Ben went up top and bathed himself as best he could. He shaved, put on his suit, and put the papers for the claim inside his coat pocket.

QUEEN'S REVENGE

When he reached Gold Hill, he glanced toward the coffee shop. He didn't see many customers. He took out his watch and glanced at it. He headed down the street to file his claim. The street was crowded as usual.

A big ore wagon rumbled past, drawn by six head of mules. He had started across the street and suddenly glimpsed the boots and legs of somebody on the other side of the wagon, waiting for it to pass. Turning sharply, he walked toward the head of the slow moving wagon, then running, he ducked around ahead of the team and stopped.

A big man stood in the center of the street with a drawn gun, staring wildly about.

"Looking for me?" Ben yelled.

People had stopped to watch as the man turned, raising his gun.

"Yes, darn you!"

Ben's side was toward him. He stood tall and alone, waiting.

Only seconds passed, yet it seemed like hours. With a kind of curious detachment, he saw the man's gun coming up and heard somebody yell. He sensed a surge of people on the street. Some rushed to see; some crowded to get out of the way. They were the smart ones.

The man's back was to the light, his face in darkness. The gun rose. Ben drew and fired.

The man's gun went off, and the bullet struck the earth with an angry thud, only inches from Ben's boot. With gun in hand, Ben walked slowly toward the fallen man, watchful but unworried. He knew where his bullet had gone.

People crowded around. Somebody turned the man over; he had a handlebar moustache and a big scar over his eye.

"I'll be darned," a bystander said. "He always struck me as a sure thing man."

"I believe he thought it was a sure thing," Ben said mildly.

CHAPTER NINETEEN

Then he walked across the street to the theater. The doorman shrugged and stepped back.

"Heard some shooting," he said. "What was it? Some drunk?"

"I don't think he was drunk," Ben said. "I think he was paid."

Albert Davis sat drinking wine in his office at the back of the theater. Davis was thinking of buying another mill. He suspected the mill operators were not as honest as they should be.

Ben Lett. At last he had seen the man. Lett was different from what he had expected—much sharper, cool. Something about the man's eyes disturbed him. Davis despised all men and held them in contempt, yet this man, this Lett, was dangerous.

The coolness he displayed killing Davis's employee—his careless employee—was not what he expected at all. By all reports, Lett had been in command of the situation, from first to last. He was quick to perceive danger and acted with deliberation with no sign of panic. Such a man, who lived with awareness, would be difficult to kill.

Johnson, his other employee, knocked at the door and entered. Johnson's reports from the mine were neatly laid on the desk.

"Lett's men have opened tunnel forty-nine at their mine and begun stopping it out. The vein is thirty-five feet wide and very rich—the best yet."

"Thank you, Johnson. That's good news."

When the office door closed, Davis got to his feet and walked to the window looking over the mountainside. He fought down panic that surged inside him. He had more than sixty thousand dollars between this safe and his private safe at the hotel. Why not take it and run?

He pushed the impulse aside. What he wanted was there. He wanted power and position. So far he had won, and he must not weaken despite this temporary setback.

The situation was desperate, and it was a time for desperate measures. Everything he had worked for, connived for—all of it was at stake. Whatever was to be done must be done now. His benefactors would not be happy if he let Ben Lett walk away again.

All three of them—Lett and his two partners—must die. When they were killed, he must be in public view, totally unconnected with whatever happened. It had to be quick, it had to be decisive, and it had to be immediate.

CHAPTER TWENTY

ED AND WILLARD cooked breakfast as Ben told the story of his encounter in town the day before. As they drank their coffee, they agreed that someone wanted to kill Ben or maybe all of them.

"We need to be careful at the new mine," Ben said.

"Some of the superstitious miners have been telling tales about the mine and tunnel forty-nine in particular," Willard said.

"I don't put stock in such nonsense," Ben said. "To work the mine properly we need to be smart and go deeper. We'll need lots of capital. I've talked to Wes Crockett, and he agreed to buy half the mine. His payment will give us the money we need for further drilling."

Ben and Ed agreed that they needed to go down into the mine and check on the newest vein.

"You'd better be careful," Willard said. "You know what trouble we've had with mud there."

"We'll just look around," Ben said. "Ed hasn't seen the new vein yet. We'll check it out and be back by noon. We'll take six candles; that will last us twenty hours."

Ben put on the jacket he always hung on the wall of the mine office. He also took a spiked candleholder for fixing candles against a wall.

It was dark and still in the mine except for the drip of water and an occasional rattle of falling rocks. They picked their way along the narrow track on which the ore-cars ran. At a fork in the drift, Ben picked up a shovel. He was thinking of the chart of the mine workings back in the office. They should be nearing the new vein, number forty-nine.

After a few more steps, he paused so suddenly that Ed bumped him from behind.

"What's wrong?" Ed asked.

"A spot like this could be a dead end," Ben said. "There are hot springs all over this area, and they deposit the gold. We have to decide whether to continue working, hoping for mineral on the other side of this rock, or stop here, taking for granted the barren ground will continue."

Then Ben stooped and picked up something from the floor of the tunnel.

"That's odd; this is a piece of Bickford fuse used in blasting," he said.

Ben led the way forward, pausing occasionally to look around. He gestured toward the ground at his feet. All along the wall a thick, black smooth stretch of mud lay at the foot of the wall, projecting almost to the track.

"Sometimes layers of mud are between rock strata. When you run a tunnel into it, the pressure squeezes the mud into the open space," Ben said.

"Then what happens?" Ed asked.

Ben shrugged.

CHAPTER TWENTY

"It just keeps squeezing. The mud keeps oozing, and in areas where this happens, you usually have one or two men busy all the time cutting it out with shovels and carrying it away. If you don't, the mud will fill the tunnel," Ben said.

"You mean it will fill all this space?" Ed questioned.

"Let's get out of here!"

They had taken no more than two steps when a dull thud sounded somewhere behind them, and a sudden puff of pushed air put out their candles.

"There has been an explosion, Ed," Ben said. "Stand perfectly still until I light up."

"That smell, what is it?"

"Powder smoke," Ben said. "I think we're in trouble, Ed."

He fumbled for a match, struck it, and lit his candle, then Ed's.

"Let's see how bad it is," Ben said.

He led the way back along the track to the opening of the cross cut, but no opening remained. Instead he found a pile of muck, broken rock, and splintered timbers.

He lifted his candle. The charge had been placed so as to block both the cross cut and the dead-end tunnel. He studied it thoughtfully, trying to recall the formation he had glanced at as he had entered the tunnel. How much had been shot down? How far were they from the other side?

Too far.

"Ed," Ben said, "put out your candle. We'll need the air."

"Are we trapped, Ben?"

"Yes, we are. And that was the whole idea, Ed."

"But they'll find us, Ben! They'll find us when they come to work tomorrow!"

"Tomorrow is Sunday," Ben said. "Nobody will be working."

"What about Willard?"

191

"He won't be back before Monday at the earliest. He went into town for the weekend."

"Then we will die here?" Ed said.

"Let's get to work and see if we can clear some of this debris," Ben replied.

The charge had gone off where the cross cut left the main tunnel. Rock that fell had not closed access to the tunnel, but only a few yards farther along the tunnel ended.

Ben was on his knees atop the rock fall, tugging rock after rock from its place and letting each roll back behind him. The stuff was too large for a shovel to be of any use. His coat, vest, and shirt hung on the shovel standing against the wall. Dust had fallen over his back and shoulders while sweat ran down his back and chest, leaving trails in the dust.

"It's ten o'clock, Ben. Hadn't we better rest?" Ed asked.

"We'll rest when we get out," Ben answered.

They needed to open a hole to let air come in before they exhausted what remained. They could expect no help. By now all the miners would have left for the day and guards would be on duty. They would permit no one to approach the mine.

Once before, Ben had been briefly trapped in a cave-in and some passing Indians had dug him out. He remembered how close the air had become, how the candle flames had burned lower, and how he had struggled for breath as the air grew thinner.

"Somebody was watching us enter the mine," Ben said. "He came into the mine and lit a short fuse behind us."

At midnight they stopped working.

"What do you think?" Ed asked.

Ben answered, "It doesn't look good."

He held the candle close, peering into the hole he had made. All he saw was more rocks beyond. The candle flame did not flicker. That meant no new air was moving.

CHAPTER TWENTY

"We've got some distance to go yet," he said. "Ed, get some rest. You can spell me later."

Ben work steadily. His muscles ached and sweat dripped into his eyes, which stung from the salt. He found himself resting more which often. Was he imagining it, or was the candle flame burning lower?

He backed out of the hole again. He was in more than twenty feet and the roof above him seemed fairly solid. He mopped his face and chest with his shirt. Ed was sleeping. Thank God for that.

His watch lay on a flat rock where he had put it before using his jacket as a pillow. It was after two in the morning.

The work had been painfully slow. Each rock he removed had to be pushed behind him, and as he worked deeper, the rocks had to be taken from his improvised tunnel.

He sat down heavily, blinking the sweat from his eyes. If the air was going bad now as it seemed to be, how much longer could they last? Another twelve hours? It would not be enough unless someone thought to look for them in the mine.

Willard might think of them when he returned to the coffee shop and missed them. Or would he? He might assume they had gone to the hotel.

Twice in the next two hours they had to take detours around rocks too large to move. Whoever had placed the charges had been shooting down rock, not trying to break it for running through a mill for mining purposes.

It was nearly seven o'clock in the morning when Ben heard a rock fall away ahead of him. Ben put out a testing hand. Emptiness!

He backed out hurriedly, got the candle, and crawled back, holding the candle out before him. Hope vanished in a cloud of despair.

Beyond about fifteen feet was another wall of broken rock. Ben crawled slowly back to where Ed lay and sat down.

He felt empty and exhausted. He was tired . . . so very tired. Resting his arms on his knees, he lowered his head and closed his eyes.

Ben felt a hand on his shoulder.

"Ben? Ben, are you all right?" Ed asked.

Ben sat up quickly. "Sorry. I fell asleep. I was dead tired."

"I can imagine."

As he stood, Ed and Ben's eyes met.

"Ben, tell me. Are we going to get out?"

"Not that way." Ben nodded his head in the direction where he had been working. "I broke through last night. There's just a small gap and another pile of rock. If we get through that, there will be another."

Ben stooped and took a pick from the floor.

"I found this, though. Some miner left it standing at the wall. God bless him."

Ed stared at him, not fully comprehending.

"Ed, do you remember that section of the cross cut we looked at on the map up in the office? Did you really look at it?" he asked.

"I think so," Ed said hesitantly.

"Look." Ben said. "This cross cut is like a bar across the top of a Y, or almost the top. How wide was the top of the Y, do you remember?"

"I don't know. I just glanced at it. I think maybe it was fifty feet. In fact, I am sure it was."

Ben took up the pick. In the low blue light of the candle, Ed's eyes were dark hollows in the pallor of his face.

"But it's rock, Ben! It's solid rock!"

"There are many kinds of rock. If this is like most of the mine, it's decomposed feldspar and clay. Sometimes

CHAPTER TWENTY

whole sections of the roof will fall in. It's pretty flaky stuff. Sit back a ways and pray."

Ben chose a spot and took a tentative swing at the wall. He prayed for just an opening, just a hole of some kind to let the air in. Ben did not know if Ed realized what that blue flame on the candle meant, but the bluer the flame, the worse the air.

Ben swung the pick, tearing loose a chunk of rock. With a double jack he could pound fifty blows a minute. He wouldn't do that well with a pick in this air.

He struck the pick into the rock and pulled away a good-sized slab.

"I've got to be careful," he spoke half aloud and to himself, "or I'll break this pick handle."

His body dripped with sweat, which was water he could ill afford to lose. With a cold, desperate fury, he attacked the rock wall. Pieces broke off and fell at his feet, some of them gleaming with silver. His body shone with sweat; his pants were dark with it. The heavy thuds of the pick and the gasps of his breathing were loud in the small space.

For an hour or more he worked without a let-up. Then suddenly he backed off and sat down, his breath coming in great, wrenching gasps.

"Ben?" Ed's voice was a whisper. "Are you all right?"

"I have to rest."

Ed got up. "I'll take over."

He took up the pick.

As the hours retreated behind them, the opening seemed pitifully small. Slowly, heavily, Ed and Ben swung the pick. Their lungs sucked at the air. Each man could swing but once or twice and then rest.

The candle flame grew bluer now and smaller. Each swung the pick and pulled off chunks of rock. Their muscles had built power; their hands were like claws shaped only for the handle of the pick. Sometimes after several blows they would fall against the wall for a moment to rest. They no longer talked. They no longer wished for freedom from the darkness. They scarcely even thought of air. They just were there.

Ben swung the pick because he knew no other way. All his life there were battles, and all his life he had worked and fought against the odds. He would go down fighting, go out trying as he had always done. Had he known how, he would have quit, but life had taught him everything but that. He attacked the mountain like a dumb brute. Bits of it splattered into his face, and sometimes it was wet.

Hours after Ben and Ed had entered the mine, Willard pushed through the door of the coffee shop in Gold Hill, bumping the man who stood with his back to it. Not until he was in the room did he see the shotgun in Kohl's hand.

"Another time, Mr. Kohl," Johnson said and went out the door past Willard.

"Thank God," Melanie said, gasping. "You stopped a shooting."

"They're gone," he blurted out. "Ed and Ben are gone, and I think Johnson knows where they are."

"You mean they're dead?" Melanie demanded.

"I don't know, but I know Johnson."

"Where could they be?"

"How long since anybody saw them?" Ed Kohl asked.

"It's been hours," Willard said.

"They must be at the mine," Melanie said. "You boys better go have a look."

The men started up the street together, calling out, "Ben Lett is missing. So's his friend Ed. We think they're trapped in their mine."

CHAPTER TWENTY

As they walked, townspeople yelled, "Hold on! I'm coming!"

Two miners, carrying lunch buckets and still dripping from the heat of the mine, turned and followed. Along the street, word passed from man to man, place to place. Two more men broke from a crowd and followed. Another one. Then three. One was a gambler in his shirtsleeves.

From this place and that they came—gamblers, bartenders, teamsters, miners, and superintendents of mines.

"Ben and Ed are always there to help when anybody else is in trouble," someone said.

Soon there were fifty, then a hundred. Then even more.

CHAPTER TWENTY-ONE

THE GUARD STEPPED onto the path as Willard and the group reached him. "Sorry, boys. Nobody goes into the mine."

"How long have you been on guard?" Willard asked.

"Yesterday afternoon sometime. I been relieved once, then I come back."

"Anybody go up there?" Willard asked.

"Nobody. Mr. Lett said nobody can go by without an order from him."

"You haven't seen him? Ed?"

"Nope. Nobody."

He paused.

"Well, come to think of it, I thought I saw somebody over on the back side, but when I walked around, there was nobody there. On a job like this, you get to seein' shadows."

"We've reason to believe Ben and Ed may be trapped up there. We're going up."

"Now, see here!" the guard said, sweating. "You just can't."

CHAPTER TWENTY-ONE

"You want to stop me, Tom, or all of them?" Willard asked mildly as he turned and gestured to those gathered around them.

Tom shook his head.

"If Lett is down in that hole, I want to help," Tom answered.

"We don't know he's there," Willard said, "although I don't know where else he and Ed would be."

Willard tried the door of the mine office and said, "This is open. Somebody's been here."

Tom pushed open the door and went in. Willard followed as Tom walked toward the hoisting-engine house.

Tom said, "They wouldn't walk off and leave the office open. Not even with guards about."

Willard pushed open the door and went in. Suddenly Tom called out, "Boys? He's here all right. Ben's coat is gone. He hangs it here to wear whenever he's below!"

Willard saw the map of the cross cut and tunnel forty-nine on the table.

"See here. Forty-nine. Folks say don't go near forty-nine, and here's the chart of it as if somebody has been studying it. All right, it's something to go on," he said.

Willard looked around the gathered men and said, "Anybody here who ever worked in this mine?"

"I did," said a big sandy-haired miner in damp digging clothes, who pushed to the front.

"What's wrong with forty-nine?" Willard asked.

Sandy shrugged. "Nothing more than anywhere else. There's a lot of dangerous ground in the mine. Everybody knows that, but it's no worse than a lot else."

"We need to take a look," Willard said, then paused. "Better only six of us go down so we don't clutter everything up."

He looked around at the assembled faces.

"You fellers stick around. We might be needin' you. Sandy, I'll take you and Rod. Sandy, you pick out three good miners to come with us."

"Build a fire," somebody suggested. "If they find them, they'll be cold when they hit the night air. Comin' out of one of those hot mines is an invitation to pneumonia."

"I'll get some blankets," somebody said and, turning, ran off into the night.

With lighted candles, the six disappeared into the opening. Sandy led the way.

"Been a few months," he spoke over his shoulder. "I quit. Didn't like the way the last mine owner operated." He gestured with a hand. "Forty-nine's up this way."

For several minutes they walked in silence until the tunnel suddenly ended at a slanting wall of muck. Sandy held his candle high.

"Well, I'll be darned! Whole darned roof fell in!"

"It didn't fall, Sandy. It was blasted. Look here," Willard said as he held up a slab of rock.

He put his finger on a small half moon of a hole.

"Been drilled, and see, that band of quartz ran right over the top."

He turned it.

"Some good values in it, too."

"Maybe," Sandy agreed reluctantly, "just maybe. But what would a man do that for?"

They looked at each other and finally Sandy said, "They had trouble with this area. She was always flakin' off. I was pushin' a car in here one time, and a slab that must've weighed three hundred pounds fell. Hit the front end of the car. I was all bent over pushin'. If I'd've of been one step further, it would have wiped me out."

"If they're back there," another miner said, "they've had it."

CHAPTER TWENTY-ONE

"How far from here to that cross cut?" Willard asked.

"Hundred and fifty feet. Maybe more. Been awhile since I worked in here."

"This is fresh," Sandy said. "I can still smell powder smoke."

He gestured with his candle. "Let's go back to the other branch. We got to try it."

"No need, Sandy."

The miner speaking was a stocky, barrel-chested man they called Blaine.

"That cross cut opened up this drift, and they hadn't broken through on the other end yet. This is the only way into forty-nine, and nobody had gone this way."

"Unless this was done after they went in," Willard said. "Somebody has tried several times to kill Lett. Took some shots at him."

"If they are back of that," Blaine gestured back toward the cave-in, "they aren't going to get out in a hurry. I know that roof, and if any of it went, fifty or sixty feet went. When we start to muck it out, more is going to come down. It's bad ground, believe me."

At the main tunnel Willard paused, turning to shine the light of the candle up the other side of the Y.

"You don't think we should look up this way?"

"No use," Blaine said. "That cross cut hadn't come through. We'd do a sight better to start getting muck out and getting some timber ready. That tunnel will have to be shored up."

Sandy hesitated and then said, "What the heck, Willard. Come on."

Two of the miners stopped.

"You have a look. We'll go topside and start things rollin'. We're in for a lot of digging," one said.

Sandy led the way, commenting, "Be a wonder if we dug all the way back there and he showed up all hale an' hearty."

"They won't," Willard said, "I know him and Ed. They never left anything lying out and never left a door unlocked. They are careful men."

The boots of the miners splashed in pools of water between the ties. This tunnel was wetter than the other, and water dripped from the roof. It was dark and wet and very hot. Willard thanked God that he had never taken up mining. How miners stood these conditions he could not guess.

Hours passed as the men got to work, while a crowd of townsfolk gathered around the campfire that had been built at the mouth of the mine.

"Ain't far now," Sandy said. "They put a few rounds in from here just to mark the spot." He paused suddenly. "Say one round. There it is, only three feet or so from this side."

They stood side by side, looking at the beginning of what was to be the cross cut—a narrow arched doorway in the rock.

Willard mopped the sweat from his face. He was exasperated and disappointed.

"I was hoping maybe there was an opening all the way through," he said.

In silence they stood, listening to the slow drip of water. Utter blackness surrounded them where no candlelight shone, and water dripped everywhere. Willard wanted to get out, to get away.

"Sandy, I don't see how you do it. You must have more guts than a country mule," he said.

"Mined all my born days," Sandy said. "I've been underground more than I've been on top. My wife's always

CHAPTER TWENTY-ONE

after me to quit, but what can I do? I don't know anything else."

He turned his head and the light from the candle on his cap shone for an instant into the arch of the cross cut.

"Sandy," Willard croaked. "For Pete's sake, Sandy, *look at that!*"

They turned their candles.

A hand—a white hand—stuck out of what appeared to be a solid rock wall!

Albert Davis permitted himself a complacent smile. Things had moved along in a manner that pleased him greatly. He straightened his gray silk cravat, pulled his vest down, and regarded himself in the mirror with satisfaction. The part in his hair was absolutely straight, every hair in place, his appearance impeccable.

He took his usual seat in the hotel dining room. On Sunday evening, The International typically filled quickly with those who could afford to dine there, but this night it was almost empty.

The waiter came to take his order and then ventured a comment. "I didn't expect you this evening, sir. I thought you would be up at the mine."

"Why?"

"Everybody is up there, sir. The word is that Mr. Lett and his partner are trapped up there."

"Oh? I hadn't heard. Trapped, you say? How could that be? I understood the mine was closed and there were guards."

"The whole town's up there. They're very well liked, you know, so everyone who is free has gone up."

The waiter went off to fill Davis's order and no doubt to spread the word that he was at dinner as usual.

Davis frowned, suddenly furious. He felt a burst of rage and frustration within. To be thwarted in any way sent him into a fury, but outwardly, he appeared as always—cold, without expression, the master of his destiny. The queen would be pleased with his work and reward him handsomely.

He ordered a glass of wine and sipped it slowly. All depended now on what was discovered. Nothing could lead to him, of course. He was pleased with himself.

He was having his dessert when the door burst open and a man came in.

"They found them! They're alive! They're coming here!"

A flurry of excited questions followed, and from the talk, Davis gleaned a word here and there. Lett had cut his way out with a pick. He'd gotten a hole through so he could get air, then had passed out.

"That's the way I heard it," one man reported. "Had one heck of a time, I guess. Been trapped in there for hours."

"Done on purpose," somebody was saying, "shot down after they went in."

"Who? Ain't hard to figure out. Davis would stand to gain if he got his hands on that mine. I don't think anyone else could get into the Solomon."

Davis had his back to the speaker and knew people stood between them. Obviously, the man did not know he was present, or if he did know, did not care.

Davis placed his napkin beside his plate and arose very carefully. Without turning around, he quickly went from the room. He went up the stairs, his heart pounding.

"Keep out of sight—out of sight, out of mind," he told himself. There'd be a flurry of excitement over this, but some other sensation would replace it in their minds. In a few days this would be an old story.

CHAPTER TWENTY-ONE

He wondered how they had discovered that the roof had been blasted. He had intended it to look like a natural cave-in, which happened often enough to warrant no comment. Somehow, Johnson had botched the job.

Davis swore, and he was not a man given to swearing. He swore slowly and with emphasis.

Johnson was a fool. The Hat. The Hat was the man he needed. The Hat was quick as a cat, utterly without mercy. Davis decided he must have the Hat. The Hat not only was in town, he was in that very hotel.

Ben recovered rapidly once out in the air. He relived again that moment when his pick broke through and he felt the rush of air against his face. He had managed a deep breath. Then he enlarged the hole. Moving aside, he held Ed up to the small opening. He remembered a murmur of voices from somewhere, but he could not rise.

It had taken the miners and Willard only minutes to make an opening large enough to get the men out. Once in the open air, Ben did not want to move. He just wanted to breathe long and deeply.

Ed had come through it well and was in the hotel restaurant now with Willard. Ben had been resting in a hotel room upstairs in The International, gathering his strength and thinking.

Ben knew this had been a definite attempt to kill them both. The time had been well chosen, the holes drilled, and the charges planted before he and Ed inspected the mine.

In that loose formation where slabs were flaking off constantly, only a small charge or two was needed. The pick left by some careless miner had saved them.

During his time in the mine, something had nagged at Ben—something striving for acknowledgment, for recognition. His brain was a vast void. One thought remained—keep trying. And he saw one image—a thin, pale shadowy face.

The face belonged to the man who had tried several times to kill him.

Ben swung his feet to the floor and reached for his socks. Slowly, carefully, he dressed. As he dressed, he put it all together. Several attempts to kill him—through the big man with the moustache and then by the man named Johnson—had not succeeded.

Ben finished dressing and reached for his gun belt. Then he remembered. He had removed it when working in the mine. Unless somebody had found it, it remained there in the muck.

He went to his saddle bag for another gun, then thrust it down into his waistband and went out, closing the door carefully behind him.

The instigator of it all had to be Albert Davis. It had to be. It fit.

"Somebody tried to kill Ed and me," he said to himself. "That somebody is still here, but it isn't only him."

He went down, glancing into the dining room of the hotel. He saw no one. Ed and Willard were gone. He paused a moment to survey the street. Nobody. He went down to the coffee shop.

Melanie got up when he came in.

"Ben! Are you all right?"

He shrugged. "Who, me? I just did two weeks' work in two days, that's all. Ed and Willard around?"

"They're around somewhere. They are worried about you," she said kindly.

Ben ordered coffee and sat watching the street. It was a warm, busy day. Ore wagons went by. Men were on foot and horseback. Three well-dressed women passed on the

CHAPTER TWENTY-ONE

opposite side of the street accompanied by a man in a black pin-striped suit.

The town was changing. He could feel it. He looked over at Melanie.

"The wild days are gone," he said. "It will not be the same again."

CHAPTER TWENTY-TWO

BEN STEPPED OUT on the street, removed his hat, and ran his fingers through his hair. He stood for a moment, thinking, the wind stirring his hair. He wanted to find Ed and Willard. He knew they had been asking for him. He must see them.

His eyes scanned the street, missing nothing. He put his hat on and hitched his belt a little, easing the position of the gun. He had reloaded it, just to be sure.

It was all going to end here, today. He knew that. Smiling a little wryly, he considered that he, too, might end right there. These men were hired by the queen and her henchmen, and he knew they would never stop trying to destroy his dreams of a new home in a new land. Would they succeed?

Albert Davis worried him most of all. Davis would never draw a gun and give him a chance to shoot back. He couldn't prove anything.

He had no doubts that Johnson worked for Davis. And he knew the Hat's reputation. They were men who used

CHAPTER TWENTY-TWO

guns—strong men, confident men. Each dangerous. Each very sure of himself with reason.

He no longer wished to kill anyone, yet he had no choice. They had tried and would continue trying to kill him. Moreover, they had tried to kill Ed. He was a fool to stay so long in one place.

The city was going about its business, mining ore, mining money from the pockets of stockholders, and freighting ore to the mills. The stamp mills were pounding and people were coming and going, all oblivious to what was about to happen. Generally speaking, it was none of their business. But after it happened, this unfinished business would be a topic of conversation for a few days.

Suddenly, a rider pulled up beside him. It was Bob Ritter.

"I heard you were in trouble the other day. I come in a hurry, but you were already out," Ritter said.

"Thanks, anyway," Ben said, reaching up to shake his hand.

"Ben, you are a special friend. On your advice I started guarding gold. When I tried for a job, I found you'd recommended me. Why?"

"I just knew you were a good man. A man does a lot of things when he's young he wouldn't do a few years later. So I put in a word here and there. It wasn't anything." He smiled.

"You're in trouble, Ben. I'm good with a gun."

"You're real good, but you just stay with what you're doing. A man's success he can share with others; his troubles are his own. I've got to do it myself. You know that better than anyone."

"The Hat is after you, you know. He's fast, Ben. He's very fast. Don't try to match him because nobody can. Take one if you must, but kill him. You may only get one shot, so put it where it matters," Bob advised. "Watch yourself on the street. He's a show-off, too."

In the evening sky, shadows reached out to reclaim what they had lost at daybreak, and the red faded to rose pink. Ed and Willard were eating in the hotel and talking about the trouble at the mine. Ed had recovered completely and was feeling great. They began talking about buying tickets for the theatre that night. It was an hour and a half before showtime.

Ed returned to his room at the hotel to clean up. He knew someone must be in his room. He could detect the smell of horses.

Pulling off his shirt, he stepped into the room and crossed to the closet door. Taking the chair by the back, he began to wedge in under the doorknob. The door burst outward, and there was Johnson.

He was even larger than Ed remembered. He smelled of stale sweat and unwashed clothing.

"How'd you know I was here?" he yelled.

"Because you're filthy," Ed said. "You left some horse manure back there. Nobody comes here right from the stables."

"You think you're so smart," he chuckled.

The room was small. No matter which way he turned, Johnson was within arm's reach of Ed.

"If I were you," Ed replied, "I would leave now while you still can. The men in this town will hang you for what you've already done."

"They won't hang me. I have done pretty much what I wanted all my life," he boasted. "I'm going to do what I want with you."

Without warning, he struck Ed on the head and sent him sprawling. Before Ed could move, Johnson kicked him.

CHAPTER TWENTY-TWO

Ed just barely managed to turn his hip to catch the force of the kick and protect his stomach.

Ed rose to grab a bowl of shaving cream and smashed it on Johnson's head. Johnson lunged and knocked Ed sprawling, his head ringing from the blow. Ed rolled over quickly and scrambled up.

Johnson said, "I'm going to take pleasure in choking the life out of you!"

"You cheap coward, I doubt you could beat a woman," Ed sneered.

Johnson swung a huge fist at Ed and started for him as a pounding started at the outside door. Johnson stopped, and for a moment his eyes were wild.

"You call out, and you'll just get 'em killed, whoever it is. You make a move toward that door, and I shoot you in your legs."

Ed jerked toward the door. Johnson moved like a panther and hit Ed again on the head.

"Think you're Lett's special friend. Well, I'll show you."

"I wouldn't."

The door swung open. The low voice belonged to Ben Lett. Johnson turned and palmed his gun, but Ben shot him twice. The explosion was loud, and Johnson fell back into the room catching himself on the edge of the bed with his left hand still holding the pistol in his right. Both bullets had hit him three inches below his belt buckle.

Ben held his pistol casually, almost carelessly.

"Ed," he said, "you'd better step outside."

Johnson's gun swung up, but Ben had been waiting for it. The swinging barrel of his own pistol caught Johnson's wrist halfway, and the gun went spinning into a corner. Stepping over, always facing Johnson, Ben scooped up the pistol with his left hand. He stepped back into the doorway.

"I'd spend what time I have left trying to make peace with the Lord. If by some chance you should live, you'll hang," Ben stated coldly.

Ben stepped out and pulled the door shut.

He paused to reload his pistol and thrust it inside his belt. He put Johnson's gun in his belt at the small of his back.

"Are you all right?" he asked his friend.

"Shaky," Ed admitted, "but I'll be all right. If I'd had anything to fight with, I might have whipped him."

Ben laughed. "Let's go," he said gently, "you need some rest. You did all right."

Willard was coming up the walk.

"You all right? I heard shooting," Willard asked.

"It was Johnson. He's in bad shape in the hotel," Ben said.

"I saw some shooting, too," Willard said. "In the hotel, I mean. Albert Davis is dead."

"Dead?"

"John Rome was in Davis' room, waiting for him. When Davis came in, he killed him."

"Just like that?"

"Davis must have been full of his own thoughts because he came in, hung his coat over a chair, and went to the sideboard for a drink. He must have been upset by something because hear tell he wasn't a drinking man. He must have looked up from his glass and seen John sitting there with his rifle.

"'No!' he pleaded. 'Not me! You don't understand! You can't,' he said, but John shot him. Folks are speculatin' that John found out that Davis had cheated him out of his interest in a mine. Anyways, Davis started forward and fell

CHAPTER TWENTY-TWO

against the table, sliding off it to the floor. He started to crawl toward Rome.

"They're saying Davis whispered hoarsely and said, 'This is wrong. It's wrong! Not me!'

"He was sitting there like that when the door burst open, and people rushed into the room," Willard said. "It was somethin.'"

"Ben Lett?"

Ben knew immediately who was addressing him. He saw a passerby stop suddenly and stare.

"Go inside, Ed," he said, "it seems there's always something left undone."

It was the Hat. He stood, feet apart, flamboyant as always, poised and ready.

"Why hello, Hat," Ben said. "Are you getting lonely, Hat?"

"Lonely?" He was surprised by this question.

"Why, yes, Hat. Your friends are all dead and gone. Do you want to join them, Hat? They're gone, Hat. That cozy little bunch of river rats and scoundrels who were your friends. A pretty shoddy bunch, Hat, just like you."

The Hat trembled; he wanted to kill. Never in his life had he wanted to kill anyone so much.

"You know what I've got here, Hat? It's your gun. The gun you left behind when you tried to visit me in St. Louis. You lost it when you were running away. *Running.* All you bold, daring thieves. You were running, and you dropped your gun. See? It has your name on it. I'll show you."

Ben drew and fired, beating the Hat by a hair. The Hat took a slow backward step; his gun went off into the dust of the street. Ben took a step closer, ready for a second shot.

"Being fast, Hat, is not always enough, is it? I'm sorry, Hat, but I didn't come looking for you."

The gun slipped from the Hat's fingers. He started to speak, turned away, and fell.

"Ben? Are you all right?" Ed said, running up to his friend.

"I'm all right," he said as he reached to hug Ed. "I'm all right now."

CHAPTER TWENTY-THREE

IF MINING COULD get any better, Ben couldn't imagine how. Before his encounter with The Hat, he had started to run a short horizontal tunnel to the outside in his mine. He thought it could improve air circulation and give the miners another way out if it was needed.

In the process, he cut into a vein of almost solid silver. It wasn't the richest on the mountain, but it was rich enough. The vein was so wide he couldn't see top or bottom of it, and it dipped right down toward the richest part of the mine.

"I'm a rich man," he said to himself that moment.

He and Ed and Willard rejoiced for a day and then got to work removing the silver ore from the mine. Days and weeks and months flew by. It had been more than two years since he and Ed had left Illinois to make their fortune. Now that they had realized their dream, Ben's heart and mind turned more toward home each day.

"Ed, have you been thinking about home and our wives and children as much as I have recently?"

"Yes! And I'm ready to pack up and start for home."

"My last letter from Debra said that her heart was breaking with longing to be held in my arms. She said all the gold or silver in the world couldn't satisfy her longing for me."

"Ben, let's start planning for our journey home. Janice has tried to be brave, but I know she'd be happier if I were home. We have enough money now to hold us for a really long time. We can sell our interest in the mine and have enough money to pay for a trip home by ship and buy that land when we get home," Ed remarked.

"Willard, will you be coming with us to Illinois?" Ben asked.

"You can't get rid of me now. I'm going to Illinois with you," he roared.

"OK! It's settled then. We'll sell the mine as soon as possible and book passage on a ship to Panama," Ben said. "Do we all agree that going home on a ship is better than crossing that desert again in a covered wagon?"

"Darn right!" Willard chuckled.

"Count me in," Ed added.

"Now that the queen's boys are all dead, we can travel without fear of being attacked during our journey," Ben said. "Traveling by water sure will be safer than traveling across country in a wagon."

The entire voyage was unlike anything Ben had ever before experienced.

His first voyage as a boy with his parents had been in the hold of a ship wallowing in the storms of winter. Then he was looking forward to a new home in the Americas but remembered mourning the loss of friends back home in Ireland. Aboard ship, days had been defined by cold, howling gales, crashing waves, moaning passengers, and his discomfort.

CHAPTER TWENTY-THREE

Sabbath fell upon the third day of their journey. Willard had not slept more than a few hours in the two nights since their departure from San Francisco. He had eaten only because Ben placed food in front of him and urged him to do so. Willard moved about the deck only when Ben insisted he get up.

At dawn, Ed drew Willard from bed with a bowl of the hot black tea called sailor's broth. He directed him toward the chamber where the other men washed and dressed for the morning service. As soon as the boson piped the morning crew on deck and the others to their breakfast, passengers made their way from their quarters.

The captain greeted them, doffing his hat and bowing to the elder of the two pastors on board. "It is my habit at sea to offer the men a Sabbath reading. But I'd be grateful for a proper vicar to bless this day."

"It would be an honor for you and your men to join us," one of the pastors said.

They began with a song, another, and another still. One of the men drew out a concertina, another had a mouth organ, and one more had a set of bagpipes. They had no hymnals, but none was needed because everyone knew the hymns by heart. These passengers shared worship and common faith, greeting the rising sun in four-part harmony. The sailors cast astonished glances among themselves. Ben sang a solo, and he and Ed harmonized on another hymn.

The younger pastor opened the Bible to the book of John and began the day's reading. Ben listened and marveled at how the words came to him with understanding from days gone by.

Ben lifted his head far enough to study the sky. Every sail was out. The great billowing mass of canvas filled the blue that appeared where clouds did not. The sun rose behind him, burnishing the sails overhead. The timbers creaked, and the deck beneath his feet was never still. A pair of great black-headed seabirds with wingspans broader than his outstretched arms flew alongside the starboard railing, their heads tilted as if straining to better hear the hymn.

Ben inhaled deeply and realized, as he thought of Debra and the children, that Christ's joy was a dominating force in his life. There would be some sorrow as long as they were apart, but he knew that they would soon be together again. With a thankful heart, he knew the glory of God was his to enjoy.

In the cubbyhole aboard ship, Ed and Ben sat facing each other on Saturday of their sixth week at sea. Ben, as usual, took refuge from the sickening movement of the plunging ship by sitting on the hard bed suspended from the ceiling by ropes. Ed straddled a straight chair, bracing himself with his legs each time the ship slid up and then down the great swells outside.

They might not reach Panama for a day or two.

Willard had fully recovered from his sickness. He had never been on a voyage before but had always thought square riggers like this one were the best looking of all sailing vessels. He enjoyed watching the crew in the never-ending effort to change the positions of the many sails.

As he washed out some clothing in Ben's cabin, Willard said, "This stuffy cabin has me wondering if I'll be able to stand the trip from Panama to New York."

Ben praised him for not complaining in front of the other passengers. They seemed to be interested in nothing but their own discomforts, railing against the hard beds and the lumpy pillows.

"By faith in the winds, we should dock sometime tomorrow or the next day. Then we'll have a week or more of travel from Panama City to the eastern coast," Ben said.

CHAPTER TWENTY-THREE

After landing in Panama City, they hired a guide. Their journey continued much as Ben had predicted. The tropical terrain was new to all of them, but they made their way steadily east. They traveled by foot, canoe, mule back, and cart. It was very hot and humid but still better than the desert.

"The jungle is full of insects and mosquitoes, and we need to be very careful. I have a concoction to help repel the mosquitoes," Ben said. "If we stay safe and don't get sick, we should make it to New York in another month."

On the third day in the jungle, Ben commented, "If we stick together and look out for bandits, we should be all right."

No sooner had the words come out of Ben's mouth than shooting began and bandits approached them.

The leader approached the men, but Ben greeted him with his guns blazing. The bandito fell dead, and two of his men on mules fell to the ground. Ed shot another bandito, and the rest turned and rode off.

"Those men won't bother anybody for a long time," the guide said.

"You have to be ready at all times," Ben commented.

"You sure took down those three men in a hurry. Nice going," Willard said.

"Banditos roam all through this country. One of us needs to stand guard at all times tonight," Ed suggested. "No doubt we'll be attacked again."

That night Ben took the first watch and Ed the second. Willard would watch last and remain on guard until sunrise.

On Willard's watch trouble found them again. Two men snuck into the campsite they shared with their guide and began shooting. Ed was grazed on the right leg. Ben began shooting back, and the gunfight lasted only a couple of seconds. The bandits both lay dead. Ed lay back, holding his leg.

"Are you hit bad?" Willard asked.

"He got me in the leg," Ed responded.

Ben went after the bandits but soon returned. Attacks like this were frequent occurrences.

"How's the leg, Ed?" Ben asked when he returned.

"It will be all right. Willard has cleaned and dressed it," Ed answered.

The ride that day was rough on Ed, but he took it like a trooper. Ben had made a mud plaster poultice, which he placed on the leg to help draw out infection. It also seemed to help relieve the pain.

They were relieved when they reached the port on the Atlantic shore and found the vessel waiting to take them to New York.

CHAPTER TWENTY-FOUR

ON SEPTEMBER 15, 1853, the three men stood on the dock amid a large crowd of people, most going aboard the American vessel *William Penn*.

"Ben," said Willard, awed by the size of the massive ship, "what does that name mean?"

"I think it's a man's name, but I don't know who he might be," Ben answered.

Ed was keeping an eye on the ticket office where Oka had gone to get their tickets validated. Oka represented the company selling the tickets to the passengers.

"Ben, here comes Oka," Ed said. "Maybe he knows who William Penn is or was."

Oka was smiling as he threaded his way through the crowd. "All right," he said. "We're all set. You can board in about ten minutes. You have cabins fifty-four and fifty-five on the second deck."

"Oka, who is William Penn?" Willard asked.

"I didn't know until I went in the office just now. A passenger from Brazil asked one of the ticket agents about the name of the ship. It's named after a famous American from New England. I believe he was a Baptist preacher."

A half hour later, the three miners had boarded the ship and placed their belongings in their cabins. They stood at the railing on the second deck, taking a last look at the city. Smoke billowed from the two huge smokestacks, and soon the gangplank was lifted into place on the ship. The dock workers loosened the mooring ropes from the dock posts and threw them onboard. A moment later, the passengers heard a sharp blast from the ship's whistle and felt a roaring rush of water at the rear of the vessel as the great power of the engines throbbed through the decks beneath their feet.

When the ship was away from the dock, people began to leave the rails and head up to their cabins or down into the belly of the vessel to steerage quarters.

Ed watched the many people heading down the stairs and said, "My heart goes out to those poor people who have to travel in steerage."

"I learned from Oka that we have 354 passengers on the ship," Ben said, "and more than 250 of them are in steerage."

"Praise the Lord we were able to afford second-class accommodations," Willard said.

"Amen," Ed said.

After a while, the *William Penn* headed toward the open sea. As the men came to the cabins, Ben said, "Men, I'll be along shortly. I need a few minutes alone."

"Sure, Ben," Ed said. "Just come back when you're ready."

Ben made his way along the rail until he could see the bow of the ship. He looked past the ocean into the beautiful sunrise. In his mind's eye, he could see Debra running to meet him down their country lane on a warm morning. A warm, stiff breeze toyed with his long brown hair. As he

CHAPTER TWENTY-FOUR

gripped the rail, a haunting loneliness came over him and tears filled his eyes.

"Oh, Debra," he said with a soft voice, "my life will never be complete without you. But I trust we will have eternity together in heaven, my darling."

Ben choked up, swallowed hard, and used a handkerchief to blow his nose. "Lord," he said in a low voice, "I need Debra with all my heart. Take care of both of us until we're reunited again in Illinois."

A scripture came to him, one he had hidden in his heart just before he left Illinois and his family. The sacred words of Isaiah 26:3 made their way into his mind: "Thou wilt keep him in perfect peace, whose mind is stayed on thee: because he trusteth in thee."

He felt better with those words of calm assurance echoing in his heart. Ben told himself he could face the future knowing that the God he served would keep him in His faithful loving care.

Looking back at the diminishing coastline, tears dimmed his eyes. He watched as the land grew smaller and smaller until it was swallowed in the mists rising from the deep blue water.

Midmorning on the seventh day at sea, the Gulf of Mexico was deep blue with sunshine dancing on the rippling waters. A warm breeze wafted across the ship, and the happy laughter of the children from steerage filled the air as they played games on the main deck.

Ben had enjoyed the journey so far. While the other men were occupied in their cabin, he decided to take a walk about the ship as he had done every morning for the past six days. He had met several interesting people on his walks and was eager to meet some more.

Only once since leaving Panama had Ben been up to the third deck, which housed the first-class cabins.

He chatted with an elderly couple from Panama on their way to New York City to join family members who had moved there a year previously. Then he left the second deck and mounted the metal stairs to the top level.

As he walked slowly along the railing, speaking to people who were sitting on deck chairs, he glanced up to the bridge and saw Captain John Dunning looking down at him. They had met and talked on a few occasions. The captain, accompanied by two ship's officers, waved in a friendly manner. Ben smiled and waved in return.

The captain said something to his officers, then wheeled and entered the pilot's cabin. Ben resumed his stroll. After speaking to a young couple holding hands, he came upon a well-dressed, middle-aged man with silver creeping into his thick blond hair. The man was reading an American newspaper. He looked up and smiled as Ben neared.

Bending over, Ben extended his hand. "My name is Ben Lett."

As the man met his grip, he said, "And good morning to you, sir. This certainly is a beautiful day."

The man gestured to the empty chair next to him, and said, "Please sit down."

"Thank you," Ben said.

As Ben was easing onto the chair, the man said, "I want you to have a drink on me. My name is Max Larson."

"I will pass on the drink, but thank you. So where do you live, Mr. Larson?"

"I was born in Germany, and I migrated to the United States in 1840. I have lived in the United States ever since. My home is in Grand Forks, Dakota Territory, which is ninety miles south of the Canadian border. Grand Forks is on the confluence of the Red River and Red Lake River on the Minnesota border."

CHAPTER TWENTY-FOUR

"And what do you do in Grand Forks, Mr. Larson?"

"I'm in the retail clothing business—Larson Clothiers. Actually, I have a total of twenty stores," he said. "The main store is in Grand Forks. The other nineteen are located in cities both in Dakota Territory and the state of Minnesota.

"The clothing business is a family tradition. It was my Uncle Max—after whom I was named—that I just visited in Costa Rica. He financed my adventure in America when I was in my mid-twenties so I could realize my dream of carrying on the family tradition in America."

Ben smiled and nodded. He had figured the man was wealthy just by the way he was dressed. The fact that he was traveling first class was also a bit of a hint.

"So what about you, Mr. Lett?" Larson asked. "Are you migrating to America?"

"No, sir. I live in the United States near Chicago, Illinois," Ben said. "I was born in Ireland near Wexford, then my parents moved to Canada near Ottawa. We farmed there until my father died in an accident. In time, all my brothers and sisters and I moved to Illinois."

"And how is it that you ended up on this ship?" Max asked.

"Two friends and I went to California to hunt for gold," Ben said. "We are returning to New York now so we can go on to Illinois and our families and our farm."

The German's eyebrows arched.

"Well, my friend, you are looking at a man who lives in potato and sugar beet country. You should consider coming to the Grand Forks area."

"We are quite happy in Illinois, but if we decide to move, we'll consider your area." Ben managed a friendly smile and said, "You are kind to invite us to settle in your area."

"Mr. Larson?" came the voice of a white-uniformed crew member.

Both men looked up.

"Yes, Gerald?" the German said. "Are you finished?"

"Yes, sir. We fixed your bed by putting some new screws in the legs. It won't tip now."

"Thank you. I appreciate your getting right on it."

"It's my job, sir," Gerald said, walking away. "If you have any more problems, please let me know."

"I surely will," Larson said, rising from his chair and folding the newspaper.

By this time, Ben was on his feet.

Larson said, "Well, Mr. Lett, it's been nice talking to you. I've got to get back to my cabin. Don't forget. Give some serious thought to moving to the Grand Forks area."

"Thanks for the conversation, Mr. Larson. I'll tell my friends about our visit."

"Good. I'm in cabin number six if you would like to chat again. You can call me Max."

"All right, Max. And you can call me Ben," he said.

When Ben returned to the second deck, he found his friends standing at the railing in front of their cabin, looking out across the vast body of water that surrounded them. The Gulf of Mexico remained clear and sapphire blue, the surface calm. The breeze was still soft and warm.

"Well, there you are, Ben," Ed said. "Did you make some new friends?"

"I met a wealthy German man up on the top deck, and we had quite a talk."

"Wealthy?" Willard said. "Now that's the kind of friends to make. Is your new friend migrating to America?"

"He already did back in 1840. His name is Max Larson. He owns a string of clothing stores in the state of Minnesota

CHAPTER TWENTY-FOUR

and in Dakota Territory. His home is in Grand Forks, Dakota Territory, just across the border from Minnesota.

"He asked me to tell you men about seriously considering moving there. He told me farmland is plentiful, sugar beets and potatoes grow well there, and the climate is a great deal like ours in Illinois."

A week later, Ben was walking the lower deck on another beautiful day when he came upon Max. He was just finishing a conversation with a deckhand swabbing a section of the bow.

Turning from the man, Max said, "Hello, Ben. Are you and your friends enjoying the trip?"

As they walked together toward the starboard railing, weaving among the crowd, Ben said, "We sure are. What about you and your family? Are they enjoying the trip? So far the weather has been wonderful."

"Well, let's hope it stays that way. I've been across these waters a few times when it wasn't so good."

"I've been told it can get treacherous when severe storms blow up," Ben added.

"Indeed," Max said as they drew up to the railing. "Did you men discuss settling where I live?"

"We don't think we're interested, but we always pray about things like that together as a family."

Ben noted the sour look that settled in Max's eyes at the mention of prayer. He was about to bring up the subject of the Lord when he saw Max's eyes take on a different look. A man came toward Max, smiling.

"Max!" the man said, hurrying to him and extending his hand.

Speaking in Spanish, Max said, "Robert! I haven't seen you since I was visiting in Panama City. When was it? Five years ago?"

227

"It sure was!" his friend said as they pumped each other's hands. "How have we been on the ship this long and not seen each other?"

"Big ship. Almost four hundred people," Max said. "I'm sure there are people we haven't seen yet. Oh! Robert Sanchez, I want you to meet a new friend of mine from America. I met him a few days ago. This is Ben Lett."

Ben and Robert shook hands, greeting each other warmly, and then Ben said, "Max, I'll let you and Robert have some time together. See you again soon."

As he walked from Max and his friend, Ben saw two familiar faces in the crowd—William Patten and Thomas Beverage from Illinois. He stopped dead in his tracks, unable to believe his eyes. They stood at an angle from him while talking to each other, but neither had seen him yet.

Hurrying toward them, he excused himself as he bumped into other passengers and called out, "William! Thomas!"

The men stopped, surprise on both their faces.

"Ben!" William gasped, opening his arms wide. "We thought you would already be home in Illinois!"

Ben embraced William, then Thomas.

Thomas said, "I can't believe we've been on this ship all this time without running into you."

Ben smiled, echoing what he had heard Max say only moments ago. "Big ship. It's possible, all right."

"We've had enough of gold mining in California," said William. "We're going back to Illinois to buy a farm and start a new life. Thomas and I have relatives in the Somonauk area, and we're going to live there."

"Well, isn't this something?" Ben said. "My friends are going to be plenty surprised to see you."

CHAPTER TWENTY-FOUR

As Ben led the men across the deck toward the stairs, William laughed and said, "No wonder we haven't run into you. Our quarters are in steerage."

"We are fortunate to be on the second deck," Ben said. "We sold our mine in California, so we could afford some more comfortable accommodations."

When they reached the second level, Ben spotted Ed and Willard and led William and Thomas to them. The meeting was a great surprise for everyone. Willard couldn't believe Ben had met someone from home.

When they all sat down to talk, Ed asked if they had a place picked out to buy back in Illinois. William was positive that the farm he had his eye on would be for sale when he got home.

The night of October 1, Ben was reading scripture when he heard the wind begin to buffet the ship.

We haven't had that kind of wind since we left California. Could be a storm blowing in, he thought.

He closed his Bible. The ship pitched to and fro and rocked side to side. Ben laid his Bible down and went to the cabin's porthole. Cupping his hands at the side of his face, he peered out. He could see whitecaps on the water. They looked eight to ten feet high.

Ben put on his coat and went next door to Ed and Willard's cabin. The men got down on their knees and prayed together for the Lord to keep them safe. They included Max Larson in their prayers, asking God to bring him to salvation and thanking Him for bringing them together.

By morning, dark clouds covered the sky and the wind blew, setting the ocean surface in furious motion. The pitch and sway of the *William Penn* made it difficult for the passengers to stay on their feet as they came to the dining rooms for breakfast.

Ben, Ed, and Willard left their cabins and, gripping the rails, descended the stairs to the main deck. The men helped other passengers toward the dining room.

While they attempted to eat, with beverages spilling and plates sliding on their tables, the captain entered. Speaking above the roar of the wind, he told everyone in the room that they were facing a fierce storm. He wanted everyone in steerage to go below and all others to stay in their cabins. He warned of the danger they faced while moving on the decks and told them not to leave their quarters unless it was absolutely necessary.

Soon the wind was slamming the ship with hurricane force and a driving rain. With the ship tossing and bobbing in the troubled sea, people were terrified. Everyone was having a hard time walking, standing up, or being heard. Many, especially the elderly, were being helped by the crewmen.

When Ben neared his cabin, he shouted above the storm for Ed and Willard to come into his cabin so they could pray together. They sat with the howl of the wind in their ears and prayed aloud one by one, asking the Lord to stop the storm.

When it was Ed's turn, he said, "Lord Jesus, you were on a ship one day with your disciples when a storm like this one hit. The wind was strong, and the waves beat into the ship. The disciples were scared, just like we are now. You told the wind to stop blowing and told the sea to be still. We need you to stop this storm for us. Please?"

Suddenly the roar of the wind ceased. Everyone in the bobbing cabin opened their eyes and looked at one another.

"I can't believe it!" Willard said. "The wind quit blowing!"

"Of course it did, O ye of little faith," said Ed, secretly astonished himself.

CHAPTER TWENTY-FOUR

Everybody laughed.

The ocean was still rough, but within an hour the clouds had broken up and the sun was shining. Much praise was given to the Lord by the men. Willard was very encouraged in his own prayer life.

The next morning, the sea was still somewhat choppy under a sunlit sky as Ben and Ed walked together on the main deck. Ben spotted Max standing at the rail on the port side and whispered from the side of his mouth, "There's Max! I'll introduce you to him."

Max smiled as Ben introduced him to Ed. Ben explained that Ed and his wife, Janice, were friends of his family from Canada and had traveled with the Letts to Illinois.

"If you decide to move to Minnesota or Great Falls, let me know. I want you folks to call on me if there is ever anything I can do for you," Max said, repeating his generous offer.

"We appreciate that," Ben said.

Looking at Ed, Max said, "Have you two known each other for a long time?"

The two men grinned at each other, and Ed said, "For many years. I'll let Ben tell you the story."

Happy for the opportunity, Ben told Max how he and Ed met when they were both neighbor boys in Salina, Canada. They played together, went to church together, and fought together. Their wives had also been the best of friends. The truth of the matter was that they both loved Jesus Christ as Savior and Lord, and their friendship was forever.

Calmly, Max said, "I don't mean to offend you, but I don't believe that Jesus Christ was any more than a mere man who lived and died like all other mere men."

Ben said, "With all respect, Max, you are wrong. The Bible says when God brought his Son into the world, he said 'Let all the angels of God worship him.' Jesus is no mere man.

"Scripture also says, 'In this was manifested the love of God toward us.' That passage is talking about the entire sinful human race, Max," Ben continued.

"'In this was manifested the love of God toward us,' means that God sent his only begotten Son into the world that we might live through him. It goes on and says, 'And we have seen and do testify that the Father sent the Son to be the Savior of the world.'"

"That's right," Ed said.

"Max," Ben said, "the sentence of eternal death is on this sinful human race. We need a Savior to save us from the wrath of God, and we need a Savior who can give us eternal life. That Savior is God's virgin-born Son, the Lord Jesus Christ."

Max shook his head. "This may be all right for you, but not for me."

"Are you telling me that you will never die?" Ben said.

"Of course not. Everybody has to die."

"Well, the Bible says there are two deaths."

Max frowned. "What?"

"Jesus is alive, Max. If you die without him as your Savior and without your sins washed away in his blood, you will burn in hell for eternity."

"Do you understand, Max?" Ed asked.

"But I don't believe any of this," Max said.

"Your disbelief doesn't change any of these facts, Max," Ben commented. "It will just put you in the lake of fire. In Revelation 21:8, God says, 'But the fearful, unbelieving, . . . shall have their part in the lake which burneth with fire and brimstone, which is the second death.'

"In John chapter 3:17, 18a, it says, 'For God sent not his Son into the world to condemn the world; but that the world through him might be saved. He that believeth in him is not condemned.'

CHAPTER TWENTY-FOUR

"Your unbelief has you already condemned, Max. You must repent of your sin of unbelief or die in your sins and spend eternity in the lake of fire," Ben continued. "All of us are sinners. We all need to be saved. The Bible says, 'For whosoever shall call upon the name of the Lord shall be saved.' The difference is eternal heaven or eternal hell."

Ed said, "Max, I was once as hard against God and the Bible as you are, but a friend showed me with scripture how wrong I was. God dealt with my heart, and I called on Jesus to save me. He did. And I've never been sorry I became a Christian."

Ben said, "Max, I want you to think about what has been said. Ed and I have given you lots of scripture to think about. Be honest with yourself. God's Word makes sense. If you are right and when we die, that's the end of us, what have we lost by putting our faith in Jesus Christ?"

Max shrugged. "You've lost nothing," he said.

"Right," Ben replied. "But if we are right, and you are wrong, what have you lost?"

"*Everything*," Max said, his face drawn.

Laying a friendly hand on Max's shoulder, Ben said, "Think on that, and we'll talk again soon."

CHAPTER TWENTY-FIVE

ON OCTOBER 25, 1853, the *William Penn* rolled gently through the waves, steaming toward New York harbor. Billows of black smoke curled skyward from the dual smokestacks.

Crewmen spread the word that the captain wanted a meeting with all the passengers at ten o'clock that morning. They were to gather on the three decks, and he would address them from the bridge. The crewmen would translate the captain's English into Spanish.

At precisely ten o'clock, the captain came out of his office just behind the pilot's cabin and, putting a megaphone to his mouth, said loudly, "Good morning, everyone!"

Using megaphones, the crewmen rapidly made their translations. The excited passengers responded by calling back the greeting.

"I wanted to inform all of you that our navigator tells me that barring any storms, we will arrive in New York harbor in three days."

CHAPTER TWENTY-FIVE

The crowd applauded and cheered, and the captain dismissed the meeting.

"It's time for me to have my talk with Max. He's had long enough for the Holy Spirit to do his work with the scriptures you and I planted in his heart," Ben said.

"I'll be praying, Ben," Ed said.

As he reached the top deck, Ben saw Max, who smiled and headed toward him.

"Looks like we have an excited bunch," Max said.

"I'll say," Ben said. "I can almost smell the sweet air in New York harbor now."

Max chuckled.

"Yes, me, too."

"There's going to be real joy when this ship arrives in New York harbor."

"That's for sure," Max agreed.

"I was thinking what joy there always is in heaven when a saved earthly sojourner takes his last breath on earth and arrives in the heavenly harbor."

Suddenly, Max's face contorted, reddened, and his eyes filled with tears.

"Ben," he said, "you told me to think on those things that you and Ed quoted to me from the Bible. Let me tell you, I haven't been able to get them out of my mind. I've had nightmares about standing before God, facing my record, then being cast into the lake of fire. I've pictured Jesus dying on the cross for me, and I realize how much he loves this guilty sinner."

Ben's heart leapt.

"You told me that God would make himself known to me, and he has!" Max said. "I know that God is most certainly alive . . . as is his Son, and I want to be saved."

Fighting his own tears, in his heart Ben thanked the Lord, laid a hand on the weeping man's shoulder, and said, "Let's go to your cabin, Max."

As they sat down in Max's cabin, Ben said, "Let me remind you that Jesus said for you to repent and believe the gospel."

Max said, "You don't have to remind me. It has gone through my mind a thousand times."

Ben then explained to him that Jesus said, "Except a man be born again, he cannot see the kingdom of God."

He quoted John 1:12 and Ephesians 3:17, making sure Max understood that it was receiving Jesus into his heart that would give him the new birth and make him a child of God. He quoted Romans 10:13 once more, explaining that it was by calling on the Lord that he would receive Jesus into his heart and be born again.

Then Ben had the privilege of leading Max to the Lord Jesus Christ.

Ben then took Max to see Ed and Willard, and Max told them he had become a born-again child of God with hope of heaven sealed in his heart. The men joined Ben in thanking God.

On October 27, the men met in Ben's cabin for Bible study and prayer time. Max was full of questions and wanted to learn as much Bible as he could. Ben and Ed answered all his questions.

Max shook his head in wonderment and said, "I am amazed at how blind I was to the truth. I was so foolish to be such an unbeliever."

Ed said, "I know exactly how you feel. I was raised to believe that the Bible was just another book, and though it had some good principles, it was not the Word of God. I was taught by my parents that man made his own heaven or

CHAPTER TWENTY-FIVE

hell right here on earth, and when a man died, that was the end of him. Oh, how wrong I was to believe such a lie."

"You know that my wife needs to hear and believe," Max said. "I want her to be saved."

"Praise the Lord!" Ben said. "I'm glad to hear you say that, Max. One of the first signs a person has been saved is that he or she has a concern for the salvation of others, especially loved ones."

Ed said, "All right. Let's pray for her."

Heads were bowed, and Ed prayed for Marlena Larson's salvation.

Just then a loud voice came through a megaphone, asking passengers to gather for a meeting with the captain.

With his megaphone, the captain said, "My navigator tells me we have stayed on schedule since I spoke to you last. We will be pulling into New York harbor early tomorrow afternoon!"

Cheering and whistling went up from the happy crowd. Then the captain explained that all those who arrived at New York Harbor would be processed at Castle Garden. Medical doctors would examine all passengers who were not United States citizens. Anyone rejected for health reasons would be put back on the ship to return to Panama.

Many hearts filled with fear upon hearing the captain's words, especially those who were traveling in steerage. No one had prepared them for such news. If they were refused entrance into America, all their plans would be destroyed. What did the physical examination require?

When the crowd was silent again, the captain explained that those who passed the medical examinations would then be interviewed. If questions were answered properly, a person would be allowed into the country. He hastened to add that because ships carrying immigrants from all over the world were continuously entering New York harbor, it might be a few days before all the immigrants aboard this ship could be processed.

Nothing prepared the men for the feeling of pride they felt when at last the ship did enter the harbor and they were allowed to depart.

"Praise the Lord! This is a beautiful harbor indeed. And it is wonderful to live in a land such as this . . . a land of the free. Indeed, true liberty is ours here," Ben said to his group.

"Yes," Max said. "I praise this country for its true liberty. But I must praise God for the freedom I now have from the bondage of sin and Satan because of my faith in the Lord Jesus Christ! He bought me eternal liberty when he shed his precious blood on the cross, died for me, and rose again to give me salvation."

"Praise his name!" Ben said.

Tears were streaming down Ben's cheeks as he turned to his little group, all of whom were weeping, and said, "Yes! Sweet land of liberty! Let freedom ring!"

Max told Ed and Willard good-bye and then embraced Ben, thanking him for caring enough about his lost soul to give him the gospel.

Patting Max's back with both hands, Ben said, "I'm just so glad you were saved. My friends and I will be praying for your Marlena."

It was October 31 when Ed, Willard, and Ben left the ship by ferry boat to Castle Garden and then went on to Manhattan Island. While the ferry crossed the bay, the ferry boat captain explained that they would take a train from Grand Central Station to Atlantic City, New Jersey. From there, Max would head for Minneapolis. Ben, Ed, and Willard would make arrangements to begin their journey west to see their wives and families.

CHAPTER TWENTY-FIVE

By November 7, the three men had made their way by train and stagecoach to Chicago. The gray sky spit snow, and a cold wind blew. Willard felt the cold blast and said, "It's just like home in the winter. I feel at home already!"

Everybody laughed. Ed hailed a carriage driver and asked him the name of the best hotel in town. The driver told him the Lake Michigan Hotel was kept up and the people were friendly. In twenty minutes they had departed the carriage and entered the hotel. After checking in, they found a good meal and made plans for the final leg of their trip.

Everyone on the Lett farm in Leland gathered at the house that Sunday morning for a modest morning meal. Funds were low, and what little cash they had was set aside to purchase seed for the spring planting.

Still, there was joy as they all gathered around the fireplace to eat gingerbread and drink hot chocolate. The happy chatter went on in the parlor as Debra stepped into the hall to answer a knock at the front door.

A smiling Ben said, "Hello, Debra. May I come in?"

"Ben!"

Throwing her arms around his neck and kissing him over and over again, she would not let him go. She just held on to him with all her might.

Ed grabbed hold of Janice and twirled her around, lifting her feet off the floor, kissing her passionately.

"Where have you been, my love?" Ed said.

"How dare you ask me that question?" Janice replied, smiling.

Willard stood holding his hat, embarrassed at being present for this great reunion.

"Let me introduce our new friend, Willard Bernanke," Ben said. "He helped us mine for gold and, when we finished, he decided to return with us to Illinois."

"We're so happy to meet you, Willard," Debra said. "Please, let's all go into the parlor. We want to hear about your trip."

Everyone sat in the parlor, and Ben, with Debra next to him gripping his hand, told their story. Periodically as he spoke, someone asked him a question, and quite often Ben's words were overridden by someone lifting up his or her voice to praise God.

With the story of their seemingly impossible journey complete, Ben explained that he was certain they had been under God's protection every step of the way.

"We especially knew that when we were in snowstorms, trapped in the mine, or being shot at by the queen's men," he said.

"You're right," Willard said. "Our journey was impossible except that we serve the God of the impossible. We prayed hard for his miracles to also cover you women and children here at home."

"Now, ladies, let's hear what happened while we were gone," Ben said.

Debra started, "We missed you men terrible and thought you would never get home. Our goal was to keep life for the children as normal as possible. Everyone had special chores, and each child did homework when school was out for the day.

"Once every month," she continued, "we made our trip to Ottawa. Janice and I attended the quilt guild, and the children went to the library to read. Jackson drove the team wherever we went. Ben, those men who were after you were gone, and no more bad men bothered us. Of course, Otto

CHAPTER TWENTY-FIVE

and Ginny and your family and our neighbors took good care of us as always, too.

"When we received letters from you men, Janice and I read the letters first and then shared them with the family," she added.

Debra also said that she had received letters every few months from her mother in England. Mother McGirr worried about Debra being out in the wilderness alone, but Debra said she had assured her that more and more people were coming west and that she and the children were in no danger.

Jackson was anxious to tell his father about how the railroads had expanded in the time Ben and Ed had been away. A railroad was being built from Aurora to Mendota, and it was scheduled to be completed late the next year. Before the men had headed west for gold, Jackson had often talked about the railroads with his father.

In 1849, a railroad line was completed from Chicago to Turner Junction, now West Chicago. In December of that year, construction began on the line from Turner Junction to Aurora. This line opened for traffic early in September 1850, and many neighbors worked on these lines to make extra money for their families. Even young Jackson had wanted to work on the lines, but he was needed on the farm.

"Now a stop might be built at Somonauk Station, too," Jackson said. "It would be the first stopping place for the railroad in De Kalb County. Another stop might be coming at Newark Station in Kendall County in a year or more."

"Around here, the talk about the railroad coming to Somonauk has greatly stimulated settlement. The prairies are swarming with land seekers," Debra said. "Not many all-prairie farms have been occupied before now, but the new immigrants are buying up the more fertile farms in our area."

"Farmers in the neighborhood called a mass meeting of the citizens of Newark last week. We heard that a committee was formed to petition the railroad company to establish a station," Janice added. "Everyone who can afford it is being encouraged to take a trip as frequently as possible as soon as it is completed. Maybe Newark station will become a regular stopping place.

"We are living in exciting times," she added.

"I agree," Ben said. "Let's have some more hot coffee and more of that gingerbread while we tell you about the gold we found and how it will help us expand our farming operations."

The children were dismissed, and Willard said he would be happy to bring in their things.

"Willard, your room will be at the top of the stairs and to the right," Debra said. "Make yourself at home."

Ben and Ed were eager to tell their wives about the gold they were carrying. They had left considerable money in Sacramento Bank of California. It would be safe in that bank until they could figure out where to put it in the Ottawa area.

This gold might buy five hundred acres of good prairie land. The men wanted their wives to each have their own new home. They would offer the present Lett home to Otto and his wife with the understanding that Willard would live with them. The men said they would build their homes next summer very close to one another so their wives could continue to live and work close together.

Debra and Janice talked about a possible trip to Canada and England after the houses were finished. Ben agreed he could not go along because of his problems with the queen.

The next morning, Debra washed and dressed hurriedly. She was behind schedule getting breakfast because she had been looking through pages of memories Ben had written

CHAPTER TWENTY-FIVE

down about the trip. She stepped more briskly than normal along the length of the long hallway and down the winding staircase. She was nearly out of breath as she entered the cozy breakfast room where their morning meal was waiting.

"My apologies," she began.

"Good morning, my dear," said Ben, who had risen to seat her. "Did you sleep well?"

Debra smiled distractedly, her thoughts still on his notes about the trip. She knew he was eager to turn the story into a book.

"Coffee, my dear? I think I would enjoy another cup."

When the coffee had been poured, Ben rose to his feet and moved behind Debra's chair.

"Let's take our second cup in front of my library fire. It's much cozier on such a morning."

Debra was happy to comply and led the way. She always enjoyed joining Ben in the library. The fire hissed and crackled as they sipped companionably in silence. Debra pulled her eyes from the hypnotic flame to look across at her husband.

Ben rubbed his brow with his thumb and forefinger. She had come to recognize the gesture as a sign of mental agitation. Both of them were thinking about the news. Otto had told them he needed to leave them before spring. A good man like Otto was hard to find. Finding another suitable hired man might be near impossible.

"How soon will he leave us?" Ben asked without looking up.

"He says he must care for his elderly parents now that his mother isn't able to care for herself. He wishes to leave by the end of February."

"Perhaps we could persuade Willard to take Otto's place," Ben offered. "He seems to like this part of Illinois pretty well so far."

"We will make do now that you're home. Things might work out well with Willard," she said, controlling the joy in her voice.

Ben rose from his chair and crossed to the room's long window, brushing aside the heavy drapery to look out on the day. Low clouds scudded across the sky just beyond arm's reach, and a stout wind pulled at the bare branches of the trees along the lane. Even the birds seemed to have taken cover.

A squirrel was digging through the snow for nuts, putting them into his mouth. The dog came around the house about that time, saw the squirrel, and made a dash for him. The squirrel darted for his tree, reaching it safely before Shep could catch him.

Ben reached for Debra, encircling her waist with his strong right arm. Perhaps with a miracle or two he might be able to carry on the farming with Ed and Willard. Ben's arm tightened for a moment before he turned from the window.

"Now I suggest you take your place beside the fire with a cup of coffee in hand. I do not want you catching a chill," he smiled.

"The fire looks like it could use another log," she said.

Ben moved to the fireplace and knelt on the hearth to balance the log on one knee and work the fire screen with the other hand.

That afternoon, Ben entered the morning room where Debra sat with handwork before the fire.

"Willard has agreed to stay on as our hired man," he announced.

Debra's fingers became still in her lap.

CHAPTER TWENTY-FIVE

"Ben, that is indeed wonderful. I am very thankful. I've been praying about what we would do without Otto," she said.

"Now that that is settled, let's take some time this week to plan for our future and the future of the children. We need to make plans for expanding the farm, building another house, and your trip to Canada and Europe," Ben said.

CHAPTER TWENTY-SIX

IN EARLY APRIL, Ben was working alone in his barn spreading fresh straw in one of the horse stalls when he heard the big barn door squeak on its hinges. He turned to see a stranger enter.

The man was in his late fifties. He had a gray head of hair with a few black streaks and was about six feet tall with broad shoulders and steel gray eyes. He was dressed in a tie and suit.

"Mr. Lett, your wife said I would find you here. My name is Wayne Brown. I'm from Ottawa, and I'm with the county tax assessor's office," he said.

The look on Brown's face told Ben he was uneasy. Leaning the pitchfork against the wall, Ben stepped through the gate of the stall and extended his hand.

"Happy to make your acquaintance, Mr. Brown," he said.

As they shook hands, Ben said, "What can I do for you, sir?"

With trembling hand, Brown reached inside his suit and produced a folded sheet of paper.

CHAPTER TWENTY-SIX

Handing it to Ben, he said, "This is a bill for back taxes on your farm, Mr. Lett."

Ben said, "Back taxes?"

"Yes, sir. The taxes haven't been paid on this place for three years."

"I have been gone to California, and my wife said she paid the taxes," Ben answered.

"Well, here is the bill. Apparently she didn't pay them. The county has been very lax in collecting its taxes for the past four years. But now, we have a new administration, so it is going to be different. Everyone's taxes will be higher, and all back taxes are due."

Ben unfolded the bill, examined it, then looked at Brown and said, "These taxes have been paid, and we will prove it."

"I feel bad about this, Mr. Lett, but the administration will make no exceptions. This bill is due and payable by April 15, and there will be no leniency."

Ben's face was a dull brick red.

"Can't your office take into account that I've been gone and my wife was doing her best to keep up with all the farm business matters?" Ben asked.

"Well, sir. I'm very sorry. I wish I didn't have to be the one to bring you the bill, but if the tax debt is not paid by April 15, the county will confiscate the farm."

"My wife and I will see you and your friends in court if necessary," Ben stated frankly and glowered, rubbing the back of his neck. "I suppose you're just doing your job, Mr. Brown. I'll come to Ottawa soon and deal with your office."

"Thank you, sir. Well, I'll be going now."

Ben watched Brown walk to the barn door and open it. Brown was surprised to see Debra standing there, tears in her eyes. He told her he was sorry and hurried toward his buggy, which was parked at the rear of the house.

Ben opened his arms, and Debra rushed into them.

She said, sniffling, "I heard every word. I didn't hear the amount, but I did hear you say we don't owe this money."

"We need another of the Lord's miracles to get this mess straightened out. We will leave it in his hands," he said.

Ben held Debra in his arms another moment, then said, "I'm almost through putting the straw in the stalls. Let's go to town for supplies and see if we can get this matter straightened out. I'll finish up in a couple of minutes and hook the team to the wagon."

Debra nodded and said, "All right, I'll see you in a few minutes."

As she turned to leave the barn, Ben took hold of her arm and said, "Sweetheart, don't worry. The Lord has some more miracles left for us."

Soon they drove toward town with Jackson and Betsy in the back of the wagon and the baby on Debra's lap. Ben explained to the children that the man from the tax assessor's office had presented him with the bill for the back taxes.

"We won't lose the farm, will we, Dad?" Jackson asked.

"We're not giving up, son," Ben said.

As they approached the town square in Ottawa, they saw a large crowd and a man addressing the gathering. Ben saw his old friend Brent Barkley speaking.

"Do you know Brent?" Ben asked Debra. "He has that big farm south of town on the road to Ottawa."

"Yes," Debra said. "I've talked to his wife a few times."

"Let's see what's going on," said Ben, guiding the wagon to the side of the street.

When they got down from the wagon and approached the crowd, they saw Ben's brother Tom and his family.

"Big protest here about the tax increase," Tom reported. "Some folks are really angry about it."

CHAPTER TWENTY-SIX

"I can tell," Ben said.

Men were waving their hats, urging Barkley on, and he spoke another ten minutes before stepping aside. Before anyone else could step up, Ben planted himself where Barkley had stood.

He lifted his voice, told his name, and said, "I would like to say something!"

Speaking loud enough for all to hear, Ben said, "I cannot believe what I am hearing here! We are making noise about our taxes when we should be praising God for the privilege of living in this wonderful country.

"America has the greatest government in the world. It takes money to build and maintain schools and to build roads and keep them maintained. The sheriff's office has to be manned, and the office with the jail maintained."

A hush fell over the crowd.

Ben proceeded to tell the story of what had happened to him and his family in Canada. He told how many of his neighbors were shipped off to Tasmania because they didn't pay their taxes. Ben told how much the taxes were in Canada for a farm.

With everyone's attention, Ben told of how his family took leave of Canada after being threatened by the government and some of the Tories.

"If any of us lose our farms for not paying our taxes, at least you won't be placed in jail or sent off to Tasmania," he said.

"Like I said a moment ago," Ben went on, "we are all fortunate to live in this country. In Canada, only the rich can go to school. In America, everyone can. Our country made it through the Revolutionary War, and I know it will become a greater country yet."

Ben went on.

"This wonderful country has freedom of the press and a freedom of worship. In Canada, the taxes are not for schools, roads, and bridges, but for the pockets of the queen's favorites. If a man does not pay his property taxes on time, the British military come and take him away. He is never seen nor heard from again, and his family no longer has a home."

There was sudden applause, accompanied by loud cheering and people crying out, "God bless you, Ben! God bless you!"

Ben rubbed a tear from his cheek and set his gaze on Debra, who was applauding vigorously. Suddenly, he saw a familiar face weaving through the crowd from the right side. It was his brother Robert.

"Ben, I have been here since the crowd first began to form," Robert said. "I heard the speeches, and I want to go on record that I agree with your speech about this great country."

Ben wiped tears from his cheeks and thanked Robert.

Robert embraced Ben, and as they held each other tightly, Ben and Robert waved their hats in the air and shouted, "God save America!"

The entire Lett family gathered at the town square. It was a wonderful reunion and the first time they had all been together since Ben and Ed's return from California. The head of each family agreed to gather at Tom's home for church, a picnic, and fun the next Sunday. Ben would bring the sermon, and Tom would lead singing. Ed and Willard would lead the stories about the trip to California.

Ben and Debra left the group and started for the assessor's office, where they saw Wayne Brown.

"Good afternoon, Mr. Lett and Mrs. Lett. What can we do for you?"

CHAPTER TWENTY-SIX

"We have come with our documents proving that Mrs. Lett did pay our taxes every year while I was in California," Ben said.

"Well, let's see your documents," Brown said. "The assessor and I will examine the documents and give you an answer by the end of the day. Could you return at four o'clock?"

"We'll be back then," Ben said.

"I should have your answer by then," Brown said, taking the papers from Ben.

Just then, some other men were meeting on the east side of Ottawa. Two men talked in the basement of a home owned by the local meat merchant. Ben and his family were shopping while these men discussed Ben's future.

The man who called the meeting was fifty years old, gray haired, slightly stooped, and angry. He had been in touch with men from Canada. His name was A. Watson; his partner was James Manier. They both hated Ben Lett.

They would not be pleased that Ben's tax problems would be resolved that afternoon. After all, they were behind his tax problems.

At four o'clock, Ben and Debra returned to the tax office as promised. Wayne Brown greeted them with a smile and showed them records that affirmed their taxes had been paid. He apologized for the mistake but couldn't explain what had led to the misunderstanding. He did, however, promise it would not happen again.

On Sunday, as agreed, Ben and Debra drove their buggy into Tom's yard, unhitched the horses, and turned them into the pasture near the barn. Debra joined the ladies, who were buzzing about the food while the children went off

251

to play with their cousins. Ed, Janice, and their children, along with Willard, had come for the picnic, too.

Merrilla rang the big triangle with her cooking spoon to call all the family and friends to dinner. The smell of coffee, baked ham, chicken dumplings, and roast beef made the family crowd around for a word of prayer and a song before the food got cold.

While eating their dinner, Ben and Tom caught up on all sorts of topics, including the trip to California.

"I don't like the looks of the clouds gathering in the west," Tom said after a spell. "I suspect we're in for some real bad weather."

"Yeah, I think you're right. All we can do is watch and hope we can get everyone to the storm cellar before it hits," Ben responded.

A towering thunderhead rapidly grew, the flattening top a sure sign of storm. Its slight green cast suggested hail, and the day had grown even more humid. The children were down by the creek, and some were riding ponies. Ed and Willard yelled for the children to come to the cellar on the run.

The sky grew black, and a single low growl of thunder crawled across the sky. Ben saw small streaks of lightning flashing across the blackened sky. When the hail started, it was pea sized, but it rapidly grew to the size of small plums.

The women hurried toward the cellar with children in hand while Tom and Ben tended to the cattle that entered the barn to move away from the pelting balls of ice and fierce rain. The rumbling sound had grown out of proportion to the number of cattle.

Then Ben saw that part of the cloud had dropped an evil-looking black tail. It was sucking up dirt and grass as it traveled. It looked about a quarter of a mile away, and it was coming right at them.

CHAPTER TWENTY-SIX

"*Cyclone!*" Willard screamed. "Get off your horse and lie flat!"

"But the children!" Ben shouted back.

"They are all in the cellar. Take care of yourself!"

The sky was black as night, and the horrible rumbling grew into a grinding scream as it came closer. Ben dismounted and tried to get his horse to lie down, but the animal's eyes were wild with fright, and he fought to get free. A bolt of lightning struck nearby, and the horse reared into the air, pawing and screaming. Ben felt the reins being ripped from his hands, so he jammed his hat tighter on his head.

Water from the deluge splashed up into his face as he flattened himself as close to the earth as he could. The roar was deafening. He thought he'd already seen the worst nature could hurl at him, but past tussles paled in comparison to this cyclone.

The roaring seemed to last forever, but even as the banshee din moved away from them, the rain continued. Great slashing curtains threatened to wash the crops away. Ben struggled to his feet, disoriented. He couldn't distinguish the house from the barn or hear any voices. He was standing still, trying to get his bearings, when someone shouted at him.

"You all right, boss?" Willard asked.

He found Willard, and they made tracks for the shelter. Ben opened the cellar door and shouted into the room, "Everybody all right?"

Debra called back, "Where were you when the storm hit?"

"I was on the ground, praying."

The rain began to let up a little, and they all began to move out of the cellar carefully. Surveying the damage to the house and barn, Tom remarked how pleased he was that these buildings had survived the storm quite well. The machine shed and chicken coop had some shingles missing but were in good shape for the most part.

"Let's all gather around and thank God for sparing our lives, our buildings, and our livestock," said Tom. "We have so much to be thankful for."

Robert, the oldest Lett brother, asked everyone to hold hands as he led a prayer of thanksgiving. Then the families all wanted to return home to survey the possible damage at their own homes.

"You can't leave until you hear Ben's sermon," Tom said.

"I will make it short," Ben assured them. "It is from a passage from the book of Romans."

Everyone found a chair or log to sit upon while Ben opened his Bible and began to read from Romans, chapter 8, verses 26-27.

"Likewise the Spirit also helpeth our infirmities: for we know not what we should pray for as we ought: but the Spirit itself makes intercession for us with groaning which cannot be uttered. And he that searcheth the hearts knoweth what is the mind of the Spirit, because he makes intercession for the saints according to the will of God."

"My prayer for all of you is that you have invited Jesus Christ into your hearts to be your own personal Savior," Ben said. "You are also given at this time the Holy Spirit, to intercede for you before the throne of God. You have it all now. God cannot let you go because he not only purchased your soul with the blood of his Son, but he has now come to dwell within your heart."

Ben continued, saying, "Verses 31-32: 'What shall we say then to these things? If God is for us, who can be against us? He that spared not his own Son, but delivered him up for us all, how shall he not with him also freely give us all things?'

CHAPTER TWENTY-SIX

"These are promises from God that we can build our lives around. The first is our salvation, the second is answers to our prayers, and the third is that God is for us. Now we can count on God freely giving us all things."

Ben closed his Bible.

"If you and I are willing to become one hundred percent his, we will be used by God to bless our world and the people we come in contact with," he said. "I've had to learn to die to myself and let God have his will and way with me. Ed and I were delivered from sure death by his almighty hand while in the mine in California. We were in his hands, and we knew it because there was no one to rescue us at the time.

"Our family and friends have all invited Jesus into their hearts, and what a wonderful heritage we have in Christ Jesus. My mother and dad would be proud and happy at all you grandchildren giving your hearts to the Lord. Let's close this gathering now with you children leading us in prayer. Jackson, you close."

All present bowed their heads. The adults all had tears of joy on their cheeks. "God bless each of you," Ben said.

CHAPTER TWENTY-SEVEN

"THE LETTS SURE know how to have fun at their family picnics," Willard said. "That was my first one, but I'll sure look forward to the next one, especially if you plan it on a day with nicer weather!"

"There will be plenty more this summer," Ben said.

After the children had gone to bed, Debra pulled Ben aside to talk.

"Sara sure looked sad today," Debra said.

"It made me feel bad down deep inside to see her that way," Ben answered.

"She looked like her heart was breaking when she asked us to sit on the porch in the wicker chairs and talk with her," Debra said.

The two of them remembered their conversation with Sara earlier that day.

While Debra had gone to get the lemonade and gingersnap cookies for her husband and his sister, Ben and Sara had discussed the hot weather and her husband's recent trip to St. Louis.

CHAPTER TWENTY-SEVEN

When Debra had arrived with the treats, she said, "I've a mind that food and drink will always bring comfort to someone who's troubled. Now, tell us what the problem is, Sara, and how Ben and I can help. We're always here for you, dear."

Sara's face had turned the color of milk, and she had cleared her throat gently.

"As the wife of a drunkard, I see my ideals and hopes being shattered and my sorrow excelled," she had said. "I am tortured, and it's truly difficult to bear the pain; but I breathe constant prayers to my heavenly Father for his mercies that come to me daily.

"I haven't been this sad since our dear sister Ann was stricken with fever and died in Natchitoches, Louisiana. That grief seemed to break my heart. At the time, I thought I would never get over her death.

"Now, however," Sara had continued, "my husband is a drunk and a mean man. He has been so ugly to me and the children."

Sara's bottom lip had quivered, and she had touched it with a trembling hand.

"Colin is making my life miserable for me," she had confessed.

"I felt for her so," Debra said. "When Sara took a deep breath and sipped some lemonade, her color seemed to improve, but the rest of her story was hard to hear."

"Colin is already a very wealthy man, but the only thing he thinks about is getting a lot richer," Sara had told them. "When he's home, he pays little mind to me because he's too busy with his cattle and land, doing whatever he can to see that they multiply and make him more money.

"I need to know what to do. I feel left out and unimportant, and it's tearing me to pieces.

"If . . . if I died, Colin probably wouldn't even spend the money to buy a coffin or purchase a burial plot. He'd just lay my body on top of one of those big rocks on the farm and let the birds eat it."

Tears had been glistening in Sara's eyes, and Debra had left her chair, put an arm around Sara's neck, and kissed the brokenhearted woman's cheek. Ben had reached over to pat Sara's arm.

"As Debra and I have told you and Colin, we are sold on the idea that without Jesus Christ in our lives, none of us can know true satisfaction in our hearts and souls," Ben had said, trying to console his baby sister.

Sara had looked off in the distance for a few minutes and said, "I've thought a lot about what you and Debra have told Colin and me about Jesus and our need to put him first in our lives."

"That's fine, honey," Debra had said, "but there's more to it than just believing that the Father exists and that his Son exists. You must do as the Bible says. You must repent of your sin and receive the Lord Jesus into your heart."

Then Sara talked about how both Debra and Ben knew that she had taken Jesus as her Savior when she was a little girl. Her first husband, David Springstead, had been a devout Christian, and she had loved him dearly. After David had died, she met Colin. Once they married, she learned Colin had lied about being a Christian.

"Ben," she had asked, "does the Bible say anything about my falling for a liar and the resulting life of sin and agony?"

Ben had gone for his Bible then and had let Sara read what it says. She had been impressed with the Bible's warnings about the pitfalls that lay in the path of the person who lived a lie so he or she could indulge in the sinful life.

CHAPTER TWENTY-SEVEN

"Thank you, Ben, for showing me these scriptures," Sara had said, smiling. "I wish you could show them to Colin."

"I'd be glad to if he'd let me."

Sara had glanced at Debra, then back at Ben.

"Could the two of you come to our home to talk to Colin?"

They agreed, and Sara shared that Colin already knew why she was unhappy. She invited them to come at 6:30 for Sunday night dinner and said she would tell Colin they were invited because she had come to them for advice.

Sara had thumbed the tears from her eyes and had said, "Wonderful! I'll have our cook prepare a special meal for you."

Ben remembered he had given Sara a hug before he left her that day.

Sara felt a slow ruffle of apprehension go through her as she rode alongside her husband toward home the day of the cyclone. She did not know exactly how Colin would react to what Ben and Debra might say to him, and she did not know what scriptures Ben would show him.

What she did know was that something had to change or her marriage would be over. She couldn't go on living that way.

"You children go play. Your mother and I want to talk privately," Colin said when they arrived. "Let's sit here on the steps, Sara."

Colin gestured toward the wide stairs that led up to the porch of their house. When they were seated, Sara looked at him and waited for him to speak.

"You need to know that I'm taking some cattle to market in St. Louis soon. These cattle will bring a lot of money.

259

I'll be gone for at least two weeks. I've asked Tom to watch over our place, and he has agreed. The cattle market is at an all-time high, and we can make plenty of money," Colin said.

"Don't you have enough money without this venture?" Sara asked.

"Why does my desire to increase our net worth always have to be a problem to you?" he fired back.

She looked him square in the eye. "It is a problem because, for one thing, you don't need any more money. You have already got more than you could ever spend if you lived to be a hundred. And for another thing, your endless search for greater riches leaves me here alone with the children."

He stared at her silently.

She took a deep breath. "Colin, do you have any idea how lonely I am? I am a discouraged and lonely woman. You and I rarely leave this place together to visit anyone. In fact, we rarely leave this farm together to go anywhere. You go riding off on some trail ride to buy or sell cattle while I sit here and pine away alone and write poetry."

"What do you mean, alone?" he countered. "Your family and mine live nearby, and you and the children can visit them anytime you want."

"The only human beings I can confide in and get solace from are Ben and Debra," she said, her eyes filling with tears. "Even when you are not out looking for more cattle to buy or sell, you are away from the house most every day, working to increase your wealth on the ranch. Most days I hardly see you."

Colin shook his head. "So I've never done a thing for you, huh?"

She wiped tears and sniffed. "Of course you have. Colin, you've been very generous with me when it comes to material things. I have more than a woman could ever

CHAPTER TWENTY-SEVEN

dream of. But I love you, and as I've told you before, I need to be with you. I need to have more of your attention. After all, I am you wife."

"As my wife, you are a very rich woman, Sara." Colin touched her shoulder. "Why can't you be satisfied with everything I've given you?"

Tears streamed down Sara's cheeks. She took a trembling breath and said, "Colin, all of the wealth in the world cannot buy love or happiness. Why is money so much more important to you than anything else? How does it compare with my companionship?"

Colin sighed, shook his head, and said, "You just don't understand, Sara."

"I sure don't! That is why I'm asking you. Why is money more important to you than anything else? I need the love and affection of my husband as well as time with him. Why don't you need that from me?"

"I do, but I want to build up a fortune while I'm able to do it. Why don't you try to understand that?"

Sara wiped her tears and set her reddened eyes on him.

"I have tried to understand it, Colin, but my loneliness overrides it. I need you close to me. I don't want anything to happen to our marriage."

When those words came from her mouth, she gasped. "Colin, I talked to Ben and Debra. I want their help to help save our marriage."

"So our marriage is in danger of falling apart, is it?"

"I want our marriage to work, Colin. I need to tell you that I invited Ben and Debra over for dinner Sunday evening, and I do believe they can help us."

"Help us? They're religious fanatics, Sara."

Colin's impudent attitude and the harshness in his voice scraped like a flint on Sara's senses and struck fire within.

"I wasn't aware that I had to check with you before I talked to my brother and his wife. I don't like being treated like a child," she said. "They are good, very wise people, and they care about others. They don't want us to go into eternity without being ready to face God," Sara said.

"You want too much from me! I'm busy. I can't hang around the house with you all the time!" Colin replied.

More tears glistened in Sara's eyes.

"I can't stand this life much longer," she said. "I want Ben and Debra to counsel us because I don't want our marriage to break up. Will you at least talk to them with me when they come for dinner?"

Sara watched as Colin stood and walked away. Wiping more tears, she said in a low voice, "Colin Cotteau, if this doesn't change, I'm leaving you."

On Sunday evening just before six-thirty, Sara stood at the parlor window watching for Ben and Debra's buggy. Colin sat nearby in an overstuffed chair, looking over his cattle ledger.

One of the maids, Sally Thompson, stood at the parlor door waiting for her mistress to tell her the guests were arriving. Sally knew that Mr. Cotteau would not allow his wife to greet the guests at the door. It must be done by one of the servants.

Sara turned from the window and said, "They're coming, Sally!"

"Yes, mum," Sally said and hurried toward the door.

Colin laid the papers aside, left the overstuffed chair, and walked to the window where Sara was peering through the sheer curtains as the Letts came up the front porch steps.

CHAPTER TWENTY-SEVEN

Colin looked out and said, "Oh, no. Ben has his Bible with him. He's probably going to preach that 'salvation' stuff to us again."

"He cares about us," Sara said. "Please don't be rude to him."

"I've already told you, I'll be courteous."

Colin and Sara heard Sally greeting them at the door, so Sara took her husband by the hand and led him to the center of the room to face the open door. Sally appeared, smiling, with the Letts behind her.

"Mr. and Mrs. Cotteau, your guests are here," she said.

Colin stepped forward and shook hands with Ben, then took Debra's hand, bowed slightly, and welcomed her.

"Let's have a drink before dinner," Colin offered.

"No, thank you. We'll pass," Ben replied.

At dinner, Colin and Ben talked about cattle ranching and other subjects. While the cook and maid came in and out, Ben refrained from bringing up spiritual things at the dinner table. With the meal complete, the Cotteaus led Debra and Ben to the parlor.

After some silence, Sara said, "I had a talk with Colin when I got home from our outing at Tom's home. I told him what I told you about my loneliness and unhappiness and that I feared our marriage was in trouble. I made sure he understood that, as I see it, I'm number two in his heart. I believe his wealth and the desire to obtain more of it are number one."

"Sara, stop bothering them about how you feel," Colin said. "You and I can work it out."

"Well, I hope you do work it out, Colin," Ben said. "But Debra and I want to help if we can."

Colin eyed his wife with a frown.

"I asked Ben what the Bible has to say about greed in a person's heart and about the results of that greed. He showed me some scriptures on it, and I want him to show them to you," Sara said.

Colin felt a surge of anger boil up within him and said, "Oh, so you want him to preach to me because you think my desire to become wealthier is just plain greed."

"What else could it be?" Sara answered.

"I told you what it is, and you still don't understand. I simply want to build up a fortune while I'm still young and able to do it."

Sara's eyes flashed fire.

"Nonsense! You already have more money than you could spend in your lifetime, Colin! You don't need any more money. What drives you to keep piling up more wealth? Your excessive desire for more money is about to drive me out of my mind!"

"As your wife, Sara is right to expect you to give attention to her and give her more of your time," Ben said as he opened his Bible. "Let me show you from God's Word how greed exists in a person's heart.

"Listen to this, Colin. Proverbs 15:27a says, 'He that is greedy of gain troubleth his own house.' Can you see the truths in those words? Your greed—your insatiable desire to continually become richer—is troubling your own house. Your marriage is on shaky ground because of it. It certainly has caused trouble between you and your wife according to what she has told Debra and me."

Ben continued.

"And he spoke a parable unto them, saying, the ground of a certain rich man brought forth plentifully: And he thought within himself, saying, 'What shall I do, because I have no room where to bestow my fruits?' And he said, 'This will I do: I will pull down my barns, and build greater; and there will I bestow all my fruits and my goods.' And I will say to my soul, 'Soul, thou hast much goods laid up for

CHAPTER TWENTY-SEVEN

many years; take thine ease, eat, drink, and be merry.' But God said unto him, 'Thou fool, this night thy soul shall be required of thee: then whose shall those things be, which thou hast provided? So is he that layeth up treasure for himself, and is not rich toward God.'

"Colin, did you notice how quickly the greedy man lost his riches when God took him into eternity saying, 'Thou fool, this night thy soul shall be required of thee?' He couldn't take his riches with him when he died, and neither can you."

Colin remained silent.

Ben said, "Let me read you something else in Proverbs that I read to Sara. This speaks of those who have flocks and herds or livestock as you have, Colin. Proverbs 27:23 and 24a: 'Be thou diligent to know the state of thy flocks, and look well to thy herds. For riches are not forever.'

"Listen to that last statement again, Colin, 'Riches are not forever.' Let's face it. Whatever earthly things we possess, we lose them when we die . . . and so often, they are lost while we live. You shouldn't set your heart on your earthly possessions, nor wrap your life up in gaining more possessions. The right thing is to open your heart to Jesus and be saved. As Debra pointed out, that will make you rich toward God."

Colin's face went dark red. Sara saw it. A shudder ran through her, and her heart began to pound.

"I have my own ideas about riches and piling up all I can, Ben," Colin said, "I will go on as I have been doing. And I have my own ideas about death and eternity. I don't believe that Bible, and I don't want to hear any more!"

Colin rose to his feet. His features were redder than ever. "I will not listen to you anymore, so this conversation is over." With that, he stormed out of the room.

Tears filled Sara's eyes, and she pressed a palm over her mouth.

CHAPTER TWENTY-EIGHT

AT THE BREAKFAST table in the Cotteau home the next morning, all Colin could talk about was his new financial venture. He intended to leave the next day for Colorado to buy yearling heifers and drive them back to Illinois. Sara looked down and picked at her food.

Colin noted it and scowled. "Sara, why can't you at least try to understand what I'm doing? The money I make is yours as well."

With tears washing down her cheeks, she ran from the room, up the stairs, and toward the master bedroom.

Colin took his last bite of breakfast, finished his coffee, and stepped into the hall. The two maids wondered what to do.

Colin said, "We're finished, girls. You can clean up the table now."

Colin left the house, went to the barn, saddled up, and rode with his hired man to look over the land to see if it was ready for plowing. When he returned some five hours later, Colin stepped into the kitchen.

CHAPTER TWENTY-EIGHT

Helen, the maid, said, "Mr. Cotteau, were you aware that Mrs. Cotteau took the children, hitched up a pair of horses to one of the wagons, and drove it herself toward town?"

Colin frowned and said, "Well, no. Why did she do this?"

"It puzzled me, too, sir," she said. "She had four bags with her. You know, the kind that you put clothes in when you travel. The children didn't say a word to anyone."

"Did she, now?"

"Yes, sir. I have no idea where she was going, but I didn't think it was any of my business to stop her and ask."

Colin shrugged.

"Well, Helen, I'm not going to try to find her. She'll be back."

That evening, when Colin came in for supper, he asked Helen if Sara had returned.

"She didn't, sir. I tried to find her, but she wasn't to be found."

Colin nodded. "I'm going upstairs to wash. It will just be me for supper."

He made his way up the staircase, washed his face, and entered the master bedroom. His eye caught the sheet of paper on the dresser. It read:

Colin:
   The children and I are going home to Tom's in Sheridan. By the time you read this, I will be there. Our marriage is over. I'll send the wagon and team back to you tomorrow.
                    Good-bye,
                    Sara

Early the next morning after Colin had eaten his breakfast, he called Helen to meet him in the parlor.

In a dull tone, Colin said, "Mrs. Cotteau has left me and gone to her brother's. She left a note saying our marriage is over. I'm sure you knew that Mrs. Cotteau was very unhappy. I should never have married her in the first place. She is too self-centered. My crew and I are leaving for Colorado to buy some heifers immediately. Take care of the house, and I'll see you when we get back."

Helen thought, *Too bad Mr. Cotteau couldn't see the prize he had in Miss Sara. Guess I'd better get back to work. I don't want him to get upset at me. I need this job.*

Ben soon learned that Sara had gone to Tom's home with the children. He and Ed had arrived at Tom's house early one morning to discuss a coming horse drive. Merrilla asked them in, and they couldn't resist her hospitality. She had prepared hot coffee, eggs, bacon, and hot rolls for breakfast, and the kitchen smelled of bacon frying and coffee cooking.

"Did you know Sara and her children left Colin and came to stay with us for a while?" Merrilla said.

"I'm not surprised," Ben answered. "Sara was pretty upset when Debra and I saw her last."

"Tom and I told her she and the children can live with us for the next few weeks," Merrilla said. "We love having them, but we have company coming from New York. Could they stay with you and Debra for a time while our company is here?"

"I would love to have them stay," Ben said. "I'll talk it over with our family."

"Sara and the children are very upset over moving from their home," Tom said.

"I know all of us will help her as long as she and the children are in need," Ben replied. "I would give anything to see my little sister happy again. She doesn't deserve to be treated so cruelly. When I think of her situation, it reminds me of Philippians 4:6, 'Be careful for nothing: but in everything by prayer and supplication with thanksgiving let your requests be made known unto God.'"

CHAPTER TWENTY-EIGHT

When he returned home, he asked Debra to gather Ed, Janice, and Willard to pray for the Cotteau family.

"We need to give ourselves to prayer and fasting," Ben said. "Tell the children to gather in the kitchen, and they, too, can pray for their cousins. I believe God will honor the children's prayers as much as ours."

They followed their prayers with singing, and adults and children all joined in with hymns and songs. Debra played the piano, and Janice led the singing. Ed and Ben both played their guitars. Jackson played his harmonica.

Ben spoke of the proverb that said, "Labor not to be rich, cease from your own wisdom. Will you set your eyes upon that which is not? For riches certainly make themselves wings, they fly away as an eagle toward heaven."

Ben told those gathered that Colin would someday lose his riches. The same thing would happen to them if they didn't heed God's warning.

The children asked Ben if God would someday forgive their Uncle Colin.

"God has already forgiven him when Jesus died for his sins. However, Uncle Colin must first acknowledge his sin and repent and turn away from his sins. God cannot do that for him. He must learn from God how to be a good husband and father. God will teach him if he asks. I was that way before I invited Jesus into my heart and life," Ben said.

The mothers scooted the children off to get ready for bed, then Ben and Ed read the Bible and Christian books to them, as they always did, before tucking them in for the night. The five adults gathered in the library for a cup of tea before turning in for the night. Ben asked them if they liked the idea of inviting Sara and the children to stay with them sometime soon.

"That is a great idea," Debra said. "We have a great family, and we should be proud and thankful for their love and faithfulness."

CHAPTER TWENTY-NINE

IN THE YEARS that followed, Ben and Debra fulfilled many of the dreams they had dreamed upon his return from the gold rush. They built their new home close to the one Ed and Janice had built. They raised their horses, and they watched their children grow. And they enjoyed some of the happiest days they had known.

Debra also made her plans to visit her mother in England at long last. That journey began in the spring of 1856.

Debra and Janice awoke as the carriage swayed around a bend in the road. Debra leaned forward to peer out the window. The lake stretched before her in the early morning light. Its expanse only reminded her of the coming farewell.

Debra looked around the stagecoach at the sleeping travelers. Janice leaned upon Ed, who rested against the opposite side of the coach, his steady snores escaping with every breath. Debra smiled in spite of herself.

The farther they had traveled through the night, the closer they had come to the ship and separation. When

CHAPTER TWENTY-NINE

Debra could hold her eyes open no longer, her last sight had been of Ben sleeping directly across from her, with Jackson sprawled across the remainder of the seat. They lay in the comforting closeness of a parent and child as the rising sun painted them in the softest hues.

She did not turn back until she had gained control of her emotions. Then she gazed at two of the most precious people in her world until the carriage lurched over a particularly deep hole, throwing them all about.

Ed snorted awake, rubbed his face, then stuck his head out the window and called softly, "I say, George, slow down for the bumps."

Ed poked his head out farther still. "So I see. And there is the lake."

"Yes, and a beautiful morning to you, sir. We've made good time," the driver called.

"Pull up, will you, and let us all stretch our legs," Ben called out.

"Yes, sir, boss. I see a wide spot just ahead."

When the coach halted, the adults climbed down to walk around, stretching stiff limbs. Debra handed around mugs of watered cider. She then took the breakfast sack from Ben and laid out their morning meal.

"What a sight," Ben remarked. "Where's Jackson?"

"Still asleep."

Ben moved alongside Ed as they stood together, gazing out over the green-blue waters.

Ed said, "It is indeed a beautiful sight."

A city of gray stone buildings lay nestled along the lake's shore. The lake curved back upon itself, and the city faced directly east. The rising sun formed a line of light and shadow over the rather still lake.

"There is no place quite as lovely as Lake Michigan on a fine day," Janice said as she joined the two men.

"This is the time of year when there are many fine days," Ed responded.

From the dock came an officer's shout and the blast of the ship's horn.

"No doubt the captain seeks to make way while the weather is with him," Ben said. "You should be underway shortly."

Just then, Debra said their breakfast was ready; soon they had eaten their bread and cheese. Jackson had awakened in good humor. When the carriage pulled dockside, Ben and Ed hurried about, helping the driver unload their bundles and chests.

With Janice nearby, Debra stood watching, holding Jackson's hand.

"Excuse me, Mrs. Lett?"

Both women turned as one at the address. No one there was to have known their identity. They found themselves facing a young man wearing a vicar's white collar beneath his black cloak.

Debra said, "You must be Pastor Jones."

"Yes, that is me." He removed his hat and bowed slightly.

"I am traveling as Debra Johnson. My friends Ed and Janice Patterson are traveling with me."

"Yes, of course. Forgive me. I have your names right here on my list."

"Once we are safely out on the water, I would be happy to be known by my true name," Debra told him.

"You are not the only ones who are departing today under assumed names, I assure you," the pastor remarked. "My wife and I wish to thank you for your most generous gifts. Madam, I cannot thank you enough. This money is making it possible for my wife and me to make this journey back to our family home in England."

CHAPTER TWENTY-NINE

"Our only request is that the gift be a secret between us and God," Debra said quietly.

"As you wish, ma'am. But I could not have possibly let your goodness go without a word of thanks." He backed away and said, "I must go see to my wife."

Debra sat on a trunk, her Jackson seated beside her. She tried not to hold his hand too tightly. He chatted away, pointing out all the fascinating things he saw. Fortunately, she was not required to answer very often. It took heroic effort to hold back her tears.

Too soon, the loading of the ship was completed. The sun was high, the day warm, the lake kind, the wind southerly, and the birds flying overhead sounding off regularly. The captain's shout turned impatient, and finally Ben came and stood by her to say, "The moment has come for you to depart my dear."

Jackson turned to look up into his mother's face. "Are you going now?"

"Yes, my dearest one. You remember I told you that you and daddy will have to take good care of your little sister and brother and the Doyle children."

"We will take care of them, Mama, we promise."

"Are you sad?" she asked.

"Yes, because I shall miss you very much. But I shall think of you every day, pray for you, and look forward with all my heart to seeing you again as soon as I can."

She felt a great distance between herself and the moment—a sense of watching herself speak. The same amazing peace kept her eyes dry and her voice steady.

"You must promise me to be good and obey your dad," she said, trying to smile.

"I love you, Mama."

He looked at her with a great longing in his eyes. She kissed his cheek and the silken hair upon his forehead. She breathed in the warm fragrance of her son. Then she did the most difficult thing she had ever done. She let him go.

They gathered together and prayed, including Jackson in their circle. They hugged and spoke final words, or at least all did except Debra. She let herself be moved from one moment to the next, coming fully alert when her husband and son got into the carriage.

Ben and Jackson's faces emerged through the open window, and the sunlight lit their hair. Debra fought to keep her eyes utterly clear, for this was the vision she wished to find every time she shut her eyes during the weeks and months ahead. This sight would sustain her.

Sailors drew in the gangplank, tossed the ropes on board, raised sails, and canted the vessel seaward. It was all Debra could do to hold to her calm. So long as the shore was visible, she would remain composed.

The harbor became merely a flat pan, and the city became a speck on the shore. Then the sunlight played upon the rolling waves, and the golden reflection gentled away her vision entirely. She turned then, buried her head in Janice's chest, and gave herself over to sorrow's flood.

Debra found herself wracked with sorrow. She experienced a small measure of the pain her mother must have felt as she returned to England without her daughter or husband. Debra had never lived such pain, though, until now. She at least knew where her husband and children were and that they were being cared for in a place that was home.

As soon as the boson had piped the morning crew on deck and the others to their breakfast, the passengers made their way from their quarters. The captain greeted them, doffing his hat and bowing.

Debra inhaled, and it seemed as though it was the first true breath she had taken since their departure. She breathed

CHAPTER TWENTY-NINE

again and found herself taking stock as one would when getting up in the morning.

Every sail was out, a great billowing mass of canvas that filled the blue sky empty of clouds. The sun rose behind her. The timbers creaked, and the roll of the ship caused the deck to move constantly.

Debra reached for Janice's hand. She knew Ed and Janice were concerned for her mental health. She gave them both a proper hug.

"I'll be just fine in a few days," she assured them.

Soon they had traveled far. To the west, the setting sun reflected upon the shimmering waters of Lake Erie. To the east, the expanse reached out to approaching night as they moved into the waters of Lake Ontario. The wind filtered through the surrounding hills in fits and gusts yet scarcely ruffled the water's surface.

Their plan was to berth in secret far enough down the Cobourg, Ontario, Canada, harbor to avoid confrontation with any British vessel. Because the waters were decidedly British, they hoped to berth and return without challenge.

Debra knew they would search for likely anchorage and landfall in the last light of day, then load into boats and finish their trek under cover of darkness.

The captain and Ed studied the bank through telescopes, conferring quietly back and forth. A nearly full moon emerged over the forested hilltop just as the day's last light faded. The two seemed to reach agreement.

The captain soon gave the order to drop anchor and lower the longboat. Debra and Janice were lowered aboard. Ed joined them, as did the crew assigned to travel on land with them.

The men rowed with the silence of hard-won experience. Ed sat in the bow, directing with one upraised hand. The tide was high enough for them to make it all the way to solid footing before grounding. The men disembarked and ushered Debra and Janice to higher ground, then heaved the longboat up and under a dense cluster of trees with as little noise as possible.

"Don't make a move," someone said in the dark.

"Steady," Ed agreed quietly. "I can see movement amidst the trees on either side."

"We come in peace!" Debra said.

"If so, why come in secret and by night?"

"These are perilous times," Debra said, keeping her voice steady. "I am both British and American."

"There is danger in making errors," one of the men said. "Make a light, I say."

Flint sparked and kindling was lit.

A second voice cried out, "By heaven's mercy! It's Debra McGirr."

She knew him then, and though she could not see him, Debra plunged through the darkness with arms outstretched. Debra's Uncle Harry gave her a big hug.

"Where did you come from?" he asked.

"We have been traveling for several days from Illinois."

"Where is your husband?"

He couldn't come because of the queen's edict to capture him at all costs," she replied. "Uncle Harry, these are my friends Ed and Janice Doyle."

"Pleasure to meet you, sir," they said.

"Let's head for Cobourg," her uncle said. "John, Sam, Russell, and Fred will guide us back to the village. These men know the region well enough to move without lights, and they have horses."

Debra, Janice, and Ed would travel on horseback while the remaining sailors would bed down nearby.

CHAPTER TWENTY-NINE

The horses were dark roans so well trained that they neither stamped nor whinnied as the unfamiliar figures approached through the shadows.

Debra and Janice rode with Ed on one side and Uncle Harry on the other. When the clouds parted and the moonlight shone through, she could see the gray in his hair and beard. He reminded her of how her father looked before he was killed.

When the way straightened and the path ahead was awash of white moonlight and calm, Janice reached across and took Ed's hand for a moment.

"We are headed for Marion Johnson's boarding house," Ed said. "You realize we are breaking the curfew. Soldiers would recognize these steeds for what they are. But for your sake, we must hold to the open road."

With the light came morning mist, rising from the ground like lazy tendrils. Debra felt the damp as she saw the sheen of dew upon Ed's coat. She and Janice drew their mantles closer about them and pulled their hoods over their heads.

Houses she recognized appeared as suddenly as silent wraiths. They passed the fence lining Janice's father's churchyard. Debra moved to the front of the group and led them through the market square and down the now-familiar lane.

In spite of exhaustion, her heart surged with joy as she saw the old boarding house still shuttered for the night when they halted. Debra slipped from the horse unaided, and her fingers trembled as she opened the little gate and moved up the walk.

Before she could knock, the door flew open and she found herself looking into Marion's face. Her eyes filled and overflowed as she felt her embrace.

"I heard God say my name," Marion said, "even before I opened my eyes."

Marion hugged Janice and Ed as Debra's eyes filled with tears. Then Debra sat by the fire and sipped a cup of Marion's special brew. She could feel the warmth of the drink seep into her stomach as the heat from the crackling logs embraced her toes. Every time Marion passed, she put a hand on her shoulder.

"The village is full of ears and eyes. Your presence is bound to come to the attention of the officials in Cobourg."

"How long do we have?" Ed asked.

"A few days," Marion guessed.

There, in the first moments of greeting, their imminent departure was already being discussed.

"Forgive me, I must rest," Debra said.

Debra awoke to birdsong and laughter. She lay and studied the room about her. Light pierced the narrow slits in the rear shutters, which was strange, for the house faced east. *It must be noon or later. Did I sleep through the entire morning?*

"Good morning, Marion," she managed around a yawn.

Marion stepped inside. "How are you feeling, Debra?"

"So much better I can hardly believe it. How are Janice and Ed?"

"They left several hours ago to visit her parents."

Marion sat down on the bedside.

"What time of day is it?" Debra asked.

"It is two o'clock and time for you to visit some of your old friends. I have invited most of them to come to my house today to prevent you from running into troublemakers out on the streets. I have some bread and cheese for you. I also have some tea and crumpets. You can sit here in bed and enjoy your meal."

CHAPTER TWENTY-NINE

Janice and Ed were talking in the lane beyond the garden gate when her father, the bishop, welcomed the couple to join him for a cup of tea.

"May God's light shine upon you, upon this day, and upon every day he grants you both," Bishop Evans said.

"Thank you, Father."

Janice embraced him, forcing herself not to let the sorrow overwhelm her. She told herself to remember the joy and the fullness of these days together.

She turned to her mother. The eastern sun shone fully upon her mother's features beneath her bonnet. Her face was far more lined than Janice had recalled. And almost all the visible hair was gray.

"I have not had enough time here in this place," Janice whispered.

"You and Ed need to enjoy your time with us, and then maybe you will get time to see Ed's family and some more of your friends," her mother said.

"We can use these few moments to give thanks that you are here for this wonderful visit," her mother said. "Your father can perform a ceremony blessing your wedding anniversary. I am so happy you are here to see him in much better health than he has been recently."

Janice nodded her assent and said, "I haven't really had a chance to speak of Father's health or yours."

"We are in God's hands."

Her mom held Janice's hand closer and asked, "Do you believe this?"

"Of course, but I am concerned that you are getting proper care."

"We are his children. He has blessed us most wonderfully. What use is there in bewailing what neither of us can change?" her mother added.

Janice nodded again, but this time she found her heart also agreeing. She was truly blessed, and her spirit was truly lifted.

She had only a short time before their departure, but she did not hurry in describing the events in her mind. She was able to see God's hand more clearly, and this she tried to seal in her memory as well.

The sun traced its way west, and Janice knew the time was coming to depart. She knew that God's hand was upon her here even as she left her father and mother, not knowing when or where they might see one another again.

"I carry with me my love for this place and my wonderful family and your love for me," she told her mother and father. "I am sustained by this and by the knowledge that a joyful reunion in heaven awaits us all."

When it was time to leave Cobourg, Marion sat next to Debra in a wagon. Ed and Janice rode nearby, keeping watchful eyes on the crew and wagons. Debra had asked to drive and, even in this old contraption of a wagon, she found pleasure in taking the reins once more.

On the way, Marion shared with Debra the tale of two diaries of Debra's grandmother's writings given her by Debra's mother years ago. They told of Debra's mother and father meeting and marrying.

Debra, in turn, told the story of her overland journey to Illinois and Ben's efforts to keep ahead of the queen's henchmen, who had made many attempts on his life. She told Marion how they had failed, but how the threat kept the entire family living on edge.

They rounded the final corner far too soon for either of them. The ship appeared through a break in the trees. Debra found herself reluctantly releasing the reins and turning to Marion. Too soon; it was too soon to leave.

CHAPTER TWENTY-NINE

Debra held Marion a very long time, willing her strength and youth into Marion's fragile frame. Marion had accepted their thanks for the visit and prayers to keep her safe. She joined them in offering their thanks to God. The little group had linked arms and hearts to pray for the mission and voyage ahead.

"The captain asks that we all board. He is hoping to make the St. Lawrence before noon," Ed said.

"I must honor the captain's wishes, Marion," Debra said with a sigh.

"Of course you must," Marion agreed. "These few hours and days have slipped away swiftly as we shared them together. A thousand tomorrows, and still it is not enough. That is both the joy and the woe of love." She enfolded Debra, Ed, and Janice in a last embrace. She drew back and looked into their faces. "Where you go, my friends, my heart is with you."

CHAPTER THIRTY

DEBRA BRUSHED A loose strand of dark brown hair back from her face and stared down at the large leather-bound book in her lap. Light fell over her shoulder through the cabin's rear windows onto the page.

She read the text out loud to herself again. "Those who go down to the sea in ships, who do business on great waters, they see the works of the Lord and his wonders in the deep. For he commands and raises the stormy wind, which lifts up the waves of the sea."

She raised her head and looked out at the wind lifting up the waves. That imagery was certainly clear enough.

Their way east from Cobourg had been sped along by a late-spring storm. To Debra's great relief, the storm ceased.

"Then they are glad because they are quiet," she read aloud. "So he guides them to their desired haven." She smiled at the welcome sound of that phrase. Certainly her marriage to Ben had brought her a long way toward that haven for her heart. His love and care for her were

CHAPTER THIRTY

evidenced in everything he said and did. But the future loomed uncertainly in the distance.

She was now on a mission to visit her homeland and especially to see her mother and aunt. If God should bring her through unscathed, she would arrive in London, her childhood home, and to her family.

"Oh, that men would give thanks to the Lord for His goodness and for His wonderful works to the children of men!" she said slowly. "Well, that is something I can do, even if I don't know how He will bring us back together again."

A knock on the cabin's door brought her to her feet.

"Yes?" she called.

"Pardon me, ma'am," came a voice through the door. "The captain is requesting your presence on deck."

"I will be there shortly," she replied. She set aside the book, tied her bonnet on her head, and pulled her cloak around her. Above she heard the sound of feet stomping to attention.

Ah, yes, it was the Sabbath, and as was custom, the shipboard rhythm was changed for the day. The decks had been scrubbed and sails carefully examined in preparation for the Lord's Day. She knew some vessels even carried clergyman or occasionally a surgeon who also was a man of the cloth.

Debra climbed the stairway and emerged into the sunlight to see several rows of seamen. Now, in the first hours of the day, she sensed her husband and children's absence. The sense threatened to be her undoing. During the sleepless hours of night, Debra had thought about how her mother had left her homeland and parents to accompany her husband to Canada. She had known the facts of her own early life in England but had never lived it all until now.

Sabbath fell upon the third day of their journey. Debra had not slept more than a few hours in the two nights since their departure. She ate when her friends Ed and Janice urged her to do so.

That Sabbath morning had begun when Janice drew her from bed. She took her to the chamber where the other women had gathered to wash and dress for the morning service.

As they returned to the main hold and gathered about the central table for a breakfast of ship's bread and brine-soaked apples and tea, Debra sensed a soft whisper within her heart telling her that all was well. It told her she should relax and enjoy the company of the other passengers.

The days took on a disciplined routine. Mornings began with tea and scripture. Midday meals were marked by prayers with Ed and Janice. At dusk, they gathered with the other passengers for prayers and scripture reading. Debra found the routine a blessing and comfort and fully involved herself in this life and this worship.

The winds, strong and southerly, blew steadily. The ship heeled over at a near constant angle, drawn forward by the taut canvas. When seabirds began congregating amidst the rigging at dawn and dusk, the passengers greeted them with cries of welcome. They had learned from the sailors that the birds foretold of more good weather and land beyond the horizon.

Three weeks into the voyage, after the evening meal, Debra chose a seat among the empty barrels lashed to the port railing. The curved staves offered protection from the wind that always grew chilly that time of day. Debra had just settled herself when she heard Janice call her name.

"Here!" she answered. "I thought you might need this."

Janice appeared, bearing her heavy cloak.

CHAPTER THIRTY

"Thank you, Janice."

Janice eased herself down beside her, her arm about her shoulders. "It is good to have this quiet moment together isn't it?" Janice asked, smiling.

The weeks at sea had browned her features. Debra imagined that she, too, was browning.

"You have become a spiritual helper to other members of the traveling family," said Debra. "You are a woman of sound judgment and impartial bearing. You seek God's will in your counsel, and you mediate with patience. Your words are a balm to the other women."

"Debra, dear, you humble me with this praise," Janice replied.

They looked at each other and smiled. Then they settled back to watch the stars blink into position.

The next morning a storm swept in hard and fast. The wind rose to such a pitch that lanyards hummed and snapped. The sailors raced across the decks and up the ropes, lashing the sails into quarter-moon shapes used to weather storms.

The captain and crew didn't seem perturbed or in any way anxious. The storm blew eastward, moving them faster still. The captain welcomed the rain, for the closer they drew to the coastline, the more likely they would be to encounter friendly ships.

Great sweeping curtains of rain fell about them, furious torrents that heeled over the boat and doused them all. But the morning remained warm enough for most of the passengers to stay on deck and revel in the first cleansing bath they had enjoyed in days. Dry and salt-crusted faces turned toward the heavens. When one shower had passed, passengers laughed and clapped in celebration.

Debra and Janice embraced. At that moment, another downpour swept over the decks, and Ed laughed with them as they hurried for shelter.

"I believe I have had enough bathing for one day," Ed said as he wiped his face. He and Janice ducked down the stairway below decks.

The stuffy cabin added to Debra's homesickness for the openness of Illinois, but after nearly ten days of stormy weather, at least the sea had calmed enough for them to walk the deck that morning. Laughing with Ed and Janice lessened some of the ache for the sound of Ben's voice.

Ed gave Debra a warm grin.

"If we have a stroke of luck, Debra, we will dock sometime tomorrow or the next day. We'll then need fewer than three days by stagecoach to travel from Liverpool to London. I promise the three of us will eat well in Liverpool," he said.

"Thanks for trying to cheer me up," Debra said to Ed. "I am homesick, but I must admit I am also worried about seeing my mother again after all these years.

"My dad, as you know, died before I married Ben. Ed, I've never found it easy to see my mother's point of view," Debra said. "I am so thankful I found Ben, and, with his love, I intend to remain only beautiful and pleasing until I'm an old, old woman."

"This separation from Ben must give you some idea of how much your mother misses your father," Ed offered.

"She is my mother, and I probably care for her far more than I've ever been able to admit," Debra added. "Ed, do you and Janice understand my feelings toward Mother? Please believe me when I say none of my alienation toward Mother has ever come between Ben and me. He can even tease me about it."

"Good. For now, that's all we need to know," Ed answered.

CHAPTER THIRTY

"I expect we'll be slammed around by every rut we hit in the road from Liverpool to London," Debra said, changing the subject. "We'll have to let the stage do its worst."

"London is lovely in the spring," Debra said when they finally arrived. "Did you notice the name on that sign over there?"

"No," Janice said, too mystified by all the noise, confusion, and crowds of people to see much of anything. Then she and Ed looked at the sign and laughed.

"Debra, how marvelous! Like something made up in an English novel, 'Swan with Two Necks.' Where do the English find these quaint names?" Janice asked.

"Never mind where they find them, they just do," Debra said.

It was the sixth of May and indeed the tender green was doing its best in the dust and racket to soften the harshness of what must be the world's noisiest, busiest city.

Janice now loved the English countryside towns through which their stage had passed on the way to London. In the two hundred miles or so from Liverpool, not one full minute passed without laughter, grumbling, or raucous shouts among the passengers.

When they had reached a wide thoroughfare that Debra said was London's famous Oxford Street, the traffic moved a bit more freely. However, few vehicles even slowed for tradesmen on foot, and the hawkers' cries didn't strike Janice as being nearly as colorful or romantic as English novels had led her to believe.

"I'll take you to see the Tower of London, Westminster, the famous London docks, and Covent Garden Theater," said Debra. "We can visit a spot that should interest you as believers in Jesus Christ. Did you ever hear of London's

Wesley Chapel? John Wesley and his brother Charles went to America in 1733 with General James Oglethorpe to help found the colony of Georgia itself."

After they'd ridden for what seemed a long time on Oxford Street, Debra said, "I'm getting awfully nervous at the thought of actually being in my aunt's home with my mother."

"Could you tell us more about your aunt's home," Janice asked.

"Well, I know they have a woman who cooks and keeps house. Her name is Flora McDougal, and she is proud to be pure Scottish. She is completely bossy and possessive, but also quite wise in her way, and she has a touch of dour Scot personality," Debra said, laughing.

"She is such a gracious and pleasant person. She keeps my mother and aunt in good spirits. No doubt Flora has had our rooms made up for days and dusts them every day at least once.

"In the area where they live, the houses are generally large with trees and shrubbery and, in season, flowers. It's a good house built about twenty years ago by Huguenot craftsmen. It's honey-colored brick with white stone facing and a brown front door. Four stories, center entrance hall."

"Does their home have a porch?"

"No, it's a terrace house, flush with the street, with such a tiny courtyard in back you'd never call it a yard. It's even brick-paved. Not a blade of grass. We're almost there. My mother and her sister will be so happy to see us. I do have real affection for her even if she never approved of Ben."

Debra talked on, preparing Ed and Janice to meet her mother.

"Her health has improved. Now she would like Ben and me to move to London. She can't believe the queen is still

CHAPTER THIRTY

seeking revenge on Ben. She is so pleased that I am coming and bringing you two with me."

When they arrived, Ed said, "I'll pay the driver and give him a hand with our trunks and valises. You ladies wait right where you are."

Debra and Janice looked up at the silent windows and the closed door. Then they went to the edge of the sidewalk and peered at the sky. The sun was setting, but they couldn't see much of it because of all the buildings, one pushed up against another, and the tall trees. A dog barked sharply, a vendor cried his wares, and four carriages rattled and careened past them over the cobblestones.

Janice and Ed labored with arms loaded to carry items to the front door. Debra hoped her mother would be there to welcome them.

"Thank the good Lord you're here safe," her mother said, addressing herself to Debra, Ed, and Janice as she swung open the door.

"Mother!"

Joan McGirr heard Debra call out in the same dear voice that had always put her in mind of music.

"Mother, we're here! Tired and travel worn to be sure, but we're here. It's good to see you again."

At once, Flora busied herself directing the driver where to pile the valises and hauling one and then another trunk to the far side of the hall. Then she stood waiting to be introduced to the visitors.

Mother McGirr hugged her visitors and then introduced Ed and Janice to her sister Mary. The sisters had lived together since their husbands had both passed away. They both were thrilled to see Debra and her friends.

"I'm sure you're exhausted, and..." Mother McGirr said.

Before she managed to get out one more word, Debra saw a smile on her face.

"And what Mother?" Debra asked.

"We're thrilled that you all came to visit us. Everyone, this is Flora," she added.

Flora, giving a curtsy, took Janice and Debra's hands and squeezed them, saying, "I'm glad to make all your acquaintances. As soon as I have this pile of luggage upstairs to your rooms, I'll heat some water for baths."

CHAPTER THIRTY-ONE

BEN AND JACKSON decided to round up some horses and prepare to move them to new pasture.

"Jackson, you are almost ready to assume the duties of my number one hired man," Ben said.

"Dad, I would like nothing better than to work with you someday as a partner," Jackson replied.

"Now that you are eighteen, I will make you a partner in the horse business, and you can have your own herd of horses."

"I would like that. It would give me an opportunity to be a rancher like you," Jackson said.

"Tomorrow we'll ride over to your Uncle Tom's place and talk to him about buying the Bark farm. I'll ask him to help me buy it for you. Then you can have your own piece of land to rent from us."

"That would be great! I know Willard will teach me what he knows about how to run my own farm and ranch," Jackson commented.

"I would be pleased to help you, too. We can all work our land together," Ben remarked.

"We'll work out a plan so you can buy the farm from us over time so it will be your own someday; we could help you buy your own cow herd. You could become the cattle man of the family. Chicago may become the Midwest cattle and hog buying center someday. You could be part of the progress bound to come as more people move here."

"Dad, I hope that someday I'll be able to think and plan ahead like you," Jackson remarked.

"Son, God will fill your mind with a vision of what is ahead if you spend time with him. He loves to share his plans with those who love him," Ben added.

"Let's move the brood mares to the pasture close to the house for foaling. We want to help them and keep them safe from wild animals."

"Dad, when will Mom get home?"

"She'll be gone about a year," Ben answered.

"It seems like she will be gone forever," Jackson said.

"When she and the Doyles get back to the United States, I'm thinking about meeting their boat in Detroit. We could take the train home."

"Can I go with you?" Jackson asked.

"No, your mother and I will use this time together for a second honeymoon. For now, you and I will start planning a winter hunting trip to northern Illinois and southern Wisconsin. I need to teach you about hunting wild game and earning money from the sale of furs.

"Together we can hunt and trap and prepare the skins. I want you to get the best price for your furs. When I travel to Detroit, I'll take the furs with me and sell them for you," Ben said.

"I also plan to spend two weeks with your mother in Detroit buying us some things for our home," he said. "I can hardly wait for her to return from her trip. I wonder what she and Grandma are doing at this time."

CHAPTER THIRTY-ONE

Debra's fine-threaded white linen had been packed for so long in a trunk that it was mussed. She was hoping Flora would attend to making her linens fresh again.

Debra bathed and dressed for a late dinner. She brushed her dark hair so it would shine. She sat before the looking glass and thought of her Ben and the children.

Debra marveled at what her mother had told her about Flora. Flora cooked the meals and also served them, and because her mother and aunt could no longer afford a butler, Flora's was the ruling hand. Mother depended entirely on Flora, and the harder she worked, the more she enjoyed being a martyr.

Debra also knew that Flora did not tolerate serving cold food. She knew she had better go down to dinner right away.

Ed and Janice joined Debra halfway down the flight of steps. Debra could tell from the dry sound of her mother's cough that she was already waiting in the first-floor dining room.

On the way, they passed Mother McGirr's personal reading room. What had been a cheerful family parlor had become the reading room when Joan moved her library and big walnut desk there. Aunt Mary told Debra that this door was closed whether the room was occupied or not.

Debra wondered if grief and isolation were still that important to her mother. Despite outward appearances, was she still as lonely as Debra thought she might be?

In the hallway, Debra stopped to show Ed and Janice what Mother McGirr had called her father's masterpiece—the McGirr family crest. It had been meticulously stitched in petit point and framed by her father with great care in a polished shadow box.

"It's beautiful!" Janice said. "And what perfect stitching!"

"You'll do splendidly with my mother by calling attention to the crest, Janice. She's absolutely pompous about my father's handiwork and his frame and the motto that swells her head with pride. See it there? 'I am ready.' Remember that, my friends. For hundreds of years, the McGirrs have been ready!"

"Stop making fun, Debra. I just thought of something," Janice said. "Your father's crest is a buck's head, and your mother's crest is a whole stag! They're so similar."

"My papa always joked about the difference."

Debra, Ed, and Janice entered the chilly dining room. Even Flora's extra Bouilotte gas lamp didn't seem to thin the darkness much. Debra's first whiff from the kitchen of rosemary and roast lamb, her favorites, made her juices flow. It was lovely that Flora had chosen it for their first meal. Joan and Mary were already seated for dinner.

"I have never purposely been late to dinner for our good Flora's sake," Joan said. "I suppose I have been known to be a minute or so tardy, but only when there was one more important matter to be attended to in my house. You all are welcome at our humble board."

"Oh, thank you, Mother McGirr," Janice said. "From what Debra has told me about your Flora McDougal, I can scarcely wait to taste the first bite! You're indeed fortunate to have Miss McDougal, aren't you?"

"Fortunate, Miss Janice? Perhaps. Flora's been with us for many years. She's a part of our small family."

"Flora, I'm speechless," Debra said, telling a little lie. "I haven't been able to utter a word since I saw you walk through that door with what must be the most toothsome leg of lamb even you have ever baked. Ed, pick up your carving knife and begin, please!"

With a snort, Flora flounced from the room and thumped down the steps for the English peas and hot

CHAPTER THIRTY-ONE

rolls. Ed and Janice exchanged a smile, his sent across the table to reassure Janice that she was doing well with Mrs. McGirr. Her smile said "Thank you" and also "There really is nothing to it."

Ed said to Debra, "I'm sure your father would be proud of Ben today as a landowner and rancher who sells horses to the military. It's too bad they didn't know each other today. Ben would be considered upper class, living in a large house and owning three farms. He really is one of the most erudite, widely read, educated men I've ever known."

"He educated himself! He came to America without houses or lands and worked hard for all he has today," Debra replied with pride.

"In England, you are born into wealth and power," Janice said. "In America, you get busy and earn your standing and rank. Anyone is given the opportunity to seek freedom and prosperity."

"America is the land of the free and the home of the brave, and I'm thrilled to be a part of the great land of America," Debra said.

Ed said, "We will take our leave now. We are tired from all our travel. Tonight we should retire early and be prepared for tomorrow."

Ed and Janice thanked Joan and Mary for the lovely meal and retired to their room on the upper level. Debra, her aunt, and her mother retired to Mrs. McGirr's private sitting room.

Upstairs, making ready for bed, Janice was perplexed at Ed's silence now that they were alone. Janice asked Ed what was wrong.

"Nothing is wrong. You just never cease to amaze me, Janice," he answered.

Slipping into a nightgown, she stood looking across the shadowy room at Ed's broad, muscled back under his nightshirt and his strong, lithe legs below it. Crawling under the covers beside her, he turned on his back.

"You just can't help performing miracles," he said. "Mother McGirr has never laughed so much as she did tonight. I remember back in Cobourg she was a mighty sick woman after her husband died."

"She'll continue to improve," Janice said. "You wait and see. Mother McGirr doesn't concern me. I do wonder about Debra fitting in with her mother, though. I feel so sorry for her I could weep."

Ed pulled her to him.

"Do we have to think such profound thoughts tonight?" he asked.

A long kiss answered his question, but they were both exhausted. The very next thing either of them knew was the glare of full daylight around the curtains. That sun meant Debra's mother and aunt were up waiting breakfast.

Ben dumped the old coffee grounds and rinsed the pot. He wasn't sure how much coffee to use, so he guessed. He found some brown paper, dampened it, and wrapped up the hardened biscuits left from the lunch Willard had cooked yesterday.

By the time the men arrived from the barn twenty minutes later, the omelets were ready, and the biscuits were soft and warm. The coffee was black and hot.

"Well, men, I fixed us a breakfast the best I could after I heard that Willard wasn't feeling up to it," Ben said. "Jason, did you talk with him this morning?"

Jason, the newest hired man, looked up to and respected Willard.

"I am worried about him," Jason said.

CHAPTER THIRTY-ONE

"Is there anything I can do for Willard?" Ben asked. "Maybe we ought to move him into the main house where I could look after him."

Ben washed the dishes after breakfast and then dug around in the kitchen cabinet next to the back door until he found some tonic, powdered mustard, and a small tin of black tea. That was all there was of any medicinal value. Whispering a prayer for guidance, he prepared the guest bedroom on the second floor.

Ben could ask Willard for advice if he wasn't so sick. Spooning tea into a pint jug, he added hot water from the reservoir in the cook stove. At least he could prepare him some tea. Sick people need plenty of liquids to drink.

Ben found a sack of rice beneath the counter. If he set on some beef to stew and made gravy for it, they could eat beef and rice. He could manage that. They might be eating beef and rice for the next two or three days. Bread was out of the question. He didn't know how to make johnnycake. He should have paid closer attention when Debra cooked.

"Jason, can you fetch me some beef?" Ben asked. "Where does Willard keep it?"

"I'll get you some from the smokehouse out back," Jason told him.

Lifting a metal basin from the counter, Jason stepped through the back door and returned in five minutes with a shapeless hunk of meat.

Setting it on the counter, he said, "Willard says he doesn't want you to worry over him. He said he'll be all right in a couple days."

"What about you?" he asked. "Do you think he'll be all right in a couple of days?"

He shook his head doubtfully. "I'm no doctor, but he looks bad to me."

Ben helped Jason move Willard into the guest room and then kneeled beside the bed.

"Ben, you shouldn't trouble yourself about me. I'll get over this in a day or so." He coughed weakly.

"I want to ask your advice about the meals," Ben said. "We'll starve to death if I don't get some help. Cooking has never been my strong point."

Willard drew in a labored breath. "I don't mind doing the work," he said.

"You won't be working today. I brought some hot black tea. Try to drink it for me, will you? Then you rest for a few hours."

Jason handed Ben the jar of hot tea and then helped Willard sit up enough to sip it. Willard gulped down half of it and then sank back. His eyes drifted closed. Jason sat with Willard to help him drink the rest.

Now that Willard was sleeping, Ben asked Jason to ride into town and get the new doctor. Ben went to check on Willard and found him awake.

"Are you in pain, Willard?" he asked, feeling the man's burning forehead.

"My chest hurts when I breathe."

"Jason went to get the doctor. He should be back in an hour or so."

The sick man's eyes closed. "Too much trouble," he wheezed.

Dr. Lanchester, a short, wiry man with a long, bony nose, soon arrived. He was too old to be young and too young to be considered an old man. Deep creases on his thin face bore witness that he'd seen his share of life.

Jason ushered him into the sickroom, and the doctor shooed everyone out and closed the door.

CHAPTER THIRTY-ONE

"Jason, go ahead and start a small fire," Ben said. "It will chase out the dampness."

While Jason prepared the fire, the doctor came out, his face drawn.

"How is he, doctor?" Ben asked.

"I'm afraid he has pneumonia," Lanchester said, shaking his head. "It will be touch and go. He'll need someone with him around the clock."

He pulled a pad of paper from his pocket.

"Here's how to make a mustard plaster." He scribbled for a few seconds. "Keep changing it every hour. Make him drink plenty of water, tea, or anything he'll swallow. That's very important. He's dried out pretty bad."

Ben took the paper from his hand and said, "Will you come back tomorrow?"

Shoving the pad of paper into his inner coat pocket, he nodded. "I have office appointments in the morning, but I'll try to get out in the afternoon. If he should go out of his head with delirium, come and get me right away, day or night."

Jason shook his hand. "Thank you, Doc."

"You're welcome, Jason."

"Thank you, doctor," Ben said.

"You're welcome, Ben," he said and hurried out.

Ben read the slip of paper. "I found some mustard in the kitchen that we can use. I hope it's enough."

Jason gazed at him and asked, "Are you going to be able to handle all of this? Cooking and nursing besides?"

"I can manage for a day or two."

Jason offered that his wife, Lucy, could come and help while he was at the farm doing the chores with Jackson, and Ben thanked him for the kind offer.

"How is Willard?" Lucy asked Ben the next day when she came to help.

"I've got to change his plaster in ten minutes," he said. "I don't think he's any worse."

"Show me what you're doing, and I'll take over. You look all in," she said.

Ben tried out a weary smile and said, "If I could sleep for two hours, I'll be able to sit up with him tonight."

Then he found the doctor's slip of paper and showed Lucy the mustard paste warming on the stove.

The sick vigil lasted for two more days. Finally, the fever broke, and Willard started coughing in earnest. As painful as it was for him, they were all relieved to see him throwing off the infection. The next day, Dr. Lanchester declared that he was out of the woods.

Lucy stayed one more day after that. While she was there, Lucy spent every minute in the kitchen teaching Ben how to cook. Soon Ben was ready to make biscuits and bread and had learned the art of cooking beans. He could throw together a fine johnnycake, too. Ben worked at cooking like he did at everything else—with intense concentration and determination. He never wanted to feel useless in the house.

Ben dished up beans, beef, and biscuits for Willard and poured him some hot tea. Willard made a face when he picked up the blue enamel cup. "Don't you have coffee?" he asked. "This is a woman's brew."

Ben smiled at him and said, "You should be thankful. The last thing you want is my coffee. When you get up you can start making the coffee yourself."

Willard savored a bite of a golden biscuit. "You'll be putting me out to pasture," he said after a moment. "These biscuits are better than mine."

"Not by a country mile," Ben told him. "I could learn a lot from you."

Willard chuckled and ended up coughing.

CHAPTER THIRTY-ONE

Sipping tea, he drew in a breath and said, "When you first brought me into your family and this farm, I was afraid you had made a mistake. But I am sure pleased you did because I love it here with you and your family."

That was the kindest thing anyone had said to Ben in a long time.

Ben was sitting in the rocking chair beside Willard's bed when Jackson came through the doorway with a scowl.

"What is it Jackson?" he said.

"Mr. Kellerman's here to see you."

That explained it all for Ben. He knew that Jackson had never liked Johnny Kellerman because of his arrogant ways. When the lawyer rode into the ranch yard that afternoon, Jackson would not have been happy.

Kellerman rode high on the back of a gleaming black gelding and wore a black suit and flat-crowned hat. The lawyer's only tribute to his Midwestern surroundings was his polished black boots.

Kellerman stepped forward, grinning, and offered his hand to Ben. Jackson took two steps back and quietly closed the door. Jackson's urge to punch Kellerman rushed up in his chest.

Ben also was very concerned about Kellerman's interest in Jackson's girl, Sharon.

"I'll shut your door, Willard, so you can get some rest," Ben said.

He turned to Kellerman.

"Please follow me and we'll have a seat. What brings you to the farm so early in the morning, Johnny?"

As Kellerman unclasped his leather case, he said, "I have the will of your neighbor Andrew Bark. The will has been sent to probate court in Springfield. Once it's recorded, the property can be sold. However, in the meanwhile, Bark's wishes for maintaining the farm are being carried out. You and your son are farming the land, and I'm totally in your service.

"I know that you and Debra would like to purchase this farm for your son, Jackson, so I brought these documents for you to sign transferring the mortgage on this farm to your name as the new owner. As you can see, there's a debt of $2,054 and a yearly payment of $463 due on October 1 every year."

Ben took his time reading through the closely written script. Ben pointed out several errors that could easily be corrected. The mortgage payment seemed huge. Just looking at the amount made Ben's stomach churn.

"Do we have to make a payment before October?" he asked.

"No, there is no payment due until October. I will assure the family that you and your son will do a fine job of farming their land," Kellerman said.

Before retiring that evening, Ben went to check on Willard. For once, Willard didn't say anything.

Ben picked up his empty water pitcher. "Do you need anything else?" he asked.

"Have a seat, Ben. This young fellow Kellerman came to town and took up the law office in Leland nigh on two years ago. The way I hear it, since he came to town, he has called on the banker's daughter, the mayor's daughter, and the daughters of four big farmers. I think he may also have eyes for Jackson's girl, Sharon.

"I think you should tell Jackson to make sure Sharon loves him and doesn't have some interest in Kellerman. He is no good and will break her heart," Willard said.

"Thanks for the advice," Ben replied.

"Jackson loves Sharon and is very jealous of Kellerman's attention to her."

CHAPTER THIRTY-ONE

When Willard regained his health, he was back in the barn helping Ben as usual. One day Ben told him that he'd like to go into town sometime that week. "Do you think you could find time to go with me?" Ben asked.

"How about tomorrow?"

"Sounds good. Let's eat at a restaurant. My treat," Ben agreed.

With Willard driving the surrey, they set off for town around nine o'clock on Tuesday morning. Wearing a cream-colored hat and a blue chambray shirt with a black string tie, Willard looked fine. He had to sit on the edge of the seat to reach the brake.

"Are you from Iowa originally?" Ben asked him.

"I was born in Farmington, Illinois. I had a good business there when I was only twenty-one years old. I had almost two hundred people working for me."

"And you gave it up to be a cowboy and cook?"

"I came north to run cows in the mid-forties. I stayed in Iowa and Illinois working for one farmer or rancher or another. I've always broken horses, branded cows, or taken a job as a cook."

"I'm glad Ed and I met you on our way west. You belong to our family now."

Willard wiped his face with his handkerchief. Ben did the same with his. The heat was unbearable.

When they reached town, Ben said, "Let's go to the bank first. I want to talk to Tom Jenkins."

The Leland National Bank was an unpainted structure in the center of the main street. It had double front doors with nine glass panes in each. A bell jangled when they let themselves in. Before them, a short counter had iron bars from its wooden top to the ceiling. A short, round man with black hair and a gray beard stood behind the counter.

"What can I do for you today, Ben?"

"I'm here to talk with Tom Jenkins."

"Yes, Ben. I'll tell him you're here."

He disappeared through the door behind him for an instant.

"He'll be right with you."

A minute later, Jenkins came through the hinged half door at the end of the counter. He resembled a bear from his shape and size to his dark eyes. When he saw Ben, he beamed.

"Well, Ben Lett. It's good to see you."

Jenkins stood aside and held the half door open. "Please come into my office."

Willard hesitated and said, "If it's all right with you, Ben, I've got some things to attend to in town."

"Of course," Ben replied. "I'll meet you at the general store."

Turning toward the banker, Ben said, "I don't know what we would do without Willard."

"A man of many talents, to be sure," Tom said.

Ben took a chair opposite Jenkins, who was seated behind his desk, and said, "I came to learn more about the terms of the mortgage on the farm we're buying for Jackson and what's required of me as the new owner."

Jenkins leaned back on the arm of his leather chair. "I sent the paperwork over to Kellerman's office," he said.

"Yes, he brought it over to me to sign. Unfortunately, I didn't understand the terms. I was wondering if you would explain them to me."

"It's pretty straightforward. We financed this farm fifteen years ago for $6,000 at two percent interest. Since that time, Bark has refinanced several times. At this date, the full amount due is $2,054 with single payments of $463 once annually."

CHAPTER THIRTY-ONE

"If we have difficulty making the payment, what happens then?" Ben asked.

"If you come up short, let me know, and we'll refinance your loan for $2,524. Your new payment will be a few dollars more the following year, but that's unavoidable."

"I see. This short-term fix will leave us with a bigger long-term problem."

"Is there anything else I can help you with, Ben?"

"No. That answered my question. Thank you."

Closing the jangling bank door behind him, Ben paused on the boardwalk, blinking in the brilliant glare. He walked down the street to the general store.

Both doors opened like the mouth of an enormous barrel with its contents spilling out. Small kegs of nails and screws sat below a table piled high with hand tools and neatly-wound lengths of rope. The young clerk, Tim Ingles, was filling a bare wooden table with stacks of enamel dishes.

Ben spent the next half hour in the tiny shop. It had a narrow counter that wound around the three inner walls. Beneath the counter, more shelves contained everything from building tools to canned goods, eggbeaters, and coffee grinders. Wooden shelves lined the walls behind the counters and were filled with dress goods, ready-made shirts, ammunition, and much more.

The front of the store displayed a wide variety of leather products for horses—two saddles, several bridles, quirts, and horse blankets—all in a neat row.

Willard arrived red faced and panted, "Sorry I'm late. I went down to the livery stable to check on something and lost track of time."

"I'm in no hurry," Ben told him.

A portly, middle-aged man with heavy jowls came through the back door.

"Hello, Zach," Willard said.

Willard and the storekeeper discussed the weather and the danger of drought to the farmers and their crops. Finally the men said good-bye.

"Let's eat lunch," Ben said when he reached the doorway.

Willard mopped his steaming face and said, "I'm all for that."

"Lead the way," Ben told him.

The hotel was four doors down the street, a two-story structure that looked more like a large home than a public building. It had whitewashed siding and a large, wraparound porch half filled with hungry patrons sitting at a long, narrow table.

The restaurant was bustling inside as well. People filled six more tables, and two young girls rushed around, serving them.

A small blond girl paused long enough to tell them, "We can serve you if you don't mind sitting on the porch. That is today's meal," she said, pointing to a menu written on a blackboard that was nailed to the wall beside the door.

Sinking onto a bench, Ben said, "I'm glad we can sit out here. It's stifling inside."

They sat in silence for a few minutes, nodding to people passing in or out. The constant topic of conversation was rain. At every meal and in every quiet moment, they prayed for rain.

CHAPTER THIRTY-TWO

ON THE MORNING of February 16, 1857, Ben and Jackson decided to head for the hills of northwestern Illinois to begin hunting and trapping. Each man led two pack horses and carried rifles, traps, and bullets. They had food enough for two weeks of hunting. If they wanted to be out longer, they would eat some of their own game.

"We'll start very early tomorrow morning. I hope to ride forty miles the first day," Ben said. "We need to reach Rockford by the evening of the second day. This ten-degree weather is wonderful to begin our trip."

The second night, as they huddled around the campfire eating their evening meal, Ben began writing down some life's instructions for Jackson's long-term benefit. The list included:

> First of all, obey orders from your boss. He is paying you for your service.
> When you camp at night, always point your wagon tongue toward the North Star.

Don't holler at your men.
Don't leave your herd for anything.
Don't get rattled. No matter what happens, keep your head clear.
Don't lose confidence in yourself or the Lord.
Be ready at all times to go.
Watch your horses; don't let your men abuse them.
Water your cattle and fill them up before night.
Never say "no" to your employer.
Keep your harness and camp equipment clean and up out of the mud or dirt.
Explain to your cook that he must be ready with his meal at all times.
Don't ever misrepresent anything to your employer; tell it just like it happened.
Look after the comfort of your men, and they will follow you; keep your mind on business.

When Ben finished writing this on his piece of paper, he gave the paper to Jackson. They spent several hours discussing these principles.

"You need to keep these thoughts in your mind at all times," Ben told Jackson. "You may soon have your own farm and family. Someday you and Sharon may become more than sweethearts."

"We'll have to pay close attention to the economy because we have the new farm to pay for," he said. "You will have to work closely with your mother and me to make sure we keep costs down so we have the money for payments due in October.

"I'm going to have some horses for sale then to make sure the money is there. It will mean we'll need at least a hundred horses to sell."

CHAPTER THIRTY-TWO

"Dad, I will do everything I can to make sure the money is there in October. How much can we make off the skins we are hunting now?"

"If we get our four-pack horses fully loaded, we should have enough skins to fetch at least two hundred dollars," Ben said. "You will be able to keep half of that for your farm.

"Let's start along the Mississippi River. Many small streams flow there, and we can trap for mink, coon, and muskrat. Their skins are worth lots of money. We also can shoot fox, rabbits, and deer. If we are successful, we will be home in three weeks."

The day Ben and Jackson left for the hunting trip, huge, fluffy flakes had already begun drifting down. They put on their heavy, wool-lined gloves and winter coats. Ben never tired of watching the beautiful flakes come drifting down with the wind.

The wind grew fiercer during the first night on the trail, and the storm continued without letup for days. When the storm finally blew itself out, several feet of snow covered the ground. They felled several deer.

"Good shot, Jackson. You just shot a nice, fat buck."

"They were just inside the first good stand of trees beyond the Rock River, Papa," Jackson replied.

No sooner had they walked over to inspect the deer than they heard a low growl and saw the lead wolf of a pack of timber wolves.

"They must be starved," Ben said quietly. "Jackson, get ready. If they charge us, I'll shoot the leader. You get the one right behind him, and don't stop firing."

Ben could see that the boy was terrified. "They'll turn tail and run if we kill the leader," he assured him.

The wolves were still growling, poised to attack. Ben waited, sighting the leader's head carefully. The wolf was large and heavily muscled. Long fangs showed through his open mouth. Ben hoped the pack could be bluffed into leaving, but he saw the muscles of the lead animal tensing. The leader's eyes glinted yellow and cold.

Ben waited only a fraction of a second before squeezing the trigger. The wolf sprung just as he fired, and it fell dead instantly into the snow, its blood staining the white blanket. Jackson fired before the report of Ben's rifle had stopped. He wounded the second animal. Ben dropped the third one, and as Jackson shot at the fourth animal, the rest of the pack made a quick retreat.

"Let's get this buck out of here," Ben instructed. "They'll be back. They're too hungry not to give it another try."

They draped the buck over one of Jackson's pack horses.

"Will they follow us?" Jackson shouted.

"Maybe."

That thought hurried them both along. That night, as Jackson and Ben stayed in an abandoned cabin along the trail, they could hear mournful cries echoing across the moonlit land.

Jackson shivered. "I'm glad we found this cabin."

"Me too, son," Ben said.

Hunting was always a dangerous venture, especially in the deep winter snow. Ben was especially pleased with Jackson's hunting ability. At the end of three weeks, all the pack horses were loaded with skins. They pulled for home, satisfied with their hunt.

Ben was especially pleased with Jackson's uncanny ability with horses. He was good at making friends with them and coaxing them to let him on their backs.

The previous fall, Jackson had been trying to work with a horse the hired men had brought in. The horse had a glazed look in his eyes, and his ears were always pointed.

CHAPTER THIRTY-TWO

This was not a good sign. Jackson managed to get the bit in the horse's mouth, but when the time came for the saddle, it was a different thing all together.

As soon as Jackson put the saddle on the horse's back, the horse fell over onto his back and lay there.

"What in the world!" said Jackson.

Willard had come to witness this strange spectacle. When Jackson took off the saddle, the horse stood up.

"Never saw a horse do that before," Willard said, puzzled.

"Whoa, boy," said Jackson silkily, stroking the horse's head. "It's only a saddle. It won't hurt you."

He eased the saddle back onto the horse, and the animal promptly threw himself on his back again, lying there calmly. He called Ben to the barn to witness this new horse's antics. Once again, when the saddle was placed on his back, the horse fell down and lay on his back.

Ben burst out laughing. "A falling-down horse?" he said. "Never have I ever seen that."

"That creature is purely stupid," Willard said.

"Better let that one alone. We've got too many good animals for you to waste time with that one," Ben told Jackson.

Reluctantly, Jackson turned the horse back into the pasture and began working with another one. But the odd behavior of the first horse poked at him. He'd never had a horse he couldn't do something with, and this was a real challenge. At different times, he tried unsuccessfully to get the horse to accept the saddle.

"Looks like you're going to have a long day," Willard said with a laugh from the top rail of the corral whenever he saw Jackson with that horse.

"Don't you have anything to do but sit there and watch me?" Jackson complained.

"I'm giving you moral support," Willard replied, "and some advice, too. I'm here to give you some of my horse wisdom. Jackson, I think you've finally found a horse that's smarter than you."

The next day, Ben told Jackson that he was sure, with enough time, he could break the falling-down horse. But Ben thought time was better spent working with the other horses.

"I'm afraid by the time you do break him, you'll find out he's too dumb to do anything," Ben insisted. "Just let the horse be. One of the sad facts of life is that a man can't always be successful, even at what he's good at. Just let him be. It'll make a good story to tell your grandchildren," he said, grinning.

Ben and Jackson put away the monies they earned hunting that winter, and as Ben had planned, they also took horses to market when good weather returned. Ben, Willard, and Jason worked the crops while Jackson, Tom, and Robert took the horses to Chicago.

The crop was pretty successful, and Ben was feeling good about all the money coming in that year even though the economy had turned bad. Ben's lips parted in a grin as the last of the hay was stored in the barn.

Lieutenant Mooreland came by that summer to pick up a few more horses as well. "You do have the best horses in the county," he complimented Ben.

"Careful breeding and tending," Ben answered with a smile.

He had come to like this brusque young man trying to do an impossible job with too few men and too much territory to cover. Lieutenant Mooreland came back a few days later with more news. The last of the remaining Indians had been rounded up, and the public demanded they be handed over for trial. They later were found not guilty and turned loose to be put back on the reservation.

CHAPTER THIRTY-TWO

Willard and Ben often sat on the front porch, talking about the past and future. "No point in trying to relive and change the past. It's over," Willard offered. "How about some lemonade to cool us off?"

"Please," Ben said, wiping his mouth.

This summer, like the one before, he worried about the lack of rain. He would be all right, but many of his neighbors wouldn't be if they didn't get rain in the next few days.

"Lord," he prayed, "we sure could use some of your cooling waters on our thirsty crops."

Two riders came toward the house, and Ben soon recognized them as his son Jackson and his girlfriend, Sharon Thomas. They tethered their horses in the shade of the trees.

"We'd like to have a talk with you, Dad. Is Willard around?"

"No, he's in the house making some lemonade."

"Good," said Jackson.

They sat down on either side of Ben.

"What am I getting hit up for this time? Some more money?" he asked suspiciously.

"No, something more important," Jackson said as he got closer to his father and lowered his voice. "We would like to talk to you about telling Mama that Sharon and I would like to get married when she returns home. We believe you could help us with breaking the news to Mama."

Ben grinned broadly. "You two have been thinking on this a long time, haven't you?"

"Yes, sir, we have," Jackson said. "But we know how Mama is. She would want us to wait until we're both at least twenty-one years old."

"You know how Mama is about getting married too young. You know her answer will be no," Ben stated flatly.

"That's why we want you to ask her if we could marry now. You have a way of saying things to her to make her listen," Jackson added.

Ben laughed out loud at that statement. He looked at his son's fallen face. "If I can work it into the conversation at the right time, I'll approach her about it. It's a good thing you started early on this project. It may take a long while to get a yes out of your mama."

Just then the screen door opened and Willard appeared with a tray of lemonade and glasses.

"I thought I heard you young people out here with Ben. You look real serious. Is anything wrong?"

"No, Willard," they answered.

"You look pretty worried about something, whatever it is," he said as he handed out the cold glasses of pale lemonade.

The young people drank their lemonade quickly and made excuses to leave.

Ben waved good-bye to them and started up another conversation with Willard. "Well, it seems the financial crash everyone has been talking about is here to stay for a while," Ben said. "When the Ohio Life and Trust Company failed all of a sudden, folks lost faith in every bank in the country. Farmers aren't getting more than twenty-five cents a bushel for their wheat. Farmers can't make the payments on their mortgages. Even though the banks are foreclosing on farms, they still can't keep their doors open."

Willard said, "In town they're saying businessmen out west of here are taking their own lives on a regular basis. It's a shame."

In England, Debra had her short black jacket beside her in case the sun should go behind the clouds looming to the west. She sat beside Ed and Janice in the bargain-priced

CHAPTER THIRTY-TWO

carriage he'd hired for their daily visits to as many of the famous London sites as they had time to see. In a week, they would be leaving for a long-awaited trip to Scotland.

Her heart felt light as a feather, not only at the thought of being alone again with Ed and Janice, but because Ed had assured her that she and Janice had truly won Flora's respect.

Debra was perched now on the edge of the carriage seat, trying as always to see everything at once.

Leaning toward the side window, she asked, "Are we passing Hyde Park? I think I'm beginning to get my directions straight in London. Everything interests me, even though I do pity the poor. Don't forget I've been reading about London all my life, and my mother's friend Mrs. Mackay in Cobourg, Ontario, talked about London when she and her husband lived there."

"I thing I've just had a bright idea," Ed said.

"Tell us!"

"Today I planned to show you girls Westminster Abbey. I can't let you miss the most breathtaking old English architecture anywhere, but today I have a strong feeling that you need to see trees."

He pointed out the window. "We're almost to Park Lane. It runs along Hyde Park. I sense that you ladies need some medicine for your homesickness."

For a time, they just rode in silence. Ed and Janice reached for each other's hand.

"Thank you, Ed, for being exactly as you are," Janice said. "What can I do to let you know how much I love you, Ed?"

"A man tries to be exactly what his wife wants and needs, but men are men, and women are women. If even one of them holds the other too tightly, distance can come," he said. "Janice, I'm a fairly independent man, but I couldn't face a day of my life now without you. I need us to be even closer than we are this minute, if that's possible."

The carriage driver took them over what must have been every inch of Hyde Park, and the women listened to Ed's explanation of its history. They passed beneath a splendid grove of giant oaks and elms on a steep rise called Buckden Hill.

"Ed, this is breathtaking, isn't it?"

He chuckled at that, and she knew he had remembered the oaks they loved on a branch of the Fox River at home.

"You're a dear to show us so many trees. It does take your breath away. Some days we have seen a lot of buildings."

"Aye, 'tis a pity," Ed remarked. "Cities do have buildings."

"Does Scotland have many buildings?" Janice asked.

"The answer to your questions is yes, they have many," Ed laughed. "I promise to take you ladies to Westminster tomorrow, but before that, beautiful Janice, we have tonight."

At home, they found Mother McGirr and Aunt Mary home early from their shopping trip, and Debra asked them if they had a special reason for coming home early.

"Indeed I do, and 'twill make you happy, Daughter," Joan said.

She stepped briskly inside, shifted her umbrella and hat to her left hand, and began fishing in her purse.

"Here! A letter from Illinois."

Debra took the letter and threw both arms around her mother's neck. Then looking at the address, she began to laugh and cry.

"However can I thank you? It's my blessed husband's script, and you brought it just in time before Ed and Janice and I leave tomorrow for Scotland."

CHAPTER THIRTY-TWO

She gave her eyes two quick swipes and hugged her mother again.

"I'm not crying for any bad reason. I'm crying and laughing for joy as a woman has a perfect right to do both, especially if she's blessed enough to have a thoughtful mother like you. I will open it this minute, and I'll read every word aloud to you."

"You don't think Ed will object?" she asked, hanging her umbrella on the hall tree. "Wouldn't you prefer to read it alone first?"

"No, I would not."

"Oh, I was only joking. I know by now that you can share anything with Ed and Janice."

Debra laid aside her letter and gave her mother yet another hug.

"Have I thanked you enough for hosting our visit and making all of us feel so very much at home?"

Her mother looked pleased and said, "Now, you haven't been given a chance to read a line of what your dear husband wrote. Are you certain you wouldn't prefer to read that without a meddlesome old woman?"

Debra grabbed up the letter. "No, no! I want you to hear it all. The last thing I want is for us to wonder what is happening to the children, Willard, and the farm."

Her mother was very pleased to hear all the news from Illinois, and especially liked the final words that said:

> We all beg to be remembered with the deepest love to your mother and aunt. I pray you will visit the Maxwell Castle. God watch over all of you and keep you safe and well.
>
> > Your husband,
> > Ben

Her mother said, "Aye, Debra McGirr, like my departed husband, your husband is a true aristocrat."

With all her heart, Debra longed to tell her mother that Ben loved her deeply, too, but she felt a stranger with her. While she was trying to decide what to say, to draw on whatever wisdom she may have inherited from her father, she reached again for her mama's hand.

"Debra, love cannot be explained or understood," her mother said. "I'm a selfish old woman trying to end my days here on earth in love and joy. Your visit has helped bring about a rekindling of that love. I would love to have you and Ben nearby, but I know some things in life don't work out the way we would like them to.

"Only you and Ben must decide where you'll spend your remaining years. Just don't let Ben talk you into anything that goes against your nature," she added.

Hoping to lighten the moment, Debra smiled and said, "Don't worry, Mother. I have a mind of my own."

"Aye," she said, returning her smile. "I believe that you do. But, oh, you do love that man!"

In bed on the third night of their stage journey north toward Scotland, almost at the border in the English town of Carlisle, Debra grew drowsy while Ed explained to the ladies that poor Mary, Queen of Scots, had once been imprisoned there.

"Ed, do you love Scotland? Are you excited that tomorrow we'll roll onto actual Scottish soil?"

"Any full-blooded Scot loves Scotland, no matter where else he's been, I suppose," Ed said. "My mother has always spoken tenderly of the 'wine-black moors' in the time of heather. I guarantee you two ladies will see it. You can write all about it to your precious Ben.

CHAPTER THIRTY-TWO

"I'm also going to show you Castle Rock. It is a ruin, but the present laird is in residence there in small quarters about three months of the year. Between the Romans and the English, the old place has stood up amazingly well."

"Maybe we can see Castle Rock our first day in Dumfries!" Janice said.

"That will be up to you, ladies," Ed said. "I'll have to arrange for a contraption to take us across the old stone bridge. Castle Rock is a few miles from Dumfries over the River Nith."

Ed put his arm around Janice's shoulder. "Every day ahead will be ours, ladies. That is all that matters."

CHAPTER THIRTY-THREE

"EXCUSE ME, SIR. I am looking for Pastor Collins." The little man with bright eyes peered up at Debra intently.

"I am Pastor Collins. And whom do I have the honor of addressing?"

Debra thought he fit her mother's description perfectly. Just seeing him there made her mother's letters come alive, inviting both a smile and pleasant recollections. But there was no room for humor this day. Now that they had returned to London from Scotland, she had come to her mother's pastor seeking help ensuring her mother's well-being and finding safe passage home for her and her friends.

Before she could respond, the pastor gave a start. "Bless my soul."

"Pardon me?"

He set down the tray he was carrying and stepped closer. "Might you be Debra McGirr?"

"I am, sir. But how . . .?"

CHAPTER THIRTY-THREE

Her words were cut off by the pastor's cry and warm embrace. When he released her, Pastor Collins's eyes were wet with tears, and he said, "What a joy and a blessing, my child."

He took her by the elbow, saying, "Come, my dear. Debra, that is your name, is it not?"

"Indeed, sir, Debra McGirr Lett."

"Of course. Of course. Your mother told me you had married a young man from America."

"I expected to see my friends when I arrived. Are Janice and Ed Doyle here?"

"They did arrive some time ago but then went off arranging for passports. My dear, your mother has spoken of you so often and at such length, I feel I might count you among my own kin," the pastor said.

"This is not the first time I have held you in my arms, as a matter of fact. When you still were in swaddling robes, your father came here to study for the military."

Pastor Collins cocked his head to the other side and said, "I am happy to see that you have become as lovely a woman as you were a little child."

He had such a warm smile that she felt her heart aching for her inability to respond in kind.

"Forgive me, sir. I wish I could be more joyful over this meeting. I have heard so much about you. Father and Mother both spoke so highly of you."

"They are too kind, too kind. Will you have tea?"

"Thank you, no."

He settled himself into the chair opposite her. "You are sorely distressed."

"Indeed so."

"Is there anything I can do to assist you?"

"I do not see how. But I did not know where else we might turn."

"Perhaps if you were to tell me the trouble. Please, begin with what lies most heavily upon your heart," he suggested.

"My husband," she managed. "My husband could not travel to England because of his troubles with the government of Canada."

"Your second husband?" he asked.

She swallowed and breathed as steadily as she could manage, and said, "Your knowledge of my family is remarkable, sir. Yes, I was married to a military man who lost his life in battle before I married Ben Lett."

"You came to England on this trip with an assumed name to cover you and your friends' identity because of Ben Lett, right?"

She nodded.

"I believe it will be best if you return the same way."

Pastor Collins' eyes opened wide, and he leaned toward her as he said, "I suppose that is why we are speaking now."

"Yes, sir."

"Were they to have known who you were when you arrived in England, my dear, they would have imprisoned you and your friends and held you for ransom."

Debra's head dropped in defeat. "I must return to my husband and children in America. Can you help me?"

"I invite you to stay here at my parsonage where there is less risk of your true identity being discovered. It is modest but clean. And you should consider going back to America as soon as possible."

Pastor Collins' expression held out little hope, but he said, "Rest assured I shall join with you in prayer for a quick departure and the safety of you and your friends." He excused himself to make arrangements for rooms for Debra and the Doyles.

CHAPTER THIRTY-THREE

Debra looked out the window, staring at the London harbor and the city rising in the distance.

"I don't care overmuch for big cities," Debra said to herself.

A mid-afternoon breeze blew in from the sea, carrying enough coolness to make even the brilliant sunshine feel pleasant.

When the pastor returned, he drew her to one side and murmured, "Is there something else that ails you, Debra?"

"Pastor, I cannot tell you all the emotions I'm feeling. I worry about leaving my mother, but I will be so happy when we find a ship to America so I can be with my husband and my children."

He studied her face, trying to understand, and then lifted his head, listening.

"What is it?" Debra asked.

She shaded her eyes and squinted against the afternoon sun, looking in the direction where Pastor Collins pointed.

"I see Ed and Janice approaching," he said, smiling.

Ed and Janice returned with all their passports and with tickets on the passenger ship *William Bilderdijk*, too.

"Our ship should arrive in three days," Ed announced.

"I cannot believe it," said a beaming Pastor Collins.

He pushed back to lean his arms on the table after they had shared a simple drink together. "This truly is an answer to prayers."

Debra reached to clasp Janice's hand. They really would be ready to board a ship for home in three days. She pushed back from the table and the chatter.

"If you will please allow me to excuse myself," she began. "It has been a very long day, and I feel that a bit of rest in my room would be most welcomed before dinner."

For a moment Ed looked as though he would argue, but he caught the message in Janice's eyes and nodded silently. "Don't be late for dinner," he told Debra, and he let her go, with Janice at her side.

Ed and Pastor Collins continued to chat about Ben and his problems with the queen. Pastor Collins wondered if Ben might someday come to England in a disguise so the whole family could visit Mother McGirr. Both finally agreed it would be too dangerous.

Three days later, the friends had boarded the ship and placed their belongings in cabins thirty-four and thirty-five. Debra, Ed, and Janice stood at the railing on the second deck, taking a last look at England. The mooring ropes were loosened from the dock posts by dockworkers. A moment later, they were underway.

Suddenly Ed pointed down to the dock and said, "Look! It's the pastor and his family and some of the people from the church! They must have misunderstood us when we told them Sunday what time we were leaving. They are waving to us!"

"Well, all we can do now is wave to them," Janice said.

When the ship had sailed, Debra stayed near the rail looking back at London while Ed and Janice headed to their cabin to unpack some things.

She looked past the city all the way to the Scottish Highlands, and she thought of Ben so far away. She swallowed tears and used a handkerchief to dab the moisture from her cheeks.

"Lord," she said in a low voice, "Take care of Ben and our children."

CHAPTER THIRTY-THREE

A passage of scripture came to her . . . the sacred words of Psalm 121 . . . and helped ease her troubled mind. In her mind, she recited:

I will lift up mine eyes unto the hills from whence cometh my help. My help cometh from the Lord, which made heaven and earth. He will not suffer thy foot to be moved: he that keepeth thee will not slumber. Behold, he that keepeth Israel shall neither slumber nor sleep. The Lord is thy keeper: the Lord is thy shade upon thy right hand. The sun shall not smite thee by day, nor the moon by night. The Lord shall preserve thee from all evil: he shall preserve thy soul. The Lord shall preserve thy going out and thy coming in from this time forth, and even for evermore.

With those words of calm assurance echoing in her heart, Debra told herself she could face the future, knowing that the God she served would keep her in his faithful loving care.

As she walked slowly along the railing, she glanced up to the bridge and saw Captain Deuningen looking down at her. The captain was a tall, bearded Dutchman with wide shoulders and a barrel chest. Debra felt he could command a ship with his physical presence alone.

The next day Debra, Janice, and Ed climbed the stairs toward the top deck together under another clear blue sky. With the bowsprit of the *Willem Bilderdijk* pointed westward as gracefully as the arched neck of a magnificent stallion, the ship glided smoothly over the water. Debra looked around at the passengers seated in deck chairs and standing at the railings. She didn't see anyone she recognized.

They decided to pull up three deck chairs and sit down to read their Bibles. They read quietly to themselves for about an hour. The clouds began to gather, so they decided to return to Ed and Janice's cabin to continue their reading.

Janice began reading scripture to Debra and her Ed, and while she was reading, they heard the wind begin to buffet the ship. Janice stopped in the middle of a verse, looked up, and said, "We haven't had that kind of wind since we left London. Could a storm be blowing in?"

Janice went on reading, and by the time she closed her Bible, the ship was pitching to and fro and rocking from side to side. Debra laid her Bible down and went to the cabin's porthole.

Cupping her hands at the sides of her face, she peered out and said, "I can see by what light is shining from the ship that there are whitecaps on the water. It looks like they're three and four feet high."

When Ed and the women prayed together, each one asked if a storm were brewing.

"Lord, please keep us all safe," they said together.

They included others on the ship in their prayers, asking God to bring many of them to salvation. They thanked him that he had used them to show many how to know Jesus personally.

By morning, dark clouds covered the sky, and the whole surface of the ocean had been set in furious motion. Safely in the cabin together, Debra, Janice, and Ed sat on the beds with the howl of the wind in their ears and prayed aloud one by one, asking the Lord to keep them safe in the storm. In time, the wind ceased.

The ocean was still rough, but within an hour the clouds had broken up and the sun was shining. Much praise was given to the Lord by the little group.

After they arrived in New York, Ed made arrangements to travel to Detroit, where they would be united with Ben for well-deserved rest and relaxation. Ed and Ben would

CHAPTER THIRTY-THREE

meet with David in the Detroit office to catch up on the progress of their trading business there.

Traveling by train and boat, Ed, Janice, and Debra hurried to Detroit as fast as transportation would allow. They spent one night in Buffalo, New York, in a hotel. Debra had gone to bed, worn out from traveling across the state of New York and filled with the excitement of soon being reunited with her Ben.

She wanted to be in Ben's arms again and hear all the news from home. The thought of it was almost more than her tired body could handle. Debra thought back over all the years she and Ben had yearned to be together. A man after her own heart. A man filled with desire for adventure, yet a strong, loving husband and father. She would treasure every minute of their time together in a new way.

They had spent years looking over their shoulders, wondering if the queen's men might catch up with Ben and murder him to collect a reward. Those troubling thoughts were enough to keep Debra awake until well into the early morning.

She tossed on the bed until she feared she would disturb Ed and Janice in the next room. She fought her pillow, fluffing it up, and then punching it down to a small lump under her neck. Still she could not sleep. She began to pray. She didn't even know what words to choose.

What did she want from God? A miracle. Yes, another miracle. She did not want to lose the man with whom she would soon be reunited.

At long last, she cried in submission, "Lord . . . Thy will be done."

From Buffalo, they traveled by stagecoach to Detroit over the next three days. No rain fell despite the chilly, gray sky. The brand new stagecoach and fairly smooth road allowed them to enjoy the drive and the company of the other passengers.

"Burlington House," the driver of the stagecoach called out in English and French. Debra saw Ben standing in front of the main door, a large grin on his face. It was the first hour of nightfall, and candles had already been lit. She could see the flickering light silhouetting the figures behind the panes, and the long twilight had lingered to light the front of the hotel.

Debra would have dashed from the stagecoach had Ed not held her arm firmly. He helped her down safely, and she rushed to the hotel.

"Ben," Debra cried.

Debra was vaguely aware of the little crowd that had gathered around them. Curiosity touched their faces. Ben put his arms around Debra and lifted her off the ground. She put her arms around his neck and looked deeply into his eyes.

After they all hugged one another, Ed and Ben took their ladies inside for a cup of coffee and scones. Ben delivered reports on the health and activities of the children, and each family rejoiced in the safekeeping of the children and family in Illinois and the safety of the travelers.

At last, Ben and Debra closed the door to their room and stood looking at each other, both feeling giddy and saying any silly thing that popped into their heads. They laughed at each other's foolish remarks and feeble jokes.

Ed said, "I don't understand it at all." He had leaped into bed to take Janice into his arms as though he hadn't

CHAPTER THIRTY-THREE

had a chance to do this nearly every single night they'd been away.

"Not even one drop of rain fell on us over all those miles in that overstuffed stage, but tonight, dear Janice," he breathed between kisses, "I predict there's going to be a wonderful—and quite terrible—storm right in this very room."

"I predict it, too," she whispered, pulling him closer, her body aching with desire and that still nameless, wholly unexplained sense of release and anticipation.

"Oh, Ed. Ed, am I crazy? Or did something amazing really change for us?"

"You're not crazy, Janice! This is so good."

In the room across the hall, Ben and Debra reunited after all their time of separation and loneliness. He kissed her throat and shoulders till she was breathless.

They both sensed that they were embarking on a new stage of life and something very good and nearly unbearable was about to take place in that moment. Maybe it would be the wildest moment of their lives. It might be even better than they had ever made happen. And indeed, it was very good.

Bodies one, souls, minds, and spirits reaching, Debra gasped, "Help me, Ben! I'm drowning in your love. *Your* love. I can't hold it all. Help me! Please help me!"

His whole being enfolding her, he groaned, "I'm trying, Debra, God in heaven knows I'm trying. But I need help, too."

When morning came, neither Debra nor Ben was surprised that rain was falling onto Abbotsford Street. Ben felt rested and yet was somehow still soaring with the high anticipation they'd both sensed while getting back together again. Almost at the same waking instant, they reached out to each other.

Ben said, "Tell me first—how are you feeling today, Debra?"

Both arms around his neck, she laughed into his face. "How am I today, my darling? Oh, I couldn't possibly be better," she said in an exaggerated British accent. "And how are you today, Ben?"

He kissed her nose and said, "I know that was a dumb question. What I meant was, do you still feel it's possible something more wonderful may be going to happen to us? I believe that something is happening to Jackson and his friend Sharon that will bring us all very great blessings. I had a dream about what they might be planning. They talked with me before I left on this trip about their future."

Ben could tell he had startled her because she gave a little helpless scream and sank back onto the pillow.

"Our son, Ben? Thinking of getting married? Don't tease! Did you really have a dream about our son? Please don't joke! I know how silly we've been acting, and I still feel that way today—almost. But don't ever tease about our baby!"

"I wasn't, darling. Honest. Debra, are you scared? You look almost scared."

"I don't think so," she said in the smallest voice. "No. I just—I just nearly choke sometimes because I long so for Jackson to be in our midst. I also know how stupid that sounds."

She held his face close to hers and said, "Our life is so perfect; I don't want the wedding of our son to spoil it. I need to think about all this."

They decided to walk to the point, which was a beautiful spot on the waterfront in Detroit near their hotel. They would walk there many times before they left Detroit.

As they walked on one of their last days in Detroit, Ben looked at his wife's face and felt there was more to this little

CHAPTER THIRTY-THREE

excursion than a mere walk. Debra seemed distracted and deep in thought, and the point was a great place to work through a dilemma or sort out an emotion. He had carried her light shawl and spread it over her shoulders.

The day was glorious and neither too warm nor chilly. The wind blew just enough to stir the leaves of the trees. Nearby a bird sang to its mate high in the branches above. Ben found it hard not to express his thoughts about the perfection of the morning, but he held his tongue. He would not speak until Debra was ready.

She settled herself on a log, and her gaze swept out over the scene before them. He watched her slim shoulders rise and fall. Then she settled back, eyes upon a small fishing boat gently rocking on the waters beyond. A strange calm seemed to relax her face.

"I have enjoyed coming here this past week," she began without looking at him. He nodded. "There is so much to think about. To try and sort out."

He reached for her hand and held it, his thumb rubbing gently back and forth against the smoothness of the skin. Ben held her hand, watching her face as she obviously struggled to find words for her emotions.

"Life can hand out some extremely painful things," she finally said, looking out over the water below them. "Once I realized that, I knew I had to stop blaming all those involved and let God direct my life. 'Submit' I kept telling myself. 'Submit to God. One day he will make it plain. Make it right.' And I was finally able to accept things as they were. To find an inner peace."

She turned to look at Ben. He nodded silently, fearing that the struggle was still going on, wondering how he could help her.

There was no anguish in Debra's eyes. There was calm. The hand he was holding was not trembling but was returning his warm grasp. She smiled, ever so slightly, and her voice held a triumphant note.

Ben could feel the tears hot behind his eyelids. Why was he weeping? Seldom did he respond with tears. This was a joyous occasion. This was an answer to many years of prayer on the part of his beloved wife. Perhaps there really was no other way to express his deep emotion than through tears.

He slipped his arm around her and drew her close. He felt Debra's own tears as she pressed her cheek to his. His arm tightened, and they sat in silence, drinking in the wonder and closeness of the moment together.

In time, Debra drew back and settled against him. He had never seen her so at peace. Ben waited a moment then said, "Fear makes people do dreadful things—unreasonable things. It becomes a vicious frenzy of who will strike first to save himself or herself from the other. God help us to never let hatred become a cancer to our souls.

"Love is a promise of good things, and the circle of love just keeps growing larger if we allow it. But we—you and I and all the others—we need to nurture it, like a garden, and tend it with care."

"Keep out the weeds," Debra said. "Weeds of bitterness and envy and hatred and greed."

"Yes, and water it with prayer," Ben said.

Ben also had some time while they were in Detroit to learn about Debra's adventures in England and Scotland and to tell her how life had been at home on the farm. He delivered a package when they were alone, and Debra carefully opened it along with letters from home.

"Why am I getting a package?" she asked.

"Who else gets packages but you?"

"Is it from Leland?"

CHAPTER THIRTY-THREE

"Of course it's from Leland and your very special son."

"Do you want me to unwrap it?"

"Yes! Hurry."

Ben fumbled in his pocket for his penknife and cut the cord someone had securely wrapped around the box. She ripped off the paper, jerked the lid from a flat, sturdy box, and took out what appeared to be a thin piece of board with paint on it. A letter fluttered to the floor.

Debra leaped up to grab it. Ben could see her hands shake as she broke the dark-red wax of the seal bearing "JL" for Jackson's name.

"Ben!" She sank back on the side of the bed, a single-page letter clutched in both hands.

"Oh, Ben, it's a letter from Jackson! Look, sweetheart, Jackson wrote this himself! I taught him to write a long time ago, but look! No, don't look. Listen, and I'll read it aloud."

August 1857
Dear Mom,

This is a cardinal I painted for you and Dad. Willard and I do lots of such things these days. I miss you so. I would cut off one of my fingers and be glad to do it if only I could be with you and give you a hug. Are you ever coming home to see us? I will take good care of you if you will only come home. I hope you like this cardinal painting.

Love,
Jackson

Debra began to fight tears, and they spilled down her face onto the pale pink collar of her nightgown. Ben could only stand there. With all his heart, he longed to take her in his arms and tell her that it was only natural for her to cry because it had been such a long time since she'd been with her family.

He knew she was painfully homesick. Debra was hungrily studying every stroke of Jackson's painting of the big red cardinal. Jackson remembered that she had always loved cardinals.

"Ben?"

He found the courage to go to her and said, "What, Debra? What can I do for you?"

A minute or so passed, and he was fully aware of her great love for him.

CHAPTER THIRTY-FOUR

IT WAS NEARLY dusk, and the odd alchemy of nature duplicated nowhere else on earth surrounded them as the sun faded in the west. They saw it now coming through the window of the coach and Ben, Debra, Janice, and Ed began singing the old hymns.

Rays of sun sifted through the land and molded into unbelievably gorgeous hues of red, orange, yellow, pink, and purple and splashed against a canvas of fluffy white clouds just above the horizon. It was truly breathtaking.

"What a wonderful homecoming," they all breathed, as much to God as to the stagecoach driver.

As they neared the farm, they heard music and saw lights in the coming darkness.

"Looks like they're havin' a git together," the driver said.

As they drew closer, Ben saw a full-fledged party in progress. "Must be our turn to host the dance," he guessed.

Ben could pick out Jackson's tall, slender frame in the distance as he mingled with the guests under the string of lanterns. His son was heartbreakingly handsome. His friend Sharon, with flowing blond hair, was strikingly beautiful. Ben saw them turn just as he and his fellow passengers came across the bridge and down the lane.

Holding hands, Jackson and Sharon loped to meet them, their faces flushed with grins spread from ear to ear.

"Mom! Mom! You're back!" Jackson exclaimed as he helped Debra down. "My beautiful mom," he whispered against her hair.

"Mom, this is my sweetheart, Sharon Thomas. Sharon, this is my mom."

"It's nice to meet you, Sharon. I look forward to getting to know you better," Debra said warmly.

"Sharon, these folks are my parents' best friends, Ed and Janice Doyle. Ed and Janice, this is Sharon," Jackson continued. "We planned this party to welcome you home from your trip to England."

While the fiddle music swirled the women's skirts and lifted the men's boots, Debra found her way into Ben's welcoming arms, and they realized how good it was to be home again together.

"Ben, the Lord has brought all this about, I know it," Debra said. "I've learned I can't live my life without his guidance and care."

"You're not the only one who's learned a few things," Ben confessed. "If you only knew how many times I've prayed lately, most of all that he would bring us back together safely. He's given us the answer to our prayers."

She smiled up into his eyes. "Ben, take down your fiddle and play with the others. You can sing for all of us." She smiled. "No more regrets. No more doubts. Let's celebrate. We're home."

CHAPTER THIRTY-FOUR

Time passed quickly, and on March 27, 1858, Jackson and Sharon were married in a beautiful ceremony conducted by Pastor Sam Packard and Ben Lett.

Snow lay on the ground. The sky was a brittle blue, and a brisk north wind blew outside the church building, but those attending felt only warmth and happiness at this most joyous occasion.

Sharon wore a dress of fine wool just the shade of her cool blue eyes. She chose blue for it symbolizes that love will always be true. Around her shoulders she draped a warm paisley shawl.

The light of heaven was on Sharon's lovely face as Jackson looked into her eyes and repeated vows to his cherished bride. This couple loved each other and had found each other by God's grace. Their ceremony was a breathtaking sight for all to behold. When the pastor told Jackson he could kiss his bride, many guests shed tears of joy.

Ben introduced the couple as Mr. and Mrs. Jackson Lett. Then Sharon looked into her husband's eyes and repeated the age-old passage from the book of Ruth 1:16b, "Whither thou goest, I will go: and where thou lodgest, I will lodge: thy people shall be my people, and their God my God."

A hush hovered over the members of the congregation as they witnessed this touching moment.

The newly-married couple made their way to the back of the church and greeted a line of well-wishers who then filed to the basement for a reception.

Fiddle music filled their ears as the guests wished the couple well. Ben offered a toast. So did Ed and Willard and Jackson's Uncle Tom and Uncle Robert. Then Jackson danced with his new bride. Ben and Debra soon joined them on the dance floor as did Ed and Janice. Willard even danced, as best he could, with Sharon's mother, a widow.

QUEEN'S REVENGE

Several hours later, Ed brought a rented carriage to the door of the community building for the young couple. A fine looking pair of matched black horses with white stockings stood patiently as Jackson and Sharon climbed aboard after saying their good-byes.

That evening, they traveled to catch a train to Milwaukee where they would start their married life in a cozy rented room that looked out over Lake Michigan.

As the couple talked about their future in those precious days, they often thought of the family that had sacrificed to pay for their wonderful honeymoon.

In a few months, the mention of Milwaukee would stir other strong emotional responses from them, but for now they enjoyed their days there together to the fullest.

When they returned to Leland, the newly-married couple took up residence in the little farmhouse on their new farm.

Hard times plagued Ben and his neighbors and family the rest of that year. When the time came for Ben to pay his share of the loan for Jackson and Sharon's farm, he came up short.

Ben went to visit Tom Jenkins at the Leland National Bank. Tom explained he no longer could offer Ben the chance to refinance his loan, as they had discussed just two summers before. He did, however, offer Ben a short extension. Ben would have until January 1, 1859, to make his payment (with a sizeable penalty added on) or lose that farm.

In late October, Ben was working in his barn, rubbing down a horse, when he heard footsteps approach.

"Mr. Lett, my name is John Severson," the stranger said. "I'm here to talk about the farm you bought for your son and his wife. My partners and I heard you are short of money and couldn't make your fall payment. Our company

CHAPTER THIRTY-FOUR

can make a generous offer for your farm. We could save you the embarrassment of losing it due to foreclosure."

Severson smiled as Ben stared at him, expressionless.

"The Letts have such a good name in the community. I expect you don't want to sully that name. We are prepared to take the farm off your hands to help you save your good name," Severson said.

"You must be a bigger fool than you look," Ben said coldly. "I have no intention of giving up the farm, especially to the likes of your kind."

"This is a copy of the note the county courthouse gave me when I inquired about your farm. You and your brother signed this note guaranteeing payment by October 1, but that date has come and gone," he said, sneering. "You know you don't have the money. The bank will sell you out because they are short of money and need your payment. Everyone is short of cash."

Ben's head jerked back and, blinking, he said, "You get out of here and tell your partners that we are not going to give up the farm we bought for Jackson. You think you have this all figured out, but what you don't know is that the bank has already given me an extension on my loan. I want you off my property."

Severson walked out as Debra walked in.

"I'm sorry you had to hear all of that," he said.

"What else can we do to make sure we have that payment by the deadline?" Debra said. "I don't ever want to see another man like that come to our home threatening to take away our property. Are you sure we can't borrow from your brothers?"

"My brothers can't help us, sweetheart. Tom and Robert are hurting just like everyone else, and I would be reluctant to ask them to help us any more than they already have."

Ben held Debra in his arms a moment and then said, "Is our little Betsy finished with the job you gave her in the pantry?"

"She was almost finished when I left the kitchen. I told her to stay there."

Ben and Debra explained to Betsy and her little brother that a man had made an offer to buy Jackson's farm.

"Papa. Mama. The Lord gave us that farm for Jackson and Sharon," Betsy said. "I know he will provide the money for us to make the payment. He won't let us lose the farm."

Both parents were proud of their daughter for her unwavering faith in the Lord's ability to take care of his children, but they found their own faith a bit weaker.

At breakfast the next morning, Ben, Ed, and Willard discussed ways to raise the money. Ed and Willard offered to chip in and lend Ben about half the money, but he said he would give up the farm rather than take money from his best friends.

Willard thought Ben's attitude a bit foolish; however, he understood why he might feel that way.

Ben then thought about selling his share in the Detroit trading business partnership he and Ed had established on their way to Illinois back in 1845. Ed agreed to the idea that Ben would sell his share to their manager, David Bristol, so Ben started making plans for a trip to Detroit.

Debra begged Ed to go with Ben to see to it the money would be safe, but Ben insisted Ed was needed on the farm to ready horses for the next drive in the spring. Ben won the argument and left for Detroit alone just after Thanksgiving 1858.

After several days of talks in Detroit, Ben convinced David Bristol to buy his share and become a full partner with Ed. As soon as the papers were signed and the deal closed, Ben wired the money home and made his plans.

CHAPTER THIRTY-FOUR

First, he found gifts for his family and partners back home. Ben bought a beautiful ring for Debra, a dress for his daughter-in-law Sharon, a gun for Jackson, and boots for Ed. For Janice he found a sweater, for Willard a jacket, and he also bought clothes for his children and shoes for Ed and Janice's children. He crated and shipped everything except the ring. This he kept on his person.

He traveled westward across Michigan by train, watching the landscape rush by in a fraction of the time he could travel it by stage. He would depart from Grand Haven at the end of the line and board a steamer that would take him across the tip of Lake Michigan to Milwaukee in about six hours.

Jackson and Sharon had told Ben and Debra how much they enjoyed this bustling town that had become a major trading center for lumber and furs. He couldn't resist the chance to see it for himself before he traveled home.

He observed two men at the dock as he waited to board the steamer. They almost appeared to be waiting for him, which seemed strange to Ben. He wondered if they might be up to some trouble, so he kept an eye on both of them.

When they were out on the lake, the men introduced themselves. Stewart Wilson was a Milwaukee businessman who shipped merchandise from Grand Traverse Bay, Michigan. James M. Manier was the other man Ben had seen at the dock with Wilson.

Ben decided to engage the men in conversation. When they talked about trading, Ben learned that Manier worked for A. Watson on Wilson's behalf. Watson was the commission merchant and meat merchant in Ottawa, Illinois. Ben realized as they talked that Watson was connected with Jerome Banister, the criminal who had attacked Ben's home back in the late 1840s and was killed in a gun battle with Sheriff Miller and his deputy.

Ben stayed on guard. The men went about their own business, and Ben decided to get some rest. He was eager for this steamer to dock in Milwaukee.

Later Ben met again with Wilson and Manier for a game of cards.

Perhaps when Ben bent over to pick up a card, Wilson managed to switch the drinking glasses. No one ever confessed the details of how poison made it into Ben's glass, but when he took his next big drink Ben started coughing. And he knew right away that something was wrong with that drink.

Ben became very ill very fast. The ship's captain was called when Ben had a hard time breathing and was doubled over with pain in his gut. Just minutes before, the captain had talked with Ben, and Ben had been fine. Suspecting an ill deed, the captain asked Ben if he thought he had been poisoned by these men, and Ben nodded his head up and down.

The captain put Wilson and Manier under arrest. They complained bitterly but to no avail. Captain John Blankenship stood six foot six inches tall and weighed 240 pounds. His bushy gray hair, dark brown eyes, bright ruddy face, and angry look made men like Wilson and Manier cower.

They went to their locked room without a whimper.

Ben writhed in pain on his bed. Captain John gave him extra blankets and some hot soup, but Ben still cried out for help. The strychnine was more than he could handle, and he sensed this might be the end for him.

When the steamer arrived in Milwaukee, the captain turned Wilson and Manier over to the authorities. Sheriff Ross put them in the city jail, bound them over to the city authorities, and charged them with attempted murder. The two men paid for an attorney from the money they

CHAPTER THIRTY-FOUR

stole from Ben's cabin after he took ill. Ben was too sick to resist.

The captain sent a telegram to Watson in Ottawa, telling him of the arrest and asking him to notify Tom Lett of Ben's illness. He also suggested Tom come quickly.

Watson received the telegram and contacted the attorney for Wilson and Manier right away. He failed, however, to notify Ben's brother of the poisoning and the need to come immediately to Milwaukee.

Tom Lett received word of Ben's death nine days after his death. When he told Ben's family and friends, a great outpouring of sorrow and grief surrounded them. All gathered to comfort his widow and children.

Tom and Ed traveled to Milwaukee to retrieve Ben's body. They left by train from Somonauk and arrived in Milwaukee the next day before noon. They returned by train.

Jackson comforted his mother and sister and little brother while Janice took charge of funeral arrangements and organizing meals. Debra barely functioned, but Jackson's wife, Sharon, became her greatest comfort. She was well versed in the Bible and had great empathy as she had lost her father recently.

Tom talked with authorities and hired a lawyer to pursue justice for Ben's death. He hoped to see Wilson and Manier hung for their deed, and he planned to go after Watson as a person of interest.

Tom and his attorney discovered many pieces of information, and many other details came to light in the investigation into the murder of Ben Lett and the trial that followed in the Milwaukee courts.

Wilson, it was discovered, was living in adultery with another man's wife. Ben had never met this woman, yet the ring Ben had bought for Debra was found on her person aboard ship. She told authorities she had it for "safekeeping."

The authorities also came to believe that Wilson had poisoned Ben and robbed him. Manier, they suspected, was an accomplice to the crime.

At the trial for these men, Manier testified that Watson had paid him money for his work. When asked where he lived, Manier said, "Michigan, Ohio, Indiana, and Illinois." When asked if he knew Ben Lett, Manier answered, "I am his partner."

This was a lie, as they were only recent acquaintances, not partners.

Circuit Judge Arthur McArthur rose and addressed the jury at the trial and said, "If you find these two men guilty, I will grant them a new trial."

This he did without being asked or without a plea being made on either side. Such was Milwaukee justice in January 1859.

The Milwaukee *Sentinel* reported, "The captain and mate of the vessel on which Mr. Lett came here expressed their confident belief that he was poisoned and doubted not by whom."

An autopsy confirmed Ben's death by strychnine.

The man accused of giving him the poison was never convicted.

Although no clear motive emerged, Tom Lett later asserted, "England had not money enough to hire any of their cut-throats to shoot him down, and they had to stoop to slander, perjury, and poison to accomplish his destruction."*

---

*see Author's Notes.

CHAPTER THIRTY-FOUR

Benjamin Lett was buried not far from his home in Leland at the Lett Cemetery located north of Sheridan on the Tom Lett farm.

The money Ben had wired to the family was enough to make the payment on the farm. The gifts he shipped and Debra's ring were kept by the family for many years.

Tom fought hard to have Ben's name cleared and make sure his brother and his love of freedom was never forgotten. Two monuments erected by Tom at the Lett Cemetery bear lengthy inscriptions—nearly 2,500 words—defending Ben's honor, and explaining his role as a patriot rebel in Canada. The money Tom spent to build Ben's memorial stones would have purchased eighty acres at that time. These monuments were the talk of the area.

Many members of the Springstead and Lett families are buried south of Sandwich, Illinois, in the Lett Cemetery on the local road known as the Sheridan Blacktop.

Tom Lett was not the only one who remembered the life and actions of Ben.

James Mackenzie, an editor, prominent citizen of Lima, Ohio, and the son of William Mackenzie, Ben's confidante during the rebellion in Canada, wrote this of Ben in a memoir:

"He was certainly a singular man; and whatever the provocation may have been beyond colonial oppression which developed under happier circumstances he would have been a man of superior energy, and a supporter of law and order wisely administered by worthy government."*

---

*see Author's Notes.

AUTHOR'S NOTES

WHEN WE CONNECT with people of the past, they can make a great impact on us, and we will not be the same because of that encounter. Such was the case with my wife, Sharon, and me when we first heard family stories about my Uncle Ben Lett. We went to work researching all the information we could find from public and private sources.

That research led to the publication of *Patriot Rebel*, a novel that tells the story of Ben Lett, his family, and his involvement in the war of 1837-39 in Canada. From Canada, Ben and two brothers and three sisters moved to northern Illinois, where many descendants lived. Ben was hounded by his enemies until his untimely death in 1858. This novel continues the story from where *Patriot Rebel* finished.

The legacy of Ben's struggles for freedom is etched in a monument that stands in the Lett Cemetery located south of Sandwich, Illinois. My great-great-grandfather Tom Lett built this monument and defended his brother Ben's name while he lived and after his death. Tom's words that appear

AUTHOR'S NOTES

in the final pages of this book are etched into the main column of this monument.

The McGirrs, Doyles, and several others in the story are fictitious, but Ben's story indicates that there were such nameless persons. I simply gave them names. Many of the facts of Ben's final days and death were gathered from newspaper accounts.

In the process of telling this story, I've drawn on many facts about the small towns and prairie farms surrounding the area where my ancestors settled about 170 years ago.

I gained insight from several passages in *History of DeKalb County, Illinois* by Henry L. Boies, which was printed by O. P. Bassett of Chicago in 1868.

From page 67:

Until the spring of the year 1835, the feet of very few white people had trodden the soil of what now constitutes the County of DeKalb. It was the home of the Indian, and the Indian agent at Chicago, backed up by companies of United States troops, was authorized to drive off all whites who should encroach upon their land. But it having been noised about in the spring of 1835 that the Indians were about to remove west of the Mississippi, no further attempt was made to restrain the immigration of the whites, and they poured into the country in great numbers.

In pre-empting and claiming land, delays are dangerous, and each landless immigrant, desiring to have the first choice of lands, and to be sure of a location inferior to none, hurried into the territory, and camping near some favorable grove and stream, began to blaze the trees on a line surrounding as much of the timbered land as he thought he should want, and then ran his plow out on the prairie, making with its furrow a tract as large as he cared for of the open prairie.

QUEEN'S REVENGE

This, according to the primitive regulations that governed the new settlers at that time, gave him a right to hold the tract thus marked out until the time when the government should have it surveyed, and the opportunity offered for a better title, by purchase of the United States.

But innumerable disputes arose under this arrangement.

Wrongs and outrages, for which no known legal redress existed, were being multiplied, and from these circumstances the claim associations developed.

From page 71:

Each settler was solemnly pledged to protect every other settler in the association, in the peaceful enjoyment of "his or her reasonable claim as aforesaid," and further, whoever . . . should refuse to recognize the authority of the aforesaid association, and render due obedience to the laws enacted by the same from time to time, "to promote the general welfare," should be deemed a heathen, a publican, and an outlaw with whom they were pledged to have no communion or fellowship.

As soon as courts were accessible, litigation began. Claim associations were not without opposition. The expenses in closely contested suits were much greater than the value of the property. Later the state legislature passed a statute legalizing sales of claims, thus maintaining the law established by the settlers' claim associations.

It was into this environment around 1840 that Ben Lett purchased his farmland near the town of Leland. Ben Lett bought his land from previous owners for about $1.50 per acre.

Brothers Robert and Tom purchased land close to the Fox River near the town of Sheridan. The three Lett sisters married Springstead brothers who settled north of Serena. This meant family gatherings and shared work were possible.

AUTHOR'S NOTES

There were times when the Springsteads and Letts helped establish local schools, churches, and town halls for dances as well as public meetings.

I found other insights in the pages of *The Somonauk Book: History of the Somonauk United Presbyterian Church* written by Jennie M. Patten in collaboration with Andrew Graham. The book was privately printed in Chicago in 1928. Jennie Patten is a great-great aunt on my grandmother's side of the family. In addition to being an author, she was a patron of the Sandwich Library in Sandwich, Illinois.

From pages 19-20:

A few efforts were made to "jump" claims. . . In one case the "claim jumper" was advised by the settlers to leave the country for his own personal benefit, which he accordingly did. In the other case a man with grown sons jumped the improved claim of a neighbor who had several small children. When a posse of citizens, bent on securing fair play, waited on the "jumper," he barricaded his door and threatened a gun fight. After some parley he changed his mind and sent out a flag of truce with his terms of surrender, which were. . . accepted and all went well.

From page 20:

The purchase of the land nearly drained the country of nearly every dollar and left the people very poor in money with which to buy necessities. . . A good deal of exchanging or trading was done to keep the wolf from the door. At times it seemed an almost impossible task to support a family, a school, and a church.

Reviewing the old records of those early days, one will note with interest their liberal contributions to missions in comparison with their meager incomes. Not only were they desirous that others might have what was nearest and dearest to their own souls, but they "gave until it hurt" to materialize this desire . . . Nor is this excellent quality of liberality deficient in their descendants; it continues in the blood.

From page 40:

The discovery of gold in California aroused a desire for riches in people in all walks of life. It swept through the country like a pestilence and during the years 1849 and 1850 the roads and trails to the great West were crowded with hurrying trains of wagons pressing on over the unexplored plains to the gold mines.

From page 41:

The "sink of the Humboldt" promised to be the greatest difficulty to be overcome. On account of the extreme heat of this part of the desert they were obliged to cross in the night. In preparation for the ordeal they rested themselves and their horses for three days. Starting at four in the afternoon, after eighteen hours of continuous travel, they succeeded in pushing their teams across the forty miles of desert.

From page 42:

After nearly a year and a half spent in the gold-fields of California . . . returned home by way of the Isthmus of Panama . . . From the Pacific side he walked to the Chagres River, took ship for New York City . . . He reached Somonauk in August 1851, two thousand dollars richer in gold than when he left home eighteen months before; a good fortune in those days.

From page 45:

Just before January 1, 1849, a railroad was completed from Chicago to Turner Junction, now West Chicago, and opened for traffic. In December 1849, construction was started on the line from Turner Junction to Aurora, under the name "Aurora Branch Railroad Company." This line was completed and opened for traffic early in September 1850. Two years later the line from Aurora was completed as far as Mendota, and placed in operation October 20, 1853.

AUTHOR'S NOTES

From page 55:

The financial panic of 1857 and 1858 came suddenly and unexpectedly. Due to over speculation many large and substantial business houses failed, as well as the greater number of the host of state, commonly called wildcat, banks.

This catastrophe added much to the burden of the settlers, and business stability did not return to the country for several years. Bank notes declined in value rapidly. Money disappeared almost entirely from circulation. Paper money, although it was all but worthless, was accepted each day on a basis of that day's rating, as published in the Chicago morning papers.

From pages 286, 288-289, and 290-291 of this book, I included some of the wonderful wording of letters sent back and forth between Elizabeth Pratt Patten and her husband, William Patten, of Somonauk, Illinois, during his trip to the gold fields of California in 1850.

Members of the Ben Lett family were adventurers who were ready to take on any challenge. They lived under the constant pressure of watching for strangers to approach Ben with the thought of doing harm to him or his family.

Their friends the Doyles helped to lift many of life's pressures. Janice especially lived to give support to Debra when she became discouraged and depressed.

Their son Jackson provided the entire family with great joy and blessings with his humor and happy attitude. He loved the farm and horses and was becoming a great man of God. He led the entire church in singing, read scripture, and occasionally preached.

Willard gave the family balance, helping where he could with farming and sometimes with the cooking. He gave the family special strength whenever they became frightened or discouraged. His newfound faith in the Lord was very strong. He, too, liked to teach the Bible.

QUEEN'S REVENGE

The crash of 1858 put all farmers in a real bind. Ben realized that the recent purchase of a new farm for Jackson could be the financial death of the entire family because Tom had helped them buy this last farm. Ben wasn't going to let the family down.

Ben's sister Sara Lett Cotteau wrote many poems during her lifetime. Many were collected and published by her daughter. This one especially captures the spirit of Ben Lett and his conviction in defending and fighting for personal liberty.

The March of Freedom

Tell it in haughty London;
Tell it in ancient Rome;
Away in a land of plenty
Freedom has found a home.

No figurehead of royalty
Impedes her growing state,
But *manhood* rises grandly,
And only *worth* is *great*.

O, say to the toiling millions,
The sons of every clime,
"You'll see the star of Freedom
In God's appointed time;

For she is marching onward,
And none shall make her stay,
Till crowns become as playthings
A child might throw away;

AUTHOR'S NOTES

Till rank of birth and titles
Shall vanish from the earth;
Till manhood shall be measured
By pure, intrinsic worth;

Till pride of ostentation,
And pomp, and circumstance,
Shall huddle in the shadows
To hide from Freedom's glance.

For she is marching onward,
And none shall make her stay,
Till crowns become as playthings
A child might fling away;

Till arrogance and envy,
Alike, shall be abhorr'd;
Till honest, noble *labor*
Shall reap its own reward;

Till children learn self-government
Upon the mother's knee,
And – perfectly developing –
Find they are *truly free*.

Cotteau, Sara Lett, *Mother's Poems* (Chicago: Robert O. Law Company, Printers & Binders, copyright by Ida Cotteau 1901 & 1906), p. 81.

WinePressPublishing
Great Books, Defined.

To order additional copies of this book call:
1-877-421-READ (7323)
or please visit our website at
www.WinePressbooks.com

If you enjoyed this quality custom-published book, drop by our website for more books and information.

www.winepresspublishing.com
"Your partner in custom publishing."

CPSIA information can be obtained at www.ICGtesting.com
Printed in the USA
LVOW061236231112

308305LV00003B/6/P

9 781414 121024